F
SETTLEMENT

FINAL SETTLEMENT

LINDA DAVIES

McArthur & Company
Toronto

First published in Canada in 2005 by
McArthur & Company
322 King St., West, Suite 402
Toronto, Ontario
M5V 1J2
www.mcarthur-co.com

This paperback edition published in 2006 by
McArthur & Company

Library and Archives Canada Cataloguing in Publication

Davies, Linda, 1963-
Final settlement : a novel / Linda Davies.

ISBN 1-55278-561-0

I. Title.

PR6054.A76823F46 2006   823'.914   C2006-900298-3

Design and Composition: Tania Craan
Printed in Canada by Webcom

10 9 8 7 6 5 4 3 2 1

For my glorious Lara, who brings boundless joy and light, with all my love.

Take me to you, imprison me,
Except that you enthral me, I never shall be free,
Nor chaste, except you ravish me.
—JOHN DONNE, *Holy Sonnet 14*

All is not lost, the unconquerable will,
And study of revenge, immortal hate,
And courage never to submit or yield
—JOHN MILTON, *Paradise Lost*

Wild is the wind
—NINA SIMONE

This is my story. It's not a pretty one. Don't say I didn't warn you.

Chapter one

I was born in the midst of a storm, on Long Island in the States, to a Welsh mother and an American father. I came into the world apparently screaming my rage at the thunder and lightning that broke the dawn into shards. My parents were young, in love, and cast with the longest shadow of all. They died here on Long Island, after a party given by friends to celebrate my birth. What a poisoned chalice I was. Three months old, and my mother just ready to face the world in her sequinned gowns and jewels. I've seen pictures of her from that night, and she was beautiful. I can almost conjure the smell of her. I imagine Joy, something expensive and French and lesser known. My father stands by her, almost shadowy and happy to be so. He is tall and slim and in profile. A gentle presence, radiating quiet strength. But there was something *sotto* about him, as if he knew a countdown had begun.

She drove the car, my mother. She hadn't drunk for months, they said, so just a couple of glasses must have gone to her head. It was late. She would have been tired. Laughing perhaps, turning to him to share an anecdote, taking her eyes from the road for that brief moment — enough to plough through the bridge and into the river below. Did they drown or did the impact kill them? I've always wondered. Was it quick and merciful, or did they know what they were leaving behind, to a life empty of everything that mattered? Me. The three-month-old. No aunts, no uncles. No-one who wanted to take me. Not a godparent. My parents didn't give me any of them. Perhaps they would have if they'd lived to my christening.

What I *did* have was a guardian, a trustee — Geoffrey Warrender — to minister to my needs. And I had money. That was always there in abundance. So I had nannies, and nurseries, and toys, and cooks in his house in Long Island. And later, a succession of tutors. That sounds antediluvian, some prehistoric eccentricity of Geoffrey's, I know. But it was purely practical. When Geoffrey inherited me he took me away from my dead parents' home in Long Island to live with him, close to his job at the bank in Manhattan. Whether it was bereavement that triggered it, the doctors would never say conclusively, but in Manhattan I developed an intense asthma and eczema that were so bad Geoffrey took me back to Long Island. Not to my parents' house, for that had been sold, but to a new one he bought himself: Mirador. He commuted from there to New York, graduating from buses and trains to the helicopter his wealth and position in the bank now allowed. Back beside the sea, my ailments vanished almost as quickly as they had appeared. But, if I spent more than a few days in the city, or far from the sea, they returned. So tutors at home it was. A succession of the finest. I was beautifully educated, erudite beyond my years, socially adept with adults, and totally incapable of dealing with the few contemporaries who came my way. So I had a largely friendless childhood, unless you count elderly tutors.

I did have one friend, but she was so transient I didn't feel I could count her, much as I wanted to. Her name was Henrietta Hobbles. She was English. We were both twelve when we met. Her mother had just married our neighbour, Charles Whitmore, if you can describe someone as such when they live — albeit in the next house — a quarter of a mile away, beyond security fences and seemingly boundless green lawns. Henrietta went to boarding school in England, holidayed during the winter in St. Barts, spent Easter in the Alps, but came for six weeks every summer to Long Island. She was magnificent, and for some strange reason we hit it off. Perhaps because she was English I didn't seem so odd to her; all Americans were odd, and she was an individualist who didn't give a damn what people thought, or about social norms, even at twelve.

But when she left I felt lonelier than ever. I was not allowed pets of any kind, since they were inimical to my asthma, so I became good at being alone. I saw little of Geoffrey. He seemed to my childish eyes a giant of a man, remote as a mountain. He was six foot seven, well built, not reedy, with a strong face ennobled by a roman nose. He was imposing to most people, let alone a child. His eyes did twinkle, but more with a dry sardonic humour than the kind of merriment that a child would understand. As an investment banker, he lived to work, and I'm not sure he found the company of a child particularly riveting, but, we did have one thing in common that seemed to keep us both sane — the sea. How I loved the sea, to look at it, to paint it, to sail on it, to swim in it. To toy sometimes with drowning in it. The tides here can be vicious, unforgiving, beckoning . . .

Geoffrey loved to sail, and starting when I was a baby, strapped into a car seat and secured in the pilot room, he took me with him. As I got older, he gave me more and more freedom aboard boat, patiently teaching me to sail. When I was seven, he bought me my first boat, a twelve-foot Lazer dinghy which I quickly learned to sail alone. Even when I had that, he would still take me out on his forty-foot ketch, the *Morganna*, named after me, as often as he could. We would go out in almost all weathers, both of us strapped in and standing at the helm, buffeted by the wind, water sluicing down our bodies, mad smiles on our faces. It was the only time he came alive and let go of the control he seemed to hold himself under on dry land.

For me it was liberation. Out there on the sea, I felt like I was flying. In fact I felt a whole slew of emotions that seemed denied to me on shore. For Geoffrey I knew was impressed by me, enjoyed my company. He rarely took anyone else sailing, and then only for business purposes, and I never sailed with anybody else.

We were members of the Southampton Yacht Club, but only because I think he thought we ought to be, and it was useful for his work. Various captains of industry and media magnates had taken to buying up great pads on Long Island, and competing with one another over who had the biggest, sleekest or fastest boat, so off we would go to the charity sails and brunches and dinners. Geoffrey didn't care for socializing. Making money and sailing was what he lived for, but he managed these things beautifully. He was so elegantly smooth and engaging, charming to everybody. I was aware as I grew up that he was utterly ruthless in his business dealings. He would talk to me on the boat as one adult to another, so I well knew his cold and calculating and mercenary side, but he masked it well, and that made him even more devastatingly effective.

I hated these social affairs, I would much rather have been out sailing alone with Geoffrey. The other children belonged to a world so different from mine. They talked a jargon all their own, radically different from the one I shared with my elderly tutors. They dressed differently, and patently found me odd, mimicking or else shunning me even though I could sail the pants off them. I wasn't wise enough, or perhaps didn't care enough to conceal that from them. Now I am utterly proficient at concealment, but I digress. Geoffrey became much more of an uncle to me than the formal guardian he had started off as. Behind his reserve he was, possibly only to me, consistently kind, honest and reliable; and I knew that in his brisk New England way he was fond of me. It wasn't the kind of love that filled you up and sent you out into the world with an all-conquering confidence, but, hell, it was a lot better than nothing. Beyond that, he was utterly trustworthy. My parents had entrusted me to him, and it was a good choice as time would tell.

As well as sailing, I had another passion to occupy me, which in some strange way kept me company. I painted. Perhaps I wanted to recreate my most treasured possessions; portraits of my mother and father, painted just after their marriage, when my mother was already carrying me. So I am in that picture, an unseen ghost. Perhaps ghost is the wrong word. But there is no good word, is there, for invisible life? Foetus sounds so leaden, so harsh. I prefer to think of myself then as an invisible sprite, a spark of life, rapidly forming — informing perhaps — the smile on my mother's face.

Muck Welsh, they call the ones with the white, white skin that tans so easily, and the black hair and green eyes. That was my mother's gift to me. Geoffrey says I am the spit of her. Wouldn't I like to be. My mother was riveting. She faces the artist, smiling her sprite smile, harbouring the secret of me. She is wearing a long, green velvet dress, peacock iridescent, livid against her white skin. Her hair falls long and straight, curtaining her heart-shaped, elfin face. A face of mischief. The artist caught her in a way no photographer ever did. My father's look is one of love. Pure and simple. He looks past the artist at the object of his love. I see the complete scene in my painter's mind. My mother languishes in an armchair, in her green splendour, watching him as he poses slightly self-consciously. His body is stiff, but his smile is sublime, utterly captivated. How he must have adored her.

When I was trapped indoors by one of the not infrequent gales that hit Long Island turning the sea to spume and the air to liquid, I would creep up to the attics, squash myself into my favourite overstuffed armchair and pore over the photograph albums; my parents' wedding, their courtship, picnics on the lawns, sailing on the Sound. I knew every feature, from every angle, and every expression.

I yearned to paint them, but something stopped me. It was not for lack of technical ability. A succession of tutors came to Mirador: charcoalists, water colourists, oil painters, landscape painters, portrait painters . . . but still I could not tackle my parents. Not yet. Perhaps never now. I painted other lovers, trying to capture such a look. But I never found a like one, never saw such a look until much, much later.

I thought perhaps if I got better, more technically accomplished, that if I trained under someone who seemed to be able to pluck the soul from a sitter and reproduce it, I might succeed.

I scoured the Internet, I ordered caseloads of books, I did my research and found the teacher I wanted.

He was called Angelo Nardizzi, one of the great masters at portraiture, and he was based in Florence. But he wouldn't come to us. Not even copious amounts of my money could lure him to Long Island. Perhaps this was the break I had been subconsciously praying for. I was beginning to feel seriously trapped on Long Island. I was twenty, for God's sake. I had so much life simmering inside me I felt I was burning up. Desperate for the wider world, for independence, for experience. I'd never had a proper boyfriend, I'd never lived on my own, I'd never really mixed with people from outside my ultra-privileged orbit. I wanted to live, to take some risks, to stretch myself. So hopeful, nervous, exhilarated, I flew my gilded cage and went to Florence. I hoped I could tolerate my ailments, drug them down, manage them for perhaps a whole month. Maybe more.

Amazingly, give or take the odd flare-up, they stayed away. Some of the tribes of doctors I had visited over the years had suggested the conditions might alleviate when I reached adulthood. I put it down to that, and so I managed to spend one whole year in Florence, under Nardizzi's tutelage. Learning about art, and life.

And how I lived. Among the smell of oil paint and

turpentine, I learned to breathe. I learned about people, what they really look like, when artifice slips away during the long sittings into the night. I learned about what they conceal, I grew to discern what passes for their soul. I learned that I was no less perfect, no more messed up than most of them. I learned that almost everyone thinks they have something to hide, and never can quite forgive themselves all things. The mark of guilt mars most faces. Only the innocent are truly radiant.

In some ways I packed more living into those twelve months than I had into twenty years. I experimented with abandon, with alcohol, with men, with pleasure, but I cannot say that brought me joy. I learned something that surprised me: people are no cure for loneliness.

So, when my year was up, I came back to Geoffrey's house, because you have to go somewhere, have some sort of rhythm to hold your life together. I had always felt myself just a little too close to going off the rails, and I feared it, especially after my experimentation in Florence. I wanted to *live*, and live well, for my parents' sake, so I clung to what passed for my history. I did not have then the ruthless certainties I now possess. So, like a tame little homing pigeon, I went back.

Mirador, the house where I grew up, was beautiful. White stucco, pillars, huge windows, oak walls and floors, strewn Persian carpets. Enough flowers to fill a mausoleum. Night-flowering jasmine, with its delicate star petals, and tuberose assailed you as soon as you entered the somnolent, dark hallway. Their scent filled the house like a narcotic. I can smell it still, in my dreams. It gave everything an almost hallucinatory quality. As if I dreamed my childhood away, as if I were in a state of suspended animation, waiting for something to happen.

Despite the flowers' rich promise of decadence, nothing much really did happen there. Until that summer.

God it was hot. The kind of heat that caused riots, and death. Not in Long Island, of course. There the sea breezes cooled fevered brows. Staff meant you sweated only if you wanted to. I loved to sweat. It made me feel alive. I would walk in the midday sun until rivulets slicked between my breasts, then I would run down the sloping emerald lawns onto the scorching fine white sand and into the shocking sea to cool off. That day, I'd just come out of the sea and, letting the sun dry me, I was walking up the lawns back to the house.

I wasn't paying attention, so I didn't notice anyone sitting under the giant oak, a hundred yards away. Her voice stopped me:

'Oi, is that any way to treat a friend?'

I wheeled round. 'Henry!' I shouted. I jogged over to her. We embraced and I dripped water all over her. She laughed. 'More, more. I need to cool down.'

'Come and have a julep,' I said, 'and tell me everything you've been up to since last year.'

'How many juleps d'you have?'

'As many as it takes.'

James, the butler, mixed up a pitcher and we took it out to the shade of the oak and talked.

'I heard about Florence,' she said. ''Bout bloody time you got away.'

I smiled. 'It was. But I'm glad to be back too.'

'You always were a homebody, even though you look like a witch–' she stopped and laughed at my look of protest.

'An incredibly beautiful one, don't worry, although God knows you could do with a bit of preening. Never heard of pedicures? Hair cuts?'

'I cut my own. It's just a straight line, for God's sake, and I don't want someone fiddling with my feet.'

She gave an exaggerated sigh. She was expensively buffed, evenly bronzed, artfully highlighted, and naturally beautiful in cut-offs and her cropped T-shirt.

'Listen, you busy tonight?'

I gave her a wary look. 'Depends. I'm not on for grubbing it in some sweaty club with a bunch of cocky Harvard boys who've still got their puppy fat.'

'Nothing like that. Ma's got an old friend staying with her son. She's out tonight at some charity meeting she can't take them to, so I've got to entertain them. I think they need a change of scene, you know, meet some of the natives.'

'They nice, interesting?'

'Wait and see,' she replied with an enigmatic smile.

I see — a grey-haired dowager and her dowdy son. Oh well, if it got them out of her hair for a bit. 'Fine. I'm sure Geoffrey won't mind. It's not as if I spring something on him that often. Drinks, dinner, or both?'

'Both, if you can have it laid on in time.'

'James could lay on dinner for forty without a blink.'

They arrived early. Geoffrey wasn't back from Wall Street, and I'd just stepped out of the shower. I heard

12

voices outside. I threw on a silk dressing gown over my wet skin, moved over to the window and looked down to the garden below.

James was serving drinks to Henry and just one guest — a woman, who stood in profile. I could not have been more surprised. The woman must have been about fifty. She was supremely elegant, beautiful still. There was something mesmeric about her. I got the impression of power. Her movements were lithe and sinuous, yet she was restrained, like a storm stoppered in a bottle. She turned then, and looked up. I was standing in partial shadow, but I felt she could see me. I stepped back slowly from the window, away from the branch-shadowed patches of sun, rippling on the dark oak. I pulled on a dress, combed out my hair and stepped into some high heels. On impulse, perhaps spurred on by her elegance, I went to my safe and pulled out the necklace of rubies I had inherited from my mother and clasped it in place. Then I went down to meet her.

'There you are,' exclaimed Henry as I walked out onto the terrace. 'Are we early, or are you late?'

'Open house, Henry. Come any time.'

She smiled. 'Let me introduce Rosamond Edge. Rosamond, this is Morganna Hutton. Most of us call her Morgan.'

She moved forward, took my hand in hers, shook it and held it.

'Morgan, what a pleasure. So nice of you to throw open your home.' Her voice was mellifluous, beguiling. Close up, she was even more radiant. She was one of those rare people who seem to carry around their own force field, energizing everything and everyone in their path. I couldn't wait for Geoffrey to meet her.

'My pleasure,' I replied, taking the martini proffered by James. 'What brings you over here?' I asked her.

She gestured airily. 'Oh, a bit of this and that, chance to see old friends, do the bare minimum of business.'

'Oh, what do you do?'

'A little light trade. Antiques, special pieces. Talking of which, that is a spectacular necklace,' she said, nodding at my rubies.

'Thank you. It was my mother's.'

She gave an almost imperceptible nod. If she found it odd that I spoke of my mother in the past tense, she didn't, as most people invariably did, quiz me, and I was grateful for that. I was sick of being the orphan, of the pity and sympathy that went with it.

I turned as I heard the unmistakeable tattoo of Geoffrey's shoes on the marble floors as he made his way towards us.

'Morganna. Sorry. Got held up by that confounded credit commit–' He stopped abruptly. He was staring at Rosamond with a look of disbelief, and something else I couldn't fathom. Then, so suddenly I wondered if I really had seen anything odd, he was his usual, urbane self.

'Rosamond. What an unexpected surprise. After all this time.'

'Geoffrey.' She came forward to him, offered up her cheeks to be kissed, then drew back. 'What is it?' she glanced at me, then back to him. 'Twenty years?'

'That would do it,' he answered. He seemed very

distant, almost lost in memories. But I had no time to wonder just what the hell was going on here, because I looked into the hall to see a man approaching. No ordinary man. No Harvard jock with beery jowls.

A whole series of impressions struck me at once: dark scrutinizing eyes, a lock of black hair falling across one, shoved back impatiently by an elegant hand. He looked like an Erté drawing, all elegant, long lines in his chinos and blue shirt. There was humour in his look, and something else, a sort of voracious searching. I tilted my glass back and took a big slug of martini.

He came first to me, with only a scant glance at everyone else. 'Hello. I'm Archie Edge, Rosamond's son.'

Chapter two

It was way after midnight when they left. 'What's the story with you and Rosamond?' I asked Geoffrey after we'd waved them off.

'No story,' he answered, glancing at his watch. 'It was just a surprise, seeing someone after such a long time.'

'How did you two meet?'

'Some party or other. She was out here staying with friends, same sort of circuit. We ran into each other a few times.' He gave an exaggerated yawn. 'I gotta hit the sack, Morganna.'

I got the sense he was being evasive, and I wondered why, but, frankly, I was too thrilled by mother and son to care overly.

'Listen, would you mind if I invited them round again? Rosamond told me they love to sail. I thought I might take them out.'

He paused just fractionally before answering. 'It's your home, Morganna. Have anyone you want round. Goodnight.' He gave me a peck on the cheek.

''Night.' I watched him retreating away up the stairs. He looked ever so slightly weary, but then it was 1 a.m. Time for me to sleep too. I went to bed, but for hours I just lay there, too restless to sleep.

Archie came over the next morning at eleven, bearing a huge bunch of the most delicate orchids.

'From my mother,' he said. 'And from me.' He

leaned forward and kissed my cheek. His kiss seemed to cut through the barriers I surrounded myself with. He moved away from me slowly. I still felt joined. 'Thank you. Come with me while I put them in water.'

I led him to the conservatory, to the old Welsh dresser filled with a selection of vases. I picked one out, busied myself with arranging the flowers, then carried them through and placed them in the hall, on the mahogany table. They glowed white and ghostly in the gloom.

'Come on, let's get into the sun,' I said. I needed to get out, to move, to move away from him, perhaps. 'Fancy a walk?'

'I'd love one.'

So we walked down to the beach, took off our shoes and wandered along the warming sand. He'd rolled up his trousers, pristine white chinos. He wore a blue shirt that matched his eyes. He was utterly beautiful. I wanted to take hold of him, rattle his composure, see again the need I was sure I'd seen flare in his eyes when he came forward to me the night before.

If I had wanted to get away, and I'm not even sure now that I could have done, I failed miserably.

Over the next few weeks, I fell in love with him. And the lust I felt, quick and painful, had more than a little to do with it.

Like all of us, I had been searching for love, but unlike some, perhaps many, I carried the memory of having been loved. Three months of love was enough to hardwire my brain. And my heart. Perhaps that is worse than never having felt love. I knew what I was missing. I remembered the warmth of my mother's arms; like sunshine in the veins. I could recall the blissful security, when all was right with the world and you were untouchable by bad. An illusion, of course, as time proved, but in those little pockets of time, true. While a small part of me spent years trying to anaesthetize the memory of love, the bigger part of me searched, as I had done in Florence, only to be disappointed.

Of course I wanted to paint him. I wanted to just look at him for hours, drink him in. And so I did. In the studio, next to my bedroom, with the windows flung open, I painted him. Back and forth, we moved, from bed to studio. That painting was drenched in our love. I painted him in love with me. Art copying reality, or making it, I never knew. And who gives a damn. By the time I completed his portrait, he was in love with me. It was not gentle adoration, like that of my father for my mother. He looked as if he were to devour me with love. What I wanted that time, I got.

And Rosamond, the storm, his mother. I painted her too, or tried to, but there I fell down. I could not capture her on canvas. Her beauty, yes, but not her soul.

'Call me Rose,' she said in that mellifluous voice of hers, as she posed. It was rare to encounter someone who was not, at least initially, uneasy under the painter's eye, but she faced me with what might have been, but could not have been, blithe innocence.

Oh Rose, you were so charming, wicked, worldly, and utterly beguiling. Your son worshipped you; Henry thought you were awesome; only Geoffrey remained immune to your charms. I didn't care. I was captivated. Motherless and susceptible. You were just the age, I worked out, that my mother would have been.

I took Rosamond and Archie out on my boat. Geoffrey had given me his old boat, the *Morganna*, and bought a new one for himself, called rather worryingly, but unchangeably, *Hurricane*. So we sailed, and when the heat was too much, or the winds becalmed, we spent long languid afternoons just chatting in the shade. Rosamond made us laugh. She was riveting, but she was soothing too. Is this how it would have been, so comforting, yet so diverting, had my mother still been alive?

When they were there, Mirador came alive. Rosamond had an almost reckless love of life. One day when they came over there was a storm. The trees were whipping wildly in the wind, bending and creaking.

'How about a sail?' she asked me.

It was a Saturday and Geoffrey was there. On the surface he was polite, for my sake, but I knew he merely tolerated these visits. He loved his privacy, guarded it fiercely. I put his reserve down to that.

'Are you mad?' he asked, his words only partly softened by his languid drawl.

She laughed. 'Undoubtedly. So how about it, Morganna?'

I smiled. 'Why not?'

So out we went, Rosamond, Archie, and I. The *Morganna* needed the three of us working like banshees to sail her, but sail her we did. She practically flew across the water, chased by the storm. Rosamond yelled out orders to Archie who seemed quite happy to comply. I was impressed by their closeness, by his respect for her. He seemed to feel no macho compulsion to order us around, and was quite happy that we both obviously sailed a lot better than he did. After the resentful competitiveness of my peers at Southampton Yacht Club, his quiet confidence made me feel I could trust him to let me be me, and to love me as I was.

Henry watched it all happen, a surprisingly wary witness.

'Don't you think you're both taking this thing a tad fast?' she asked one afternoon when we were alone together.

'What, sleeping with him?'

'No, not that,' she snapped impatiently. 'The love thing.'

I laughed. 'I don't think you have much choice, do you, who you fall in love with?'

'Of course you do. My mother only makes sure she falls in love with seriously rich men. Charlie's her third super-rich husband, and each one's richer than the last.'

'Henry, the last thing I need is more money.'

'Just as well.'

'So what's the problem?'

'The problem is there's a great big ocean out there which is fun to fish in.'

'I fished enough in Florence. I never met anyone who I felt a connection with, and let me tell you, that kind of anonymous sex is more depressing than celibacy. I feel connected to Archie, and to his mother in some strange way.'

'Oh, everyone falls in love with her, with her charisma. But after a few weeks of her, I think my mother wants her out of the house, PDQ.'

'Oh no. They're not leaving, are they?'

'In two days, honey bunch. As far as my mother's concerned, not a day too soon.'

The fear that hovered around me now clenched my gut like an illness. I had tried not to think of what I would do when Archie left. I had lived for the moment, and the moment was almost gone.

So I wished and I dreamed and I prayed and when I think of it now the words of the Greek Gods come back to me; be careful of what you pray for, because you just might get it.

Chapter three

I defied tradition and went to be married not in the environs of what passed for my home, but in the north-west tip of Scotland. I left Long Island with an armoury of Vuitton trunks that had belonged to my mother. I felt grown up, excited, strangely bereft as I waved Geoffrey goodbye. He'd been reserved for days, and I got the feeling he was biting something back, but when the time came for me to leave, that reserve cracked. I saw tears in his eyes and they undid me. The Olympus of my childhood had become a mere mortal. I had never seen him cry. I blinked away my own tears and resolutely looked forward. Geoffrey should have been coming with me. He'd offered excuse after excuse as to why he couldn't. He hid behind the shield of work commitments, so I travelled solo as perhaps every bride-to-be should.

I was bound for Archie's ancestral home, in Sutherland, overlooking Cape Wrath. In one neat crossing of the Atlantic, I exchanged my history for his. We travelled up three days before the wedding so that Archie could show his birthplace to me. We took the sleeper train from Euston. We sat in the train, in the bar, looking out of the window with suppressed excitement as the guard strode up and down the platform blowing his whistle. There was something magical in that sound, and in the slamming of doors that followed it. Time was being counted out, the last few seconds of my old life, before, at seven o'clock exactly, the train gave a gentle lurch and pulled out of the station.

As I had done with Archie, at first sight I fell in love with his birthplace. Cape Wrath was a wild place, aptly named in retrospect although, as Archie told me, it was named by the Vikings. In old Norse, Wrath meant turning point, for it was here that their long boats turned and headed down the Scottish coast bound for rape and plunder. But the contemporary English meaning resonated with me. You only had to take one look at the rugged coastline, dotted with outlying islands, ranging from the large Orkneys, to the deadly small rock formations all too ready to scythe through the hull of any vessel fool enough or unlucky enough to encounter them. Here the full might of the Atlantic smashed into the shore, grinding the rock to endless miles of golden sand beaches, or serrating the cliffs into gullies and overhangs and echoing caves. The air was rent by the sound of sea-gulls, wheeling through the air, riding the wind in wild abandon. Every so often you would hear a deep booming sound, as the waves thudded into the caves, exploding in the confined space. And then, almost inescapable, there was the sound of the wind, roaring in, buffeting the cliffs, racing on across the miles of bleak moorland.

It was not a comfortable place. Ruined cottages testified to inheritors' desires to move away to somewhere more temperate. I would have hated to be elderly or infirm there. It demanded youth, vigour, and resilience, which is what I thought I possessed. I found it exhilarating. In three days we saw every kind of weather save snow. On the first day we were dazzled by sunlight reflecting off the golden beaches, on the second the sky brooded, magnificently overcast, and on the third the rains came, sluicing down, soaking us in seconds. We laughed, retreated to our hire car, and with the heater blasting, drove back to our hotel in Durness.

That night, Geoffrey telephoned. Archie was in the bath. I was glad he wasn't there to witness the call.

'So, Morganna.'

'So, Geoffrey.' His urbanity had deserted him, and he was floundering. He blew out a breath. I knew this wasn't easy for him, but I was damned if I was going to help. He should have been here in Scotland supporting me, not thousands of miles away lecturing me.

'So tomorrow's the day?' he asked.

'As you well know.'

'Look, Morganna, I'd be failing in my duty if–'

'Oh, your duty. God forbid you fail at that.'

'Please, Morganna. Just listen to me. I'm saying this because I care about you, because I love you, Godammit, and I can't just sit back.'

'If you loved me you'd be here, handing me away tomorrow.'

'That's just it. I cannot hand you away with a clear conscience.'

'Why are you saying all this now? Tonight of all nights? And what the hell do you mean?'

'I tried to say something on Long Island. I just couldn't get the words out right. And I know my timing stinks and I'm sorry for that. But it's now or never, I guess.'

I bit back a response. I couldn't let this escalate. I

felt alienated enough from Geoffrey as it was, without saying things that would live on like wounds in our memories. I took a few deep breaths and let him speak.

'Go on then.'

'Are you *sure* this is wise? There's still time to change your mind.'

'Why would I want to? I *love* him.'

'I don't doubt that you love him, but this is so precipitate. You're so young. Wait. Get to know them better. Because you don't *know* them, this family you're marrying into.'

I laughed. I was marrying the man, not his mother, and as far as I was concerned, she defied the old mother-in-law clichés. I adored her. And, anyway, how much time is enough when the things worth knowing are the things best hidden? And what difference does knowledge make, when over one marriage in three fails?

I *was* young. I had all the answers. I wanted to *live*, to *love*, to *feel*. Couldn't he understand that? I was twenty, for God's sake! What twenty-year-old who had lived her entire sorry life as I had wouldn't have jumped at the chance of love? I was burning inside, even then. Though I didn't know it. And Archie was gorgeous. Inflammatory himself. A pyre for my childhood.

So the next day, as planned, we married. In a reversal of convention, it was Rosamond who gave me away. She was mother to both of us that day. It was a day of gales, rain, sun and rainbows. Man and wife, we left the church at two thirty after a service that was short even by lay Scottish standards: a quick hymn, a five-minute oration by the Reverend Graham Leaves on the subject of trust — all or nothing — absolute, or dust — *Had he known, I wondered? Had he the eye like some in these parts were rumoured to possess?* — the vows, at which I smiled solemnly, while he looked enchanted — another hymn, then the elaborate signatures, both schooled in copper-plate, in the dusty book, then out into the elements. No confetti. No rice. Rosamond decreed both common, but perhaps the seagulls felt the lack, for screaming they flew, high and low, wild in the wind, darting white against the lowering sky. Nearly dark at two thirty. It was October, and felt like frigid February. I shivered in my silk dress. Who got married in northern Scotland in bleak October? We did. Archie Edge. Morganna Hutton.

I said my new name, mouthing the sound to the wind as I walked the slippery, uneven cobblestones back to the street. We posed. I threw my bouquet high. It spiralled like a Frisbee on the back of a gust, and came to land in the hopeful hands of one of the village children. A girl of seven, who caught it, unsmiling. Long wait, I thought.

Not like me. Scarcely turned twenty. I hadn't planned on falling in love, had little thought of mar-riage, other than something that might happen some-time in the future. I didn't know what marriage was like, I had no model. No preconceptions, good or bad. Perhaps that was why it was so easy for me to take the chance. Against Geoffrey's advice.

I spent my wedding night in a castle. Wrath Castle stood on the edge of a cliff, looking north towards

Cape Wrath. It seemed to be standing sentry, guarding the mainland from all sea-based marauders. It was built as a fortress, Archie told me, in the thirteenth century. It had four towers, one at each corner. In between were six slitlike windows, ideal for firing arrows from. It was enormous, grey, implacable, ugly but impressive. It was also crumbling, and shuttered up. But Archie opened it up for us, and we were to spend the night in the one arguably habitable room. I could think of many places where I would rather have spent my wedding night than in that damp, forbidding prison, but it was my husband's castle, and this was some form of rite of passage, beyond the normal. I thought little of it. It seemed a simple enough thing. Our few guests drove fifty miles to the nearest decent hotel. Archie and I lay in bed, warming each other, listening to the howling wind. It sounded angry to me, a wind of rage and lamentation. I thought to myself that the fates were angry that we had dodged what had been mapped for us both. Married. I had done it. *Escaped*. I thought I saw in his eyes the same gleam of flight.

The next day we left Sutherland and headed to the Caribbean to honeymoon on Peter Island. Two weeks alone, an interlude, hot and blissful, and then we came home. Not to Scotland, but to the November streets of London. To Archie's bachelor pad in Chelsea — one bedroom, one bathroom in an Edwardian block overlooking the Thames. It looked like a set. For one. It was tiny and unloved but I didn't care.

The traffic on the Embankment roared by in a never-ending noxious torrent, but the presence of water, even if it were the sludge of the Thames, I found reassuring. Anyway, Archie and I were so consumed in each other I scarcely noticed my surroundings. During those long nights as winter closed in, we had the slow luxury of getting to know each other, body and soul. There was a gas fire in his bedroom, and we would lie with the curtains drawn against the world, with the firelight flickering on our naked bodies and make love, first with wild frenzy, and then, later, only partly sated, with delicious slowness. Then we would talk, tell each other tales from our childhoods, talk of places we wanted to go together, things we wanted to do. We did what all happy lovers, and newlyweds, do. We cemented our love with history and dreams.

After the whirlwind of our courtship and marriage, there was a great joy in just being with each other, in falling asleep entwined, in sharing a cup of breakfast coffee, in dining in one of the tens of restaurants that thronged the King's Road, in walking in Battersea Park in the interminable rain that seemed to fall, but which still, then, failed to dampen our spirits.

Our love calmed and deepened, and in that I was truly happy. I felt I was right and Geoffrey was wrong. There was no price to be paid for haste. But as the weeks passed, and November turned into December, the rest of life began to intrude.

However much I tried to mask it, the reality was I didn't take to London. It was too big, too restless. The indifferent streets alienated me. I didn't know what to do with myself in the long hours when Archie was at his office. I was a country girl, not a city girl, and the major pastime in cities — shopping — left me cold. As for work, I was too unschooled to get a job of any interest, and spared of the necessity of having to work for a living, I languished. I tried to paint, and to my despair, I found I couldn't. I tried, gripping the paint-brush as if it were a lifeline. But it failed me. The grey reaches of the Thames that I chose for my subject lay like mud on my canvas. So I gave up, before I forgot altogether that I once could paint. The days began to drag.

Archie worked, or tried to, as an architect. Monday to Friday he went to his poky office under the arches in Waterloo every day and touted for jobs. The country was in the grip of recession, the fiercest since the Wall Street Crash of the nineteen twenties and thirties. The stock markets crumbled, property prices tumbled, and no doubt lives foundered. The only commissions Archie picked up were a few paltry extensions, a garage conversion. Soon he was as dispirited as I.

I could see the same storm brewing in him as had blown up, but remained contained, in his mother. The rage of promise unfulfilled. He would come home from Waterloo and pace, or else sit and brood. I caught his agitation, like a disease. And then my eczema came back, and my asthma, full-blown attacks that left me wheezing and covered in red weals.

Archie was horrified.

'What's brought this on?' He asked, appalled.

'I've always had it, or been prone to it. That's why I had to live in Long Island, by the sea. It went into remission there.'

'I had no idea.'

'I thought I had grown out of it,' I said sadly. 'It did-n't seem worth mentioning.'

'But what about Florence? You spent, what, a year there, didn't you?'

I was struck suddenly by how little we still knew of the exact details of one another's lives.

'I did. For some strange reason, it stayed away, more or less. That's why I thought I'd gotten over it.'

'Go and see a doctor. Ma'll know the best, she'll intro–'

'Archie, darling, I have seen the best.'

'So what do we do?'

'Live with it,' I answered.

He caught one of my hands in his and grimaced at it. 'But it must hurt, no, and the asthma attacks. They scare the shit out of me, if I have to be honest.'

'I'm not a big fan of them either.'

He let go of my hand and turned away from me to gaze out at the Thames, flowing by in silent disapproval, its slick blackness flecked by the reflection of the street lamps.

'Perhaps you should go back to Long Island for a little bit, see if it calms down.'

'Is that what you want?' I asked him, leaden-hearted.

'Of course I don't. I want you here with me. But I can't just up sticks. I have to work, or at least bloody try to.'

'Look, London's full of all these places doing complementary therapies. I'll try some of those.'

'You haven't tried any before?' he asked, suddenly hopeful.

'One or two.'

'And?'

'Well, they didn't really work. But there are still loads I haven't tried.'

'And in the meantime?'

'God, Archie, there are worse things. I'll be fine.'

He ran his hands through his hair. 'You're not fine. I hate seeing you like this. It's miserable, and I can't help you, and not only that, I'm not a whole hell of a lot of support at the moment. My work is shit. This whole economy's going down the tubes. Nobody's doing anything. Garage extensions! Not exactly what I spent seven years training to do, fantasizing about.'

'What would you like to do?' I asked.

He leaned forward, arms on knees, eyes gleaming. 'Something big,' he answered. 'Something I can really get my teeth into. A proper challenge. A major house, a restoration. Making something beautiful.' He gestured at the world outside. 'This all feels so pointless, such an anticlimax.'

I looked out at the river, my eyes coming to rest on the Buddhist temple in Battersea Park, lit up like a giant bauble. I stared until the edges became blurry, and I began to see another image altogether. Perhaps it had been forming in my unconscious mind for weeks. Perhaps it had to be shocked into life. I saw a castle, by the sea, emerging from the mists brilliant and intact.

'What if we went back to Scotland?'

'What?' he snorted. 'Where would we live? On what?'

'We'd live in that castle, of course. It can be your project, your labour of love. You can restore it.'

'With what? Do you have *any* idea how much that would cost?'

I smiled. 'I don't need to. One thing you never knew

about me, my love, is that when my parents died, they made me a very rich girl.'

I didn't tell him how rich. Of the fortune that would be mine when I turned twenty-one in a few months. That much Geoffrey had successfully drummed into me.

Chapter four

In the weeks that followed, Archie became like a man possessed. We flew back and forth to the castle five times. He drew up floor plans, tried to convey to me his vision. I found the details hard to follow, the interminable, but beautifully drafted plans frustrating, but I had visions of my own. Archie's excitement was infectious. We both fell in love with our project. He dealt with all the practical details.

I rang Geoffrey, warned him there would be some serious calls upon my trusts.

'What? Already? Jesus, Morganna! Couldn't you just let the ink dry on your marriage certificate?'

'Oh Geoffrey. Please support me. I hate fighting like this. I hate your animosity.'

'I wouldn't take this line unless I thought it best for you.'

'Geoffrey, I am covered head to toe in eczema, my asthma's back, I—'

'Oh Morganna, I am sorry.'

'Then support me. Quit this attack on Archie. I love him. We're happy together. We're making a dream together, something good for both of us. I cannot stay in London. In Cape Wrath I'll be by the sea. I'll be better.'

He blew out a long breath. 'You always have my support. I might not show it in the ways you want, but, I promise you, all I want is your happiness, your well-being.'

'I know that, Geoffrey, but I'm a big girl now. Please, just trust my judgment.'

'Morganna, money is what I do. You don't get to my age without having seen a few things, developing a sense about things.'

He just didn't get it. He was jaundiced, the old fool. He was a banker, in love with his money. It seemed to me that he wanted me to revere mine, not to spend it. He could have stopped me, but it hovered between us unsaid that in a few months I would be free to dispose of my money as I wished. All he could do was talk, and all I needed to do was say *hmm-mmm*, and ignore him. Of course, I couldn't see him, pacing his study with the phone in a death grip, the worry pinching new lines on his face. I couldn't, or would not, hear the love or concern that underlay his words.

He wanted to talk, to meet, to counsel me. I was in my usual hurry, but he managed to extract from me a promise to meet next summer, June at the latest. I would go to him, as I always did in the summer. I agreed without argument. It seemed at the time a small enough price to pay. I was so busy, so full of my new life that I didn't have time to miss him, so in the selfish ways of the young and the newly in love, it didn't really occur to me that he was missing me. Besides, he had always tried to appear so self-contained. I justified my actions easily enough.

The weeks leading up to Christmas sped by. I busied myself with provisioning the castle, which was completely bare. Every morning I would go to Starbucks on the King's Road to drink cappuccinos and compose my lists. I couldn't buy much, because the castle was so damp, there was nowhere to store anything, but Archie had got a team of Polish builders together, who had already gone up to Cape Wrath, an advance guard, to make two or three rooms habitable, so I had a few rooms to fit up.

I decided to try to make it fun, so I rang Henry's mother's house in London on the off chance that my friend was around. The next morning she phoned back.

'You're here!' I said with delight.

'Down from uni for the holidays. Always spend a week here for the parties.'

'And then recover in St. Barts. Fancy some more shopping?'

'Name the place.'

'Peter Jones.'

She groaned. 'Not quite what I had in mind.'

'I know, I know, but I *have* to buy all this housey stuff and I might at least get some fun out of it if you're around.'

'Well, shopping is shopping, I suppose,' she replied, trying hard to muster enthusiasm.

'And we can reward ourselves with a decent lunch afterwards.'

'Now you're talking.'

I met her a few hours later on the King's Road.

'Bloody *hell*! What happened to you?' she asked, peering at me in horror.

'My eczema's back. And my asthma.'

'I can see that. Why?'

'City living. The pollution.'

'God, Morganna. Can't you do something?'

'Not really. Not here.'

'You look terrible.'

'Thanks.'

'Sorry, sweetie. I didn't mean it like that, but it must be awful.'

'It isn't fun, but it's not permanent. I hope. Come on, let's go shop.'

I was fed up with the reactions I was getting: sympathy, distaste — both were equally unpleasant. I was beginning to feel almost like a leper. Since the eczema had covered my body, Archie had not made love to me. He said it was because he feared hurting me, abrading my already raw skin, but, although I did my best to cover it up, I was hurt. It lent an urgency to all I did. We *had* to get out of London, and quickly.

I put it out of my mind, pulled out my list, and Henry and I hit Peter Jones. I ordered a bed, sheets, pillows and duvets, a wardrobe, towels — white, huge and fluffy — and basic kitchen stuff. I felt at a bit of a loss. Homemaking was not one of my skills. I couldn't cook, so I had no idea what saucepans I would need, and what the differences were between the tens of different kinds on display. Henry was just as clueless as I was, but we amassed a selection, and I arranged for delivery in the first week in January. I felt like I was play-acting the part of wife, and not very well. But I felt too, that some other, more real, life was waiting for me and Archie.

I surveyed my purchases with a mixture of satisfaction and embarrassment. Those that I had managed to haul off the shelves made a great obstacle course round the till, earning me frowns from Alice-banded matrons who clearly thought I had no business buying goose-down duvets and Le Creuset. I stifled a giggle as one audibly tutted me, and then Henry and I headed off to Walton Street for lunch.

'So, give,' she demanded after we'd ordered huge restoring bowls of pasta.

'We're going to Scotland. We're going to do up his castle, and live there.'

'In Scotland? All year round?'

'Yes. Why not? It'll be perfect. Archie'll have something real to use his talents on, and I'll be by the sea. My asthma and my eczema will clear up, they always do by the sea, and I'll be able to paint.'

'Jesus! It all sounds very empty to me. For you, anyway.'

I shook my head. 'I love it up there. It's incredibly beautiful.'

'Cape Wrath, or something, isn't it? I remember Rosamond talking about her castle. Very grand, it sounded.'

'Well, not really, not now. It is huge, but it's pretty tumble-down. Properly restored, it will be amazing.'

'Who's paying for it?'

Our pasta arrived. 'Bon appetit,' I said, taking a forkful.

Henry sat with hers untouched. 'So?'

'It's good. Tuck in.'

'Morgan. Answer me.'

I swallowed angrily. 'Well, who do you think?' I replied.

'That sort of thing costs a fortune.'

I said nothing.

'Come on, Morgan. Don't be like that. I'm only trying to look out for you.'

'Well don't. I don't need it and I don't want it. Why does everyone feel they have to protect me? I can look after myself.'

'You think? Morgan, look, you've led about the most sheltered life of anyone I know, closeted away in Long Island.'

'Maybe, maybe not, but that doesn't make me an imbecile.'

'No-one ever said you were.'

'So what are you saying then?'

Henry looked at me for a while. It felt like she was trying to delve into my head.

'Nothing, really. Forget it. How's Archie? He must be thrilled. I know how much his mother loves that place. How are things going with you guys?' said Henry in an uncharacteristic gabble.

'Fine. He's really well. He *is* excited. This is the kind of work he is cut out for. He couldn't be happier.'

She gave a thin smile. 'I'm glad for him. And you?'

'I can't wait to get out of London, get healthy again.'

'I'll bet.'

Henry and I finished our lunch, and I left her in Walton Street, feeling strangely glad to get away. She'd been oddly reserved, not her usual light-hearted voluble self.

I flagged down a taxi and went back to Embankment Gardens, lugging the portable purchases up to the third floor. Archie was in the sitting room, poring over his drawings. He looked up with a smile.

'Good God, you should have buzzed up to me and I'd have helped you. What is all that?'

'Housey things. Nothing you'd get excited about.'

He took the bags from me, gently held my arms and kissed me. 'I'm excited about everything these days. Come and have a look at this. Tower rooms. I've designed a studio for you, where you can paint.'

'Oh Archie, you are an angel. Show me.'

We sat down together on the sofa. Archie showed me his plans, conjuring the image of a room in a tower, north-facing, with huge picture windows overlooking the sea. I could see myself there, I could almost smell the sea salt, and the oil paints, so clear was Archie's vision.

'North-facing too. You thought of everything.'

Archie smiled. 'I consulted a great tome entitled *Architecture for Artists*. It said you simply had to have light from the north.'

I quickly forgot Henry's words, her caution, in our joint euphoria.

On Christmas Eve, exhausted but excited, we piled into Archie's ancient BMW, and headed out of the city, seemingly with half of London, for Rosamond's cottage in Southwold. I'd never been there. It was where Archie had grown up, and I was keen to fill in some of the yawning gaps in my knowledge of his childhood. When I asked him, he always replied that there was little to tell, and not sufficiently subtly changed the subject. I'd always believed though, that bricks and mortar had their own tale to tell, so I was looking forward to a little harmless detective work.

I was looking forward too, to spending a week with Rosamond. The mad dashing about in the last few weeks had left me exhausted, in serious need of a little nurturing, something that Rosamond was so good at. Archie had told me too that she was a brilliant cook. Home cooking, long chats by the fire and walks along the beach were just what I needed. Hopefully, the eczema and asthma would go into remission too. By the end of the week, my skin might just be clearing up.

At Archie's insistence, we had told Rosamond nothing of our plan for the castle. It was to be our Christmas present to her. Some present. Archie had drawn up a complete set of plans for her, with pages of explanations written beautifully in copperplate in his black fountain pen. This he had bound in red leather. He had worked into the night for a week to finish his present. Now his skin was more pallid than ever, with dark shadows crescenting beneath his eyes

'I hope it's enough for her,' I said, absently eating a packet of crisps, passing them to Archie, who was glaring angrily ahead at the stationary traffic. Perhaps I should have brought a more immediate offering; scent, a silk scarf.

He turned to me with a look of sheer incredulity. 'Are you mad? This is what she's dreamed of ever since she was a little girl. Although I think she's probably given up on it by now.'

The vehemence of his response silenced me. I was conscious of undercurrents, of eddies of history and emotion here that I couldn't begin to decipher. Archie felt my need for explanation, filled the silence. 'You've got to understand that her father's ancestors built that castle and occupied it for nearly six hundred years.

Can you imagine that? All the generations of Edges that lived there, the marriages, the births, the deaths?'

I imagined a long line of my in-laws. Their breath, blood, and tears must have seeped into the very fabric of the castle. They had weathered it with their lives.

'Their occupation of it ended with her,' Archie continued. 'They shut it up sometime after I was born. I'm hazy on the details; she doesn't like to talk about it. Feels cast out I think. Although she hasn't lived there for nearly thirty years, she still thinks of it as home. I grew up with stories about it. Other boys would have *Thomas the Tank Engine* — I'd have Wrath Castle, every night for years. She peopled it with knights and fair ladies and vengeful ghosts,' he laughed and edged the car forward as the interminable queue shifted slowly. 'She drip-fed it into my blood.'

'Why did they shut it up?'

He gave me that look again, slightly toned down this time.

'Money, of course.'

'Ah.'

I felt uneasy then, unsure of quite what I and my money had set in motion.

'Archie, just one thing I don't get. You said generations of Edges have lived there, but I thought that was your father's name.'

'Oh, no.'

'But didn't you take your father's name?'

'Originally, yes.'

'And?'

'My mother had it changed back to hers, after he died.'

As if he never lived, I thought. 'Why?'

'She feels strongly about the name. Wanted some-one to continue it.'

'Like a dynasty?'

'Exactly.'

Chapter five

Southwold was a pretty place, slightly melancholy like all summer resorts out of season. Rosamond appeared at her front door the moment we pulled up. She came out to meet us, opened the door to me and beamed at me as I stepped out.

'Morganna, darling,' she gave me a great big hug, and kissed my cheek. It was as if she was quite blind to my eczema, totally unsqueamish, unlike everyone else it seemed.

'Come on in. You must be exhausted poor thing, all those hours cooped up in that wretched car.' She turned to her son.

'Archie, my love, how are you?' she kissed and embraced him warmly, and led us into her home.

I was surprised by the modesty of Rosamond's house: a whitewashed cottage, overlooking a bleak common. It didn't suit her. It seemed like a staging post, and, surprisingly, she seemed to regard it as such, showing me around with casual indifference, as though the house had little to do with her. Surely she couldn't have been holding out for Wrath Castle all this time? How did she think it would fall into her lap? After the brief tour, she installed us by the fire and brought us steaming bowls of stew.

'I thought you'd like to sit soft after being stuck in the car.' She handed us broken-up pieces of French bread, warm and drenched in melting butter to dip in the stew. I took a mouthful and moaned with pleasure.

'Eat up,' she said, just a glint of worry in here eyes. 'You're thin as a rake.'

'A week of this and I won't be.'

'Good. Then I shall make it my personal project,' she replied.

After dinner, Archie went out into the garden to get some fresh air. Rosamond came upstairs with me as I headed for bed.

'You get some rest, won't you, sweetheart. Don't feel in any rush to get up in the morning.' She kissed my cheek again, still saying nothing about the disfiguring red patches. I blessed her for it.

I undressed and almost fell into bed. I think I was asleep seconds later.

I slept so deeply that I woke wonderfully refreshed and unusually early. I left Archie asleep, dressed silently and with quiet delight headed out for a walk along the beach. It was still dark. I was utterly alone, and blissfully content. This is what I did almost every day in Long Island, year round. I felt there was a rhythm here I could slip into immediately. The surf pounded in, and the air was biting cold, but I found it exhilarating. I must have walked for nearly an hour. Dawn was only just breaking as I let myself back in.

I found Rosamond in the kitchen in her dressing gown, struggling to put a huge pan containing a large goose into the oven. I hurried over to help her.

'I'm fine, darling,' she said briskly, fending me off. She closed the oven door with a slam. 'Right, time to get dressed,' she said, hurrying off.

It might have been the early morning that made her

snappy, but I had a feeling it was because I had caught her toiling, and in her nightclothes. Rosamond liked to give the impression that she achieved everything effortlessly. Her house was spotless. I bet she cleaned it herself, but would never admit it to anyone. I felt my admiration for her grow. I brewed some fresh coffee and poured her a cup when she appeared ten minutes later, looking immaculate in perfectly pressed, thin grey wool trousers, a creamy silk blouse and kitten heels. Her hair was brushed, swept back from her face as if by its own volition, curling gently on her shoulders, and she smelled of something by Guerlain. It struck me then that she was rake thin, just as thin as I was. It was the thinness not of the periodic dieter, but of someone with lifetime iron discipline, and an unquiet mind that would devour calories like a fever. Her thinness and her rigid posture made me think of the Duchess of Windsor. The difference was that while Rosamond was to get her castle, she never did have her king.

'Thank you, darling,' she said, taking the coffee, sipping it gratefully. 'You're up early,' she observed over the brim.

I shrugged. 'I woke up. I can never go back to sleep.'

'Neither can I. Bugger, isn't it?'

'Bugger,' I agreed.

Lunch was delicious. We finished by two, and then went for a walk on the beach. We returned in time for the Queen's speech. Only then did we turn to our presents.

'Champagne first,' said Rosamond, getting to her feet. She came back with a bottle of vintage Pol Roger.

For all her apparent lack of money, she entertained lavishly. We clinked glasses, and I flicked a nervous glance at Archie. I could sense his excitement, wondered what it felt like to be the only child, presenting his mother with something she had dreamt of all her life, probably never thought she'd see. I felt then, the measure of his love for her, and it only made me love him more.

He reached behind him and handed her the file, wrapped in crisp, pale gold paper. She gave him a long, quizzical look, as if trying to divine exactly what he was presenting her with. She must have felt his excitement, and wondered. She took a long sip of champagne and peeled away the gold paper. It slithered to the floor. She caught it up and tossed it into the fire, where it hissed and flared, like a charm.

And then she opened the red leather cover, and her eyes widened in disbelief. For a while, she just looked at the first page. I could see her eyes flicking back and forth, across images and words, as if unable to take them in at first sight. Then she turned the next page, and pored silently over that. It must have taken her ten long minutes to look at the whole file. I could see, as she neared the end, that she was trying to compose words. I had never seen her less than bitingly eloquent at all times, and her hesitancy gave her a vulnerability that I found discomfiting. Finally, she wrenched her eyes from the file, and looked up at Archie. She blew out a slight breath, and shook her head.

'Is this really going to happen?' she asked.

He nodded. 'It's begun already.'

The two of them just gazed at each other for a while, and it seemed to me that worlds of meaning passed between them. For the first time, I felt strangely excluded. I almost wanted to leave the room, leave them to enjoy this, and all it seemed to stand for, alone together. Rosamond reached for her champagne glass, and I saw then that her hand was shaking. She turned to me suddenly, with a glittering smile.

'You, my dear, are amazing.'

She saluted me with her glass, and then repeated the gesture to Archie.

'To Wrath Castle,' she said, draining her glass. 'To the best present I could ever have.'

I blinked. I had always thought of the castle as a new life for me and Archie, not as a present to her. But I upbraided myself quickly. Of course she was delighted. With her background, it was only natural that she be dynastic; a gift to Archie was a gift to her.

We drank the toast. She hadn't asked the obvious question. She must have guessed then, that I had money. It didn't occur to me that she might already have known.

So we tied up the castle in a bow, and presented it to her on Christmas Day. Her ancestral home. Her, and my, destiny.

Chapter six

The remainder of the week in Southwold passed in a blur. Rosamond and Archie went into practical paroxysms of delight poring over the plans together. I took long, solitary walks on the beach, swathed against the bitter north wind that froze and exhilarated me, filled myself with Rosamond's delicious food, read books, and slept. By the time we were ready to return to London, I was feeling wonderfully refreshed, but, I have to admit, keen to have my husband to myself again.

I kissed Rosamond goodbye.

'Thank you for a lovely week,' I said, 'and for my bracelet.' She had given me an antique filigree silver bracelet, which I had hardly taken off. It was as fine and delicate as a spider's web, and as captivating. I loved it.

'My darling, my pleasure, I promise you. And thank you for your incredible present. Quite beyond the realms of imagination, I must say.'

I smiled. 'I can't wait to go there, to live there, and get stuck in.'

'I bet. Hard work, but I hope you feel fortified, just a tad.'

'I do. I feel much better than when I arrived. And, by the way, thank you for saying nothing, about my eczema, and my asthma. Very sensitive of you.'

She gave me a complicit smile. 'My dear, I simply cannot abide sympathy. It's too often laced with ill-disguised *schadenfreude*. The only people that seem to get off on it are the self-pity junkies, and I'd never have you down as one of them. Far too much backbone.' She turned to Archie, hugged him to her. 'Goodbye, darling boy. Good luck, and *courage*.' She pronounced it the French way, which seemed to emphasize it, somehow.

Why would he need it, I wondered. He kissed her, pulled away, and we began the long drive back to the city.

We left London for good at the end of the first week in January. We stole away in Archie's car at 5 a.m., in the black predawn. As we left London, and stiff hours later England, behind, I watched the countryside changing, growing progressively wilder. We spent the night on the borders, and set off before dawn again, keen to arrive in Cape Wrath before nightfall.

All we took with us was a few untidy suitcases, packed with the haste of fugitives. We felt something of the glee of escapees too, as we bounced along up the old road that led to the castle, and parked with a screech and crackle on the ancient gravel. Archie took out a heavy three-pronged key, grey with age, opened the enormous oak door studded with nail heads, and swung it open upon our new life.

We walked through the empty rooms, our footsteps echoing against the frigid walls. It seemed to me that we should have felt like intruders, disturbing a long peace, or awkward strangers at least, but we didn't. We moved as if we belonged, knowing what every room had been and was to be again. If the ghosts of Archie's ancestors were watching, I felt sure they would be pleased. And in Archie, if not in me, Edge blood would flow once again, within these ancient walls.

One room had been made ready for us by the builders; the bedroom where we had spent our wedding night. The team of Polish builders that Archie had hand-picked had plastered, painted, and primed it in a week of frenetic activity. The bed from Peter Jones was there, with a pile of bedding and pillows atop. I made it up; the flannel sheets were smooth and comforting against my chilled hands. There was a fireplace. While Archie marshalled the builders, I went off in search of driftwood.

The moorland leading up to the castle offered nothing but scrubby heather. I skirted along the cliffs until the precipitate rocks gave way to a steepish slope of rock and thin soil, anchored in place by wiry grasses. I found what seemed to be an old path dotted with sheep droppings. Delighted, I made my way carefully down, using my hands in places. The path twisted and turned, switchbacking down until it gave onto a beach that made me catch my breath.

Golden sand stretched away to either side in a crescent at least two miles long and five hundred yards wide. Just out to sea, a giant rock stood proud of the water. It looked like a totem pole. Hard to imagine that this was the work of the sea alone. It seemed hewn by a much more specific hand. At the far end of the beach there were small dunes. I noticed white shapes dotted amongst them — a herd of sheep drawn by something irresistible.

The sky was grey, the sea steely, and while the wind was only moderate, great rollers boomed and crashed into spume in the shallows. I stood, riveted, firewood forgotten. This was a place of magic, the secret kingdom of every child's dream, mine to share with sheep and seagulls.

Finally the cold dislodged me, and I remembered my mission. I gathered up as much firewood as I could, and headed up the steep path.

When the Poles heard of my plan, there was much gesticulating and cautioning, and, when they saw I was set, two of them went onto the roof, prodded the chimneys and hauled out a bird's nest, unoccupied, thankfully.

That night, as Archie and I got ready for bed, I lit the fire. The wood I had collected was damp, but the boards the Poles had ripped down from the windows and chopped up for me were just right. I lay them in a pyramid over crunched-up newspapers and struck a match. I loved lighting fires. This one took with a breath that soon became a roar. Archie and I lay there and gazed at it, naked under the flannel sheets and alpaca blankets. We looked at each other, and smiled in the firelight. The first night of our new life. Outside, the wind roared, while we lay side by side, hands touching, safe.

I woke to the cry of seagulls. I turned to look at Archie. He lay on his back, arms flung out, frowning, faraway in sleep. I eased out of bed, stifling a cry. The stone floors were freezing. I burrowed around in my suitcase and yanked out clean clothes. I dressed as quickly as I could, pulling on my down parka and gloves over my numbing hands.

I headed down the staircase, making for our rudimentary kitchen, passing the builders on my way. I dipped my head and smiled and said *hello* to each one of them, until I begin to feel a bit like one of those nodding dogs in the back of cars. There must have been thirty of them.

As I padded around the kitchen, finding homes for Peter Jones's pots and pans, I heard them start work, with a series of bangs and clangs and drilling and thuds that sounded like a minor war.

Archie appeared, looking blue with cold. He kissed me, grinned at my gloves, and put the kettle on. We tried to talk, but, even shouting, we could scarcely make ourselves heard. I began to wonder whether the castle could withstand such an assault. I managed to say as much to Archie, during a brief lull.

'It's a fortress,' he replied, laughing. 'Don't worry.'

'Yeah, but what are they *doing* to it?'

'Creative destruction. You wait, you'll see.'

He poured out a cup of coffee, sugared it for me, and we stood together, hands clasped around our mugs for warmth, frozen breath pluming from our mouths like wreaths. There was no food in the house.

'I'll go and forage,' I said. 'Where are your car keys?'

He hunted them down, threw them through the stirring air. They glittered like a dragonfly and landed in my hand. With a kiss and a wave, Archie went off to join the Poles. I escaped the sound and fury with relief.

The village was five minutes away. There were perhaps thirty small houses, whitewashed with varying degrees of diligence, a pub, a self-styled bunkhouse called *Surfdom*, a tiny school, a petrol pump outside a post office, a fish and chip shop/café, and one grocery store.

Good job food didn't mean that much to me. Although I enjoyed good food, I could exist quite happily on basics. There would be no balsamic vinegar here. But the aisles were stacked with the tinned and frozen food that I knew I would rely on, and there was a small section of fresh fruits and vegetables.

'Better in the summer,' said a voice. 'We get a lot of local produce then.' The speaker was a woman in robust old age. Her pale skin was scarcely lined. Her hair was triumphantly red.

'I'm not a vegetable person anyway,' I said.

She nodded, keeping her eyes on me, curious. I felt slightly awkward. I smiled, and moved down the aisle. I filled two shopping baskets. I wondered who was feeding the army of Poles. I hoped it was not to be me. I couldn't cook for one. Ready-made frozen meals made up most of my haul, plus loads of milk, bread, butter, eggs, and marmalade.

'Who's all this for then?' asked the woman. At least I think that's what she said. I didn't dare ask her to repeat herself.

'For the castle,' I answered, as if it had hungers of its own.

'Ah,' she said slowly. 'I had heard. So there's to be Edges at Wrath Castle again.'

I nodded.

She studied me closely, without embarrassment.

'And you'll be the wife, then?' she asked.

I stretched out my hand to shake hers. 'I am. Morganna.'

'McMullen. Ellen,' she said, taking my hand in a

surprisingly strong grip. Ignoring my protests, she helped me to the car with my shopping. I got in, rolled down the window, and said goodbye.

'Good luck,' she said, by way of parting.

I made toast, and coffee, and stood for a while, my head pounding in the throbbing kitchen. Perhaps it was my upbringing in Long Island, in Geoffrey's hushed, sepulchral house, but I never could stand man-made noise. That's one of the reasons I hated London. Even at night, it was unquiet.

I drained my coffee, ran up to our room, and grabbed my paints and brushes, a canvas, and my easel. I put everything I could fit into my backpack, and strung the easel over my shoulder. Feeling vaguely truant, and delighted with it, I hurried downstairs and out of the castle. While I was inside, the clouds had parted, giving way to dazzling sun. I found my cliff path, and headed on down. The wind had picked up, churning the sea into whitecaps.

I put down my easel and backpack and ran down to the sea's edge. I took off my glove and plunged my hand into the shallows. It was so cold it bit. I withdrew my hand, laughing. I studied the waterline for a while, determining that the tide was coming in. Even so, I calculated I would have hours before the tide forced me back to the cliffs.

I walked back to set up my easel and mix my paints. I lifted my brush, hesitantly, flicking my eyes back and forth between the sea and my naked canvas. Until London, and my abortive attempts to paint the Thames, I hadn't quite realized how much my painting meant to me, how much my sense of well-being depended on it. Now I knew, and for a moment felt quite sick as I sat, brush suspended in mid-air. But then, quite simply and easily, I began to paint.

I must have sat there for hours, unaware of the cold, of the approaching tide. It was only when the water was perhaps twenty feet from me that I came to, jumped up, turned in panic to regard the cliffs behind me, and my tiny path, which looked more perilous from this angle. Quickly I gathered up my paints and my palette, folded up my easel, and, trailing my wet canvas in one hand, I hurried up to my path and, breathing hard, I scrambled up.

At the top I turned and stared down. It seemed to me that the sea had already covered my footprints in the sand, and filled in the holes left by the legs of my easel. Were it not for the painting in my hand, wet but completed, I might not have been there.

Chapter seven

Over the coming weeks, it sometimes seemed to me that the castle was Archie's mistress, while I went to the sea with my paints as to a lover. I filled my days with it. There was no privacy in the castle; it literally hummed with the teams of builders knocking down, putting up, drilling, hammering, running up and down stairs, watched by Archie, patrolling, the mad conductor of this cacophony. I *had* to escape.

I would climb down the crumbling path to the beach. Archie would warn me on a daily basis. *The path is unsafe, the cliff crumbles, spectacularly, unpredictably. The pounding it takes from Atlantic storms sends shock waves through fault lines, and on one perfect, clear summer's day, with a crack like a shelving glacier, it could slice off and crash down.* I laughed. It wasn't that I was unafraid of death. I just didn't think it could happen to me. I was blessed.

So every day, apart from when there was a storm and the beach was claimed by the foaming ocean to itself, I would climb down, precarious but determined, my easel under one arm, my paints in a backpack, often a packed lunch.

I painted the sea in all its moods and colours. On a sunny day, it would be iridescent turquoise, purer and more brilliant than anything the Med had to offer, but when the skies were grey it was dark and foreboding. On the rare days when it was calm, it appeared sinister, as if trying to lure you in under false pretences. It was unfailingly beautiful.

I grew to love the castle, and its wild landscape. I liked to stand with my back to the sea and gaze at the castle with its distant backdrop of mountains. Their serrated outline seemed to cut into the sky like a knife into fabric. Like the sea they changed colour with the elements and the light, transforming themselves from black at night, through dark red on a clear, rosy dawn, to a whole series of blues on a sunlit day, and greys in the rain. I could have painted all day, had I the time.

The only tiresome chore I had was the constant shopping for food, and the rudimentary cleaning I engaged in as little as possible, but which seemed to be endlessly necessary. Trouble was, the activities of the builders — even in another part of the castle — meant that almost as soon as I had hovered and dusted the ubiquitous grey film returned to swamp everything. I tried to do my simple cleaning when Archie wasn't around. I felt stupidly self-conscious doing it. But one day Archie caught me with a duster in hand, cursing under my breath.

He burst out laughing.

'What's so funny?' I demanded.

'You. The heiress. Dusting.'

'Well, someone has to do it.' I answered, seriously riled now. I hated the word *heiress*, it made me sound as if I were nothing more than the sum of my money.

'My God, Morganna. We'll get someone in to do it. There's enough unemployment around here. There'll be plenty of people glad to do it.'

'Well, find them then. You don't think I enjoy this, do you?'

He smiled. 'No, I don't imagine you do. I didn't know you were doing it to be honest.'

'I know,' I reply ruefully. 'I do it, and then ten minutes later it's as if I was never here.'

'Why bother then?'

'I just sort of felt I ought to. Do something, you know . . .'

'Wifely?' He asked gently.

'Yes. Exactly.'

He took the duster from me, put it down, and kissed me. 'You are the perfect wife, just as you are. I'll find a cleaner or two. You content yourself with the fun bits.'

'What fun bits?'

'Interiors, furnishings, that sort of thing.'

Ah, and there was the rub. Neither dusting nor interiors were really my thing. The castle was not decorated, of course. Bare, plastered walls stared at me unforgivingly. Archie and the builders were doing only structural work at this stage. Rosamond rang many times, avid for progress. She and Archie endlessly discussed structure; that I knew. He gave her daily updates, but she looked to me for reports on colours and fabrics and furnishings. I knew she and Archie were waiting for me to opine, to fly down to London, and trawl through the interior design shops, or else to take on some chic designer, worthy of Wrath Castle.

Wouldn't they love it. A perfect story for the glossy pages of *Interiors*. Morganna Edge, chatelaine of Wrath Castle, poses before the twelfth-century fortress with her interior designer, Justin Camp. Thing is, for all my painter's eye, I had no interest in furnishings, soft nor hard. I enjoyed them, but don't ask me to choose them, or a suitable designer.

That innocent indifference was my next mistake.

Not that it was remotely evident then. Archie and I were renewed, fulfilled in our own ventures, and, once again, together. Weeks of living by the sea, and, I suspect, my own happiness with my painting and Archie's with his work had banished my eczema and my asthma. My skin was clear again, and my inhaler sat untouched in the bathroom cabinet. I was in love and I was happy. Who but a fool looks beyond that? Dissect and kill. You put a rose in a vase to admire. You might bring your nose close to sniff it, but the minute you pick it apart, the beauty is gone.

At the end of every day, when the Poles departed with grins and waves to the barn they were converting, and sleeping in, Archie would show me round, pointing out the progress, which was sometimes hard to see. Rubble lay where walls had once been. Destruction was a kind of progress. I could see that. Archie's cheeks flushed as he ran up the ancient spiralling staircases ahead of me, throwing open doors with a flourish, and a 'Look, Morgan, look what we've done today.'

I could feel the progress of the castle in the calluses on his hands as we made love. They scored my skin in triumph.

He was happy too that I was fulfilled by my painting. He rarely saw my canvases. I chose to keep them to myself. I wasn't sure anyone would understand why I painted what might seem to them like the same scene over and over again. Of course the sea changes every second, and I could see the differences, could smell, hear and feel the different moods of sea, wind and sky and rain. I would paint, indifferent to the cold and the sluicing rain. I rigged up an umbrella over my canvas, so it stayed pristine, while I grew bedraggled. Like a wild thing, said Archie, kissing the raindrops off my nose, when I reappeared.

I *was* wild, and I was happy. In some unfathomable way, I felt I had come home. The castle, for all its inviolable austerity, felt secure and tomblike inside. Its six-foot-thick walls, where they were not crumbling, were a fortress against the elements. For five days a week, the Poles toiled, repairing them, and the roof. And it almost seemed to me that in the dark of the night, as we slept, the castle repaired itself too; that the fabric of it grew together like skin over a wound. Perhaps it was gratitude that I felt, or else just the elemental comfort of something getting better, strengthening, but I felt a balm in that castle, as if it knew what I was doing with my dead parents' money, my husband's skill, and the toil of the Poles.

When gales struck, as they so often did, I would stand in my favourite tower, the one closest to the cliff, gazing out of the arrow slits at the screaming sea. When a particularly huge wave smashed into the cliff, the spray would rise up so high. I could slide my fingers through the arrow slit and touch it. I imagined the castle trembling to its foundations, as I sometimes did, when the wind cried its lament all around us.

I grew addicted to the shipping reports. When the Poles had finished for the day and retreated to their barn, the castle became mine again. I would take a radio up to my tower, and stand listening to Fitzroy, Dogger, Cromerty, Forties, Viking, Wight, Plymouth,

Humber, the strangely mesmeric incantation, and I would search the sea for the incoming weather, and teach myself the portents of storms. Then I would watch them roar in, often as not from Cape Wrath, screaming across the moors, across the bay, to us.

We grew into a routine, Archie and I. We would breakfast together, then separate for the day, and regroup in the rudimentary kitchen, where we would knock up something easy for dinner, and carry it upstairs with a bottle of wine to the room next to our bedroom, with its fastened walls and its view.

There, with the sea our backdrop, we would eat and talk.

'Morgan, the Poles need paying, and I need to order more supplies.'

I got to my feet and came back from the bedroom, chequebook in hand.

'How much?'

Archie looked momentarily awkward. I knew he hated these moments.

'Seventy-five grand.'

I wrote out the cheque to him and passed it over. He glanced at it and then pocketed it without a word.

'Look, why don't we dispense with this ritual. It would be much easier if you had direct access to my accounts.'

His dark eyebrows shot up in surprise. 'Are you sure, Morganna?'

'Of course I'm sure.' I laughed. 'You're not going to run off with it, are you, with some village totty?'

He gave me a wicked smile. 'Well, now that you suggest it . . .'

'Mmm. You really wouldn't want to cross me, Archie Edge. I would haunt you through this life and beyond.' And we both laughed.

Chapter eight

The next day, I rang Geoffrey. It was early morning his time. I imagined him sitting at his gleaming mahogany table, with his newspapers, masticating breakfast and news, frowning at the interruption of the phone. I surprised myself by feeling nostalgic.

'Hi Geoffrey'

'Morganna. How nice.'

'No it's not. I'm disturbing your communion.'

He laughed. 'Disturb away.'

'Well, I'm just ringing really, to say hello, and also to say that I'm giving Archie access to my bank accounts. It's not good for him to have to keep coming to me and asking for money.'

Whoever said silence is neutral must have been the aural equivalent of colour blind. There are so many different qualities of silence. This one was frozen, ice blue.

'Morganna, I have to object.'

'You don't *have* to do anything.'

'That's where you're wrong. On two counts. Number one, I care about you. I do not want you doing anything precipitate, and number two, as your legal guardian, I would be negligent if I did not counsel you against this in the strongest possible terms.'

'And just why would that be, exactly? On principle, or do you have something against my husband.'

'On principle. I don't know your husband, that's part of the issue, and, given that you two have know each other for the grand total of six months, and been married for just over two, I don't think you know him very well either.'

'I am married to him, for God's sake. I share his bed every night. Of course I know him.'

'Oh, Morganna. If only it were that simple.'

'Stop patronizing me.'

'Well stop being so damned naïve. You think sharing a bed with someone makes you *know* them.'

'Yes, as a matter of fact I do.'

'Well, I disagree. The world is full of disillusioned lovers.'

'You think Archie's going to rob me blind?' I demanded. 'Why don't you just come out with it?'

'No, Morganna. That's not what I think, but what I know is that as a matter of standard operating procedure you do not open up you bank account, even to your partner.'

'What are you talking about? Most married couples have joint accounts.'

'Most married couples do not have such a staggering disparity in wealth between one partner and the other. Just for the record, will your husband be putting anything into this joint account?'

'He's working full-time here now. How could he?'

'Quite.'

'Geoffrey, please, you must try to understand, I don't want my money to cause problems, with anybody. I'm trying to do the best thing for my marriage.'

'But not for your bank balance.'

'Jesus. That *has* to be one of the certainties of life. My bank balance can handle it. We won't be spending any more money this way, Geoffrey. Just in a less humiliating way.'

'Spending hundreds of thousands of pounds, no doubt many millions by the time you're finished, can be humiliating, can it? What a very high-class problem your husband has.'

'Geoffrey, come on.'

'It's your money, Morgan. I'm just urging you to caution, to look after it.'

'I will. I will. It's just the current account I'm talking about. I'd like to feed in a certain amount every month. That's all Archie will have access to.'

Geoffrey blew out a heavy breath. 'You'll be twenty-one in a few months, in control of all your money yourself.'

'So back me now, please?'

There was another long, pained silence. I had a slight sense then of the dilemma facing Geoffrey, but I thought in terms of awkwardness, not of heartache. 'All right,' he said wearily. 'I'll authorize a monthly feed. That's containable, I suppose. Will you speak to Chip Bennet, or shall I?'

Bennet was my personal money manager, Hutton Bank's finest, hand-picked for me by Geoffrey.

'Oh, Geoffrey, I know how busy you are. I'll speak to him. I need to discuss some of my investments anyway.'

'Right. Everything else okay?' Geoffrey's voice lightened. Like me, he was keen to move onto safer ground.

'Fine. It's really beautiful here. You must come to stay.'

'I'd like to.'

'I'll get some rooms fixed up for you. Oh, and Geoffrey, before I forget, please could you send the portraits of my parents? I need them here.'

'Of course. I'll FedEx them. You should have them in a few days.'

'Thanks, Geoffrey. You okay?'

'I, Morgan, am fine. The shenanigans of the funny little people running some of the biggest companies in this country keep me endlessly entertained.'

'Hmm. How's the bank's bank balance?'

'Surviving, even if I say it myself, thanks to my distrust of anything I can't personally understand, or explain to a reasonably intelligent seven-year-old.'

'I remember.'

'You never stayed still long enough.'

'I picked it up by osmosis. It flavoured the oxygen at home.'

'You would have made a good banker,' he said. 'You look beneath the surface. You understand people. Most of the time, anyway.'

'I thought you were worried that I didn't.'

'You're young, you're in love, and you're rich. That's a potentially dangerous combination.'

'What, as in love is blind?'

'Something of that order, yes.'

'I cannot be that cynical, Geoffrey. And, by rights, that should make everyone who ever loved cautious, regardless of money. There are many ways to break a heart. I'd rather be an optimist and run that risk than die by slow pessimism. That would kill love as surely as any betrayal.'

He sighed. 'You have a point there.'

'That's a big admission, coming from you.'

He chuckled. 'I make mistakes too, but if I get it wrong, it's not my heart, but the bank that goes down.'

'Which is worse?' I asked, teasingly.

'Mmm. On that note, I'll say goodbye.'

I put down the phone. Philosophizing apart, I had what I wanted: access for Archie to my money, or to a part of it. I called Chip Bennet, and set it up. Such a simple thing. It took just minutes.

I headed off to the village for some fish and chips. I ate them on the low stone wall, gazing out at the sea. The Savoy could not have produced anything more delicious. I finished every scrap, binned the newspaper, and crossed the road to Ellen's.

I stocked up on essentials and headed for the till.

'Morganna, morning to you. How're you?'

'I'm good, Ellen, thanks. And you?'

She laughed. 'Alive. Creaking, but alive.'

'Don't knock it.'

'Blessed girl, that I don't. Now, tell me what I can do for you.'

'Am I that obvious?'

'You've got something racing round that head a' yours. Anyone with half a brain can see tha–.'

'Mmm. Well. Coupla' things. I need some help around the place. Dusting, cleaning and all that. Know anyone?'

'I'll put the word out. Next.'

'I need food, proper food,' I said, handing over some Vim, scouring cloths, and new mop pads. 'Where do I go?'

'I wondered how long a soul could live on frozen shepherd's pie and baked beans.'

'This soul, indefinitely. My mother-in-law's coming.'

Her pale eyes widened with interest. 'I wondered when she'd grace us,' she said crisply.

'You won't be wanting me. You need Paul McIntyre, the butcher. Better'n that, you need his brother, Ben. The shepherd.'

Most things here seemed to come directly from source. The anonymous filter that separated us from the stuff of life has been removed. While the entire castle was being re-plumbed, we collected rainwater in a series of drums. We washed in the water we carried up to our bathroom, as Archie's ancestors had done, only they, I supposed, had someone to do it for them, probably to scrub their backs as well.

I found Ben on the moor, roughly where Ellen had told me he would be. How did she know, I wondered? The flock grazed hard on the unyielding ground. Two collies ran up to me, noses low on the ground, tails unwagging. I crouched down, stretched out my fingers, let them smell me, until they seemed satisfied.

Ben approached slowly. He was wearing a Gore-Tex-type jacket and weathered jeans. He was medium height, wiry build, and as he got closer I saw that he had the most remarkable blue eyes: clear and brilliant. His skin was weathered, his hair short and roughly cut, I bet by himself. He smiled at me, a small, half-smile that reached lips and eyes. Put this man on the silver screen and he'd have a fan club of millions. Yet he seemed totally oblivious to his appeal.

'You'll be wanting a lamb or two then?' he enquired in a gentle burr.

'How did you know?'

'Why else would you seek me out?'

I toyed with a number of answers to that one.

'Did you know I was coming?' I asked.

'I knew that sooner or later you'd be needing some real food.'

'How did you even know I existed?'

'Everyone round here knows.'

'And does everyone round here know about my cating habits?'

He grinned. 'No doubt. Not much news round here, see. Not lately. Opening up the castle got folks' interest.'

'Mmm.'

'Leg or shoulder?'

'Er, both, I think.'

'Who will it be you're feeding?'

'Well, me, my husband, and his mother.'

His eyes widened too. 'She's come back then.'

'Day after tomorrow.'

'Fatted calf you'll be wanting. Not a lamb to the slaughter.'

'She's not exactly prodigal, is she? And who's the lamb?'

He looked away and muttered something. I couldn't hear what it was.

The next morning, as I was hurrying out of the back entrance with my paints, Ben arrived, not his brother. I took him into the kitchen. He looked round, unimpressed. He walked up to the cooker.

'Know how to use this?'

'I know how to turn it on.'

He studied me and decided to grin.

'Right, well that's a start.' He unwrapped a leg of lamb, and dangled it before me. He also took out from a bag a sprig of wild rosemary. 'Now, this is what you do with it.'

Armed with Ben's instructions, I put the lamb in the pantry. We didn't yet have a fridge, and until the height of summer I doubted we would need one. I was just about to grab my paints and head out again when the great bell rang. I wandered through the huge hallway and hauled open the door. A man in a brown suit stood gazing at me with keen interest.

'Mrs. Morganna Edge?'

'That's me.'

'FedEx. Got a package.'

'My parents!' I shouted, leaving him dumbfounded. He backed away, then turned and opened up his van, extracting a crate.

'Sign for it?'

I took his pen and clipboard, signed hurriedly. He nodded, backed away again, and quickly got into his van. He drove off with a squeal of tires.

I rushed back in, hunted down the Poles. Two of them hauled the crate up to my bedroom, levered out the nails, opened it up. The portraits of my parents were there, but also the Augustus John portrait of a young girl they left me in their will.

Thought you might like this one too, to keep you company,' Geoffrey had written in an enclosed note.

Bless him. I was so delighted I could hardly keep still. Fifteen minutes later, my parents were hung on the wall facing the huge window out to sea. I think they would have been pleased by the view. The Augustus John I hung on the sea wall, beside the window. My first bit of decorating, and I was delighted with it! I thanked the Poles, and sat admiring the paintings for a while, before finally heading down to the beach.

I spent the morning painting, but without managing to lose myself in it, or to turn out something I was particularly pleased with. I decided to give up, and headed back to the castle feelingly oddly listless.

I was picking my way up the spiral staircase when, like a dog, I froze suddenly, hyperalert. I heard nothing, just sensed a presence. Not one of the builders, I can always hear them a mile off in their clunking boots, but someone else. I spun round. A humming rose up the stairs to greet me, then Rosamond herself appeared, trailing her hand against the replastered walls.

She didn't seem remotely surprised to encounter me there. It was as if she could see round bends.

She reached out her arms to me.

'Morgan. *Isn't* this a triumph?' She pulled me in, gripping my arms hard, kissed both cheeks and released me. She gazed in delight at the dull gleam of plaster.

Today was Tuesday, wasn't it? She wasn't due until Wednesday.

'Rosamond, am I going mad? I wasn't expecting you until tomorrow.'

'Pah! Drove through the night. Couldn't be bothered to stop.'

'You must be exhausted.'

'Darling, I never sleep much. Spend most nights pacing the floorboards. What's the difference?'

'True.'

And she didn't look tired. Her eyes glittered. She exuded vitality. She would have saved money too, I decided, by not staying in a hotel. I smiled and took her arm, gently.

'Come and have a coffee.'

Armed with our Nescafés, we advanced upstairs to the habitable room next to our bedroom.

Rosamond gazed about her, entranced.

'An Augustus John?' she asked, striding up to my painting.

I nodded.

'Mmm. *Very* nice.'

I suddenly felt uncomfortable. There was something faintly lascivious in her appreciation of it.

'Thank you.'

'You've been busy,' she announced, collapsing sinuously on the least comfortable chair. She set a gleaming black leather handbag down beside her, and I was reminded of her elegance.

'Not me. Not really. This is practically my sole bit of decoration. It's not really my scene,' I said, keen to lower her expectations. 'Your son has been busy though,' I added, sitting down on a wonderfully baggy overstuffed armchair.

Without asking, she lit up a cigarette, greedily breathing in the smoke. I got up, foraged, emptied the soap dish from the bathroom next door, and proffered it as her ash elongated worryingly.

She nodded. 'So what are you getting up to?'

'This and that. I walk. I paint. I love the sea.'

'Glorious, isn't it.'

'What have *you* been up to?' I asked.

She gave me her cat's smile. 'This and that,' she echoed with a mechant smile. 'Seeing friends, dreaming dreams. Living.'

'That's enough.'

'For some.' She got to her feet. 'Is that where you sleep?' She nodded to the room next door.

'Yes,' I answered, unwilling to lead my mother-in-law into our bedroom, self-consciously aware of the tousled sheets, the clothes strewn around. She showed no such delicacy. She strode on so confidently, that I rose and meekly followed. I stood behind her in the doorway as she scanned the room, so intently, I wondered if she was searching for something long lost. Her eyes came to rest on the freshly hung portraits of my parents. She let out a small exclamation and moved towards them.

I walked after her. She moved closer, and then stepped back, tilted her head to one side, more distant now, as if she were in a gallery, studying a Van Gogh, but still she was avid.

She turned to me, eyes alight with something I could not fathom. 'Your mother and father?'

I nodded.

'Magnificent.'

'Aren't they?' Again, I felt uncomfortable. She walked past me, back to our sitting room, and took something out of her handbag. She hunted round and collected a couple of water glasses, into which she sloshed something white and viscous.

'Sloe gin,' she said with an inviting smile. 'I concocted it myself.'

I took the proffered glass and bit back a mouthful. It scalded the back of my tongue. Slowly, and more pleasantly, the heat seeped down my throat and into my stomach. She raised her glass.

'To Wrath Castle!' she said with a flourish.

'To the castle,' I repeated, and sank some more ruin.

'I'll show you to your room,' I said, getting up, suddenly conscious that I was the hostess, not her. 'It's rather basic, I'm afraid, but the best we can do for now.'

She nodded and followed me down the staircase, across the great hall, and up the south staircase.

Practically nothing had been done to this room, save putting in a bed, but Rosamond had given me the grand total of two days' notice of her visit, so nothing much could have been done.

She was not impressed and made little effort to conceal the fact. Her beautiful face looked oddly sour.

'I'm sorry about the room,' I said. 'I know it's pretty basic, but give us a bit more time and we'll do up a guestroom in grand style for you. I'll get Januscz, he's the head builder, onto it.' I began to pace with excitement. 'I'll make sure it's all done up, interior design and everything. We were going to do it anyway, obviously, but I'll bring it forward, then you shall have your own room, next time you come.'

I turned to her expecting to see a mirror of my own excitement.

'A guestroom,' she intoned slowly, in her cut-glass perfection, as if pondering the concept. Then she warmed and beamed back at me. 'How absolutely lovely. But, darling, you won't be expecting me for some time.'

I laughed. 'Januscz can have a room done in three weeks. It might take a tad longer if we're doing specialist painting, or panelling. We need to book in the experts, but hey, there's a recession on. No-one's *that* busy.'

'I shall look forward to it. Have you a room in mind?'

I paused. 'You did live here, didn't you? It was still habitable when you were born?'

She raised her eyebrows. 'My darling, did Archie never tell you? I was born in your bedroom. One birth, one death.'

A pall fell over the room. 'What do you mean?'

'I killed my mother, didn't I, in birth.'

So did I, I thought. But it took me three months. I didn't know what to say. I hadn't known. Like me, she was motherless. I felt a pang for her, for a baby that hadn't even had her mother the three months I had. But I knew Rosamond scorned sympathy, so all I said was, 'Oh. I didn't know.'

'Now you do.'

'Well, I suppose you wouldn't have wanted that room anyway,' I finally said.

Rosamond laughed. 'Darling, it wouldn't make any difference to me. I'm not afraid of ghosts.'

Chapter nine

That night, slavishly following Ben's instructions, I cooked the lamb, cabbage, and roast potatoes. I was nervous as hell. Rosamond's cooking was a hard act to follow at the best of times, and I was a complete novice. But, after a whole week of her delicious nurturing, the least I could do was reciprocate for one meal. Added to which, I had the distinct impression that ineptitude of any kind would be despised by Rosamond. Here, in the castle, she seemed subtly altered, not as homely as she had been in her little cottage in Southwold. She was more the grande dame, and I got the feeling that I too was expected to be chatelaine, not ingénue.

Ten minutes before it seemed ready, I ran up to tell Rosamond and Archie to come down. I was mildly pissed off that neither of them had seen fit to offer a hand, but I pushed it from my mind. As I rounded the bend in the staircase that gave onto the hallway where Rosamond's room was, I heard her voice. The cold fury in it halted me. I should have turned and walked away, but I didn't. I'd never heard her angry before. This was a side I didn't know. I tried to decipher her words. *I will not have —— in my castle. Do you understand —— necessary evil, but that —— really, I'd sooner put out my eyes.* Then I heard Archie's almost plaintive come back: *Ma, please, be reasonable. It's ——* she cut him off. *Bugger reasonable. I'm going to deal with it, Archie, even if you don't have the backbone to.* Then his voice again, angry too. *On your head be it, Ma. I'll have nothing to do with it.*

I knew a parting shot when I heard one, and I backed quickly and silently down the staircase, retracing my steps until I was safely back in the kitchen. What the hell were they on about, I wondered, as I strained off half the lamb juices and attempted to make a gravy. I stirred ponderously, still shocked by the venom I had heard in Rosamond's voice, and her viciousness towards her son. Only one thing was plain; it was not a conversation I was meant to overhear.

Archie appeared a few moments later. His face was flushed and I could feel the anger radiating from him.

'Hi,' he said, brushing his hair back from his face, flashing me a quick smile. 'Got any wine?'

'Open,' I said, 'on the table.' In front of his nose.

'Ah.' He poured himself a glass, waved the bottle at me. I indicated my nearly empty glass beside me and he filled it up. He took a long glug of his own, half draining it.

'Smells good,' he said, nodding at the lamb joint, reabsorbing its juices as directed by Ben.

'Perhaps you could carve,' I said, handing him a knife.

'Sure.'

He started hacking away. 'Fuck,' he shouted, dropping the knife with a clatter. I turned to see blood spouting out of his finger.

'Ah, darling,' said Rosamond sinuously, appearing behind us. 'War wound. Let me see.' She grabbed his finger, dropped it dismissively. 'You'll live,' she opined, helping herself to wine.

I watched Archie open his mouth to speak, then wordlessly close it.

'Come here, my love,' I said. 'Here's the first-aid box. I'll stick a plaster on it.' He came to me almost meekly.

I stuck on a plaster and gave his lips a light kiss. Then I attempted to carve the lamb myself. I filled our plates with my offering, placed them on the table, which I'd covered with a clean sheet for want of anything better, and then I lit the candles I'd bought from Ellen. The three of us took our places. I'd seated Rosamond at the head of the table, Archie and I to either side.

'Bon appetit,' I said, crossing my fingers under the table.

Miraculously, dinner was more than edible. Rosamond, humour restored, complimented me, eyes wry with amusement, as if I had conjured rather than cooked. It felt to me rather as if I had.

'That was delicious,' said Archie, as he took me to bed.

'My pleasure,' I replied, replete with my own food, and relief.

He leaned across to kiss me. 'It was a lovely idea as well to offer Ma a room of her own. You're very good to her. To me.'

I paused. There seemed to be some deeper meaning in his remark that I could not fathom.

'Her blood runs through the veins of this place. How could I not?'

'By the way,' he said casually, turning away from me to switch off the light. 'I thought we needed another car, a bigger one, so that I can haul stuff around, and so that you can be independent, have your own.'

'Oh, right,' I replied in the darkness
'It's coming tomorrow.'
God, that was fast. 'Fine. What is it?'
'Something nice.'

Nice it was. It arrived after breakfast: a brand new, top spec Range Rover. It was for him, he explained. I got the old BMW. I did wonder, just for a moment, but then I saw the logic. The Range Rover held more. But still I heard Geoffrey's voice in my mind saying: *What's wrong with a pickup truck? Second hand?* But then I silenced that voice. That was not a direction I was prepared to go down in my marriage. I knew where that would lead: to emasculation, suspicion, a corroding of love.

It wasn't the only surprise I had that day. Leaving Archie and Rosamond to admire the car, I went back to our bedroom to grab my coat and gloves. As I swung the door open I came face to face with a woman who must have been all of five-foot-nothing, at least sixty, and armed with some kind of aerosol that she was spraying around with intent. I stared at her in amazement. She just looked back at me, wordlessly.

'Er, excuse me asking,' I said, mustering my best Long Island politeness, 'but I don't think we've met.'

Her response sounded like a grunt. Still trying to give her the benefit of the doubt, I reached out my hand.

'I'm Morganna Edge,' I said.

She looked at my face again with her watery inscrutable eyes before taking my hand and shaking it. She didn't even bother to remove the yellow rubber gloves she was wearing.

'And you are?' I asked.

'Mrs. McTaggart.'

'The cleaner.'

'Aye.'

As if to make the point, she turned away and began to blast the mantelpiece with her noxious aerosol. Right. Fine. I grabbed my coat and gloves, and, coughing, retreated quickly. I headed down to the beach, breathing in deep lungfuls of sea air, trying to expel the bitter taste that stayed in my mouth.

'I see you found a cleaner,' I said to Archie at dinner that night. It was a light supper, at Rosamond's request: smoked salmon, brown toast, scrambled eggs, and salad — a cinch for me after last night's effort.

'Not me. Ma. Still plugged in after all this time.'

'The redoubtable McTaggart,' said Rosamond, smearing the thinnest glaze of butter over her toast. 'She's a treasure. If anyone can beat the dust, she can.'

'You know her?' I asked, amazed that she would have picked such a crone.

'She used to clean here, in the old days. She's been around since I was born.'

'She's getting on a bit. It's a lot for someone her age to take on,' I observed.

'Not a bit of it, darling. She's fit as a fiddle, and loyalty is something to reward, don't you think?'

Loyalty to whom, I wondered, and with respect to what, exactly?

Chapter ten

It took Januscz and his team four weeks to get Rosamond's room done. I'd guessed at her tastes, thrown myself into the daunting task of decorating for her. I surprised myself. Growing up amidst luxury and beauty did seem to have rubbed off just a tad. I was pleased with what I'd created. I just prayed she would be too. I'd chosen pale yellow painted and oak-panelled walls, Persian carpets strewn on the oak floors, primrose-speckled curtains. As spring unfolded slowly, so did the room come to life. We invited her back, to the castle of her ancestors.

On the day she was to arrive, I carried up a bowl of yellow crocuses and placed them on the table beside the bed. I glanced round the room. To my untutored eye, it looked beautiful. A room to be happy in.

It stank, though, of McTaggart's noxious aerosols. I really must do something about that, I decided. I knew it played havoc with my asthma, I had suffered three attacks I could put down directly to the chemical blasting she gave my bedroom, but to date I'd let apathy and a strange reluctance to confront her hold me back. I threw open Rosamond's windows and turned with a jump when I heard someone come in behind me. McTaggart in her yellow marigolds. She turned to go when she saw me.

'Wait, Mrs. McTaggart.'

She stopped slowly.

'Could you please not use all these sprays. There are

perfectly good wax polishes that do the job just as well, and just dampening a cloth with water is fine too.'

She seemed to look right through me.

'Did you hear me, Mrs. McTaggart?' I was forced to ask.

'I heard ye,' she replied, and walked off.

I felt a slow anger rising. I had been unfailingly polite to this woman from the outset, and received nothing back save attitude and condescension.

I heard, or perhaps I imagined, the slamming of a car door off in the distance. As if caught somewhere illicit, I ran from the room and down the stairs in time to see my mother-in-law unloading two heavy Vuitton cases from the trunk of her ancient estate car and handing them to Archie, who had arrived at a skid.

Archie carried them up the stairs as one given a test, angry and reverential, combining uneasily the roles of porter, and, literally, architect of her dreams. Rosamond smiled at me, embraced me warmly, and took my arm as we ascended the staircase behind Archie. 'Don't worry, darling. I'm not really moving in. Just brought enough stuff to be comfortable on my occasional visits, and, I promise, they will be occasional.' I must still have looked doubtful, for she stopped, cupped my face in her palms, and laughed. 'I'm off on Friday.'

Four days. A short, but respectable stay for one travelling up from the South. Archie set down the cases by her bed. She gazed round the room, with that hyperscrutiny of hers, eyes narrowed, but lips smiling. Archie and I exchanged a quick glance. She walked to the windows set in two walls. I'd left them open after my confrontation with McTaggart, and now the room felt suddenly icy. Archie had had them enlarged, so that it almost felt as if the sea and the elements were blowing in. Rosamond pulled them closed with a snap, then turned back to us. I waited anxiously for her verdict.

'Very acceptable. Now bugger off and let me settle in.'

That was praise, I told myself, given the English love of understatement.

When Archie disappeared off with the builders the next morning after breakfast, I made my suggestion.

'I'd like to try to paint you again, Rosamond, as a birthday present for Archie. Then you can hang in the great hall.'

'Like a gargoyle, keeping you from evil spirits.'

'I hope I can do you better justice than that.'

'Don't knock it. Gargoyle is fine by me.'

'Do I need a gargoyle?'

'We all do, darling. Only the naïve think otherwise.'

I took her to the room I had set up as my studio. It was in my tower, at the top. The window was huge, north facing as decreed by Archie, smashed from the ancient stone by the Poles. The dust had long since settled, but somehow the smell of it never left this room, as if in demolishing masonry we had disturbed something more durable that refused to be blown away by the ocean winds I let in. I'd cordially requested that

McTaggart needn't trouble herself with this room, so at least it didn't reek of chemicals.

I positioned Rosamond on an austere oak chair. She sat straight as a mannequin, amber eyes watching me, amused, but not unkind. She wore the ever so slightly patronizing air of one who was indulging me, an impression I was determined to shock out of her by creating, this time, a brilliant portrait of her. In Long Island, I had tried, and failed.

The cold north light fell upon the planes of her face, rendering her white as alabaster. And, she sat there, so still, she could have been a sculpture adorning a Roman square. She could hold a pose like no-one. What self-discipline, or self-containment, held her so? For a while I did not touch my paintbrush to my canvas. I just watched her, and mixed my colours, trying to discern in her what I had missed before.

Her beauty was there for the world to see: the still luxuriant chestnut hair, falling in soft waves to her shoulders, the large, almond-shaped almond eyes glittering with life and intelligence, her heart-shaped face, the high cheekbones, the wry lips — they weren't full, teased up by collagen like so many of her fading contemporaries, but they were beguiling, seeming to hint at some hidden knowledge, not quite the meaning of life, but not far off. She was utterly compelling. In her youth she must have had the pick of any man. Still she could have enthralled any number of choice husbands. Yet she had chosen to live in comparative poverty.

'Tell me about your husband,' I said.

'Archie's father,' she intoned, with a trace of wistfulness.

'I feel there's something of Archie I can't know, because I never met his father.'

'What of you then, Morgan? You must be in large part unknowable.'

'To myself as much as to anyone,' I replied. I did not want to go in for lengthy discussion of my character, least of all the hidden bits.

'Archie's father was beautiful, dark, like my son, with quick green eyes. He was twenty-four when we met. We married six months later.' She smiled. 'Scandalously quickly. *Indecent haste*, said my father, but I was impatient, like you, in love. And I'd always been in a perpetual hurry.'

I didn't think, somehow, that her love was like my love.

'We couldn't live here full time, of course. Needed to make money, so we based ourselves in London, in what is now Archie's flat. We took up as antiques dealers, by default really. We both had a good eye, and not much else we could usefully turn to profit.'

I smiled. I could imagine Rosamond wheeling and dealing, excelling at what she appeared to disdain. *Trade, my darling, surely not?* But she was honest enough to admit she was doing it for profit.

'You were good at it?'

'I was.'

'Did you enjoy it?'

'Darling, it was great fun. Roddy trawled the U.K., while I did France, Spain, and Italy. France was the best. Place hadn't been done to death and you could find some great bargains tucked away in little villages. I'd spend weeks at a time rattling round in my ancient

Citroën, garnering up things small enough to fit, valuable enough to make it worth my while.'

'Didn't you miss each other?'

She gave me a slow look, to check I was not judging her.

'Of course we did. I'd recommend it to anyone. We weren't in each other's pockets. Fatal for a marriage.'

I could see her, wearing culottes and a white shirt, trawling elegantly through the villages, gloriously independent, Gitanes trailing in her wake, dining on red wine and cassoulet, warm sun to wake her, and a baguette and vicious coffee for breakfast.

'Getting away from dreary London must have been pretty good too.'

'Oh, you have no idea,' she replied with warmth. 'Exchanging the strikes and the unrest and the miserable damp streets of seventies London for the South of France.' She took a deep breath as if inhaling the scent of sand and pine and hot pavements.

'Must have been quite social too.'

'It was. Not like it is now, cheapened and overcrowded. Back then you could actually see the mountains. Now every square inch is built up. And the people were a damn sight better. Picasso, Dali, Somerset Maugham. Not that they were good,' she laughed, 'but they were fun.'

'Sounds idyllic.'

'It was.'

'What did you do with Archie?'

'Oh, all this was before he was born.'

'And after?'

She dropped her pose and her hands fell limp by her sides. 'After Archie was born, Roddy died. And everything stopped.'

I put my first brush stroke to canvas just as she rose from her chair.

'That is enough for now, darling,' she said, wrenching up lightness. 'I never could sit still,' she added with a smile.

She disappeared to 'her' rooms with an airy wave. I brewed myself a cup of the instant coffee I loved. I stood with my hands wrapped around a steaming cup, in need of sudden warmth.

I stared in frustration at my blank canvas. I wondered if Picasso had ever lifted Rosamond's veil of secrecy and sketched her. Someone possessed of her prodigious beauty made a natural subject. How could he have resisted her? How could anyone? I imagined her with him, laughing, tempting him perhaps, and my thoughts turned to Archie's father, back in the U.K. and I felt a pang of sympathy. The worse side of the bargain, followed by . . . death. Had he adored Rosamond, as my father had my mother? Did he find the joy of life in the time he did have with her, and then with his son? How old had Archie been when he died? I suddenly realized how little I knew of my husband's childhood. He tended to be evasive when questioned, and out of respect I hadn't pushed what would have been painful. But my ignorance made me uneasy.

I finished my coffee, headed to the window and gazed out at the sea. The sky and sea were darkening, turning a bruised black.

That night I cooked for Archie and Rosamond: roast chicken. I was getting more proficient in the kitchen. It tasted good, especially washed down by the copious amounts of alcohol Rosamond had procured from somewhere.

Chapter eleven

That night I fell into a heavy sleep. I tossed and turned, disturbed by the wind and rain lashing the windows, by the creaks and groans of the castle around me. Normally I found the sounds of a storm strangely reassuring from the safety of my own bed, but not tonight. I lay somewhere in the wasteland between proper sleep and wakefulness. I wanted to wake up, but I cannot seem to stir myself.

When morning came, I dragged myself from bed, exhausted, hungover, but relieved the night was over. Archie stayed in bed, still resolutely asleep.

I headed for the door, and cried out. Even in the gloom of the heavily curtained room I could see the portraits of my parents were gone.

'Archie,' I shouted. 'Oh my God, *Archie.*'

'What? Morgan, what's wrong?' he pushed himself from bed, gazing round, alarmed.

'Look,' I said, pointing at the walls. 'My parents. They're gone.'

'Fuck,' he muttered.

'Did you move them?' I asked, heart thudding in my ribs.

He shook his head. He looked sick.

I paced up to the wall, threw up my hands, dropped them, tried to speak. I gulped in air, almost choked on it.

'Where?' I managed to say.

He disappeared, came back belting his dressing gown.

'Let me check the castle,' he said, hurrying off.

I doubled over in front of the empty wall. They could not be gone. They were my talismans. All I had left of my parents. They were worth more to me than the entire heap of my money.

Archie came back ten minutes later, white-faced.

'They've gone, Morgan. The portraits. Other things too.'

The sounds in the night, my sense of unease. I saw gloved hands, reaching up, raping what was sacred to me.

Nothing much else was taken. There was nothing of value in the whole bloody castle. Apart from the Augustus John. Strangely, that had been left. Some candlesticks, and, more sinisterly, some kitchen knives *were* taken. The police came, hours later they left. They found no visible forced entry. But none of us could swear that we checked every ground floor window to ensure that it was closed before we went to bed. It had never seemed an issue. Crime in Cape Wrath was practically unknown. Even they, as policemen, attested to that.

I alternated between wanting to sob and scream, and feeling utterly hollow. Archie flailed around me, dripping sympathy. Rosamond was brisk.

'No broken bones,' she said. 'Nothing living.'

She didn't understand that, for me, my portraits were just that.

'Beef up your security here, I would,' she intoned. 'Especially when you start getting really valuable things in.'

'Like what?' I said.

'Well, furniture, rugs, other paintings, silver. All the things that Wrath Castle needs to bring it back to life.'

The castle was her equivalent to my portraits. I wonder how she would feel were it razed to the ground. Would I turn to her and say efficiently — *no broken bones*?

Rosamond decided that one of the Polish workmen was the culprit. I came upon her later that day berating him, in a voice like a whiplash, pacing before him like some predatory animal, threatening him, trying to force him to tell her where he has hidden the portraits. I wondered what possible proof she could have. I knew she was doing this for me, but I was horrified by her ferocity. The man was practically cowering. He looked frightened, not guilty. He shook his head, stumbling over his limited English, denying vehemently her accusations.

'Liar!' she concluded. 'You're fired, as of now. Go.'

With that, she wheeled around from him, caught sight of me.

'Here's your thief,' she announced, triumphant. 'I'm sure of it. Anyway, even if we don't find where he's stashed your portraits, he won't do it again.'

I nodded slowly and watched her go. I turned back to the man before me, who was watching her too, not with the anger I would have expected, but with fear.

'I didn't,' he said, switching his gaze to me. 'Mrs. Morganna. Promise you.' He crossed himself. 'On my mother, her life, I did not.'

I looked at him. I wanted so much to find a culprit,

to get my portraits back, but I could read the truth in his eyes.

'I know you didn't,' I said. I was angry on his behalf, and privately appalled at Rosamond's bullying rage. It was the second time I'd witnessed her temper. Archie had been the recipient the first time. I found myself wondering if she would ever try it on me, and how I would react. Perhaps I wouldn't have to wait long to see.

'Go back to work,' I said, deciding to back my own judgment. It was the first time I had done anything remotely against the wishes of my mother-in-law, but I didn't see that I had any choice.

He reached out, touched my hand. He thanked me profusely.

I tried to keep myself busy, to keep one step ahead of my misery, but of course I failed. I drove to Ellen McMullen's for food and at the checkout burst into tears.

'What the divil?' she asked. I told her. She was horrified. She seemed to know instinctively what the portraits had meant to me.

'You poor angel. Come here.'

She put her arms round me and held me tight.

'Come in the back. Sit yourself down for a moment.' She brewed up a pot of tea and made me drink two cups of sweet tea before she would let me go. She also refused point blank to take payment for the items I had left at the checkout. This touched me even more and once again reduced me to tears.

'You go home and let that husband of yours take

care of you. Shock like that you should tuck yourself up in bed with a hot water bottle and a healthy Thermos of toddies for a few days.'

Wouldn't I have loved to. But I knew I had to keep going, to show the backbone that Rosamond so valued in me.

I drove back to the castle, and went straight out for a long walk on the beach. Lunchtime came and went but I stayed out. I had no appetite and no wish for company. Finally I went back, snuck up to my bedroom, and tried to ring Geoffrey at the bank.

'Not here,' said Mary-Beth, his P.A.

'Where is he? I really need to talk to him.'

She paused awhile before answering. 'Well, since it's you. He'd hate anyone else to know. Officially he's out of the office. In reality, he's ill.'

'Ill? Geoffrey's never ill.' I felt a wave of panic sweep me. 'God, Mary-Beth, tell me it's not serious.'

She said nothing.

'Mary-Beth? I'm panicking here, please, help me out. I've just been burgled and I need to talk to him and now you tell me this and I'm—'

'Morgan. Stop. You really need to talk to him.'

'He's at home?' Not in some hospital with tubes . . .

'He's at home.'

I hung up without another word and rang Long Island. The butler answered.

'What's wrong with Geoffrey?'

'Headache, Miss Morganna. Bad one. He's in bed, asleep. I'd rather not wake him if that's all right.'

I was torn. I wanted to have Geoffrey woken, demand to hear from him what was wrong. Headache was a bromide and I didn't believe it for a second, but if he was really ill then the last thing he needed was me ringing and waking him and telling him I'd just been burgled.

'Of course. Please just tell him I called, when he wakes.'

'Shall I ask him to call you?'

I wouldn't be able to conceal the burglary from him if we spoke, at least not for a while, not till I'd got myself under control.

'Er, no. I'll ring back. Thank you.'

I hung up and immediately rang Mary-Beth again.

'It's me. Look, I got nowhere. The butler says he has a headache, which I don't believe. Now, *please*, level with me. What's wrong with him?'

She was silent a long while, clearly agonizing. 'I really shouldn't tell you this, but perhaps you can help.'

'What, please, just tell me. Whatever it is, not knowing is worse than knowing.' I profoundly hoped that was true.

'Okay. Here goes. But listen, first, will you swear to me you won't tell him I told you?'

'I swear.' I would have sworn to just about anything right then.

'It's his heart. There's a murmur. A baddish one. I've had to arrange all the ECGs; had to get a doctor right here to the office six weeks ago. It's stress. The docs want him to retire, or step back, at least for a while, but you know him. Stiff upper lip and all that b.s. He just keeps on going.'

I could imagine. 'He thinks illness is all in the mind, that to acknowledge it is to give in to it.'

'Exactly. But maybe you could find out about it from him, and make him slow down. If anyone can, it's you.'

'Maybe. Maybe not. But first I have to find a legitimate way of appearing to find out.'

'Please. Do that,' she said.

I hung up, sank my head into my hands. 'Oh, Geoffrey. Please be all right,' I had thought him indestructible. His existence was a given in my life. For twenty years, he was all the family I had. He had been there, an unquestioned rock of stability in my life, one I had taken utterly for granted. To have his life thrown into question shook my already unsteady world to its foundations.

I did what I have always done when I cannot face the world or my thoughts. I curled up in bed and sought sleep. Mercifully it came. When I woke it was seven. The sleep had helped, but I was still trembling inside and my mind kept leaping about. I wanted so badly to ring Geoffrey, but I held off. I wondered where Archie was. Tucked away with the builders, no doubt. In the meantime, dinner needed preparing, and it seemed to me that I was somehow expected to do it. I hurried downstairs, and dug out some of my purchases from Ellen's: fish fingers and beans. No culinary performance that night.

Rosamond appeared just as dinner was almost ready.

'That was not wise,' she said, by way of hello.

My head felt thick, befuddled. I didn't feel up to dealing with her, and it took me a while to tune in to what she was saying.

'What's that, Rosamond?' I asked.

'Keeping that man on.'

I paused, palms down on the work surface as if to brace myself before I replied. 'I happen to think he's innocent.'

'Well, you're a fool then,' she snapped.

I took the fish fingers from the oven, put them down, and turned slowly to her.

'Really.' I tried to keep my voice neutral. The last thing I wanted was a confrontation, a blow-up, but I wasn't about to cower as the poor man had done.

'You'll just have more problems until he goes. I know about these people. I'm used to dealing with them. This is beyond your ken. You're young and–'

And you're so much older and used to dealing with armies of staff, workmen, huge building projects, I thought, but managed not to say.

'I'll deal with it, my way,' is what I actually said.

'You don't control this project, Morganna. Your husband does.'

So I was just the wallet. Pay up and shut up. That really made me start to rise. The theft of my paintings had left me raw, exposed and ultrasensitive, added to which I had always had a temper of my own. It had been rigorously subjugated by Geoffrey's meticulous East Coast politeness, his almost constant *sang froid*, but it was still there.

'I control the money. I think that gives me a vote or two,' I said, struggling to keep my voice level.

'I think you'll find it is not a good idea to throw your financial weight around.'

'It's never a good idea to throw weight around, of any kind,' I replied. I walked from the kitchen and called up the stairs. I was trembling on the outside too. I needed to stop this before it really escalated.

'Archie, dinner.'

Please be near, I thought. He normally appeared in the kitchen at this time anyway. I remained in the hall for a minute, taking deep breaths, trying to calm myself. Archie did appear, mercifully quickly.

I smiled with relief. 'Ah, there you are.'

'Hey, sweetheart. Where've you been? I was worried about you.' He pulled me to him and kissed me. 'Couldn't find you this afternoon, then I had to drive in to Inverness to load up on bloody supplies. Only just got back.'

I let him hold me, composing myself in his arms. He pulled away to study my face, saw the tears in my eyes.

'Oh, Morgan. I'm really sorry I had to go off. This is wretched, I know. We'll try really, really hard to get the portraits back. I promise you.'

I nodded, said nothing, rubbed my face, took another deep breath, and returned to the kitchen together with him. While he chatted with his mother, I busied myself with pots and pans and opened a bottle of wine. Archie sat between me and Rosamond, an unconscious buffer. I found myself thanking Geoffrey for the lessons he had so painstakingly instilled in me. I had always been able to make small talk with adults, to entertain them at dinner with inconsequential chatter, no matter what or how I was feeling. So that is what I did. Rosamond, for her part, did the same, but she wasn't quite as blithe as normal. The eyes she turned on me were just a touch narrower, more thoughtful, less indulgent. If Archie noticed any of this he was wise enough to say nothing. I hoped it was just a phase that would pass. Discussing it would merely give it more substance, so I in turn said nothing to my husband. I trusted that any oddness in my behaviour he would put down to the theft.

Geoffrey rang me the next day.

'Hi, Geoffrey, how are you?' I asked, trying to sound breezy.

'I'm fine,' he snapped. 'Damned headache got me down, but I'm back at the coalface now.'

'Can't you give yourself just one day to get back on an even keel?'

'My keel is just fine, Morgan, believe me.'

That was just it. I didn't.

'Now, how are you? Everything all right?'

I must have paused, just a second too long before answering that, yes, I was fine, because he was onto me like a sniffer dog.

'Morganna. Stop. Hold it right there. Something's wrong. I won't get off the line till you 'fess up.'

'Nothing's wrong,' I replied stubbornly, wishing I could lie as well as he could.

'Morganna,' he said softly. 'I have known you since you were a tiny, wrinkled little thing. I know you better than you think, better than you know yourself I sometimes think. And I know now that something is wrong.'

'Oh, Geoffrey, please, let it go. It's nothing serious.'

'Then you can tell me.'

I was trapped in my lie, and not quick enough to think of a plausible but small problem.

Damning myself as I answered him I spluttered out, 'It's my portraits. They're gone.'

'Gone as in stolen?'

'Yes.'

'Both of them?'

'Yes.'

'When?'

'Yesterday.'

'Why didn't you tell me?'

'I didn't want to worry you.'

'I'd be a damn sight more worried to learn about it from the insurers. You weren't harmed?'

'I was asleep. I knew nothing of it until I saw the blank walls the next morning.'

'Anything else stolen? The Augustus John?'

'Funnily enough, they left that.'

'Did they now?' he hissed. 'So what else *did* they take?'

'Nothing much of value to take, besides the portraits, but yes, a few bits and pieces.'

'Such as?'

'Candlesticks.' I paused. 'And knives.'

'Jesus!'

I've seldom seen or heard Geoffrey angry, so great is his self-control. But I knew he could become so. Colleagues had spoken of his temper, rarely unleashed, and all the more terrifying for its rarity, but I could feel the waves of cold fury emanating from him even down the telephone wires.

'Morgan, will you promise me you'll be careful.'

'Yes, of course I will, but–'

'I want to come and see you.'

'You're being ridiculous now. I'm fine.' Dear God, this was not what I wanted to happen. 'Please,

Geoffrey, don't worry. We're beefing up security. I'll be careful. I promise.'

'If you see, or you hear anything you don't like, promise me you'll get out of that castle, go somewhere safe. Is there somewhere, someone you could go to?'

'Well, my husband of course,' I answered, puzzled and not a little upset by the vehemence of his reaction. Perhaps his own bad heart had unsettled him.

'Yeah, yeah. Besides him.'

'Why would I go anywhere else?'

'If he's not there,' he snapped.

'Well, I could go to Ellen's or to Ben.'

'Good.'

'Geoffrey, please. You're scaring me. This was an opportunistic theft. That's what Archie says, and Rosamond thinks it was one of the builders.'

'Is she there?'

'Yes, she came up a few days ago.'

'I have to go, Morgan,' he said abruptly. 'Please, remember your promise.'

'I will, and please take it easy. I don't like the sound of your headaches.' I desperately wanted to broach the subject of his heart, but wasn't sure how to do it without upsetting him.

'Morganna, will you quit. It's nothing that a Tylenol can't fix.'

Liar, I thought, hanging up the phone slowly, now profoundly unsettled.

I spent the next few days trying to keep busy, trying to act as if everything was fine. I wept in private for my stolen portraits. I tried not to worry about Geoffrey, while plotting what I could do to get him to slow down. I continued my sessions in my studio with Rosamond, in a vain attempt to distract myself and to pretend that everything was the same between me and her. We both spoke cordially to each other, but there was a distance now, a new reserve. I had, I suppose, if not hero-worshipped her, then admired her — perhaps to excess. I still did, but now the rose-tinted glasses were off. Perhaps every relationship went through a honeymoon period and came out the other side with just a tinge of disillusion. No-one was perfect, and I told myself to cut her some slack, but our unforced closeness was gone, at least for the moment. Just when I needed it.

When she left four days later I had little more than shadows of her on my canvas. I had failed again to paint her, partially because I was depressed and uninspired, but also because something fundamental to her remained elusive to me. I waved her off with immense relief, watching her elegant hand wave jauntily from her open window as she sped away. Archie kissed me and headed off into the castle. I just stood and gazed at the empty track.

Chapter twelve

One evening over dinner, a few days later, Archie made a casual announcement. 'By the way, I think I might go south for a week or so, hunt down furniture. Ma showed me a Sotheby's catalogue. Some good-looking pieces. I'd like to see them myself.'

'Oh good. Let's have a look.'

Archie looked blank.

'The catalogue.'

'Oh. Ma took it with her.'

I was disappointed.

'So when are you going?'

'Tomorrow, I thought.'

'So soon,' I found myself saying, sounding to my discomfort like a petitioning wife.

'Don't worry,' he said, covering my hand with his. 'I'll be back soon, and you won't miss me, what with your paints . . .'

'I'll miss you,' I said. 'I don't take my canvas to my bed, do I?'

'Would you like to take me to your bed?'

'Would you like me to?'

'Very much.'

We did not take our eyes off each other during that entire exchange. I wanted to soak him up. I felt as I had the first time I had seen him. I saw him with a stranger's eye, his cool beauty, his need. He had for weeks seemed so consumed by the castle, especially during his mother's visit, that I had felt edged out of his life. To be desired so keenly put me back where I wanted to be. I wanted to be the obsession, the passion, hot skin not cold stone.

We pulled off our clothes and fell shivering into our bed. It seemed that he too wanted to devour me. He dug his hands into my flesh and gripped me like he was saving me from a fall. He murmured my name; he sank his face into my hair and breathed me in. I felt that he was rediscovering me. His need for me was urgent, immediate. I ranged my hands over the fine smooth skin of his back. He felt hot, almost feverish to my touch. I spread my fingers into his hair, pulled his head back so that I could look into his eyes. And there I saw the voracious searching that had first drawn me to him. I felt a mirror of it in my own eyes. I pulled him back into my arms. Just as he needed me, I needed him, needed to feel that everything was the same as it had been.

We made love with a fraught passion that left me drained, but I did not sink into restful sleep. The wind battered at our windows, and I tossed and turned as if buffeted by storms of my own. I got up and hauled on my oldest, warmest dressing gown, and hunched it round me. I looked down at Archie. He was frowning slightly, as he often did, awake or asleep, but his body lay relaxed. I walked to the window, and stared through my reflection at the hump-backed waves, slicked with moonlight. Around me, the castle creaked and groaned, as if its old bones were being tormented by the chill wind.

The cold bit into my feet and I hurried back to bed but still I could not sleep. It was on a night like this that my paintings were stolen. The sense of security you carry around you in order to survive had been breached in me, and not even love-making, or love, could heal it. I'd tried to go back in time that night, to find in Archie's arms a security that I now knew never could be there. When I'd fallen in love with him, and him with me, I had hoped, like all innocent lovers, that it would make me complete, seal me up, protect me from life. As I lay there awake while next to me — he might have been a thousand miles away — he slept, I felt for the first time the limitations of love. You think when you fall in love your love is like the universe — infinite, then you realize that it has its boundaries, and beyond them is nothingness.

I waved Archie off the next morning. 'Be sure to lock the windows and the doors,' he called to me.

'I will.'

I thought of my missing portraits, and of the stolen knives, and I shuddered.

I returned inside to make myself a cup of coffee. I froze when I heard a movement at the back door, then I saw it was Ben and relaxed. He had with him a puppy. A tiny sheepdog. I crouched down, reached out my arms to her and she ran to me, snuffling happily.

'Another shepherd I know, one of his bitches whelped. Five pups — have to find homes for them all. Thought you might like this one. Little bitch, sweet as they come.'

I fondled the little black head, and fell in love.

'Oh, Ben. She's beautiful. I'd love to keep her. I've always wanted a pet, and she's just perfect.'

'Good. That's settled then.'

'Er, what does she eat?'

He laughed. 'Little bit of meat, vegetable scraps. Don't worry, I'll keep you supplied.' He set down a plastic bag on the kitchen counter.

'That'll keep her going for a while.'

'Ben, you think of everything.'

'Not quite. How are you?' he asked, the smile gone from his face.

I straightened up and reached for my mug of Nescafé.

'Fine.'

'I know about the burglary. Your portraits. I'm sorry.'

'That's okay. I've—' suddenly, unleashed by his gentle, unshowy kindness, I could not hold back my tears.

He led me to the table, eased me gently into a chair and sat down beside me. I cried for a good few minutes while he just sat quietly by my side. I think I cried too because Archie had gone when I needed him here. He had known I was frightened, still in shock, and, while he could easily have invited me to go with him, he hadn't. Locking doors and windows was no solution to fear. Finally, I stopped, blew my nose, and offered Ben a faint smile.

'Sorry.'

He shook his head. 'What for?' We fell silent again, and then he said: 'Why don't you have your parents to stay, make you—' his words ebbed away as he saw my face.

'What? What have I said?' he asked, looking stricken.

'It's all right,' I answered. 'You weren't to know. My parents died when I was a baby.'

He looked away, at the floor for a few moments. 'Oh, Morganna. I'm so sorry.'

I shrugged. 'That's life. Shit happens.'

'Too much, to some people.'

'That's why I loved my portraits so much.'

'They were all you had left of them.'

I nodded. Tears threatened me again.

'You have a nice little companion now,' he said, ruffling the puppy's sleek fur. 'She'll watch out for you, be a little guard dog.'

'You think I need one?'

'Can't hurt,' he said. He looked at his watch, and gave me a regretful smile.

'I'd better be off. Look after yourself.'

'I will. Thanks for this little one,' I said, cuddling my new puppy.

'If there's anything I can ever do for you, let me know,' he said slowly.

'I will,' I answered, touched, and worried by his offer.

Chapter thirteen

My new puppy watched Ben retreat, then she turned back to me, and looked up at me expectantly. I crouched down and stroked her gently.

'Right, you lovely little thing. I think what we need is some fresh air, and a walk. What do you say?'

She looked at me with limpid trusting brown eyes that seemed to say whatever I came up with was just fine. I gathered up my canvas, easel and paints, and a backpack with water and a packed lunch. I looked down at my puppy.

'Will you come with me?' I made a movement towards the door. She gave a little yelp and followed me.

I led her down to the beach, checking that she was following, that she didn't find the path too tricky. I needn't have worried. She was sure-footed, nimble, and keen to follow me. She looked as happy as I was to be outside. It was a glorious sunny day, with the promise of spring warming the normally vicious breeze.

I set down my kit, and then took my little pup for a walk down to the sea's edge and along the foaming border between sand and water. She had great fun chasing the retreating waves, and then scampering back when a fresh one broke and tumbled towards her. I watched her, laughing with pleasure, marvelling and grateful, so grateful to her and to Ben, who between them had lifted my mood so profoundly, and so immediately. The gloom, the fear, the loss, and the sense that I had somehow been violated wouldn't disappear altogether, I knew that, but at least I had a respite.

After a while, we headed back to my paints and I set them up. She watched intently as I squeezed out my oils and mixed the colours on my palette. I turned to the blank canvas before me and contemplated it. My puppy seemed to pick up my stillness, for she lay down on the sand beside me, head on paws, and started to doze.

My last effort at painting had failed dismally: Rosamond. The sea, for all its mystery, seemed much more knowable than her. I settled my gaze on it with relief.

That day it was a new colour as if spring was stirring within it too. The faintest hint of turquoise enlivened the grey. And as I had so often done, I lost myself for a few blissful hours in my paints, oblivious of all else, save the scene before me, and my puppy at my feet. When I packed up after a few hours, I had a completed canvas, and turquoise-grey tips to my hair. My puppy wriggled with delight as we headed back to the castle. I gave her some of Ben's meat and watched her eating happily.

That night, my first night alone, she escorted me as I locked all the doors and windows, and then when I went reluctantly to bed. The phone rang just as I was climbing in, making me and my puppy jump. It was Archie.

'How are you, my love?'

'Not too bad,' I answered. 'Been busy. Painting. How're you?'

'Tired. Drove all day. Staying in some dodgy motel, but a bed's a bed, I guess.'

'Get a good sleep.'

'I will. You'll be all right, won't you?'

He wanted me to reassure him that charging off down south and leaving me alone in the castle was just dandy, but some stubbornness that surprised me made me hesitate. I looked across at my puppy, who was watching me with her gentle eyes and I softened.

'I'll be fine.' I didn't tell him about my pup. I wanted to keep her as my special secret, just for now.

'Good girl. Right then, you sleep well, you hear me.'

I gave a wry smile. 'You too.'

I hung up, and settled myself in my bed. My little dog jumped up beside me, and curled into a contented ball on the covers. I turned off the light and lay there, listening to her breathing. As long as she was calm and peaceful, I knew I would be all right.

And I was. All night. I awoke at six, wonderfully rested, my puppy still beside me, awake herself, watching me. For a while I just lay there, in the flannel sheets I still used to keep me cosy, even though it was April and technically warming up. I had deliberately left the curtains open, so that the rising sun flooded in, pouring what looked like a pool of gold onto the old oak floors. I picked up my puppy, slipped from bed, and padded over to that patch of sun so that it gilded me. As I stood there, I felt that the sun was pouring into me too, filling up all the gaps in me.

I dressed in my jeans and heavy boots, a thermal T-shirt and a heavy fleece, and with my now permanent escort went up to the high tower to gaze at what I couldn't help myself thinking was my kingdom. Is this what they thought, Archie's ancestors, as they gazed around? It was their kingdom, wasn't it? Two hundred thousand acres of hill and sky.

The sea was glass calm, the only flecks of white where the gentlest of waves licked the stone shore. I watched the day glow into life, the seagulls wheeling and screaming, then ran downstairs to make coffee. Archie always chided me for this, told me I might fall, but I loved the feeling of flight, of being slightly out of control, at risk of tumbling at any minute. But I hadn't so far, and I didn't that day.

My puppy watched me as I prepared breakfast for the two of us. She stood behind me, wriggling her whole body.

'Jelly, that's what you are,' I said, giggling at her. And so she got her name.

The sun rose as we ate, slanting into the kitchen. It seemed even the weather was conspiring to make Archie's absence easier. After breakfast, Jelly and I headed down to the beach. The tide was out, and the sand stretched out ahead of me, shimmering pale gold. I set up my easel and got back to painting what I loved best. I'd never seen the sea the colour it was that morning. It was so pale and clear it was almost iridescent. I felt almost as if I were in a trance painting it. The susurration of the waves gently breaking, and a light wind, bearing a hint of spring warmth, lulled me completely.

So we settled into a routine, my new puppy and I. And, boy, did the weather help. It was relentlessly sunny that week, so Jelly and I took ourselves out by day, and back to the fastness of the castle by late afternoon when the sun dipped down to meet the sea and we found ourselves tired and famished.

Archie rang every night. We spoke of the restoration like besotted parents discussing the first steps of their firstborn, but Suffolk, or London, I was beginning to lose track of where he was, and his growing collection of exquisite this and just perfect that seemed to belong to a different world. I had my dog, the shimmering sea, spring sunshine and boundless fresh air. I preferred my world to his, but I *did* miss him, and found myself counting the few days left till his return.

The one serious irritant was Mrs. McTaggart. She had persisted with her arsenal of toxic products despite my repeated polite requests. I was building up for another confrontation, but she forced my hand when I found her one morning berating my precious Jelly.

'What's going on here?' I demanded, picking up my cowering puppy.

'Knocked her water over, she did.'

'She's a puppy. She's playful, sometimes a bit clumsy, she's–'

'She's a dirty mess, paint on her, muddy paws, she–'

'Right, McTaggart. I think that's enough. I'd like you to go, please.'

'Go where?'

'Leave. Leave the castle. Leave my employ. Now. Tell me what I owe you, I'll pay you, then I want you gone, and your key handed over.'

'It's Mr. Edge who pays me.'

In a manner of speaking, I thought. 'Well I'm paying you now, directly, and telling you, directly, to go.'

She looked at me as if she might somehow resist, but I think the outrage in my eyes finally convinced her I was serious.

'Fifty pounds,' she announced.

I had no way of knowing if that were the true amount, but I just wanted her out, so I dug into my purse and handed her the notes. She took them wordlessly and marched for the door.

'The key, Mrs. McTaggart.'

She turned slowly and cast me a look of such hatred I felt my cheeks flush, but she put her hand in her pocket and took out my key and dumped it on the table.

I watched her go with relief.

I felt shaken by the exchange, by the undercurrents of viciousness and ill intent I had felt. I made myself a cup of tea, cuddled Jelly as I drank it, then, feeling better, I hunted round the fridge for something that might approximate lunch. There really was nothing and Jelly's supplies were running low, so I grabbed the keys to what I still thought of as Archie's ancient BMW and drove off over the bumpy track.

Ellen was standing beside her open door when I arrived.

'Enjoying the sunshine?' I asked.

'It's grand. Good for old bones.'

'And young ones.'

She nodded. 'Running low?'

'Running on empty,' I said.

'Lord and Master away?'

'How did you guess?'

'You'd keep a well-stocked larder for him, wouldn't you?'

I raised my eyebrows. 'I should, Ellen, being the perfect wife. Don't always manage it. But I do need a serious stock-up. Shepherd's pie, big-time.'

'Ben'll be upset.'

'I'll make it up to him, next time my mother-in-law's in town.'

'I can hardly wait.'

'Oh, Ellen, can I ask you something?'

She gave me a considered look. 'You can ask me, sweet one.'

'Mrs. McTaggart . . .'

'Eileen McTaggart?'

'Small, sixty-something. Cleaner.'

'Aye. I know the one.'

'And?'

'What do you want to know?'

I glanced round. The shop was empty. 'Well, this is a tad awkward, but I've just had to fire her. I really did not get on with her. I just wondered what she was like in general, with other people.'

Ellen leaned back on the counter. 'Well, depends on who you're asking. Ask your mother-in-law, for example, she'd say she was wonderful.'

I nodded. 'She did. She hired her.'

'Figures. But other folk're not so keen.'

'And you?'

'Let's just say they'd be plenty I'd give a seat in my lifeboat ahead of her.'

I smiled. 'Thanks, Ellen. At least I know it's not personal now.'

Ellen gave me a long look. 'I wouldn't be quite so sure of that.'

At that moment the woman who ran the fish and chip shop waddled in with her equally well-fed daughter, and the chance to ask Ellen to explain was gone. I collected my purchases and headed back to the castle, mulling over her words, the sunny mood I had worked hard to conjure quite gone.

Called by the Durness grapevine, Ben turned up early the next morning with lamb chops and his rosemary. I reached into my kitchen drawer to take out some notes to pay him, but he raised his hand to stay me. I felt touched by his kindness, with no idea why I deserved it. I wondered how to repay him. I came upon my answer as I looked at his dogs, sniffing my backpack that contained my painting kit.

'I've never painted a dog, Ben. Could I practise on yours, just watch them on the hills for a while? They don't need to be still.'

'Never thought of something like that,' he said, scratching his cheek. He smiled slowly. 'Be grand.'

And so that morning, Jelly and I followed them onto the moor. Ben occasionally wandered over to watch me working. He stood silently behind me, just for a short time, as if not wanting to intrude. At twelve o'clock, he shared his sardine sandwiches with me and the dogs, and gave me a snifter of the whisky he carried in a hip flask. It tastes of the heather we sit on and the wind we breathe. This is the life, I thought, gazing around me, my good mood restored.

'You're happy here,' said Ben.

'Yes. Burglary apart, I am. Very.'

'Not lonely, so far from home?'

'Nope. I have everything I need here.'

He nodded, and for a while we both just gazed out over what sustained each of us — the moors, greenly undulating, speckled with the gold of newly flowering gorse, and in the hazy distance beyond, the enormous blue of the sea.

'You're not what we were expecting,' he said.

I laughed. 'What were you expecting?'

'Someone distant. Someone who would do the whole laird and his lady bit.'

'Such as?'

'Dinner parties. Socializing only with other lairds and their wives.'

'I wouldn't know a laird's wife if she washed up on the beach.'

He laughed. 'You're one yourself now.'

'Good God. I'm not even used to being a wife yet.'

'When the castle's finished you'll be the most sought-after wife and chatelaine in the North.'

'I hope the castle will never be finished then.'

'You want to do it up just for yourselves?'

'Yes. Terrible, isn't it? I don't want to show it off. I'm very happy just living there alone. Have you ever been inside?'

He shook his head, strangely vehement. 'No. When I was born it was shut up.'

'Well, you should come and have a look round sometime. It doesn't feel like some soulless vast thing. It is magnificent, but it's also incredibly reassuring. It's my fortress. And my haven.'

'From what?'

Back then of course, I didn't know the answer.

In late afternoon, he and his dogs walked back with me to Wrath Castle, and bid me a formal goodnight. That night, I cooked the lamb chops and devoured them with a hunger born of a day outside. Then I carried my canvas up to my studio to finish off the painting from memory. It surprised me how the contours of the mountain background had imprinted themselves on my memory, as if I'd known them for years.

Chapter fourteen

The next morning the police called. There were two of them. One I remembered from the day of the break-in, a thin, anxious-looking ginger-haired one. PC Jordan. The other, heavy-set, older, dark, thinning hair grey-flecked at the temples, disconcerting in his authority, I'd never seen before.

'Detective Spratt,' he said, introducing himself.

I welcomed them into my kitchen, ever hopeful. Jelly settled herself into my arms and surveyed the newcomers carefully.

'We've not got any closer to your portraits, Mrs. Edge,' Spratt said quickly, declining my offer of tea.

'You've no idea who might have taken them?'

'No idea of who, no.'

'Then what?'

'A type, perhaps,' answered the ginger one.

'What type?'

'Someone who knew what they were looking for,' replied Spratt.

'What makes you think that?' I asked, almost aggressive in my desire not to believe them.

'Well, what do you think're the chances of an opportunist just happening by a castle, in a remote part of northwest Scotland, and finding two valuable portraits on a building site?'

I studied my feet.

'It could have been a builder,' I ventured.

'A possibility we explored, fully. And rejected. These

builders aren't exactly plugged into the art scene. And we've searched anywhere round here they might have stashed it, and nothing.'

Reluctantly I looked up. 'And they left the Augustus John.'

They nodded.

'So you're saying you think someone knew what they were, knew they were here?' I asked them both.

'That's about it,' answered the ginger one.

'But who?' I asked, my voice rising.

'We were hoping you might tell us that,' replied Spratt.

'I have absolutely no idea,' I answered.

They nodded in unison, as if they expected me to say that.

'Were you fond of the portraits?' Spratt asked me.

I looked at him in sheer incredulity. 'They were of my parents,' I answered, not attempting to keep the disbelief out of my voice.

He shrugged, as if that were immaterial.

'They were worth a lot, I understand.'

'They were by de Greubel.'

'Which means?'

'It means in financial terms they were worth a lot.'

'How much?'

'I have no idea.' I found myself getting angry now. Why was he missing the point?

'But they're insured.'

'My guardian would have insured them for here. He always takes care of things like that. Look, what–?'

He cut me off, glancing at his watch. 'We'll be off now.' He got to his feet, surprisingly gracefully for such a heavy man. 'Think about it,' he said. 'If you get any ideas, ring us.'

I didn't want any ideas. I didn't want to think about it.

'Wait,' I called, as they were heading out. 'One thing you're saying is that, you don't think whoever took them will be back?'

They glanced at each other. 'Working on the assumption that they have what they want, that would be true. But I wouldna go round thinking you can just leave open your doors and your windows.'

'What are you telling me?'

'Nothing more than we'd tell anyone sitting alone in a property where there's serious spending going on.'

'How did you know I was alone?'

Detective Spratt smiled. 'In a community like this, everyone knows everyone else's movements practically before they know it themselves.'

'That's comforting.'

'It can be. It makes outsiders easier to spot.'

I thought about what they'd said long after they were gone, but got nowhere with it. He had seemed sometimes to be almost talking in riddles. It hit me then, that I was an outsider. The thought, for all it was obvious, left me feeling strangely vulnerable, and unsettled. Spratt had pronounced the word as he might have said *undesirables*.

I tried to put them out of my mind. I took Jelly and wandered out onto the moor, my painting dried and rolled up in my backpack. I didn't find Ben, but his dogs found me. After I'd been walking for about forty minutes, they came, like arrows through the heather. They made no noise, no barking, but they sniffed then licked my outstretched hand. Jelly cavorted round them with glee. A few minutes later, Ben appeared.

'Morganna.'

'Hey, Ben. Nice morning.'

'That it is.'

'I had a good dinner last night.'

'Glad to hear that. Make a healthy eater out of you yet.'

I grinned. 'Still need my vices. Fish and chips tonight.'

'If that's the worst you can do.'

I looked at him standing there, all weather-beaten, rugged, calm and strong. His presence instantly made me feel better.

I smiled quickly, to defuse the moment, and I fumbled in my backpack and brought out my painting.

'Here you are.'

He took it uncertainly, unrolled it with his brown hands. He looked at it, unreadable. I'd never given anyone a painting before, and suddenly began to regret it. I felt hideously vulnerable.

He looked up at me, eyes bright. 'You've a gift, Morganna.'

I felt a surge of happiness, and relief.

'Oh, Ben, thank you. I don't know about that, I just love doing it.'

He began to hand the canvas back to me.

'Ben, it's yours.'

'No,' he shook his head, not resistant, but unwilling to believe.

'*Yes*. Unless you were just *saying* you liked it.'

He grinned, and took it back. 'I like it well.'

I thought then of telling him about the police visit, about their suspicions, but I didn't want to break my mood, and anyway, I didn't think there would have been anything he could have said to have made it any better.

That night as I got ready for bed the phone rang. It was Archie's last night away and keen as I was to talk to him I was even keener to see him, to have him back here with me in our bed.

'Hi, Morganna.'

'Archie, hey. What dump are you ringing from this time?'

'Dump?'

'Motel.'

'Ah. I'm not in a hotel, I'm in London.'

'God, you didn't get far.'

There's a slight pause.

'Darling, listen, could you bear it if I spent another week up here?' He continued before I had a chance to reply. 'I'm on a bit of a roll. Got so many good pieces,' he laughed. 'I'm feeling inspired.'

'Mmm-hmm.'

'Might as well do as much as I can in one trip instead of spreading it over two, hey?'

'I guess so.'

'You all right? You sound down.'

'Well, I'm disappointed. I was looking forward to seeing you.' *God*, I sounded plaintive.

'You will, soon.'

'Yeah, I will,' I replied casually, trying to regain ground, wondering why it mattered.

'What have you been up to?' he asked.

'Oh, this and that.'

'Seen anyone?'

'Oh, the locals, you know, Ben, Ellen . . . you bump into everyone round here, don't you?'

'*You* do.'

'Hey, don't knock it. Stops me feeling too lonely.'

'*Feel* lonely,' he said, voice low.

I remembered the night before he left, and I did. Loneliness, lust and love. Powerful alchemy.

'You feel lonely too,' I replied.

'I do, Morgan, I do.'

'By the way, I've–'

'Oops, got to go,' he said suddenly. 'Call you back.'

I hung up. A strange humiliation burnt my cheeks. What was so urgent that he had to practically hang up on me at ten o'clock in the evening? I had been keen to tell him about Jelly, finally let him into my secret, into a legitimate balm to my loneliness, but he didn't call back that night.

Chapter fifteen

Archie returned on a Sunday night. I was standing in the high tower, the one with the 360-degree views. I saw his car coming a long way off. It was pulling what looked like a horsebox. Puzzled, I watched him pull up, and step out of the new Range Rover. He slammed the door, and stretched. He seemed to be breathing the air into his every pore. He relaxed, and moved towards the huge oak front door, loose-limbed, confident. I felt a sudden urge to hide, to surprise him. He looked so much like the returning hero, confident of his welcome. And why shouldn't he, I thought, surprised at myself. But I stayed where I was, waiting in the dark. I squatted down on my heels. I heard distant sounds of doors opening and closing. I heard him calling my name. Finally, I heard his footsteps approaching. He stopped abruptly when he made me out.

'Morgan. What the hell are you doing down there? Didn't you hear me?'

I stood slowly and pushed my hair back from my face. I smiled, and he took hold of me, drew me to him, and wordlessly pushed me down to the floor. He knelt over me and began to trace the contours of my face with his finger, as if he wanted to reimprint me on his memory. His hands moved down to my throat, down to my breasts. He unbuttoned my shirt and began to kiss me, gently at first, and then hard and hungrily. I lay there, deliberately passive, giving myself to him as a gift he craved, allowing him to pleasure me, until I could stand it no more and pulled him down onto me and into me. We took each other with animalistic greed on the hard, unyielding floor.

I carried the bruises of that encounter for a good week.

The Poles unloaded the contents of the horsebox the next morning, chased by Jelly, who was wildly excited by this new game. Archie watched with amusement.

'What do you think?' I asked him, swooping her up for a cuddle.

'Whose is she?'

'Mine, of course.' I showered her with kisses. Archie gave me an indulgent smile. I didn't tell him Jelly was a gift from Ben. I thought it wiser not to. Archie quickly turned his attention back to the horsebox.

When I saw what it contained, an Aladdin's cave of rugs, lamps, silver frames and candlesticks, small side tables, I was amazed that Archie risked leaving it out all night, unsecured. But then he probably hadn't intended to. After our love-making we had both fallen into an almost drugged sleep till dawn on the rough floor.

The Poles toiled away, carrying in Archie's haul to the exact positions he must have planned for them in advance. I watched amazed as he breathed more life into the rooms.

'There's more to come,' he said, smiling at me. 'The Sotheby's stuff.'

He took charge of the rugs, unfolding them for me, throwing them out in grand gestures in the library, the morning room, our bedroom, and, best of all, in my tower. He had picked the most beautiful rug for my tower, and he watched with quiet pleasure as I stroked the warm, heavy, finely woven wool. He didn't even seem to mind when Jelly, my little shadow, peed on one of them.

He was also puzzlingly solicitous of me over the next few days, cooking me healthy and deliciously tempting things as if he wanted to build me up. He seemed to delight in being back, and in being with me.

I didn't ask what any of the new treasures cost. I was too happy to care.

That didn't last long. Geoffrey rang on Tuesday afternoon.

'Morganna.'

'Hello, Geoffrey. How are you?' He sounded stronger than the last time we had spoken, but troubled still.

'Well, I'm fine. You?'

'Great.' I waited.

'Look, Morgan, we have to talk about finances.'

'Talk.'

'Are you fully aware of the size of some of the recent expenditures?'

'We're restoring a castle, Geoffrey. That doesn't come cheap.'

'No, it doesn't. Neither does the furniture, it seems.'

I felt a cold flutter.

'In the past two weeks, your husband has signed cheques for over nine hundred thousand pounds. On furniture. Books, candlesticks. Not to mention another sixty thousand on a Range Rover and a few thousand more on a horsebox, which I suppose in his lexicon must count as loose change nowadays.'

I felt as if someone had punched me in the solar plexus. I literally could not speak. I gazed around as if I might find an answer in the mahogany bookcase and the First Editions it held, trying to buy time, to frame a response that would explain it all, to me as well as to Geoffrey, in a way that wouldn't blow my world apart.

All I could manage was: 'I didn't know that, Geoffrey.' I wanted to shout and scream, but I kept the lid on myself and my emotions, for fear of letting them out.

Geoffrey's voice was surprisingly gentle. 'I thought you might not have.'

'I wish you hadn't told me.'

'Morgan, how could I not?'

'You could have, dammit. You could have just said nothing.'

'Not by my lights.'

'I have to go,' I said, and hung up. I doubled over on my bed, and roared into the suffocating embrace of my pillow.

For a week I said nothing to Archie about his spending. I just couldn't tackle it. I wanted to rail at him, demand an explanation, but I couldn't see a way of confronting him without damage. I wanted to give him the chance to come to me and explain it, say it had been a one-off, just to get some key pieces, to say he got carried away, couldn't help it, but it wouldn't happen again. But he didn't. And each day he kept silent, my anger grew and the chance to deal with it without causing harm receded. I knew all this, but still I did nothing. The following Sunday night, finally, I tackled him. We were in bed, we had just made love, but neither of us was particularly sleepy.

'Archie?' I said, taking a deep breath.

'What is it?' he asked.

'I wanted to have a word about the furniture.'

'Mmm.'

'Archie, we really don't have the money to buy that kind of stuff.'

He sat up in bed, instantly alert. And disbelieving.

'Why are you bringing this up now?'

'Was there a better time?'

'I didn't know I was subject to any kind of *allowance*.'

'Christ, Archie, a million and some is hardly an *allowance*.'

'Right. Fine. So how much *can* I spend?'

'Knock a nought off everything, and you'll be in the ballpark.'

'So much for the twenty-first century,' he said.

'Meaning?'

'Meaning that if I had the money, your spending wouldn't be questioned. It's quite accepted that women share in their husband's wealth. Not it seems the other way around.'

At that, he got up, pulled on a dressing gown, and disappeared. I lay there burning with confused fury. He was behaving as if I had done something wrong. Finally, I fell asleep. When I woke at six o'clock, I was alone.

I didn't see Archie until the afternoon when I returned from Ellen's with supplies. I was loading the newly delivered fridge when he came up behind me and put his hands on my waist. I straightened up and turned in his arms to face him. He looked contrite, and my anger faded, just a touch.

'I'm sorry, Morgan. I wasn't very impressive last night.'

'No,' I agreed.

'I find it difficult, sometimes, this money thing.'

'I know.' A high-class problem, if ever there were one.

'Look, it's a beautiful day. Let's go for a walk on the moors.'

'All right. I'll just get my jacket.'

With Jelly dancing at my heels, we headed out as the sun was sinking towards the horizon. I could feel the watery warmth of the sun, but the wind blew in a chill. I pulled my collar up around my ears as we headed up onto the moor. We didn't speak much. I didn't want to. I just hoped being together would be a salve.

When we reached the high tor, I noticed Ben sitting with his back to us. He turned, with no show of surprise, almost as if he had known we were coming. He got to his feet. Jelly launched herself at him in a way she never did with Archie, covering him in licks. Archie groaned, but I headed on in Ben's direction, so all Archie could do was follow.

'Hey, Ben.'

'Morganna.' He nodded a greeting at Archie, who just nodded back.

'Nice day,' I said. I found myself wondering whether he had a wife and children, and if he did, why they weren't sitting with him on so perfect a day. I felt sure he hadn't though. There was a solitary quality to him, and a loneliness. He might have been loved once, but not now.

'Aye, that it is,' he replied.

He seemed strangely reticent. This encounter felt downright awkward.

'Well, we'll be on our way. Better get back before it gets dark,' I said. 'See you, Ben.'

'See you, Morganna.'

He and Archie exchanged nods again, and we moved on. The Laird and his Lady. Again, we spoke little, but we were at least together and trying.

Weeks passed. Spring came in gently, the days grew longer, the destruction in the castle continued apace. Archie and I muddled along. In the lengthening evenings, we drank our drams in the second tower room he had made into a kind of den. He had had much of the stone removed, and the narrow windows enlarged so much that it felt as if we were sitting in a telescope. The view was amazing. The changing sea and sky, the scudding clouds and setting sun entranced us both, obviating the need to talk. We *could* talk, but only really about the castle, about our project, not about much else.

After dinner, when the sun had set, I would go up to my own tower, alone, and feel less lonely than I was growing to feel with him. I felt alarmed by what was happening to us, unsure what to do about it. I had known subconsciously that the confrontation over his spending would be damaging, but I'd had little idea of just how great and durable would be the harm. The lust we had felt seemed to be ebbing too. I tried to avoid love-making, while Archie, despite the mental distance growing between us, seemed to want to make love every night. It felt mechanical, not real.

I wondered what would happen when the renovation was complete. What would he do all day? What would we talk about? What would we have in common?

Then everything changed. I discovered I was pregnant. It didn't occur to me that I might have fallen pregnant, especially given the paucity of our love-making. But then I began to wonder. My breasts had grown and were tender. I thought this just signalled an imminent period, but the period never came. So I drove to Durness, bought a test, found a secluded spot by the roadside and peed on the stick there and then. And God, amazingly, wonderfully, I discovered I was going to have a child.

I drove home. Archie was in the kitchen, sipping tea.

'Morgan. Everything all right?'

'More than all right.'

'Tell me?' he asked, eyes suddenly bright with curiosity.

'Archie. I'm pregnant.'

Wonder rose slowly, lighting the features of his face. I could see him thinking furiously, and then he leapt up, came to me, took my face in his hands and kissed me, passionately. Then we both laughed out loud, for joy.

'Champagne, we need champagne,' he said, hunting round. 'And I must call Ma, immediately.'

I thought that could have waited, but I didn't want to do or say anything to break the mood, so I shut up, and walked off, as he hit speed dial.

'Ma. The best news. You'll never guess,' he said, as I moved away. I headed for my tower. Conversations with his mother rarely lasted less than half an hour. I gazed impatiently out to sea, my fingers working on the wooden sill.

'Ouch. Damn!' A shard of wood had splintered off into my index finger. I could see it lying black and ugly under the skin. I tried to pull it out but it broke off under the skin.

'Blast it.' I'd just have to wait for it to come out itself. I glared angrily at my watch. Damn Rosamond too, interposing herself between me and Archie, even in our most precious moments. By the time I returned down to the kitchen, I was seething. I'd given them their statutory half-hour, but he was still speaking away. I walked up to him, made a scissoring motion, tried to accompany it with a gracious smile.

'Oops, better go,' he said.

'Wifely demands,' I heard Rosamond say, and then she chuckled in her throaty way. 'Tell her congrats' she added.

'I will,' said Archie. 'Bye, Ma.'

'Well,' he said, turning to me. 'Better find that champagne, hadn't we?'

He didn't seem to realize that the moment had passed.

Chapter sixteen

My stomach swelled as Scotland roared into high summer. There was nothing like a perfect summer's day on that wild coast. The gorse came into bloom, blazing gold, coconut scented. I would walk on the moors with Jelly and the air was literally filled with the scent of gorse, and with the sound of birdsong. So many birds, spiralling their happiness into the sky. Mirroring mine. I watched the arrival of lambs with a mother's hungry zeal. The moors were dotted with rapidly growing babies frolicking and bleating. I thought of the baby growing inside me and my love bloomed too. I felt so vibrantly alive, so excited by the life inside and so protective too. My child. My baby. My love. *I will be there for you*, I promised my unborn child. I will not leave you as my mother did me. I felt a sudden chill as the shadow of death passed through my thoughts. I banished it quickly. I was young, I was healthy. No harm would come. But then a voice inside my head said that's what your mother would have thought too. I remembered her face in the portrait, where she was smiling with the secret of me. She looked so sublimely happy and content, and safe. Nine months after she sat for that portrait, she was dead.

I forced those thoughts from my head, and busied myself with living.

June passed languidly in a haze of good weather and pregnancy hormones. I had never felt so relaxed, but Archie seemed more driven than ever. Determined to finish as much of the castle as possible before the baby was born in November.

In July, he announced he needed to go away again. 'Just for a week or so, darling, track down some stuff. You'll be all right, won't you?'

'Of course. I'll miss you though.'

'And I will you, but it's not for long, is it?'

A week, I thought, no doubt dragging into two, like last time. We were getting on well enough, the earlier rift papered over by hormones and excitement and sheer weight of time. It was exhausting to stay at odds, so much easier to push difficult things from your mind and move on, and, let's face it, the baby had moved us on, supercharged our love, and our love-making. But still, I could do with a break, I thought. I could do with being the one who goes away.

'You know, I think I'll go and stay with Geoffrey then. It's beautiful in Long Island now, and I haven't seen him since the wedding, and God knows when I'll see him next after the baby's come.' I could also try to do something about the whole heart issue. I hadn't heard of any problems since the 'headache' at the time of the burglary, but that was scant comfort. I wanted to do something and now was my chance.

Archie didn't say anything. He was always a bit cool where Geoffrey was concerned. I got the impression he didn't like him much, which was, I suppose, understandable. Geoffrey hadn't exactly been ecstatic about Archie, and his no-show at our wedding spoke for itself.

'But Morgan, Scotland's so lovely now too, and should you really be travelling?'

I burst out laughing. 'Archie, I'm pregnant, not ill. I'm fine. The–'

'It's not just you though, is it, there's the baby to–'

'*Archie*, that's just what I was about to say. The baby's fine. I'd never do anything to threaten my baby. Flying to the States is *fine*. Living in luxury on Long Island is fine. Anyway, it'd be good to get away from the builders and the banging and the dust for a while.'

He nodded, reluctantly.

'What about Jelly?' I asked suddenly. 'You'll look after her for me, won't you?'

'I don't think so, Morgan. Auction rooms and cities are not suitable places for a puppy who is still not perfectly house trained, if I remember.'

'Fine. Okay, I'll make other arrangements.' His reply had smarted, as if by rejecting my puppy he had rejected me.

A few days later, I saw Ben on the moor. I asked him if he could take Jelly.

'My pleasure. She'll pine for her mistress though.'

'Probably nowhere as much as I'll miss her.'

We talked for a while about Jelly's favourite foods, her idiosyncrasies, arranged a time for me to drop her off, and then Ben went on his way. It occurred to me that he always seemed to be there when I needed him.

I rang Geoffrey to tell him I was coming for a couple of weeks. I suddenly remembered that I'd been meant to come anyway, we'd arranged it months ago, and in my excitement with my baby, I'd simply forgotten. Geoffrey hadn't reminded me, and I saw in that his diffidence, not wanting to pressure me and I felt a flash of love and compassion for him. He sounded delighted.

I became excited about my trip. I would be able to see for myself how he was, and, hopefully, either reassure myself that he was fine, that the problems were minor, or history. And, if they weren't then I would do my damnedest to do something about getting Geoffrey to slow down. Then, selfishly, two weeks without the builders would be blissful. And the simplicity of slipping back into being the child in my childhood home, with no role to play, just time to enjoy being me, a new, pregnant me was just what I craved.

The night before I was due to leave, Rosamond arrived.

'Surprise,' she announced, throwing her arms around my neck. 'Thought I'd come to look after your husband for a while.'

'Does he need looking after?' I asked, feeling suddenly miffed. I had had no idea she was coming to my home, and I disliked the implication that somehow I was neglecting my wifely duties by going away. After all, he was the one who first announced he was off. Was I supposed to wait passively, the loyal, immobile, pining wife?

'Who looked after your husband while you were off antiquing?' I surprised myself by firing back.

She narrowed her eyes at me as if readying herself to retaliate, but then she smiled benignly. 'Needs must, back in those days, darling. Different set-up, if I may say so. Right, now, let me look at you.' She held me at arm's-length, and turned me slowly round. I felt like a prize cow at a show.

'You look well,' she pronounced. 'Merest hint of a bump. Just as you should be.' She planted a kiss on my cheek. 'Well done. Truly splendid news, another Edge at Wrath Castle.'

'Thanks,' I replied. I hadn't thought of my baby that way, and it struck me then that for Rosamond, my baby was not merely a baby, but, more importantly, an Edge, part of a dynasty, her dynasty, the dynasty she had perpetuated by the simple device of changing her son's name back to her maiden name after his father's death. So now I was an Edge, carrying an Edge. I laughed out loud. I couldn't help myself. I had done well, hadn't I, conceiving for her.

'What's so funny?' she asked.

I shook my head. 'Nothing,' I replied. She gave me another measured look, but then Archie appeared brandishing a champagne bottle and three glasses and the moment passed.

'How long are you staying?' I asked her as we ate a scratch dinner later.

She waved an airy hand through the air. No itinerary would trap her. 'We'll see, won't we, darling,' she said, turning to Archie.

Wouldn't she just love it? I imagined her, the chatelaine she had always dreamed of being, restored to her destiny. Would she imbue the walls with her spirit, mould the cells of the place to her being?

That night Archie and I made love sweetly, tenderly, drawing it out as if that way we could slow down the dawn, but morning came defiantly quickly. I showered, dressed, and followed Archie downstairs as he carried my suitcases to the waiting taxi. Rosamond was there, on parade, dressed and made up at 6 a.m.

'Bye, darling,' she said, kissing my cheeks. 'Have a wonderful break. Come back refreshed.'

'Bye, Rosamond.'

She went back into the castle, leaving Archie and me to our goodbyes.

'Bye,' he said cheerily. 'Take care of our baby. And yourself.'

'I will. Have fun in the castle, you and your mother.'

'Oh, we will, don't you worry.'

I waved goodbye, and as the taxi bumped away down the track, my quick pang of separation sadness disappeared and I felt my spirits soar. An innocent trip, I told myself, feeling an almost guilty pleasure. Two weeks away. What could be the harm in that?

Chapter seventeen

The beautiful house in Long Island was just as I remembered it. The air was still and giddy with tuberose and jasmine, but this time I found it soothing. Everything about the house, the long drive, the emerald sloping lawns, the sea susurrations beyond, the quiet luxury, I found soothing. After my long and fragmented journey — Inverness, London, New York, Long Island — I was tired, and I was worried about Geoffrey, about the changes I might see in him.

I hadn't told him I was pregnant. As he hurried across his echoing hall to welcome me, he stopped and gazed at me in amazement, and that was my renewed first impression of him: my familiar, beloved Geoffrey, filled with tender wonder.

'Good God, Morgan. Look at you.' Then he came to me and embraced me. 'Congratulations. Fantastic. Wonderful!' Now I held onto him and studied him. He looked older, his face slightly thinner. It made him look more hawklike, more ferocious than ever, but the worry lines that had always creased his forehead seemed deeper, grooves now. He had lost something of the wry, dry, almost inscrutable countenance that was his trademark in business, and the domestic mask that only slipped to show his true feelings when we went sailing together. He looked care-worn, and the change shocked me.

'Aren't you the one for secrets,' he said, as I smiled at him, hoping my face didn't betray my shock.

'Some things are better shared face to face. The telephone wouldn't have done for this.'

'It wouldn't,' he agreed. 'Your room's all ready. Lie down, rest. Do whatever you need to.'

'Thanks, Geoffrey. I'll just call Archie, tell him I've arrived okay. I won't be long. And I don't need to rest. I'm dying for a lemonade on the lawn, all the trimmings.'

'I'll have it ready and waiting.'

I headed up to my room, my childish pleasure at being back muted by the change in Geoffrey eight months and a flickering heart had wrought. But while part of me worried, another part unwound as I found myself surrounded by all my old talismans. I gazed around, touching familiar objects. My silver hairbrush set that Geoffrey gave me when I was 'grown up,' for my thirteenth birthday, my mother's old tortoiseshell comb, the high mahogany sleigh bed, made up in the crispest linen, topped by a rose-sprigged quilt. There was just one jarring note: the two patches of empty wall where the portraits of my parents had hung. It wouldn't have been so bad if they were at least safely ensconced in Scotland. I'll paint something myself to hang there, I resolved. No substitute, but something, at least.

I sat down on my bed and rang the castle. It took an age, but Archie finally answered.

'I was about to give up on you,' I said, with mock exasperation.

'Morgan,' he answered, panting. 'I just ran up four flights of stairs.'

'There's a phone downstairs.'

'Out of order,' he replied irritably.

139

'Ah. Well, anyway. Bit of exercise, good for you.'

'Yeah, if it doesn't kill me. Good flight?'

'Yeah, all right. No weirdoes sitting next to me.'

'Yes, well that's the benefit of flying first class.'

'I never fly first, Archie. Might as well set fire to a suitcase of notes. Besides, there're plenty of rich weirdoes too.'

'I wouldn't know. How's Geoffrey?'

'Seems fine,' I replied. I had told him nothing about Geoffrey's heart. It would have seemed disloyal, and, anyway, Archie would not have been first in the queue with sympathy, given his and Geoffrey's antipathy.

Archie paused as if about to say something, but then seemed to change his mind.

'Er, good. What're you about to do now then?'

'Why, lemonade on the lawn, of course.'

'How could I forget? Drink one for me will you.'

'I think I can manage that. I'll call you later, say goodnight.'

'I'll already be asleep. Five hours ahead, and all that.'

'Okay,' I replied, feeling slightly dashed. 'Goodnight now then.'

''Night, Morgan.'

I hung up, walked over to the window and gazed down at the spot where I'd first set eyes upon Archie. I stared out at the empty lawn. I tried to recreate the moment, but it wouldn't come.

Geoffrey and I sat out under the leaves of his ancient oak and sipped our memories. For a while we sat in pure, companionable silence. It might have been my imagination, but it seemed to me that as we sat there, the sun setting beyond us, Geoffrey began to look a little better, the tautness in his face and the depth of the grooves lessening.

I found myself unwinding too. After seasons in the north of Scotland, the heat was wondrous to me. I felt my body begin to loosen. I'd had no idea it was so furled. Geoffrey for his part, just seemed happy to have me here.

Geoffrey had laid on all my favourite foods: a fresh green salad to start, lightly grilled tuna and French fries, followed by ginger crème brûlée. Over dinner he regaled me with all the local gossip — who has left who for whom, who has moved in, up, or out. I laughed, glad of a bit of lightness.

After dinner, we headed for the library, and a nightcap.

'You know, you look just like your mother, when she was carrying you.'

'Do I?'

He nodded. 'Happy, excited, beautiful.'

And unaware that she was living out the last months of her life. I felt a chill go over me. I took a gulp of chamomile tea and tried to banish those rogue thoughts that would not leave me alone. I wondered how she would feel now, my mother, about her growing grandchild.

'How is everything?' Geoffrey asked, pouring himself a Calvados. 'You look troubled.'

I shook my head. 'Just roving thoughts. I'm fine. I'm pregnant, beyond the danger period, and I'm glad as heck to be here.'

'I'm glad, Morgan.'

'You know, it's strange, I love the castle, but I sometimes wonder if it's good for me. Sometimes I get this
sudden sense of unease, probably fanciful, but I almost
feel there's some kind of bloodlust there, almost embedded in the walls. There've been so many deaths there.
Rosamond's mother died having her, and, hundreds of
years ago, there was this great slaying where a neighbouring clan broke in and murdered every living occu-
pant of the castle. The line only survived because one of
the clan was pregnant and she was away when it happened. Thirty-three people. Men, women, babies. Can
you imagine?'

Geoffrey closed his eyes. 'There is no limit to
human depravity.' He opened his eyes and continued.
'I don't think there's bloodlust in a place, Morganna,
just in men. And women.'

'Archie's father died there too. There seems to be no
end to–'

'I don't think we can blame that on the castle.'

'What do you mean?'

For the longest while, he said nothing. I could see he
was having some kind of debate with himself. His
silence spooked me.

'There is a grave suspicion that he did not die of natural causes,' he finally said.

'What are you talking about? Rosamond told me he
went to bed one night, and never woke up. Heart attack
in his sleep. She was away in the South of France, digging up antiques. Cleaning lady found him.'

Geoffrey shook his head. 'There was an inquest,
because he died so young. Only thirty-two.
Postmortem, everything, but they still couldn't find a

cause of death. There were some circumstances that made the coroner uneasy, and he refused to say death was due to natural causes. He returned an open verdict.'

'What were the circumstances?' I asked. I felt as if someone had thrown a black cloak of fear over me.

'Husband and wife were not getting on. Rosamond had been caught having an affair with someone in the South of France. Eight months before Roddy's death, she had taken out a life insurance policy on him. And there was a witness, well, a quasi-witness. One of the young women who worked in the castle thought she caught a glimpse of Rosamond that night, thought she heard her voice, heard her and Roddy talking.'

'Thought?'

'It was late, apparently, and a storm was blowing. It was dark as hell, and hard to hear anything over the wind.'

'I know that wind. It's like a banshee when it gets up, but even so, *thought*?'

'She was young, unsure of herself, but aware, no doubt, of the trouble she was creating.'

'What could the police, and the coroner do with *thought*?'

'Not much, though it's pretty clear they wanted to. That's why the Coroner returned an open verdict.'

'Who was she, this girl?'

'Can't recall her name. Mc something, but then who isn't, up there? Newly married to a local shepherd. That I do remember, 'cos I recall thinking it was such a shame.'

'What was?' I asked, my heart hammering.

'She killed herself, eight months later. Of course, who can say if the whole episode had anything to do with it, maybe she was a total depressive anyway, and — hey, what's up?'

'Was her name McIntyre?'

'That's it. McIntyre.'

'I know him, the shepherd. Ben. He brings me lamb; he taught me how to cook. He . . . he's a friend.'

'Morgan, I'm sorry. The whole business is bloody.'

I ran my hands over my face. 'Jesus.'

Geoffrey continued, determined to finish his story. 'So, thanks to Mrs. McIntyre, in large part, the Coroner returned an open verdict, the insurance company refused to pay up. Rosamond ran out of funds, had to leave the castle. It was boarded up, stayed that way ever since. Until you came along.'

I got up and walked across to the mantelpiece. I tried to marshal my thoughts, to look for holes in what Geoffrey was saying. He was a rigorous man, a lawyer by training, not given to wild accusations. Geoffrey *couldn't* be saying what I feared he might be. I felt angry with him for telling me this, for always telling me bad news, for shattering the calm that I had so badly craved. I turned back to him.

'I'm not quite sure what you're telling me here. Or why, come to think of it. Are you saying that Rosamond murdered her husband for his life insurance, and then somehow spun a web, over decades, waiting for the right spider to happen along? I hope not, because that is idiocy. Pure and simple.'

Geoffrey looked out towards the darkening garden before he answered.

'Well, that's where we differ. I do not think it is idiocy. I would like you to think on it, when you feel calmer. I'm sorry to spring it on you like this. I know this is a shock for you. I didn't intend for it to come out this way, so soon.'

'So why are you telling me?'

'Because I'm worried, and I think you'd do well to know who you are dealing with.'

'Are you talking just about Rosamond, or my husband too?'

'I know nothing untoward about him. It's Rosamond who concerns me.'

'Let's assume for just one moment that what you're saying is not pure idiocy,' I replied belligerently. 'Do you think Archie knows any of this?'

'What do *you* think?'

'God, I don't know. The whole thing's unthinkable. He doesn't talk about his father much. When we first got together, he told me his father had died when he was eight, didn't elaborate and I didn't push him. Then, when we got married, I said to him it was a shame his father couldn't be there, and he nodded, and said that's what happens when your father dies young. He misses all the landmarks, said it had been just him and his mother, that she'd tried to be both mother and father to him, as far as anyone could.' I thought back through our brief marriage, and shook my head. 'No, he can't know anything about these, these wild ideas. He wouldn't have the relationship he does have with his mother if he thought anything of the sort.'

Geoffrey nodded, but said nothing. I could not shake the feeling there was a lot more he wasn't telling me.

I studied him carefully. 'Geoffrey, why do you happen to know all this?'

He blew out a long breath. I'd never seen him look so uncomfortable.

'I wasn't happy about your marriage, you knew that. So I did whatever I have to do in the bank when we're about to do business with a new party. I got the PIs onto her.'

I could not contain my incredulity. 'Private investigators? Jesus, Geoffrey. She's a person, not some bloody tacky corporation.'

'Those tacky corporations pay for this house and that boat of yours that you love so much. Never talk of those companies with that scorn. Without them you'd have nothing.'

I bit my lip, chastened. 'Sorry.'

He nodded, placated. 'You seem to have become contaminated by English snobberies about money and how it is made. Please, don't go down that path, Morgan.'

'I'm sorry,' I reiterated. 'I was shocked by what you told me.'

'Yeah well, wise up, don't be.'

I began to feel as if I were floundering way out of my depth in a world whose cynicism and corruption I did not want to admit. I just wanted to close my eyes to it, to keep closing my eyes to it, but I knew it was too late for that now.

'And they told you all this?'

He nodded.

'Do you really believe she killed her husband?'

'Well, she had an alibi. She was in the South of France, on a boat. Were it not for that, I would have no trouble whatsoever believing it.'

'But she wasn't there, supposedly, and Roddy could have died of natural causes?'

'That's one interpretation.'

The other lay between us in the air, unsaid. If her alibi was false and Rosamond had killed her husband, justice apart, where the hell did that leave the rest of us? Even the best case was bad. Rosamond was an adulteress, who took out life insurance on her husband, who then conveniently, and coincidentally, but incriminatingly died, thereby invalidating the life insurance. A murder in vain, or just untimely death?

'So what the hell am I supposed to do now that I know all this stuff?'

'You're supposed to be careful.'

'Careful of my money, or my life?'

'I would say both.'

'Come on, Geoffrey, that's absurd.'

'Probably, Morgan. I know you think I'm a cautious old fool, but take care, keep your wits about you. Do that for me? Especially now.'

What could I say? 'Of course I will. But Geoffrey, there's no way she would harm me. She's thrilled I'm pregnant. There'll be an heir or an heiress for the castle, won't there, a little Edge to keep it all going.'

'There is always that,' he replied, but he didn't look much comforted.

I thought about my endless, fruitless attempts to paint Rosamond, to capture her image. She remained enigmatic, but just how much was she hiding? The crimes and misdemeanours of a normal life, or something altogether more sinister?

Chapter eighteen

I awoke the next morning with the looming sense that something was very wrong. Then I remembered Geoffrey's revelations. It was dark still, not yet dawn. I fumbled for my watch and checked the luminous dial: 4 a.m. I wanted to slide back into sleep, but jet lag and worry had left me wide awake. I pushed myself from bed, donned my robe and headed softly down to the kitchen for some milk. As I passed the television room I stopped. The door was ajar and I could just see Geoffrey, sitting profile to me, slightly hunched, features pinched, gazing at the television. I pulled back, conscious that he would not have wanted me to see him like this. I had *never* seen him up in the predawn like this. Was he now insomniac too? This didn't feel like a one off, more like some weary routine. I returned silently to my room, without my milk, with a whole slew of new worries.

I sat up in bed, trying to lose myself in a book, waiting impatiently for daybreak, and for some sense of normality to return. As soon as the first rays of dawn streaked the sky with arrows of pink, I pulled on my swimsuit, and hurried out onto the dewy lawn. I ran down to the sea, and plunged in. I wanted to wash everything away, my worries, my doubts, the lingering legacies of the theft of my portraits.

The sea had always been a balm to me, and I looked to it now as much as ever. That morning it was reasonably calm, but the waves were still big enough to tumble me around a bit. I emerged fresh and revived after ten minutes or so. I felt buffered and relieved, as if some of the weight of last night has been washed off me.

I showered, dressed, and headed down for breakfast. Geoffrey was finishing his fried eggs on toast, ensconced in his customary *New York Times*. He looked up at me as I came in and called out a cheery 'good morning' to him. He appeared tired, but not unduly so. Whatever had him up at 4 a.m., he was coping with it, but it couldn't be conducive to long-term health.

I kissed his cheek and got his customary breakfast grunt in return. I helped myself to coffee and croissants.

'Wind looks good,' I said. 'Fancy a sail?'

'You all right with that, in your condition?'

'Geoffrey, I'm pregnant, not ill. I'll let you do the heavy stuff.'

His face brightened. He got up. 'I'll just get a weather fax. If it's good, shall we go straight out? We'll give the *Morganna* a spin, boat's feeling neglected.'

'Not *Hurricane*?'

'My boat's harder to handle solo. Let's take yours.'

'You're on.'

The outlook was good: light westerly winds, freshening just a tad mid-morning. So out we went on the *Morganna*, for two hours of blissful bashing around Long Island sound. The sea and the boat worked the usual charms. Standing at the tiller, Geoffrey held up his face to the wind and the sun and smiled in pleasure. At his insistence, I was just a passenger, not a crew member. No hauling sails for me, but he did allow me a stint at the tiller.

'Big of you,' I said.

'Well, someone has to take care of you.'

'I'm a big girl now, Geoffrey. I *can* take care of myself.'

'Hmm. Everyone needs a bit of extra cosseting now and then. And by my lights, you need it now.'

'What about you?' I asked.

'What about me?'

I took a big breath and plunged on. 'There's no diplomatic way to say this, Geoffrey, but you look tired. You look a bit strained. Is everything all right?'

'Pah. I'm just getting older, get tired like the next man. You getting any sailing in over there?'

It wasn't going to be easy, I knew that, but I would pick my time again and not give up. There and then I allowed Geoffrey his abrupt change of subject.

'No, actually. But it might be an idea, sometime post-baby, to get a boat. Ferocious waters round the coast there though, but if I picked my weather it could be wonderful. It's so beautiful. I'd really love it if you would come and stay.'

'One day.'

We brought the *Morganna* in just before midday. We were walking through the hall, happy and exhilarated, when James, the butler, coughed discreetly at us.

'Misters Brascoe and Cohen are here, Mr. Warrender, waiting in the drawing room.'

I glanced up at Geoffrey. His face had tightened back into its grooves.

'Morganna, excuse me, will you,' he said, heading off.

'What is it, Geoffrey? Not work on a Saturday. Can't they give you a day of peace?'

'Not work,' he said, walking on.

I turned into the kitchen and helped myself to an apple. I sat on a bar stool and chewed ruminatively. I wanted to go and eavesdrop, or invite myself in, but I knew that was a boundary I couldn't cross. Geoffrey had always kept his business affairs strictly to himself. He shared the odd amusing anecdote, but from childhood I had been schooled never to interrupt a meeting. I thought perhaps the time had come to change all that when Geoffrey himself appeared in the kitchen, sombre-faced.

'Could you join us, please, Morganna?' he asked, almost formally.

Christ, what was going on? I felt unease clench my stomach. I followed Geoffrey into his study. Two men were sitting straight-backed on his sofa. They got up when I came in and Geoffrey introduced them.

I shook hands with Bud Brascoe, a thickset ex-footballer-type with a huge neck and bulky forearms showing through his suit, and Marty Cohen, a wiry intellectual-looking man who smiled at me almost apologetically. I sat down opposite them and waited for what was shaping up to be some kind of bombshell.

'Bud and Marty work for Kroll, Morganna. Marty's a fine art pro, tracks down stolen pieces for insurance companies and private individuals. They think they've found yours.'

I felt relief, wild relief. I don't quite know what I had feared. More revelations about Rosamond, and, worse, Archie, but this was pure, unalloyed good news. At least I thought it was.

152

'Where? Who has them?'

'They're closer than you could imagine. Here on Long Island. They're hanging in the home of one Buffy Vegas.'

'She's some kind of socialite, isn't she? What the hell is she doing with my portraits?'

'Her interior designer bought them for her. In good faith. We've been following a long trail, Mrs. Edge, and it led to her.'

'Do you know who stole them?' I asked. They both exchanged a glance with Geoffrey.

'Bud and Marty have traced the chain a long way back, Morganna, but not quite to source,' said Geoffrey.

'Meaning?' I asked.

'We don't have the gloved hand that took them off your walls,' explained Marty, 'but we have the first fence, the first person to sell them on.'

'You have as in you know who did it and you've spoken to them?'

'On many occasions,' answered Marty.

'And?'

'And they won't sing,' answered Geoffrey. 'Not a word about who fenced them to them. Interestingly though, they offered up the next link in the chain on a platter.'

'So why wouldn't they spill about who'd sold them in the first place since they seem to be the spilling kind?'

Another quick exchange of glances.

'Fear,' replied Marty. 'Pure and simple.'

'Well, that's one big fat comfort. Do you have any idea, even a guess as to who this person might be?'

'We do not,' answered Marty. 'Nothing that Kroll could hang our hats on.'

I knew professional scruples when I hear them. 'Oh come on, that means you have an idea, a hunch, a feeling at least.'

'Feelings don't cut it,' answered Bud. 'We'll keep at it, and let you know if we make progress.'

'And my portraits?'

Geoffrey gave me a wolfish smile.

'Let's go get 'em.'

I looked at him incredulously. 'What, just like that?' I clicked my fingers.

'Get your glad rags on, Morganna. It's showtime. Lawrence Fisher's on his way. Soon as he gets here, we'll go visit with Buffy Vegas.'

Fisher was our lawyer, who handled all Geoffrey's and my private business.

'They might not be mine, Geoffrey. I don't want to get my hopes up.'

'They're yours,' replied Marty.

I headed upstairs and pulled off my sailing gear. How do you dress for a reverse heist? I wondered. I decided on a loose summer dress and espadrilles. I combed the salt from my hair, sprayed on some scent, and went back downstairs just as Lawrence Fisher pulled up.

He nodded a greeting to the Kroll guys and shook me and Geoffrey by hand, and then we all set off in Geoffrey's Lincoln for the drive to Sag Harbour.

Buffy Vegas lived in a white stone house four stories high with huge, ugly, plate-glass windows glaring out across tonsured lawns. A Filipino maid answered the door and asked us to wait while she checked with her mistress. Geoffrey gave her his name, which, as always, opened the door. The maid showed us into the drawing room and a few minutes later Buffy Vegas appeared trailing a cloud of scent.

She looked like the showgirl she had once been, all pneumatic curves and teased peroxide.

Geoffrey performed the introductions, and then Buffy bid us all be seated.

'What can I do for you guys?' she asked, sweetly puzzled.

I gazed around. No sign of my parents on these pale walls.

'We understand you recently purchased two portraits, Mrs. Vegas,' said Lawrence Fisher, 'via your interior designer.'

She smiled. 'Ah, those two. Not for sale. I love 'em.'

'Yeah, well, unfortunately for you, our client loves them too,' said Marty, indicating me.

'So?'

'The portraits were stolen, Mrs. Vegas,' intoned Fisher. 'I have documentary evidence here that they originally belonged to Mrs. Edge here, and we have police records as well as sworn testimony from a number of dealers down the line that they on-sold the portraits, ultimately to your interior designer and to you.'

Buffy got to her feet. 'And you think you can just stroll into my house and shout about your documenterizing evidence and that I'll just hand them over? I paid good money for those portraits and I did not know they were stolen. I had no idea and neither did Pascale. So,

155

far as I can see, they're mine.' She turns to me. 'Sorry, honey, if you lost your portraits, but that's not my problem.'

'Oh, but I'm afraid it is,' said Geoffrey, speaking for the first time since he'd been introduced. He gave her his special smile, the one I'd always fancied a shark gave its prey as it opened its mouth ready to bite. 'We can make it one very big problem for you,' he continued silkily. 'The press would like this one, don't you think? Buffy Vegas, handling stolen goods. Not good for the rep. Then there's the statutory jail sentence. Five years. No spas in the state penitentiaries, I do believe. Not good for the bod. In many ways.' He shrugged, as if he couldn't give a toss. 'Your choice.'

He was magnificent. He sat back and allowed her brain to grind into gear. 'Of course, if you just hand over the portraits, we can just forget the whole thing. No cops. No press.'

'And my three hundred grand?'

'Consider it the cost of a lesson well learned. Next time your Pascale buys fine art, tell him to make sure it carries a certificate of authenticity. That way nobody'll get burned.'

She was trapped and she knew it. She knew who Geoffrey was. She knew he wouldn't pull a heist on her, and there was something so wonderfully, ruthlessly compelling about him. He had really made life very simple for her. She had no choice and knew it.

'Come with me,' she said, and led us to the tall staircase. There, halfway up, were my parents.

'Alarmed?' asked Marty.

She shook her head. 'Not right now.'

He went up and with Bud's help simply unhooked them from the wall.

Buffy watched them leave with a moue of regret. Thank God for a certain kind of American and their hankering for the right kind of past.

We drove my portraits back to Geoffrey's house. The Kroll men, and then Lawrence Fisher, took off, business successfully transacted.

Geoffrey and I sat down together. He looked triumphant. I shook my head at him in wonder.

'You are quite something,' I said. 'I'd hate to cross you.'

He laughed. 'You never could.'

'But those who do . . .'

'Pay the price. Pure and simple.'

I nodded. I could well imagine.

'Those Kroll people, they seem everywhere at the moment. It's as if you have them on retainer.'

'As a matter of fact I do.'

'God almighty. What kind of world do you live in?'

'The same one as you, only you never knew it before.'

'I never had cause to.'

'Well, you do now, don't you?'

I did. Whichever way I looked at it, tried to evade it, I did. How many different levels of innocence were there? How many of them had to die in a lifetime?

I was ecstatic to have my portraits back, but that night, with them hanging apparently safely in their allotted spaces in my rooms, I dreamed of the gloved hands fingering their way through Wrath Castle and I wondered whose they were to inspire such fear. I knew that sooner or later Geoffrey would find out. Even in my dreams I knew that would be a bad thing.

Chapter nineteen

The next day I woke early again. I found myself craving an apple, so I headed downstairs towards the kitchen, but again I stopped as I heard the sounds of television emanating from the TV room. And again, Geoffrey was there, eyes fixed on the screen in a kind of grim meditation. I quickly backed away, got my apple, and headed back to my room. I sat in my bed, worrying about Geoffrey, my apple untouched, my appetite gone. I must have fallen back into a deep sleep because when I surfaced Geoffrey had already left for the bank, leaving me to the quiet solitude of home. I swam, I dug out my old paints and daubed a bit, unsatisfactorily, and I dozed for a while in the sun.

I rang Wrath Castle as soon as I thought they'd be up to tell them the news about my portraits, but the phone rang and rang and nobody picked up. I tried Rosamond's number in Southwold and got nothing there. Last of all, I tried Archie's mobile, only to find it turned off.

'Great. Just great,' I muttered angrily. It was as if they'd disappeared from the face of the earth. Archie always kept his mobile on. He was one of those technophiles who got off on being permanently plugged in to the world. The ringing of his mobile made him feel wanted, important. I paced around my rooms in frustration. I'd never made that observation about my husband before, had never seen him with the light of distance and perhaps the clarity offered by my growing, seemingly enforced cynicism.

I tried Archie on and off all day, and finally when Geoffrey came home at six, especially early in honour of me, I gave up for the night.

We took drinks as always on the lawn. As I sipped my lemonade, watching the lowering sun, Geoffrey brought up the subject I was dreading.

'Like to talk about finances?'

'Must I?'

'Sooner or later.'

'Let's get it over with.'

'I think it would be a good idea if you reduced the monthly feed into your current account. Your joint current account, that is.'

'Geoffrey, that's just not practical. We'll never finish renovating the castle if I start cutting back.'

'There's renovating and renovating, Morgan.'

'Look, why don't you just tell me what exactly is bothering you.'

'Well, first off, we had that Sotheby's episode, the nine hundred grand, the museum pieces, and–'

'We *dealt* with that, Geoffrey. I spoke to Archie.' I got to my feet and filled my glass with fresh lemonade and Geoffrey's with a julep. I remembered how Archie had stormed from our bed, his face pinched with shame and anger. I remembered the damage, and the distance between us it had created. 'I'm not sure how many of those conversations a marriage can take.'

'You do what you have to do, one way or another, but I'm your main trustee. I have to report to you.'

'Okay, okay.'

'There have been five cheques over the past two months, made payable by Archie, to Rosamond, totalling one hundred and six thousand pounds.'

'Stop, stop.' I really didn't want to hear this. I got up and walked off down the lawn towards the limpid sea. I felt wracked by confusion, by ten different explanations competing in my head. There seemed to be so much going on that I wasn't quite recognizing, that I didn't understand, like a face glimpsed in a crowd, like a snippet of overheard conversation. I forced myself to calm down, and walked slowly back to Geoffrey. I sat down heavily.

'You can't just fling these things at me out of context. There must be an explanation, a kosher one,' I added quickly, wracking my brains. 'She found pieces,' I said, inspired. 'Archie was trying to cut back. Rosamond probably picked up things on our behalf, and Archie reimbursed her. She's got a great eye,' I finished, sounding lame even to myself. 'I'm sure that's it.'

'She has an eye, all right.'

'You're suggesting that my husband is effectively stealing money from me to give to his mother?'

'That's about the size of it.'

'Jesus. What does that say about my marriage, if it is true? About the kind of idiot they must think me. No, don't answer that,' I said quickly. 'I will not jump to conclusions. I am certain there's an innocent explanation.'

'Fine, but I do suggest you ask a few questions, if your husband doesn't volunteer such an explanation. And a credible one at that.'

'That will be fun.' I could hardly imagine the scene.

'Is there anything else?' I asked wearily. 'If so, let's get it all out now, so that I can enjoy my stay here, and not feel like I'm about to get ambushed by another bout of bad news at any time.'

'There's nothing else. At least not that I'm current-ly aware of.'

'Are you sure?' He was twirling his julep, not look-ing at me.

'Positive,' he said, meeting my eyes, but I was not convinced.

'Right, then.' I was determined to be upbeat, to assert some sort of control, and, most importantly, not to leap to the conclusions swirling round my head. For the sake of my marriage, which, now that I was going to have a child, was more important to me than ever, I just could not afford to.

'We'll keep the monthly feed to the joint current account as it is,' I concluded, 'and for my part, I'll watch it carefully.'

Geoffrey nodded. 'You might think your fortune is so great, Morganna, that you will never go through it, nor need to give it more than a casual thought. But you'd be surprised how easily even many millions can trickle though your fingers, especially when someone else is siphoning from below.'

'I won't let them siphon, and I really don't think that's what they're trying to do. They both are in love with the castle. As I am.'

'Yes. And you know what they say about love.'

I did, and quite possibly I was blinded, just a little. Fool for love? Maybe, but I also adhered to the belief *innocent until proved guilty*, and Geoffrey wasn't offering proof, just facts that could be interpreted in a number of ways, some innocent. I knew too that some kind of prejudice, what I believed to be an unfounded prejudice, lay behind Geoffrey's bitterness, and that the truth hovered somewhere in between the two.

Geoffrey had put me in a position where I would be forced to confront my husband again. I was cornered and I was angry and I saw no reason why I should not dish out to Geoffrey what he had just served up to me.

'Right, Geoffrey, if you are going to play hardball in my private life then you have to be ready to have the favour returned.'

'What the heck do you mean?' he asked sharply.

'I mean you're ill. Something's wrong. I've been up early twice with jet lag and I've seen you watching TV at 4 a.m. and you look worried about something, and tired, and all these headaches you've apparently been getting. I don't believe a word of it. A headache would never keep you off work. Something's going on and I want to know what it is. And I will not let up until you tell me.'

Geoffrey got to his feet.

'Dammit, Morgan. I will not be interrogated in my own home.' He stormed off towards the house, emanating anger. I had never in my whole life with him seen him like this, nor had I experienced his fury directly. I stared after him. Perhaps it was the shock of his outburst, perhaps it was the pregnancy hormones and the strain of having to live with what he had just told me of Rosamond and my husband, but I began to sob. Once I'd started I didn't feel as if I could stop. I held my head in my hands and let all the pent-up sorrow, the sense of betrayal that had been building for some time, and the fear all come together and flood from me on a tide of tears. I only stopped when I felt a hand on my shoulder and looked up into Geoffrey's remorseful eyes.

'Morganna, I'm sorry.'

'Tell me,' I said. 'I *know* something's wrong and not knowing is the worst thing. It has to be worse than knowing. *Please* tell me.'

And so he did. He sat down slowly, with the jerkiness of a man much older. He folded his arms across his chest, and leaned towards me.

'This isn't easy for me, Morganna.'

'I know. But you *must* tell me.'

He blew out a long breath. 'I've always been so fit, so strong. I've been at the top of Huttons for ten years now and I thought I could go on for another five, at least.' He unclamped his arms and gave a gesture of despair. 'Now it's all up in the air. I'm just not sure if I can go on holding it together.' He fell silent.

'Holding what together? Is the bank in some sort of trouble, because if it is, it's not the end of the world. It's not flesh and blood.'

'Flesh and blood is the problem. The bank's fine. It's me. There are two things. One is my heart. I have some kind of murmur, not terribly serious but not terribly good either. The other is my head.'

'What's wrong with your head?'

'Panic,' he said simply. 'I get these panic attacks that feel as if they're going to kill me. I lie in bed and they come from nowhere like ghouls out to get me and all I can do is get up, get out of the room, go to my television and sit there, trying to breathe, trying to shut out

what's going on in my head, to slow down my fluttering heart, to breathe, to concentrate on whatever crap
they're showing at 4 a.m. and to keep this thing at bay.'
He ran his hands over his face and I saw the full weight
of his terror as he looked at me, utterly unguarded,
unmasked.

'Oh, Geoffrey.' I went to him, kneeled by his chair
and took hold of him, as I would a child. I held him like
that for some time. He made no sound, or movement,
but it felt to me like he was crying, silently and stilly,
and my heart broke for him.

Finally, I moved away from him, but still I held onto
his arms.

'What do the doctors say?'

He gave a snort. 'They prescribe sleeping tablets,
beta blockers, diazepam. A whole cocktail of drugs you
wouldn't believe.'

'And?'

'And sometimes they work, sometimes they don't,
but if they do work it's at the price of leaving me like a
zombie, so out of it I'm no use to anyone.'

'Geoffrey, there will be something we can do. I'm
here now. I'll stay for as long as it takes, but we'll do
something, I promise you.'

He nodded and the faintest of smiles touched his
lips, but it was a smile not of comfort, but of despair.
That night as I tried to sleep I wondered if what I'd
offered were just hollow words, if anything at all could
be done.

Chapter twenty

It took me a long time to get to sleep that night with the result that the following morning I slept in and missed Geoffrey. He came home in time for dinner and I tackled him then.

'Have you thought of throwing the whole thing in?' I asked him. He looked momentarily alarmed until I added: 'The bank. The pressures.'

'Many times.'

'Then why don't you?'

'Because it would be running away.'

'Why so?'

'Running away because I cannot hack it anymore.'

'Or choose not to.'

'Cannot.'

'So, even if you look at it that way, what does it matter?'

'It matters to me.'

'Pride?'

'Don't knock it. Pride can keep you alive. Pride can keep you going long after you would have given up.'

'Should have given up.'

'What would I do? You've gone, I'm not married, I don't have a companion.'

'You tell me. Isn't there something you've always wanted to do, but have never had the time for?'

I saw a light in his eyes and I knew I'd hit on something.

'One thing,' he said. 'It's a possibility.'

'What?'

'Well, I've always wanted to go on an epic voyage, not just coastal sailing, day sailing, but cross an ocean or two. Single-handed.'

'Wow! What about your heart?'

He gave me a withering look. 'It's the panic attacks that are messing with my heart, not the other way around. If they went my heart would be fine.'

'So, what are you waiting for?'

'Morgan. Come on. It's not that simple. I can't simply get up and walk away from the bank after all this time and just–'

'Indispensable?' I ask.

He gave me a sheepish grin. 'Perhaps not. There'd be enough young guns angling.'

'Let them angle. Take a sabbatical, for as long as it takes. You may want to go back, you may not. What's the worst case? They don't want you? Someone else has taken root in your office? Come on Geoffrey. There's more to life than the NASDAQ and corporate politics. You can play that game at the highest level and you have, but is it worth giving your life for? Shortening your life for? Trouble is, when you're in it so deep, you can't see any alternatives, you're as blink ered as a pony down a pit, the only difference is, it knows it has no peripheral vision, you don't.' I fell silent. Geoffrey blew out a long breath.

'Wow. That was some speech.'

'Tell me one word of it was not true.'

'I cannot.'

'Then Geoffrey, please get away. Sail round the world. Do not keep putting these kinds of pressures on yourself. It wouldn't surprise me if the panic attacks were your subconscious screaming at you to listen.'

'Could be,' he mused.

'So?'

'These things take time, Morgan. It'd probably have to be next year. There's a small window to get away in, the winds have to be right, the seasons right for the kinda things I might have been thinking of.'

I nodded. 'So, when would be the ideal time to go?'

'Before the fall.'

I smiled. 'Right, that gives us plenty of time. Don't tell me a man who runs one of the world's top invest-ment banks couldn't get his ass in gear by then?'

He laughed and for that moment he sounded like the Geoffrey of old, but then his face furrowed back into its recent wrinkles.

'But Morgan, even if, just suspend disbelief for a moment, if I did pull this *insane* stunt, what about you?'

'What about me?'

'I'd be leaving you, I'd be away for maybe eight, nine months.'

'And? Haven't I gone off? I've been gone for eight months.'

'And it hasn't been great. I've been worried about you, as you know.'

'About my finances. I can control that, Geoffrey. Please believe me. Look, I'm pregnant, I'm happy. What I could not stand is to leave you here like this, suf-fering in the way you clearly have been. That would damage me far more than these financial indiscretions that my husband and my mother-in-law may, just may, be guilty of. Those things are just money. They are not flesh and blood. You are. Your life is. The way I see it, you really don't have any choice.'

He smiled at me and I could see a new respect in his eyes. Maybe, just maybe, he thought I was growing up, that I could be trusted, could be left.

'I'd be away when you have your baby.'

'My baby will still be here when you get back. Hey, why don't you plan it so you end up in Scotland, sail to Cape Wrath?'

His eyes lit up again and I could see I was slowly, very slowly, getting somewhere.

He raised his hand. 'Quit, will you, while you're ahead. You've done well. You've got me thinking. You've watered a seed that maybe was thinking of germinating. Now quit fussing and let me think, let me gestate, like you.'

I laughed and when I went to bed that night I felt lighter than I had in a long time. I had a feeling I might just have thrown Geoffrey some kind of lifeline, and, in doing so, I had reminded myself that my troubles were not so crippling as his. As I'd told him, my troubles were all money-based. They had nothing whatever to do with flesh and blood. I was alive, I was beginning to feel the slightest butterfly sensations in my stomach that I thought might just be my baby quickening inside me. Next to that, what did a bit of overspending matter?

Chapter twenty-one

The rest of the two weeks with Geoffrey eased by. I slept better, and I really believe he did. His face seemed lighter, not quite so furrowed as before, and it seemed to me he had a new purposefulness to him. I didn't bring up the sailing again. My instinct told me to back off. I let him be and he let me be. There were no more lectures about money. I spoke to Archie periodically, not as often as I would have liked, but in a strange way the lack of contact made things easier. No issues could arise if we didn't speak. That way I avoided confronting him about the cheques to his mother, and I could just be. Maybe it was blissful denial, maybe not, but either way I didn't care. I just wanted to have a nice, quiet, restful time, and that I managed.

The heat made me languid, and distance from Cape Wrath calmed me. I swam every day; I ate well. On the night before I was due to fly back to Scotland, Geoffrey and I celebrated my twenty-first with a quiet dinner at home. Quiet is exactly how I wanted it. I'd never been a party girl, never inherited my mother's apparent gregariousness. I missed Archie, though. I would have liked to have celebrated with him too, especially on such a landmark birthday, but we'd agreed to have a delayed celebration back in Scotland. *We can cheat by a few days*, Archie had said. It made sense. If I'd cut short my trip I would not have got the rest I needed. So I reassured myself and sat back to enjoy the feast Geoffrey had laid on for me — lashings of caviar, lobster, the freshest salads, French fries, and an enormous chocolate mousse.

Then, after dinner, Geoffrey took me into his office, and showed me a map he'd tacked to his cork board. I literally held my breath with disbelief and with joy as I followed the progress of red and blue pins across wide blue expanses of sea.

'Wow! Quite ambitious,' I managed to say. I felt like whooping with delight.

'Gonna do something, might as well go for it.'

'Geoffrey, you have no idea how pleased I am. How happy this makes me.'

He grinned. 'Yeah, well I feel pretty damn good about it too. And, you know what, since that damned night you took me on, the panic attacks have been getting better. Not so many, and not so severe. I've been managing them without drugs, and I have a real good feeling about this.'

'You've told the bank?'

'I have. I'm off in two weeks.'

This time I could not resist a whoop. 'That is brilliant. Oh, Geoffrey. What did they say?'

'They knew a fait accompli when they saw one. They huffed and puffed, but let me tell you, when the door closes behind me they'll be sharpening their knives like it's Thanksgiving.'

I laughed. 'Let them.'

'There are worse things at sea,' he joked.

'Which reminds me. Be careful, won't you, on this voyage. Don't take unnecessary risks, push yourself on if the weather's bad. Don't try and meet a schedule just for the sake of it.'

'I will be prudent, Morganna. That's what I excel at, remember?'

'*Touché.*'

'Now, Morgan, time to move on. This is a big day for you in more ways than one. Not only twenty-one, but now you are fully in control of your fortune.'

I nodded. I hadn't really thought much about this aspect of my birthday, but then, I suddenly became conscious of the great weight of my fortune. The freedom it gave me I had always taken for granted. To the responsibility it brought with it, that with my birthday I had assumed, I had scarcely given thought.

Geoffrey handed me a raft of documents. I moved to sign them. He held up his hand.

'Morganna. Read them!'

'I don't need to read them. I trust you.'

'You shouldn't. Not that I am not to be trusted, but as a point of principle you should always read what you sign.'

I thought of the realms of paper Archie put before me every month, in one great sitting. Indemnities for us against the Poles, insurance for them, promises to Scottish Heritage to do or not to do God knows what. I soon gave up reading them. It made me wonder. So for Geoffrey's sake, and in a sudden wish to placate the fates, to make up for my past negligence, I read, scrupulously, all about the trusts that then fell under my control. And I signed.

Then Geoffrey fell quiet and took out a small unwrapped box from a drawer. He handed it to me with a solemn smile. It was dun-coloured leather, old. I opened it. Inside were two rings. A gold band

and a glittering sapphire. I looked up at Geoffrey in surprise.

'Your mother's,' he said.

I pulled off Archie's rings, and slipped on my mother's. They were a perfect fit. I turned and twisted my hand and watched the sapphire glitter.

'They're beautiful.'

Geoffrey nodded.

I did not want to take them off. I put Archie's rings on the fingers of my right hand. They were a bit tight, but I managed to squeeze them on.

I'll switch them round when I go back to Scotland, I thought.

'You've had these all along?' I asked him.

He nodded. 'Your mother married at twenty-one. I thought you should have them at the same age. There's something else,' he said, handing me a blue Tiffany box. I opened it. Inside was a long silver whistle. I took it out. I saw Jelly's name engraved on it. It was perfect, the right thing to lighten the moment too. The past had suddenly made both of us become too sombre. I laughed, and gave it a sharp blow. The sound that issued forth was pure and crisp as the cry of a bird.

'Geoffrey, you clever thing. It's just what I need for that naughty puppy.'

'Good.' He glanced at this watch. 'Past the witching hour. Time for bed.'

The ringing of the phone dragged me from sleep. It was Archie.

'God, what time is it? One a.m. Jesus, Archie. Everything all right?'

'Fine. Just called to wish you happy birthday.'

I rubbed my eyes. He didn't seem to notice he'd woken me up, that it was no longer my birthday. Perhaps he just didn't care.

'Right, okay.'

There was an awkward pause. 'Er, look, Morganna. May not be worth you coming home yet, I, er, I'm staying with Ma for another two weeks.

'Two weeks?' That woke me up. 'Archie! Why so long?'

'God, Morgan. I've had flu if you must know. That's why I haven't rung you that much. I could hardly speak. And it depresses me to be ill. I think it must be the stress of the whole bloody project, the dust, the hassles. Anyway, I've bought nothing, not done a single thing on my list. Now, frankly, I need to rest a bit and then I need to get busy. I really don't think two weeks is much time to squeeze all that in.'

'No, I suppose not, if you put it like that.'

'Well how else can I put it?'

I couldn't work out why he seemed so aggressive.

'It's all right, Archie. No big deal. I'll stay on here. I'll ring Ben and make sure it's all right with Jelly.'

'Yes, Ben. Let's not forget him.'

I stared at the phone in incomprehension. What the hell had got into him?

'Right, well it's obvious you need some sleep, so better get off. Goodnight, Archie.'

He muttered goodnight, and I hung up.

It took me ages to get back to sleep.

I joined Geoffrey at breakfast feeling knackered.

'Morning, Geoffrey.'

He looked up, smiled, greeted me warmly. I poured a mug of coffee for myself. I couldn't face food.

'Is it all right if I stay on here for a few weeks? I could be here to see you off?'

He laid down his paper in unconcealed surprise. 'Of course. As long as you like. You know that. But may I ask why? I will go. You don't have to be here to push me into my boat.'

'I know that. It's Archie. He's had the flu. He's way behind on all the shopping and stuff. Needs more time.'

'Doesn't seem all that behind on the shopping to me.'

'*Geo*ffrey.'

He raised his hands in surrender. 'All right, all right. Forget I spoke. Stay. Happily.'

'I will.'

And I made myself happy, determinedly so. I felt my baby moving and fluttering inside me, I painted, I lay in the sun and swam, I ate delicious food, yet still, somehow, I felt banished. Archie and I spoke, every few days, but we filled our conversations with the old padding — this purchase and that. My money oiled the wheels of our conversation.

And so two weeks passed. The night before Geoffrey was due to set sail, and I to fly back to England, he invited me into his study after dinner. He paced around and I caught his agitation. Finally he sat down.

'You nervous, about your trip?' I asked, praying he wasn't about to announce he'd changed his mind.

'Not really. What makes me nervous is you. Your situation.'

'Geoffrey, please. I can handle it. I will handle it. I promise.'

He shook his head slightly as if that meant little. 'What I want you to promise me is this. If you see anything at all that doesn't smell right, even if you have no proof, I want you to get on a plane and come here.'

'Oh, come on. How can I do that? For some time before the baby's due and for some time after I won't be allowed to or want to travel. I'm not going to leap on a flight anyway without a really good reason.'

'I'm talking about a really good reason.'

'Such as?'

'Such as you're very suspicious of something. Or frightened.'

'*What* would I be frightened of? You're harking back to Rosamond, this wild idea that she killed her husband.'

'Perhaps I am.'

'Look, even if, and I actually don't believe it, but even if that were true, she doesn't live at the castle, and she's not going to inherit anything from me. You've got my trusts so tightly sewn up they wouldn't get a penny.'

'Morganna, it's very simple. I won't go unless you promise me to take what I'm saying seriously. I perceive there to be a very real financial threat to you. That bothers me. If I genuinely thought the threat was more than that, I simply would not go, and I would do everything I could to neutralize that threat. As it happens, my rational mind thinks you're safe enough–'

'Well, thank God for your rational mind.'

He held up his hand. 'Please, don't interrupt, don't mock.' I could see the hurt in his eyes.

'I'm sorry.'

'I'm trying to protect you, can't you see that?'

'I can, Geoffrey, of course I can. And I'm being churlish, but you've got to realize you upset me with some of the suggestions, the implications. And you frighten me. Wrath Castle is my home now. I'm married to Archie, he's the father of this child,' I ran my hand over my rounded stomach. 'I want to make it work. I have to make it work now. All this makes it hard.'

'No. What makes it hard is what he and his mother are doing with your money.'

'Geoffrey, they're besotted with the castle. They have gone over the top, I acknowledge that and I promise you I will control it.'

'And?'

'And I promise that if I feel any threat, I will get on a plane.' If I can, I added silently.

'He nodded. 'Then I will go. Tomorrow. I'll have my sat phone and I'll have my computer. Get yourself one, get it wired up, so you'll be able to e-mail me, and I'll e-mail you. Any immediate problems, ring the sat phone, or Mary-Beth. The bank should always be able to raise me, via the coast guard, in an emergency.'

I didn't think the coast guard would somehow get to him on his ocean crossings, but that wasn't an observation I was about to share. He knew that as well as I, but he was so caught up in protecting me that it seemed he really wasn't thinking completely straight.

I got to my feet, yawning widely. 'I've got to hit the sack. Long day tomorrow. And I want to be up extra early to see you off properly.'

I went to bed, but I tossed and turned for a long time, seeing in my nightmares gloved hands, phantoms planted by Geoffrey's irrational fears.

Early the next morning I kissed goodbye to Geoffrey as he stood at the helm of *Hurricane*. Then, feeling a strange cocktail of joy and sadness, I walked back onto dry land, and got into his Lincoln to be driven to JFK, and to my flight home.

I tried not to worry through my long journey. I tried not to entertain the suspicions and fears Geoffrey had planted, but it was hard not to. I wanted to arrive back with an open mind, eager to see my husband, my love for him unclouded by all the crap that had been flying around. He was the father of the child that I was now carrying visibly, the child that stirred within me, making me smile with joy and filling me with love.

That is what I would focus on, my love, and everything that was good. I believed firmly that the more you thought about phantoms and fears, the more you breathed life into them. I had promised Geoffrey to be careful, and I would be, but I would not live by suspicion and doubt.

By four the next afternoon, armed with my determined philosophy, I was back at Wrath Castle.

Chapter twenty-two

The taxi driver helped me carry the portraits of my parents into the great hall. I wasn't willing to let them be couriered again; I didn't want them out of my sight. I tipped him handsomely and closed the door behind me with a bang that reverberated through the great hall. Archie appeared from one of the side rooms. He brushed a lock of hair from his eyes and gave me his dazzling grin. I found the motion strangely studied.

'Welcome home,' he said.

I should have been ecstatic to be home, but I'd been away so long and we'd been so distant in more ways than space that I still felt cut off. I felt like I was acting. So I said little. I kissed him, and followed his lead.

He took my hand. 'Come on. I've a surprise for you.' He led me into the castle, but instead of turning right, into our wing, he headed left. The left hallway, normally closed off and shrouded in dust sheets, now echoed to our footsteps. We crossed the flagstones gleaming dully. On we went, to a mahogany staircase I had never seen before, the gleaming steps covered in the centre by an antique-looking Persian runner. The effect was stunning. Geoffrey's voice suddenly echoed in my ears. I dreaded to think what it had cost.

Up we went. The walls had been plastered, and painted in a dark sand colour. Here and there were spectacular paintings, sheep ambling along a shady path, a girl sitting beside a stone wall. I stopped to peer at the inscription — Millais. I sucked in my breath. I knew little about the art market, but enough to know that a good Millais never went below seven figures. In pounds sterling.

I felt my pulse begin to quicken, felt my skin grow warm. Archie kept on walking. I followed him to a dark door. He stopped, and threw it open. Before us was a small hallway, painted a warm yellow, beyond that I could see a drawing room, lavish, ornate, with more paintings on the walls. I walked in; Archie followed a few paces behind me. I turned to my right and saw a bedroom.

Everything was beautiful, tasteful, impersonal. Our old wing, with its lack of water, and rough walls, felt more real. Where was my home? This felt like a hotel. And I suddenly felt like a guest.

I turned to Archie, a question in my eyes.

'Our new wing,' he said. 'Complete with nursery. All done, all wired. Heating, power shower, decorated.'

'So I see.'

'We literally just finished moving all the stuff over.'

I nodded. 'And our old wing?'

'Poles are rewiring and plumbing now.'

'My studio?'

'Got you a new one in this wing. We moved all your stuff.'

He showed me.

My pulse began to race and I could feel the colour rising in my face.

'Archie, I can't see the sea from this one. The old one was north-facing, with a huge window.'

'This has light.'

'Not much, and not north-facing.'

'So what's the big deal?'

'What do you mean? You researched it. You studied what was the best kind of studio for a painter and you made one for me. All painters would kill for a north-facing studio, with light like my old one had. You *knew* that. You *knew* how much that meant to me.'

'Yes, well, professionals maybe. But you don't make a living from it. I would have thought this one would be fine for hobby painting. And, anyway, you'll be too busy with the baby to paint.'

I don't know how I managed to restrain myself, but the idea of a fight the moment I returned was abhorrent to me, so I *did* manage, although I wanted to shout and scream and rail at him. I blew out a breath. I said nothing until I could frame the words of least damage.

'Well, this one's all right for now. I'll move back to my old one as soon as the Poles have finished in that wing.'

Archie looked awkward.

'What's the problem?'

'The Poles are doing up that wing to my mother's specs. It seemed a good idea for her to have her own wing, separate from ours.'

I felt what was left of my self-control slipping perilously away. I felt as if my mind had risen somewhere out of and above my body, propelled there by disbelief and by rage.

'Darling, you're back. And, goodness. Look at the size of you.'

I turned, and there was Rosamond, all sharp grace and elegance, eyes glittering, did I imagine it, with triumph.

'You've been busy,' I said, not moving forward to greet her. A month away from my husband, and she saw fit to muscle in on my homecoming.

'You have no idea.'

'It would seem not.'

Her glittering smile vanished.

'Darling, you seem upset.'

My mind still felt as if it was hovering above my body. Perhaps it was tiredness, or jet lag, perhaps it was just the recklessness born of anger, but I had a sense of being cut off from consequence, dangerously free from normal reserve and conventions. But I was lucid enough to see two paths I could take. I could attack, or back off.

'Well, let's put it this way, shall we? I leave home for one month, and on my return I find that I have been moved out of my bedroom, out of my studio, and that my mother-in-law has moved herself into it. Not content with a suite of her own, she wants a wing. I hear the one thing that keeps me sane described as a hobby. Oh, and I see a Millais on the walls too. I wonder who paid for that?' I paused. 'Or perhaps it's a belated wedding gift from you, Rosamond. I don't remember you giving us one, come to think of it.'

Archie was staring at me white-faced with shock. Rosamond was smiling faintly, as if she were enjoying this. Her eyes were hard, battle ready.

I turned to Archie. 'Did you not think to even *consult* me on all this?'

For a while he just looked at me coldly before speaking.

'Have you ever shown any interest in the details before?'

'You think where I sleep, and where I paint, and where a cool mill, at least, of my money goes–' I saw him flinch at the *my*, and I smiled, even as I felt shamed by myself, 'is a mere detail? You think my mother-in-law moving in is a mere detail? And speaking of which,' I turned back to Rosamond, 'did you not think that perhaps after nearly a month away from my husband, I might like to find him alone?'

'Darling, I should have thought having a mother around was comforting, when the cat chooses to absent herself for so long.'

I laughed. 'So Archie's a mouse, is he? And I should fear him playing?'

'A wise woman takes precautions.'

'I thought a wise woman just insured she didn't get caught,' I replied levelly.

Did I see a flicker of shock in Rosamond's eyes? I saw something, but I was too clouded by rage to decipher it, and anyway, she had always been a mistress of inscrutability, as she remained, even under fire.

'Speaking of which,' she said, mimicking me, 'now that you're back here, you might think to wear the wedding ring and engagement ring your husband gave you on the appropriate finger, or have you entered into a bigamous marriage in Long Island, to Geoffrey perhaps?'

'I don't think Geoffrey's in the market for a wife, actually, Rosamond. No, these are my mother's wedding and engagement rings.' I fluttered them in front of her nose. She recoiled like a vampire from a mirror. 'They only fit this finger, whereas my own seemed more shiftable.'

I saw her take a deep breath. She started to say something and was interrupted by two of the Poles, lugging my portraits.

'What the hell have you got there?' Archie demanded of them.

'The portraits of my parents,' I answered. 'You'll be pleased to hear we tracked them down, got them back. Shouldn't be too long before we find out who pinched them. Geoffrey's got Kroll on their trail.'

My words fell into a sudden vacuum of silence. Finally, Rosamond broke it.

'I think, perhaps I will leave,' she said, coldly. 'I was intending to anyway, to let you catch up with each other.' She turned to go, and then stopped herself.

'By the way, the Millais didn't cost a penny. The Boston collection has eight, but no Augustus Johns. I happened to know that they were desperate for one, so I swapped the John for the Millais, a bargain that put us up about two hundred grand, by my calculations.'

'Ah, and I'm sure your calculations would have been accurate down to the last penny. Quite a coup, Rosamond, swapping my painting, but you know, despite the fact that we, as you put it, are up two hundred grand, *I* am down my painting, the one *I* inherited from my parents. Is there anything else you have done with my assets, in my absence?'

'I took care of *your* husband, *my* son, but then in *your* schema, that probably counts for nothing.'

With that, she turned, and stalked off.

'Well done,' says Archie. 'That was good.'

'Oh, I'm supposed to feel bad, am I? In what kind of Alice-through-the-fucking-looking-glass world is that?

Oh, wait, let me work it out. That'll be the one where the woman who is utterly and totally taken advantage of is the one in the wrong. Not those who take advantage, of course. They're the innocents.'

'Is that how it seems?'

'No. It's not how it seems. It's how it *is*.'

'I thought you'd be delighted. We've got a beautiful home, made from a wreck. We have a Millais on the walls. I knew you loved Millais. And that picture, of a little girl . . . I thought you'd love it. I intended it as a sort of twenty-first present.'

I closed my eyes. 'The Augustus John was part of my inheritance. You had no right.'

'It's swelled your inheritance, it's–'

'Swelled it by two hundred grand. Do you think I care about that, next to something of immense sentimental value? Or is money the only thing you value?'

'Only someone with more money than they know what to do with can make a comment like that.'

'And there's the rub. I might not know what to do with it, but you and your mother sure as hell do. Did you think I was malleable, at twenty? Is that why you married me? Rich, and malleable. The perfect combination for your mother. The route back to her inheritance.' There. I'd said the unspeakable. Now let the heavens fall.

'Bloody hell, Morgan,' shouted Archie. 'How much damage do you want to do? I married you because I loved you.'

'Loved me.'

'I still bloody love you, though God knows, you make it hard sometimes.'

I ran my hands over my face. 'Archie, I don't want to argue, but you shanghaied me. You and your mother. I feel like I have no free will here. Every decision is taken without even thinking of consulting me.'

'Morgan, I know what my mother's like. She's a force of nature. She's used to getting her own way. I know most people can't handle her. Ex-girlfriends have been steamrollered by her. Malleable was the last thing I ever thought of you. It's laughable. You have the same force of character she has. More, if anything. Just younger. I'm sorry you feel steamrollered too. I'll consult you in the future, I promise.'

'I want the Poles to stop work on our tower. Now. That's meant to be our tower, Archie, not hers. They can start again when you reconfigure it to include a nursery.'

I could see a muscle working in his cheek. I hadn't meant to give him an ultimatum. It just came out like that.

'All right. I'll tell them.'

I felt flooded with relief. I couldn't quite believe that Archie had agreed, without a fight. In the distance, we heard a car door slam, and then an engine revved, and eased away.

'Will she come back?'

'You won't get rid of my mother that easily.'

That night, in our new bedroom, after we had made love, a compulsory act to convince us both that everything was all right, I lay awake, replaying the scene with Rosamond. I tried to recall her look when I made my comment about a wise woman not getting caught. I suddenly found myself thinking that it was not outside the bounds of possibility that she *had* killed her husband. And, of course, I thought about Geoffrey, seabound. I wondered what he would say if I told him about today's scene, about what had brought it about, but I knew I wouldn't say a word. I would ride this out, alone. The last thing I wanted was him aborting his trip and flying over here on a tide of rage.

But I couldn't help wondering . . . what if I did a little digging of my own? What might I might find out? The gloves were off now. Rosamond was no longer my ally. Today we had squared up to each other as enemies. I'd seen it in the flash of her eyes. And I'm sure she'd seen it in mine.

Convinced, as I'd always been, of my own invulnerability, it never occurred to me that I might be placing myself or my baby at risk.

Chapter twenty-three

The next morning, determined to get back into the rhythm of the place, I headed down early to the beach. I spent the day there, with my paints and picnic lunch. It was only when the tide drove me back that I began to pack up, a finished painting slowly drying. A furious yapping made me look up.

Running towards me at full pelt was Jelly. She was pursued, in a more stately fashion, by a grinning Ben. I caught up Jelly into my arms and smothered her with kisses.

'Oh, Jelly. I have missed you so much.'

Ben arrived. Impulsively, I took hold of him, pulled him to me and kissed his cheeks.

'Thank you, Ben.'

'Pleasure. I'd have come sooner, but I had a problem with a lamb.'

'All right?'

He shook his head.

'What happened?'

'Fell down a cliff.'

I shivered. 'Poor little thing.'

'Aye.'

He turned to Jelly, and ruffled her coat. 'She's a lovely little thing. Be happy to keep her,' he said.

'No chance. I'm back now. Sticking around for a while.'

Ben studied me with his serious eyes. 'Good. You look well.'

'Oh, do I? Well, sun, swimming. Rest. It was good to get away from the castle for a while.'

He nodded, as if that was self-evident.

We fell silent for a while. I could not stop myself thinking about what Geoffrey had told me.

'Ben, you were around when Rosamond lived here first time, weren't you? After her marriage.'

'I was.'

'Will you tell me about it?'

'It?'

'Everything.'

'Everything's a long story, some would say better untold.'

'Will you tell me?'

'I can't refuse you, Morgan, you know that.'

'So?'

He glanced at the sky. 'Want to get wet?'

'Not really.'

'Would you like to come back to my cabin then, for a dram, or would that not be right for the Laird's wife?'

'I don't know the rights and wrongs of it, Ben, but I do know I'd like to. I'd also like to give you this.' I handed him the painting.

His cabin lay in a sheltered hollow, about a quarter of a mile back from the cliff, and about one and a half miles from Wrath Castle. It was cosy inside, with sheepskins on the floor, bookshelves lining the walls, and a large fireplace, above which hung my portrait of his dog, Gin. Ben held the new painting up next to it.

'Perfect. I'll make up a frame. You couldn't have given me anything better,' he said simply. He set the painting down carefully on his table and then poured a whisky.

'One for you?'

'Tea? Of any sort?'

Jelly made herself at home and curled up with Ben's dogs whilst he moved around in his kitchen.

He came back and handed me a cup of milky tea. 'This do?'

'It's great, Ben. Thanks.' I took a sip and then settled back into my armchair. 'This is nice, Ben,' I said, indicating the cabin.

'Built it myself, and it's mine. And the land around it.'

'I thought it was all Rosamond's.'

He shook his head.

'She sold me five hundred acres when she was trying to flog everything she could to hang on there in the castle after her husband died. So I've that, and I've got tenancy over a thousand. It's enough to make a living, keep me and the dogs going.'

But it should have been filled with a wife and children. I quickly changed the subject, and for a good hour, we talked of other things. We talked and we drank tea and whisky. I took a little whisky in my tea and it warmed me. It felt wonderfully secure in his cabin as the rain beat down outside, and our dogs lay coiled at our feet. Ben lit a fire against the sudden encroaching cold.

'What is it you wanted to know?' he asked. 'About Rosamond?'

'I want to know everything you know.'

'Why?'

I blew out a breath.

'I'm uneasy, Ben. I'm not quite sure what or who I'm dealing with here. I don't like her. I don't trust her. It could just be a mother-in-law and daughter-in-law thing, or it could be something beyond that.'

He took a slow sip of his whisky, thought for a while, and then began to speak.

'She was four when I was born. Don't really remember much of her till I was eight or nine. Then I'd see her with her father. Only child, her mother died birthing her. The father doted on her, took her everywhere with him, taught her everything she would need to know to run the castle, and the estate. Taught her to shoot, to fish, to sail, to gut an animal. Taught her to walk the moors and look out for the weather. My own father would take me out with him, and I'd see them. We'd wave, or course, doff our caps. They would nod, but we scarce exchanged a word. I know my father didn't like him, nor her. He didn't say much, but I knew. Nobody did, much. And they never did anything to make me have a different view. When she was nineteen she went away, came back married at twenty, had Archie at twenty-one. Husband was all right Roddy,' he said, brightening. 'Don't think he belonged here, stayed here for her sake, I reckon, travelled a lot besides, but he was all right. Friendly. Then he died.'

'So I heard.'

For a while neither of us spoke. Ben got up, made me another cup of tea, and refilled his glass.

'I've heard the rumours about her,' I said.

He nodded.

'We all of us here know what we think.'

'And?'

'That she did it.'

I caught my breath. I knew I wasn't going to be able to dismiss his belief in the same way I did Geoffrey's, which I still thought to be rooted in prejudice and overprotectiveness.

'Backfired, though, didn't it,' Ben continued. 'She was after his money, but couldn't have got a penny. Had to board up the castle then, move out. Never saw sight nor sound till you moved here.'

'The Coroner returned an open verdict,' I told him. 'He wasn't satisfied there was no foul play, but the police had no proof of murder. He went as far as he could, and, as a result of the open verdict, the insurance company refused to settle. So no life insurance goes to her, and he obviously left her nothing in his will.'

'I didn't know that, about the Coroner.'

'Not many people do. My guardian had some people do a job on her, go digging. They found it out.'

He nodded, and got up.

Enough had been said. I could see the ghost of his wife hovering in his mind so I didn't push any further.

'Thanks, Ben.'

'I haven't been much help,' he said.

'You have. Now I know that it's not just me being a difficult daughter-in-law.'

I glanced at my watch. 'Shoot. I'd better get home. They'll be thinking I've fallen off a cliff.'

'Like my poor lamb. Let me drive you.'

'Thanks, Ben, but drop me out of sight.'

'I might be a shepherd, Morganna, but I'm not a fool.'

'I never for a moment thought it.' I took his hand, squeezed it briefly, and followed him out. Our dogs ran out and leapt into the back of his jeep.

In the jeep, he turned to me. 'Be careful. Watch who you talk to about her. She's rich, powerful. Castle employs a lot of people. All the building work has brought money in here.'

'Yeah, my money.'

'Doesn't matter. The castle is hers, everyone knows that. She's an Edge. The Laird's daughter. They've always run things here. For centuries. They've their own bloody methods. People think more than twice before they cross them.'

'And I'm just an outsider?'

He nodded.

I swallowed back the bitter taste that rose to my mouth.

'I'll consider myself warned.'

I got home at eight. Archie was pacing round the kitchen.

'Where the *hell* have you been?' He came up close, and sniffed at me. 'Have you been drinking?'

I stepped back. 'What *is* this? You sound deranged.'

'I thought you might have fallen on the cliff. I've been out searching for you.'

'Archie, it's bloody eight o'clock, not midnight. You often don't appear from the depths of your office until seven or seven thirty. I had no idea you'd be waiting for me.'

'So you thought you could slip in a quick drink, no, make that a long drink, and I wouldn't notice.'

'Since when has having a drink been a crime?'

'Who with?'

'Archie, this isn't like you? What's going on?'

'Rather what I wanted to know.'

My head was spinning. I felt confused under Archie's tirade, and angry.

'You know what? I think a drink's an excellent idea. I'm going down to the pub. In fact, I think I'll have my dinner there.'

I walked out, leaving Archie staring after me open-mouthed.

At the pub, I got dinner, delicious sausages and mash, served up by Beatie, the landlady's daughter, who was my age, but shy as a thirteen-year-old. Despite my insistence that she call me Morgan, she kept trying to call me m'lady. After I polished off my sausages, I headed reluctantly home. I didn't particularly care that Archie didn't come to our bed that night.

Chapter twenty-four

Archie walked into the kitchen the next morning as I was making myself coffee and toast. I hadn't readied myself for him. I felt unarmed, and vulnerable.

'Morgan.'

'Archie.'

He looked from me to my cup of coffee as if searching for something to say, something innocuous to comment on.

He sat down opposite me. He looked strained, tired. I wondered where he had slept last night, if he had slept, or, like me, had tossed and turned the night away.

'Look, Morgan, I'm sorry about last night. It wasn't good. I—'

I tried to say something, to apologize back. I knew how hard he found it to apologize, but he held up his hand to stay me.

'Let me finish. Please. I think I need to get away from here for a while. Sometimes it feels like being in a lunatic asylum, with all the banging, the shouting, the Poles arguing. I need a break.'

I nodded, my heart racing. This wasn't about the bloody builders, and we both knew it. He'd just been away from the castle for several weeks. I heard a high-pitched ringing in my ears. The melodramatic part of my mind told me it was the death knell of our marriage. I tried to silence that voice, to think. But something seemed to be unravelling, and I felt powerless to stop it.

'How long for?'

'Oh, not long. Just a week or so.'

'Archie. I've only just got back.'

'I know. I know. It's not great. Look, I didn't feel like myself last night. I don't like feeling that way. I just want to get a handle on myself, and then I'll come back. I'll be back in good time for the baby, don't worry.'

'Where will you stay?'

He looked surprised. 'With Ma, of course.'

I nodded. I didn't trust myself to speak.

That night we slept in the same bed. He might as well have left already. At nine the next morning, he was ready to go.

'Drive safely,' I said, kissing his cheek. 'The sky looks bad.'

He nodded.

'What will you do?' he asked.

'I don't know.' I shrugged. 'Get myself a computer. Geoffrey's gone off sailing. Serious sailing, for months. I need a computer to e-mail him, and him me.'

Archie smiled. 'Has he, now. Well, good on him.'

'Exactly. But I'll miss him. I want to stay in touch.'

'You don't know the first thing about computers. I'd better get you one.'

'Okay. Wired, and all that.'

'Fine. Not a problem. Look after yourself, then.'

'I will. Bye.'

He raised his hand in parting, got into his car, and drove off. With the sound of the car in my ears I headed back to the kitchen. I made myself a mug of coffee and sat with my hands cupped around it. Was this how marriages disintegrated? It seemed so banal. And so heartbreaking. Were we both just giving up, letting whatever we had left die, bit by bit, or were we taking a step apart, to come back together stronger? And all this when in just over a month, I would have our baby. I gazed unseeing at the silent walls of the castle.

Finally, I got up, planning to head off for the beach. The sound stopped me. A wild, maddened beat. I hurried to the window. Rain was falling. Rain like I'd never seen. The drops seemed to be the size of Ping-Pong balls. No painting today. I would be incarcerated.

I headed up to my old tower. The Poles were working at the other end of the castle now, so, mercifully, it was quiet. I gazed out at the churning sea. Huge waves rolled in, smashing themselves against the serrated rocks in a suicidal frenzy.

It occurred to me for the first time that this view wasn't mine to own, to love, to live and die with. I had a lease on this castle, for as long as I was married to Archie.

I loved the castle, and I had loved him. Underneath all the shit going on, I was sure I still loved him. Rosamond stood between us, an invisible, malign presence, even when hundreds of miles away. I felt sure I could lay most of our troubles at her door. If we could get her out of our lives, and keep her out, we stood a chance.

It rained for three days. I couldn't paint. I couldn't even go out to walk, save letting Jelly have a brisk pee and poo in the lee of the castle. For three days, gales raged around us. They brought down the telephone wires, so I was completely cut off. All I had was the radio. With Jelly whimpering at my feet, I spent hours in the tower, watching the ferocious seas, listening to the shipping news.

I did little, save think. By the third day, I began to feel cut adrift. Whatever happened to my marriage, I knew I needed something of my own. Something that wasn't to do with the castle, or Archie, or Geoffrey and his suspicions, or having children. I needed a lifeline.

I stared at my ranks of paintings, my hymn to the sea. As I studied them, an idea began to take form. I went to bed and slept the sleep of the blessed. Next morning, I woke to clear skies. It felt like a sign. I was free to go. I fed Jelly. I rolled up ten of my best paintings and after a brief breakfast and chat with the Poles, Jelly and I set off in my car.

Chapter twenty-five

I was so excited as I drove. And nervous. I loved my paintings, and the sheer act of painting was enough to satisfy one part of me, but another part of me wanted the satisfaction of knowing they were good enough to have people pay money for them. I knew Van Gogh never got money for his, and they were masterpieces. Mine weren't, but I felt they were good, and I loved them. I hoped other people would too.

And maybe I might make some money. Money of my own. And prove that I am something more than a *hobby painter*, to be derided and indulged. But there was something more than that too. As I drove away from the castle, I realized how much of my life it had become. The castle, the sea, Archie, painting. I had been living my entire life on one small piece of cliff edge that would crumble with my marriage. I needed something to anchor me to a wider world. Other people, other places, other things. And I wanted to set it in motion now, before my child came, and my will was subsumed by loving it.

I hardly noticed the drive, the long hours behind the wheel, as I sped towards my plan.

Jelly and I spent the night in an anonymous hotel just outside Heathrow. Somewhere I could park, and arrive late and dishevelled, without attracting judgment from some snotty receptionist.

I slept badly, nervous as I was, and set off early to beat the rush hour. I got to Cork Street at seven thirty, and took my pick of the parking meters outside the galleries. I chose one outside a gallery called Toby Hood because I liked the paintings in the window — the Black Mountains, all from the same angle, under different weather. *Painted by an obsessive*, I thought, in recognition. I checked my paintings were well covered by the blanket I'd thrown over them, as if to keep them warm on the long journey. I locked the car and Jelly and I headed off in search of breakfast. I found a café open around the corner.

'Can I bring my dog in? She's very good.'

The grizzled Italian waiter gave her a good looking over, and nodded. 'If she's naughty, she goes.'

'Deal.'

I ordered a full fry-up, hoping it would unknot my stomach, begged a newspaper off the waitress, and sat down to eat. Covertly, I slipped Jelly my sausages.

I tried to read the paper, but all I could see were headlines about the imminence of war. Depressed I put it down, ate up, and at eight twenty Jelly and I headed back to my car. I was reading the meter, checking when I would have to start feeding it, when a voice made me jump.

'Ten minutes grace.'

I turned round to see a tall man with a shock of unruly grey hair, watchful blue eyes, and a mischievous smile. At his side a scruffy collie appraised me with seemingly only slightly less insight than its owner. I reached down to rub its neck. The collie turned his interest to Jelly, who was half-hiding, peeking out shyly from behind my legs. I noticed its owner's shoes, sturdy country brogues, half-hidden under long, baggy beige cords. A heavy, tweed, loose jacket of the type bird shooters wear completed the outfit. I wondered what on earth he was doing on Cork Street.

Then I noticed the rolled canvas under the man's arm.

'Are you here to see Toby Hood?' I asked.

'Are you?' he replied.

'I am. I've driven down from Scotland with some of my paintings. I'm probably wasting my time. I bet he's one of these horrible urban types, black polo-neck, black everything, twenty-four, just outgrown his spots, cappuccino maker and highlighted assistant.'

The man let out a guffaw of laughter.

'Too early for that crowd.' He rummaged in one capacious pocket and drew out an enormous set of keys.

I watched, too entertained by his hilarity to feel like the idiot I was, as he nimbly unlocked the four locks on the door before us, swung the door open, setting off the warning bleeps of an angry sounding alarm. He tapped in a code on the alarm panel, silenced the beeps, and grinned out at me.

'Well, are you coming in?'

I gave him a sheepish grin. 'Let me get my paintings.'

We sat opposite one another, across a burnished desk. His collie curled herself into a basket lined with an old Black Watch tartan blanket by the side of the desk. She rested her head on her outstretched paws, her eyes moving between us, as if following a silent conversation. It seemed to me she had been strategically placed so that she could keep an eye on him, and on anyone he entertained. Jelly sat silently at my feet. My second.

The gallery was cold, as if it were too early for heating, for business, but then I heard the creaking and groaning of the radiators that flanked the walls clicking into life. I found Toby Hood's, and his gallery's, lack of slickness comforting. He wasn't slick, but he was elegant. I watched as he took out a silver cigarette case and withdrew a long, slim, brown cigarette. He lit it with an antique gold lighter, and the acrid smell of cloves filled the room. He didn't ask if I minded. It was his show, after all.

I bent to pick up the first of my paintings. I unrolled it so that it faced him. He gathered up four heavy paperweights and placed them at every corner, pinning it to the table, like a butterfly. I got up to go round to his side of the desk, as if to see my painting with his eyes. I held my breath, trying not to make a sound, to do anything that might distract him. He looked at my sea with narrowed eyes, head tilted, lips pursed.

'May I see more?' he asked, freeing this one and handing it back to me.

Wordlessly, I unrolled all the other nine in succession, until they lay by the side of his desk like papers discarded by someone trying to write a Dear John letter. For ten, perhaps fifteen minutes, we hadn't uttered a word to each other, apart from his one request. Time enough to compose himself for the words he must have said a thousand times. He raised his eyes to mine.

'I could look at these for hours.'

'You like them,' I said quietly, not quite believing.

'I don't think *like* is the word.' He took a long drag on his dubious cigarette. And then he smiled. 'People will either love them, passionately, or not want to be near them.'

I looked at him quizzically.

'Not comfortable, are they? I'm not sure if I want to plunge into your sea and be smashed against the rocks, or run from it. There's something mesmeric about them. I feel a bit as if I'm standing on the edge of a very high cliff, fighting the urge to hurl myself over.'

'So, will you jump?'

He laughed. Not some polite chuckle, but a roar. 'With pleasure, but not until I know your name.'

'Morganna Hutton,' I say, using my maiden name, on impulse.

'When would you like your exhibition, Morganna?'

'Well, I'll be a tad busy for a while.'

'I had noticed. Congratulations.'

'Thanks. How about next October? My baby'll be nearly one.'

We shook hands. 'It's a deal.'

I had my lifeline. I left my paintings in his care. I'd been with him for over an hour. I'd completely forgotten to put money in the parking meter, but, miraculously, I didn't have a ticket. Someone was looking after me.

As Jelly and I drove away from Cork Street, I replayed his words. Twenty more paintings. Exhibition. Next October. God, I must have had at least twenty at home, and good ones, as good as the ones I've left with him. All I needed to do was courier them to him, or, even better, drive back with them, shepherd them to him, and view the ones I'd left with him, grown-up in their frames. And return, next October, or sooner maybe, when he would cast them before the public, and wait for them to love or run. I laughed out loud, part of me still wondering if I'd imagined it all.

This wasn't what I had prepared for. I had imagined a long and depressing trawl around Cork Street. At best, an ambivalent response from the black polonecks. Perhaps, *promising, but needs some work, and what art school did you say you went to?* Knowing that unless it was St. Martins or the Slade that I would lack critical credibility. Florence was where the rich sent their offspring to daub. It was not the spawning ground for contemporary painters, just amateur wives-in-the-making.

Perhaps that was why I had used my maiden name. I wasn't the wife who painted, but the old me. I had wanted an identity of my own, and now, perhaps recognizably, I would have it. I couldn't quite believe my luck. I wondered what price I would have to pay for it.

Chapter twenty-six

Suddenly I felt tired. The long drive had taken its toll, and I needed to lie down. I headed for Embankment Gardens. I quickly scanned the cars parked in the crescent. Thankfully, there was no sign of Archie's car, but I hadn't expected to see it. He was meant to be with Rosamond in Southwold.

I let myself in and looked around. Jelly darted here and there, sniffing out Archie. She'd never really liked him, and I could tell she was uneasy here. The flat smelled of him. Not me.

I decided sleep would have to wait. I needed to clear my head and give Jelly some fresh air and exercise. We walked round Battersea Park twice, slowly, because my increasing size was beginning to make me gravid. Then we headed to the King's Road, bought a takeaway pizza which I ate back at Archie's flat while Jelly munched on the contents of one of the tins I'd brought for her. After I finished my pizza I felt desperate for a nap.

I crawled into his bed, into the tumble of sheets. It smelled even more of him, but the smell of him did not comfort me. I missed him, I missed the man I had fallen in love with, and I railed against the man he now seemed to be. Where had the old Archie gone, and why had he changed?

Jelly crept up onto the bed beside me, and slept in solidarity. Her whimpering woke me, four hours later. It was dark. I sat up in bed, turned on a light, and wondered what to do. Staying here, in my husband's flat, effectively estranged from him, would be unbearable. I felt like weeping for what we have managed to lose, even before the birth of our first child. And then I felt angry. I would not give up on my marriage without a fight. If we could try again, without the poisonous presence of Rosamond, but with each other, and our baby, I thought me might make it. I had to start now, when I had the will, and the impulse. I wanted to share my good news with him, celebrate the prospect of an exhibition in Cork Street. I decided there and then to head for Southwold.

It was nearly eleven when I drove into the outskirts of the little Suffolk town. I found Rosamond's cottage. I got out of my car; Jelly hopped out nimbly beside me. I shut the door gently, walked through the darkness to Rosamond's door like a thief in the night. I knocked but there was no answer. I put my hand on the doorknob, turned it, and, to my surprise, it opened. Who left their doors unlocked at eleven at night? I was surprised at Rosamond. I walked in. It was dark, but there seemed to be a light on upstairs, and it cast a weak pall, enough for me to see my way.

Jelly stuck close to me as I turned and walked up the stairs. I suddenly felt uncertain. I paused before Archie's bedroom door. There was a chink of light under the door, and a slight sound of movement. I smiled as I opened the door.

Before me was a sight that made me doubt my own eyes. I wondered madly, for a moment, if I was in the wrong room, the wrong house. But I was not. It *was*

Archie, it was my husband, who lay in bed, unravelling from the arms of a skinny woman with long blonde hair.

Archie called my name. He jumped out of bed, he stood before me naked while she lay there, making no attempt to cover her naked body.

I stood there staring, my eyes feeling as if they would explode, my ears filled with a roaring sound, like static on a record, full blast. I think I cried out, as I spun around, as I ran, almost tumbling down the stairs. I heard Jelly running down beside me. I saw Rosamond appear in the hall, I heard footsteps behind me, yelling, I couldn't decipher what. I felt my keys in my palm, I gripped them harder, ran for the car as if my life depended on it. I got in, watched Jelly leap in beside me. I slammed the door, locked it, turned the key in the ignition, which caught just as Archie came level with me, grabbing at my door. I saw his face, white, at my window. I screamed something, I don't even know what, and then I put the car in gear, floored the accelerator, flung him off, and drove.

I don't know how I found the motorway, but I did. I drove, making myself breathe, making myself see, making the blood flow round my veins. I did this, and I just kept going, telling myself that I would be all right, that I must just drive, must not hit anything, must above all protect my child.

I have no idea how the hours passed, I scarcely registered anything around me save the red taillights of the cars in front, and there were mercifully few of them. I drove until the dawn began to streak across the sky. I found a service station, pulled in, checked into the motel, smuggled Jelly in, and then slept for most of the day.

I set off again at night, fuelled with caffeine, desperate to get back to the castle. The next morning dawned cold. To keep awake I drove with my window cracked open. As I drew nearer to the castle, I could taste the sea in the air. My home, I thought bitterly.

I saw the bend coming, I tried to slow, but there was black ice, and I hit it. One and a half tons of car hurtled to the stone bridge, and, like an echo from twenty years ago, flew through the parapet, sailed into space, and came to rest with a roar of destruction in water.

Chapter twenty-seven

There was crying. Something hurt. I was cold. There was a dog, somewhere, whimpering. Water, there was water, running. It was hot, sticky. Didn't smell like water. That sound again. That roaring. What, what? Oh help me. Someone. Something was wrong. I couldn't . . . I was losing . . . oh my God, my baby. My baby. Hands on me. Holding me. A voice. Another voice. Then brilliant white, stripes of blue. Then nothing. Nothing.

Suddenly, I was awake. I thought I was. I'd been asleep, I knew, for a long time. So long I could not make myself move. Something was in my head. There was a sound. Was I hearing it, or was it a memory? There was a scream, a terrible long scream, a scream of death. And then there was silence. And pain. I hurt, so much, all over. My head. What was in it? Stopping me. Everything. I must have been asleep, but it didn't feel like it. There was light in my eyes, but I couldn't see. Where had the light gone? Then it hit me. I was dead. This was death, only it couldn't have been, could it, because I could still think. Sort of. Heaven? It didn't feel nice, so no. Hell then? But it didn't feel too bad, and where were the other people? God, devil, the place must be overflowing, but here there was just me. Or was there? Sometimes I thought I heard voices, far away. I even thought they were talking to me, but I couldn't quite make them out. Perhaps they were speaking in a foreign language. I tried to move, to blink, to get some sight into my eyes. But nothing happened. Was I buried? That was it. I remembered something, landing, water. I couldn't get out, I couldn't breathe, help me, help me, I tried to scream, to shout, but nothing happened. My body did nothing. It did not obey my mind anymore. Was this death then, the death of my body? I seemed to fall asleep then, because when I started to think again, it seemed a lot later. Where was I? I wanted to know, and me, me. . . . What has happened, and who was me?

Slowly it came, in scattered pieces that alone made no sense. I used all my strength to try to put them together again. I did not know how long it was taking, as I tried. Time had lost all meaning. It seemed that I was given little pieces of time, cut out of some great universe of time. Pockets were all I got. I knew I was Morganna. I knew I was having a baby. I knew I had a dog called Jelly. I knew my parents were Vivian and Peter. They were young and they were beautiful. I knew something bad had happened, but what it was, I did not know. I could not get at it. Every time I tried, it hurt. I knew there was love, somewhere. Something warm and good. I felt a hand on me. A warm, good hand, and it lit my soul. But I was not sure that was enough.

I knew that I occupied a no man's land between life and death and I was honestly not sure which way I would go. I could drift, or I could fight. But I was so tired. I thought I had been tired before. I would have laughed if I could have at that pathetic ennui. *This* was tired. This trap I lay in, my prison where I was so tired I could not move a muscle. Literally. So tired I really could have died of it. So tired that I felt I was decaying, that the atoms and the molecules that made up my body were simply evaporating into the ether. And nothing replenished itself.

I could move my brain muscles. I *could* think, but for such pathetic short times. I knew I used them up, then I lost it all again. The blackness returned. The sounds went, and I was drifting towards death again. And then I felt, with everything I had got left to feel with, the sorrow of what I was losing. I could not die. I must have my baby. I must show my baby the cherry blossom, the smell of a fresh apple, the taste of its juice. I could smell the sea and feel the thrilling cold of waves as they broke over me. And I could feel. Anger. Something in me felt angry. There was something I had to do. Something. Oh . . . it hurt to think. Blackness again.

Chapter twenty-eight

I felt myself awake again, and for a glittering group of moments, I could think. My brain worked in a frenzy of calculation. Anger burned through me like acid. Someone had done me wrong, and it had brought me to this, this dissolving, inert mess, this dying bed. I had lost my baby. That much I knew. The emptiness I felt was not possible to describe. To have life torn from you, to have the one thing you loved and above all wanted to protect, longed to see, to hold, to love, to lose that, to be emptied of all but your grief was something that I feared I could not live with, if living really was what I was doing. The grief churned my soul. Anger was my only salvation. Who had done this to my child, to me? How could I find out what had happened? It wasn't justice I was searching for, but revenge, old, cold and biblical.

What could I do to live? Would I have sold my soul to live again? And who would have bought it? Would I have being doing an angel's work, or Satan's? Was there justice in heaven, or just forgiveness? What had happened to the avenging angels? Could I have become one? There was so much to do. If I had possessed wings, and invisibility, I could have seen, and existed. But how could I have delivered the stroke of vengeance? Would my wings have been lethal, like a swan's, breaking an arm? A neck? Would they have heard me, as I swooped down? Those psychiatrists who said the route to happiness was acceptance, forgiveness, had never tasted the redemptive powers of revenge. It would be my salvation. The Old Testament meets the New. Could I have done this, dead? Could I take that chance? I was not sure. Perhaps I should survive . . . but only if I recovered completely. Then I could plot my vengeance from a healed body. I wanted to live, suddenly and desperately. *She* should know. *They* should know. Nothing was as powerful, and as dangerous, as someone who has looked death in the face, and survived. I knew what death felt like. I knew I could summon it, and visit it upon someone else. That was the card I held in my hand.

But how could I live, how could I put life back into this dead body? This body that had lost life itself? I wanted to weep, I wanted to drown in my tears, but I could not even cry. It was so hard, and I was so tired. I needed help. I needed the old, vengeful, Christian God to help me. Not Buddha. None of the others. I needed the one in Michelangelo's paintings, the beautiful, strong one, the colossus, who delivered life with the mere touch of his fingertip. Touch me too, God, let me live, make me strong. If you could do a deal with the devil, then, surely, you could do one with God too?

Chapter twenty-nine

It was working. The pockets were getting bigger. I was getting stronger. Who said you could not do deals with God? Maybe it was the devil I did my deal with, for it was satanic in nature, even I knew that, but hell, it was working. I'd pay the price later. I could hear now. I could understand, not everything, but something. It still seemed that they all spoke two languages. One I understood, one I did not. But I was learning their words. If they stayed long enough, I could start to work out who they were. I could gather the pieces together, and I could make a picture. Now all I needed was the accompanying pictures of my life, to make a scene, a series of scenes, a life.

I knew I was in hospital. I know I was very ill. I knew that I nearly died, I knew my baby was gone, and I knew that they still talked about me dying, but I knew they were wrong. I wouldn't die now. Not even from the grief I felt at losing my baby, that all-consuming terrible grief that made me ache with a pain I would never have believed. But I knew I would not die from this, or from anything. Not for a long time. People said what doesn't kill you makes you stronger, and I was waiting. I knew I would recover, and that I would be stronger.

I knew too, there was the woman, and that I hated her. I knew her name was Rosamond, that she had something to do with me. She was not my mother. I remembered my mother. Where was she, my mother?

Why wouldn't she come to me? There were men. One who prodded me, but spoke kindly. One who came and stayed and talked for ages. One who came, muttered, left quickly. I only knew four names; Morganna, Jelly, Rosamond and Wrath. I did not know what Wrath was. I knew it was anger, rage, but I thought it had some other meaning for me. I just didn't know what.

But I could see lots of other things. I felt I could see into other lives. All that moved, that travelled, was my mind. Now that my body was trapped, my mind was free to wander. I could fly like a bird. I could soar over the waves. Fitzroy, Dogger, Cromerty, Forties. What did they all mean? I said the words over and over in my head, I heard a noise, gigantic, like crashing waves, like a storm roaring in. Storm. There was a storm contained in someone's head. Was it mine?

Today, I felt something for the first time. I felt the rasp of a rough tongue on my hand, the sticky residue of saliva. And I knew it was my dog, Jelly. In my mind, I cried with joy. I knew people touched me every day, but it had been as if they were touching stone. Every day, there were nurses. They turned me, washed me, massaged my inert body, and I had felt nothing. But today, the palm of my hand felt. Perhaps God, the Colossus, had reached out his fingertips, and touched mine.

I felt that someone was happy. I heard words, and barking. I strained. What was he saying, this man?

'Morganna, Morganna, I know you can hear me. We're here, me and Jelly.'

Who was me? Who was this man, with my dog?

'Ben says hello. I've brought one of your paintings

in today, the one you did for me. I love it, but I think you need it here.'

My paintings, one I *did*? I painted? I painted. Something good, and something bad. Too close, it hurt again. What happened? Someone called me a painter, wanted my paintings, then . . . blackness.

I awoke. The voice was speaking again.

'Bye, Morganna, I'll be back tomorrow, with Jelly.'

And he put his lips to my forehead, and he kissed me, and that was the second thing I felt; his lips, warm, soft, alive against my quickening skin.

There was silence, and another voice. The prodder.

'Morganna. Time to check you. We're taking you for a little journey, put you into a tunnel, have a little look at your brain.'

I felt movement. My bed was being wheeled somewhere. The voice continued.

'So you've seen your Ben. He's a good man, in here every day, isn't he, with your dog. He's–'

Ben. Ben. And it came back to me. A scene on a bleak moor. A man talking to me. He was looking at me, squinting.

Later I heard them talking. 'Brain scan. Increased activity. Good. Good.'

'Don't tell them,' said another voice. 'Do not tell Archie and Rosamond.'

I heard an argument. Who was Archie, and why was he not to be told?

I decided to listen out; I waited for this Archie to come. Days passed, and nights. I could tell the difference

216

in infinitesimal changes in temperature, in the ambient light. There was no light and dark for me. Nothing so marked. It was all just shades of grey. But not in my mind. There, I could see all the colours. The red of a postbox, the iridescent blue-green of a peacock's tail, the yellow of a primrose, the green of spring grass, the orange of the setting sun, the lucent sea at dawn. I could feel all the sensations. And of course I could feel the grief that never really left me as I thought of my baby, as I saw in my mind a tiny body, lifeless. I sometimes thought that if I ever came out of this, the normal sights and sounds and smells and sensations of normal life would blow me away.

I waited for this Archie, but he didn't come. Ben came. I knew it was him. He brought my dog. He talked to me, Jelly barked, and then she licked my hand. Again I felt. Then they went. And this time, Archie came. I knew it was him, because suddenly the air felt charged. He was not comfortable. And he was with her. It was as if he were afraid to come on his own. Who was he? And what did he want with me?

'Look at her,' he said. 'She's still the same. What's the point?' he was asking her.

'The point is we need to make sure she's still the same.'

'Ssshh. Someone will hear you.'

'There's no-one around.'

He must have indicated me, for she answered with scorn: 'Her? I don't think so. She's a vegetable, for God's sake.'

At that, I felt her grab my hand, haul it up, and let it

217

drop. It fell, my elbow banging the edge of the bed, my forearm dangling at an uncomfortable angle. Soon the blood flow would be cut off. I felt pins and needles already. This was the third thing I felt. Even pain was progress.

'See. Completely inert,' she said.

God I hated her, I felt it flow through my body like a poison. A revitalizing poison. That bitter alchemy would cure me. I knew it.

I wanted to move my arm, but I could not. And then it occurred to me, that, even if I could move it, I should not. There was power in my state of blankness. Let her think I was impotent, utterly and completely. Let her talk before me, and let me discover. She did something to me, I knew it. I just could not remember what.

'Can we go now?' he was asking.

'For God's sake, we only just got here.'

'So, what good are we doing?'

'We are observing the proprieties, that is what. If I must spell everything out.'

'So I'm supposed to play the grieving husband, while you offer stalwart support. Is that it?'

'That's about the size of it.'

'For whose benefit? Not for hers. She's a vegetable, like you say. Look at her. What little skin isn't swathed in casts or bandages is riddled with eczema. If she's not at death's door I'll eat the proverbial hat, and, even if she did recover, which, I remind you, the doctors say she has less than a one percent chance of doing, what if she remembers?'

'She won't.'

'Someone might tell her. She wasn't discreet, that girl. God, what a nightmare.'

'Come on, Archie. Pull yourself together. This is far from a nightmare. More of a massive opportunity, if we play it correctly.'

'What do you mean?'

'Well, we have power of attorney over her money now, don't we.'

'What are you planning to do?'

'What do you think? Secure my future. And yours.'

Chapter thirty

It was morning. And I was remembering; Rosamond's house. Southwold. Archie. My husband. In bed with someone. And then I remembered something else they said, another bullet to my soul: *less than one percent chance of recovery*. I thought of that. I lay alone and I thought of that. I tried to move. I tried to see. But there was nothing in my limbs, nothing in my eyes. My mind alone was not enough. My body was useless. It had let my baby die. Back came the utter despair that terrified me so much. I felt it engulf my body like a black wave, contaminated by all the foulness of human emotion. I wanted to sleep. Forever.

I was awakened. I strained to orient myself. Then it all came back. Hospital. Everything. But something nice was happening. I knew it before I was aware of what it was. I tried to zero in. My body. My arm. My hand. Rasping, sticky, then noise. A bark. JELLY! My dog was licking my hand. In my head I laughed with pleasure, with a wild joy, and I knew then, that while ninety-nine might not make it, one did.

The alchemy of the body was a strange thing. There was still so much that doctors did not know. What most acknowledged was that the mind was a powerful force for recovery, or for self- destruction. We all knew about psychosomatic illness. What about psychosomatic health? If you could think yourself unwell, then surely, you could think yourself well. I decided to start with my toes, and work up. I didn't know how long it would take, but hell, time was all I had. Day by day, I would try to awaken my frozen body. So that I once again could run, swim, make love. And get my revenge, for what they did to me, and for my baby, who never even saw life.

I didn't know how many days it took. I had no way of recording time, especially since I thought I missed some days, that the blackouts that assailed me lasted for more than twenty-four hours, but, one morning, I could move the toes of my right foot. I could wriggle them. Four times.

How poor was memory that only worked backwards. Who said that? Geoffrey quoted it to me once, I remembered that, sitting on his lawn at Mirador drinking juleps. Geoffrey, Geoffrey, the name and the memory leapt out at me with all the jagged speed of a damaged synapse firing. Someone good. Someone strong. My guardian. Then *guard* me. Where were you, now that I needed you? Why weren't you here? Had you gone, somewhere? I struggled to remember, but nothing came. I would have to fight alone. I would have to create new memories, create in my leaden head my memories to be. My wriggling toes were the beginning. Those toes would be part of a body that ran, and jumped, and smote.

Chapter thirty-one

I was getting better, but I didn't want her to know. But if the doctors discovered it, wouldn't they tell her? I wanted her kept away, but I also wanted her to come and visit and betray more of the truth to the inert me. I waited for her visits, silently, motionlessly avid, like some creature of prey who waited with endless, lethal patience for her victim to happen by. Perhaps she came when I was in blackout. Sometimes I had this feeling of a malign presence, but I could not raise myself from the pit of my consciousness. If I could have done, I would have been able to muster myself against it, to marshal some mental defences, even if my body were weak. Physical strength had its limits. How much did we rely, after all, on mental attitude to screen us from evil. When we walked down the street, if we saw someone we did not like the look of, we would try to walk tall, to appear strong, not as a Victim, to avert our eyes.

But, lying there, I could not avert myself, nor appear as anything other than victim. I felt sure it was her, standing over me, gloating. Would I have killed her if I had held a gun in my hand, and had been capable of pointing it and pulling the trigger? I amused myself for a while with that thought. But no. I wouldn't have. Not then, anyway. There was too much I had to learn first.

She was there. She came when I was clenching and unclenching my fist under the covers. At first I thought she must have seem me, because she reached under, grabbed my hand, which I had just, I hoped, in time made inert. She raised it high, and let it drop.

'Good,' she said, in the tone of a cook who had just run a skewer into a cake and decided that, yes, it was done. I was done. Only I was undone, and she was pleased.

'Still one hundred percent vegetable.'

'I'm not sure,' said another voice. Archie. The bastard. 'I get the feeling sometimes that she can hear everything that's going on around her.'

'Don't be fanciful. There's no evidence of that, and, besides, she won't recover, will she? So what would she do, even if she could hear us?'

'Nothing, maybe, but it can't be very pleasant.'

'Pleasant, I'll tell you what is not pleasant. Being thrown out of your home is not pleasant. Have to slog my guts out for years to support you in your expensive schools. Having to do bloody house clearances. That was not pleasant.'

'You almost speak as if it were Morgan's fault.'

'It is, indirectly.'

'What on earth do you mean?'

'Do you believe in sins of the fathers?'

He blew out a breath. I felt it brush my cheek. 'Sins of the fathers, or of the mothers, for that matter. I bloody hope not.'

She laughed. 'We'd better do our obligatory fifteen minutes. Got to kill the boredom somehow. So I might as well tell you. I knew her father. It was another age, another life. I'd gone to the States to stay with some old friends of Pa's. They gave me a foothold in New York. I met people through them, including Morganna's father.

He was quiet, thoughtful, intelligent. And incredibly rich. That whole lifestyle was straight out of the Great Gatsby, and he *was* Gatsby. Elusive. Handsome in an almost English, buttoned-up way.' She gave a snort. 'Don't worry darling, I won't start talking about sex. Directly anyway. He took me out. I think he found me interesting. I was a tad older than most of that crowd, the women anyway, and, let's face it, infinitely more sophisticated. I think he liked that. Things were going well. We'd been together for about three months, and then there was this party. Harrison Waldorf the third. Twenty-fifth birthday. Long Island. One of those great houses, with a lawn like a prairie, sloping down to the sea. Blazing torches lining the drive. Waiters painted like Greek statues, naked but for a vine leaf. Fireworks. The wrong kind. Geoffrey was there–'

'Morganna's guardian,' interrupted Archie.

'Exactly. He was an old school friend of Peter Hutton. I'd met him three or four times. He came over. He was with a woman, his second cousin, he said. Her name was Vivian.'

'Morganna's mother?' Archie asked.

'Morganna's mother. A witch herself. Geoffrey introduced them. I swear she put a spell on Peter that night. He literally could not take his eyes off her.'

'Humiliating for you, mother.'

'You have no idea,' she hissed.

I heard, in her vicious sibilance, all of the hatred that I now realized she had felt for me.

And so they spoke. I was witness to their confessional. I was their priest. I was the inert, unquestioning body over which they purged themselves. Why couldn't they talk like this when they were alone together? And then I realized something that surprised me. Rosamond did not revere her son, did not love him with a selfless passion. He was not the cherished, indulged, beloved child I imagined. He was a part of her, part of her domain. In some strange was he was her instrument, her agent, and it seemed to me that he was the powerless one, the petitioner, always seeking to please. He sought her approval like a child who had never truly grown up and developed an independent destiny. He was like a cat, bringing the corpse of a mouse to its owner, laying his offerings at her feet to be met with revulsion. What would have satisfied her embittered soul? What would have been enough? He would have had to roll back time and allowed her to win the prize that should have been hers: my father. Nothing less would have done. Couldn't he see that? I remembered his joy, and his nervousness in drafting the renovation plans for Wrath Castle. His great gift to her, paid for by the blood of my parents. I suspected that much of what he did was to please her. I almost felt sorry for him.

Had she used her own son to get to me, and my money? Why had she turned up with Archie at the neighbouring estate to Geoffrey's practically as soon as I was of marriageable age? I never had believed in coincidence. It was too often the refuge of liars, or self-deceivers. I didn't believe in it now. Had Rosamond hand-picked a wife for her son? A wife with whose family she had unfinished business?

She would have hated me from the start. Loved my money, which of course, if things had gone her way, would have been *her* money, and hated me. And of course, she hated my mother. I suddenly stopped. A car, lying in water, the wheels still spinning, not one, but two broken bodies lying within? Could she have engineered that? What would she have gained? I knew the answer, because I felt in myself the same mad yearning: destruction.

But she had failed. She hadn't destroyed me. She should have read her Machiavelli. If you are going to destroy the parent, then better be sure to wipe out the entire line too — women, children, infants, the lot.

Then it occurred to me. Perhaps she had not finished yet?

Chapter thirty-two

I think weeks must have been passing. There was little to punctuate time. No growing child. They came, perhaps once a week. They talked about the castle, mainly. They used visiting hours to have an off-site meeting. I lay there and listened to them spending my money. There was no budget now. There was to be gilding here, and there, a specialist was being flown in from Venice for two months. I lay there as my bank accounts were plundered and the balance of my rage was fed.

I felt like a prisoner in a jail cell. In my mind I drew another stroke on the bleak wall each time I could move another part of my body. I still could not see. I could not engage that part, but I was making progress. I felt the end of my sentence did exist, even if it was not in sight yet. I was not in here for life. What crime did you commit then, asked the interrogatory voice in my brain. Stupidity, was my answer. And trust. But no more.

One morning I emerged from the blackness. I felt like I was skiing down a mountain, out of control. I could almost hear the wind whistling, and the blood roaring in my ears, feel the cold air on my cheeks. I was rushing towards something and I was terrified. Was this death, this headlong descent? It was so fast, there was no time for goodbye, to myself, to the world, no time to ready myself for whatever was coming. Would I see my dead child, where I was going? And then something clicked in my head, and the terror was replaced by awe. I could see. Not in my head, but with my eyes. I could see. I saw a window, pale, washed out green walls, a grey sky. Snowflakes falling like confetti. It looked so beautiful, and at once, so alien and so familiar. Was this how babies felt when they hurtled into the world, trailing clouds of glory? Was this how my baby should have felt, rather than plummeting to death? I knew this moment for what it was. But for me, this birth would not be a death and a forgetting. I would remember. Most people just got one shot at life. This was my second. And I would not waste it. I was alive. Life ran through me like electricity. I called out, in joy, and in shock, and they came running. A doctor, with brilliant eyes, stethoscope flying, a nurse, eyes wide with shock. More doctors. They beamed at me, took my hand, told me, over and over, *well done*. I smiled. I tried to speak. Thank you came out, *K ouuu*. They seemed to understand.

They fussed, they beamed, they prodded, gently. A flurry of activity took place, physio, a speech therapist, it was hours before the last one filed out. When, finally, I was left alone, I ran my hands down over my stomach, my flat stomach, and then I wept, fully and freely as I never could have in my coma for the baby that was gone from me forever.

Finally, I stopped. My baby was dead, but I was alive. I was fully conscious. I owned my body and my mind once more. They did not work perfectly, by any means, but they worked. They would get better still. Someone had delivered. God or the devil, and, for my baby's sake, I would not let that gift be in vain.

But then I realized, if the wild musings of my comatose mind were correct, if I *had* really heard what I thought I had, I was now truly at risk. As a vegetable, I posed no risk. Now I did. I didn't want them told, Rosamond and Archie. I had to convey this to the doctors. I could only hope it was not too late.

Chapter thirty-three

I had my answer the next morning. By then, anyway, I'd worked out the blindingly obvious fact that they'd have to know, sooner or later. The doctor with the brilliant eyes came in and gestured to the chair beside my bed. 'May I?'

I nodded.

He sat down. 'We've rung your husband, and your mother-in-law. Took a while to track them down. Paris, I think. They'll be back in a few days.'

'Hmm,' was all I could manage to say.

'You don't look exactly thrilled by the prospect,' said the doctor. He spoke to me as if he knew me. His voice was comforting, familiar too.

'Have you been here, as my doctor, all the time?' I asked him.

'Since you were brought in.'

'How long?'

'Seven weeks ago.'

'God.' Seven lost weeks.

'He may well have had something to do with it. I don't quite know how you did it.'

'I have a feeling you must have had a hell of a lot to do with it. What kind of doctor are you?'

'I'm a brain doctor.'

'And it was my brain that was hurt worst?'

'Everything was hurt. You had five broken ribs, two broken legs, one broken arm, and a fractured skull. The breaks heal quickly. Two months and they're done, your casts came off just three days ago, but not the brain, not when it's as badly damaged as yours was.'

I paused. I had to ask the next question, but I was not sure I could bear the answer.

'And my baby. Did it suffer?'

'Your baby went into trauma, but we delivered her by emergency C section.' He smiled at me and my spirits went into some wild loop. I could scarcely believe what I might have been hearing.

'You have a perfectly healthy seven-week-old daughter, Morganna.'

And then I sobbed, tears of joy, tears of sorrow for what so nearly happened, for my nearly choosing to die, for what I might have missed, and for the existence, the secret existence all this time, of a child. My child. My daughter. Those words were like sunshine in my veins. The joy of them, the joy of *her* was almost uncontainable.

Finally, I managed to stop crying. My doctor just sat there, looking out of the window, glancing at me from time to time.

'I want to see her,' I said. 'Is it all right for her to come in here?'

'Morganna, this is a brain ward, not contagious diseases. Of course it's all right.'

'But where is she? Is she in Paris, with them?'

'That I don't know. But they must have someone who helps take care of her, because they come in here, once a week, for ten minutes without her.'

I nodded. Some person, I did not even know who, was taking care of the child I never knew I had.

'I've got to get out of here. When can I get out?'

He raised his eyebrows at me. 'Morganna, you've just come out of a coma, you very nearly lost your life. You will get out, but you've a way to go. You've done incredibly well; be pleased with that, but be patient too.'

'One percent chance, and all that.'

He looked at me sharply. 'Where did you hear that?'

'I remembered someone saying it.'

'When you were in a coma?'

'Yes. I think so. It's all a bit blurred now, but I seem to know things I didn't before, so I must have heard them then.'

'Do you remember who spoke?'

'I remember who said the bit about one percent. My husband.'

'Ah.' He seemed to want to say something, but held back. He got up to look out of the window. 'Many people maintain that coma patients cannot hear, or process sounds,' he said, returning to sit in the chair by my bed.

'I could. I know I could. Some of the time.'

'I always thought you could. I spoke to you as if you could. I do to all coma patients. That's why it's not such a good idea to speak of patient trauma in front of them, or their prospects, which normally aren't great.'

'Oh, I don't know. It helped spur me on. I *could* have died. It would have been easy. Not even a decision, just letting things go the way they wanted. I had to make the decision to live.'

'What made you choose life?'

'Well, I would have chosen automatically it if I'd thought my baby was alive. But I knew she was gone from me, and I thought she must be dead.'

'She was a month premature, had to stay in hospital for three weeks, but she's very much alive.'

I fell silent. *Where were you, my baby, where were you?*

'So what made you want to live, then?'

'Things I have to do,' I said, coming back to him.

'You sound like a woman with a mission.'

I smiled. 'You have no idea.'

'Well, we'd better do our best to get you fighting fit then. Fit for yourself. Fit for your baby.'

'How long till I can go home?'

'That depends on a lot of things.'

'Like what?'

'Well, for a start, seven weeks in bed and your muscles have atrophied. You'll have to do a lot of physio in order to be able to walk, stand, take care of yourself, climb stairs, cook. Pick up your baby and walk with her.'

'All right, fine. And?'

'It also depends on the level of help and support you will find at home.' He said this levelly, but I could see what was left unsaid in his eyes.

'Yeah, well. That's what it is. But, there are some things money *can* buy.'

We shared a wry smile.

'I happen to know a couple of very good freelance nurses.'

'I'm sure you do,' I replied with a smile. 'One favour, please,' I asked him.

'Name it.'

'When my husband and my mother-in-law do come to visit next, could someone warn me, a few minutes before they're let in to see me?'

'I'll try to make sure they do. Sometimes it's difficult, if we have someone filling in, but I'll try to brief everyone.'

'And I want to ring the castle, see if my baby is there, get her brought in if she is.'

He nodded. 'There's the phone.'

I looked at it, paused.

'I can't remember the number,' I said.

'That's all right. Not unusual. I'll get someone to bring it to you, now I'd better be off.' He got to his feet, and with a smile and a wave, was gone.

A nurse came in with the number. Heart racing, I dialled. A woman answered, but no-one I knew.

'Wrath Castle.'

'Who is this?' I demanded.

'I'm Melissa, the cook,' she replied.

Jesus, they didn't waste time, did they?

'Can I help you?' she was asking.

'Yes, I hope so. It's Morganna Edge here. Is my daughter there?'

There was a shocked silence before this uncertain-sounding Melissa managed to collect herself.

'Goodness. Right. Er, Miss Georgiana is with Mr. and Mrs. Edge, in Paris.'

'Is she now? And do they take care of her themselves, or do they have a nanny?'

'There's Mrs. Myot, a qualified nurse. She's with them.'

'Right. Where are they staying?'

'At the Crillon,' she answered, as if no other answer were possible.

'Of course they are. When they return, will you

kindly inform them that I would like to see my daughter, as soon as possible.'

'Yes, Madame, I'll do that,' she replied. 'Er, anything else?'

'No. Just that.'

Just everything. I hung up, and lay back on my pillows, burning with rage and impotence.

The same nurse popped her head in.

'Everything all right?'

'Fine,' I answered.

'Would you like a shower, and a hair wash?'

I looked at her as if she were an angel. The thought of water sluicing over my aching body was almost too wonderful.

'Would I ever?'

And so she helped me. She called in another nurse and together they carried me as if I weighed nothing to the bathroom, took off my nightdress, sat me on a special seat, pulled the shower curtain, and turned on the shower.

'I'll stay here. My name's Emma. I'll just sit here while you shower. If you need me, just shout.'

I sat under the blissful stream of hot water. My body itched. I was covered with the familiar red weals of eczema that I had hoped were a thing of the past. I looked down and saw the scar where they had cut my baby from me. I washed my hair, and then Emma and Juliette, as she was called, fished me out, dried and dressed me, then blew dry my hair. Then Emma handed me a mirror.

'See! Beautiful,' she said, with glee.

'Hardly, but maybe compared to when I came in.'

'That's in the past. Don't you go hanging on to all that.'

I glanced back in the mirror. I knew it anyway, just hadn't seen it before. My long black hair had gone. My entire head had been shaved, and now had spiky regrowth. I had lost weight, my cheeks were sunken hollows and my skin was chalk white, speckled with the eczema eruptions. I looked for all the world like an ailing ghost. A skinhead ghost. I threw back my head and laughed. The pretty girl had died. Someone entirely different had been reborn.

Chapter thirty-four

They came to see me on a Friday, hotfoot from Paris. I imagined them strolling along the boulevards, the nanny, Mrs. Myot, pushing the Silver Cross pram, my husband and my mother-in-law sipping café au lait, luxuriating in their suites at the Crillon, passing the afternoons in a succession of antique shops, impressing the supercilious patrons with the size of their cheque-book. Frieda, one of the nicest nurses, was on duty. She stalled them, and came to warn me. I had been reading, slowly tracing my eyes across the words and letters, which still had the ability to jumble themselves into indecipherable hieroglyphics. I thanked Frieda.

'And my baby?'

She shook her head. 'Not with them.'

I felt as though my blood was literally beginning to boil.

'Give me five minutes, could you Frieda, before you let them in.'

'I certainly will.' She left with a determined look on her dour Scottish face.

How *dare* they. Not for the first time, I felt a murderous rage. At the very least, I wanted to fly at them, rake my fingers down their faces, scream blue murder at them. And then what? Even through my fury, I knew that wasn't exactly smart. But how to play it? I'd agonized over little else for the past few days and still hadn't come up with a solution. Now I had five minutes and counting. Okay. In the absence of a brainwave, I decided to play it cool, let them wonder. She thought you were a vegetable, wanted you to be one, made the most almighty blunder thinking you were one. There was power in apparent weakness. Let them think you were weak. Let them think you could not remember.

And so, I composed myself. I lay back, pulled the covers up, and pretended to sleep. A couple of minutes later, I heard them come in. They stopped, presumably staring at me. For a few moments, neither of them said anything. Then I heard Rosamond's sarcastic tones.

'Great. After all that, she's asleep.'

I lay stock still, opened my eyes and locked onto Rosamond. She let out a small shriek, and I swear she jumped.

'Good God, Morgan.' She passed her hand rapidly over her hair, smoothing her exterior, composing herself, her eyes never leaving mine. I forced mine to soften. I forced out a smile. I turned to look at Archie. His own face was a rictus of smile, apprehension, and awkwardness.

'Morganna,' he exhaled.

'This,' I said, including them both in my smile, 'is simply wonderful.' The tension ebbed from their faces, and they smiled back, taking their cue.

'You're all right now, Morganna,' said Rosamond, taking my hand in hers. 'Everything's all right.'

I nodded, smile in place. I think they believed me.

'How are you?' asked Archie, nervously moving towards me, and then stopping a foot from my bed.

'I'm not bad at all. Doctors say I'm recovering very

well.' I noticed movement in the corridor. Dr. Beeston. He smiled at me, and moved on. 'Still lots to do,' I continued. 'Still fuzzy. Lots of black holes in my memory.' I stopped, hoping I was not overdoing it. 'Can't read properly, can't speak all the words in the right order, but . . .' I shrugged, and they smiled, deeper this time, before glancing quickly at each other.

'How are you two?' I asked.

'Much better, for seeing you doing so well,' replied Rosamond. Seeing how well she lied inspired me.

'I'll do even better now, with you two around.'

'Oh, we've been around, lots,' said Rosamond. 'Obviously, you couldn't take it in.'

I shook my head. 'Big black hole.'

'Well, all behind you now. Forget about the past. Concentrate on the future. On getting better. We'll help you all we can, won't we, darling,' she said, turning to Archie.

'Of course,' he replied quickly.

'And my baby. My baby's alive,' I said with wonder, not needing to act this out.

'Miracle child,' announced Rosamond with proprietorial pride, as if my daughter's survival were somehow her doing.

'How is she?'

'Simply wonderful,' she said.

I turned to Archie.

He smiled. This smile was genuine. 'She is gorgeous, Morganna.'

'Mmm. Why didn't you bring her in? I specifically asked.'

'Darling. Morgan. Come on. A baby in a *hospital*?'

'I think you'll find that most babies are born in hospitals these days, Mrs. Edge,' says Dr. Beeston, appearing in the doorway.

'I do know that, Dr. Beeston,' snapped Rosamond. 'Maternity hospitals, not, not–' she was actually struggling for the word.

'This is a neural ward, Mrs. Edge. Not contagious diseases. Bringing a baby in here is fine.'

She glared at him, outflanked, unable to gloss over the vehemence of her dislike.

'Well, maybe next week. See what Mrs. Myot says.'

I shook my head. 'No. If Dr. Beeston says it's all right, then I'd like to see my daughter tomorrow. She's three months old. I don't want to miss another day of her life.'

'Well, you hardly missed it, did you? You weren't conscious of a thing, were you?'

'Not a thing,' I lied. 'But still.'

'Fine. All right,' she conceded. 'Five minutes,' she said, as if granting visiting rights to a prisoner, and I realized that's how she thought of me. Powerless as a prisoner.

I didn't think I could take too much more of this. 'Mmm,' I replied, breaking into an enormous yawn. 'Tired still,' I mumbled. 'Sometimes I just . . .' I closed my eyes, and once again feigned sleep. Only when I was absolutely certain of their departure, did I open them again.

Dr. Beeston came in a while later.

'You, Morganna Edge, are an enigmatic woman.'

'Why so?'

'Well, forgive me if I'm treading on any toes here, somehow, I don't think I am, but, before I'd seen you conscious with your mother-in-law, I got the distinct impression that you loathed the woman. Now either I'm deluded, or else you've just put in an Oscar-winning performance as the dutiful, and loving, daughter-in-law.'

I smiled, but I felt a chill cross my heart.

'Could you close the door, please?'

He got up, did as I bid, and returned to his seat beside my bed.

'Look, you know things about me I don't even know myself. You know what my brain looks like, for God's sake. You care for me and you have helped me more than you know, but, you also know things that might not be good for me, and that is one of them.'

He eyed me closely.

'Is there anything specific you want to tell me?'

I shook my head. 'No. But I will say this. And I am trusting you here, not to tell another living soul. I am certain that my mother-in-law does not have my best interests at heart. It suits me very well if she thinks I adore her, and her son, and if she thinks I can remember little, or nothing about what happened before my accident, and even the accident itself.'

He nodded. 'How much do you know about your accident?'

'Not much. I figured out I had a car crash. I know I ended up in cold water, because I've had nightmares about it. I also remembered bits of it when I was in a coma in the first place. But I don't know where I crashed, or why I crashed. Do you?'

'I know where. It was on a bridge. You were nearly home. It was early, 6 a.m. There was ice on the roads. It had been unseasonably cold. But what in heaven's name were you doing on the road at that time in the morning?'

'I don't know,' I answered. I'd already told him enough. Whether he saw the lie or not, I did not know, but he had the grace to nod.

'Look, I don't know what's going on here, but I want you to know that you can trust me. I won't let anyone know about your feelings for your mother-in-law. That's just between us.'

'Good. Not even your wife.'

'Particularly not her. I'm divorced.'

'Ah.'

'You made reference to what happened before you crashed. Do you remember that?'

I closed my eyes.

'Every last detail.'

There was a knock at the door. We turned in unison.

'Come in,' I call.

My physio, Lyn, poked her head round. 'Oh, hello, Dr. Beeston, shall I come back?'

He got to his feet. 'I'm on my way.' He turned to smile at me. 'See you soon.'

'See you.'

'Right, physio, Miss. You up for it?'

'As always.'

Lyn helped me into a wheelchair and pushed me along to the gym. There she got me up between two long, low parallel bars. I held on, and, trying to take as much of my own feeble weight as possible. God it hurt.

Physical effort of any kind seemed to be an assault upon my body. Muscles, bones and sinews were simply not used to it, and sending the signals from brain to body felt like the greatest mental effort imaginable. But I was determined. I had willpower that I'd never known. I walked, back and forth, back and forth, as many times as I could bear. I did it for ten minutes, two minutes longer than the day before. And then, trembling violently, drenched in sweat, I collapsed again into the wheelchair.

Later, back in bed, I replayed the visit. I remember the look in Rosamond's eyes, when I opened mine: pure, visceral terror. It was as if I had risen from the dead. She would look at me anew now. Perhaps, she would see that I had power of my own. I was no longer the vegetable. My awakening had not been gentle in her eyes. It would cost me, I was sure of that, but, God, a million times over, to see her fear was worth it.

Chapter thirty-five

I hardly slept that night, for imagining my daughter. Nothing I could conjure came close.

Archie brought her in, cradled sleeping in his arms. I was sitting in my bed. I gazed at her in disbelief. I reached out my hands.

'Can I hold her?' I asked.

He looked doubtful. '*Can* you?'

'Of course. The bed will take her weight. I'm strong enough to hold her in place.'

And so he handed her to me. My daughter.

I took her in my hands, and I hugged her tight, and I studied her. She was so tiny, but there was so much life in that little frame, so much wriggling vitality. Her hair was black, thin and wispy. I could see her head through it. I took her hand, studied the miniature fingers. And then, suddenly, her eyes flew open. Green eyes, like mine. They widened, and locked onto mine with an intensity I would never have thought an infant capable of. As I studied her, she studied me. I smiled. She looked uncertain, and then she smiled at me. At that moment, I felt my heart turn over. I fell in love, and it was like nothing I had ever felt before. This was passion. This was enslavement. And I knew I would do anything I could to have this child as mine, to take her as far from Archie and Rosamond as I humanly could. I put my lips to her downy head. I kept them there, breathing in the sweet smell of her. I wanted to hold her in my arms forever.

Archie glanced at his watch. It took all I had to surrender her to him.

'She is beautiful, Archie.'

'She is.'

'Will you bring her in tomorrow?'

He sighed. 'Look, Mrs. Myot says it's disruptive to her routine. It is half an hour each way, then parking, getting her out of the car seat, time here, back in, and home. She'll be late for her feed as it is.'

I felt like saying, 'I can give her a bottle here, let her stay with me for a few hours,' but I knew I couldn't push my luck.

'Every other day?' I asked.

'How about every third day?' he countered.

And that is what I had to settle with. The only blessing in that was that I wouldn't have to see him, or his mother, every day, or the phantom Mrs. Myot, whom I loathed already.

They left. I broke out into a muck sweat, and I began to shake. Five minutes that changed a life. Then something strange happened. I felt as if I was falling, and that was the last thing I remembered.

Next thing I knew, Dr. Beeston was staring down at me.

'What happened?' I asked. 'Did I pass out?'

'You had a blackout.'

'A what?'

'You became unconscious for a while. For forty-five minutes, to be precise.'

'Shit. What's it mean?'

'I don't know.'

I looked at him in amazement. Doctors were not meant to say that.

'Morganna, there's still so much we don't know about the human body and brain. We're not omniscient, even if some of us behave as though we are.'

'Will it happen again?'

'I can't answer that either.'

I felt an unfair fury coursing through me, directed at him, as though this was all his fault. I wanted to rage, to scream and shout, but I managed to restrain myself. His pager went off, out he went and I was left by myself, wondering what the hell happened to me, and what other tricks my body might have up its sleeve. Just as I imagined I was getting better. The loneliness of illness, of hospital descended on me. I ached for my daughter with a pain I could never have imagined. I desperately wanted someone to hold my hand, to tell me everything would be all right, and for it to have been true. Geoffrey, I thought. Where were you? And then I remembered. The ocean voyage. He would have been at sea, probably knew nothing of what had befallen me. But surely he would have called to find out about my baby, giving birth, how we both were? Before I could agonize anymore, I fell asleep.

That night, at about nine, Dr. Beeston dropped in again.

'How are you?' he asked.

'All right.'

'Not furious with me anymore?'

'Was it that obvious?'

He nodded.

'I'm sorry.'

'Don't be. You've a lot to deal with.'

'Mmm. So have you.' I glanced at my watch. 'Do you live here?'

'Sometimes it feels that way.'

'Is that why you're divorced?'

He laughed. 'One of the many reasons.'

'Know much about divorce?'

'Chapter and verse on messy divorce.'

'Good. Have you got five minutes?'

He gave me a wry grin. 'Chapter and verse takes a bit longer than that, but, as it happens, all I've got in store is a takeaway that I probably shouldn't even eat in the first place, and something crappy on the box. Let me just get something edible in here.'

He returned five minutes later with an apple and a banana.

'Not much of a dinner.'

'No, well I need to lose weight anyway. So,' he asked, biting into a Granny Smith apple, 'what's going on?'

'I want to divorce my husband, and I want to get custody of my daughter. Sole custody.'

'Ah.' He paused, finished his apple. 'Morganna, before I go on, I just have to let you know something.'

I was wary. I didn't like his tone. 'Go on.'

'Some patients who are in a coma for as long as you were, with such severe damage to the brain, if they come out of it, can find they have personality changes.'

I laughed. He looked shocked, but I laughed on. That was not what I had feared.

'You find that funny?'

247

'Sorry. I know I shouldn't laugh. I *have* changed. You're right. Without wanting to sound pompous, I think I now have a better idea of what life means. And I have no intention of wasting mine. So I'm impatient, and I'm ruthless, far more than I might have been before, and you know what, that suits me just fine.'

'But divorce? Maybe you should wait until you have lived together with your husband. See how things work.'

I shook my head. 'I would have divorced him if I hadn't crashed.' I stopped, I took a deep breath.

'You want to know why I was on the road at 6 a.m.?'

'Yes, I do.'

'I was getting away from him, from my husband. I'd found him in bed, with another woman.'

For a while he said nothing. I could see professional reserve battling outrage. Outrage won.

'What a prize shit.'

'Exactly. And there's plenty of other shitty stuff going on too. So tell me, please, how I can divorce him, and get my daughter?'

He blew out a great breath. 'If that's what you want, you're going to have to put up one hell of a flight, and play seriously dirty.'

I smiled. 'I'm more than ready to do both. But why so negative? Women normally get custody in this country. Why shouldn't I?'

'Right. You're going to hear this in court, put without care and concern, so you might as well get used to it now. You're a coma case. Your brain was so severely traumatized you should, by rights, be dead. Your prognosis is uncertain. You might go on to lead a completely normal life, but as of now, you're suffering what we might call mini-relapses, blackouts. Today wasn't the first, it was just the first you were aware of, the first you remember. But the nurses and I have observed you having others. You probably just thought you fell asleep, if you remember anything at all.'

'I have a vague idea.'

'What's worrying is that it seems to happen without warning. You suddenly lose consciousness. Imagine if you were with your baby, carrying her across a busy road and that happened, carrying her down the stairs, bathing her.'

'But, but I'd have a nanny if I had to, someone to help, someone–'

'What, and you'd never be alone with your child? She'd be there, a constant shadow? Twenty-four hours a day, seven days a week? You'd need two or three, for a start, to have that kind of cover.'

'You'll have to cure me, and I'll have to cure myself. Anyway, I'm sure I wouldn't conk out with her in my arms. I wouldn't let myself.'

He laughed. 'Morganna, willpower can only take you so far. Pathological illness is not a cold that you can talk yourself out of.'

'I *know*.'

'Now your husband may give up your daughter without demur, but somehow I doubt it. I think he will fight you tooth and nail. He will say that you have not bonded with your child, that you simply were not there for the first however many months of her life it is until you get home. He will say you recklessly endangered her life by crashing in the first place. He will deny his affair, deny the circumstances that made you run from him late at night and undertake an epic drive while eight months' pregnant. He will say you stormed out after a tiff, he will make you look wild and demented for doing what you did.'

I raised my hand. 'Jesus! Enough already.'

'Enough? I haven't even started, and I'm your friend. I'm on your side. *They* won't be, I promise you.'

'They?'

'Your husband, his Lady Macbeth of a mother, and whatever high-priced lawyer they hire.'

I laughed despite myself. 'Lady Macbeth? Are you always so wonderfully indiscreet?'

'I'm old, I'm tired, and diplomacy always was way down on my list. I save lives not egos. I've seen her for three months, remember, coming in for the statutory ten minutes, not even bothering to conceal her impatience, her profound dislike of the whole performance.'

'My husband is no Macbeth, though, apart from the thought being too incestuous, he's too weak, not enough backbone to be Macbeth.'

'Even so, divorce makes monsters out of people, believe me, I know.'

'Were you the monster, or were you monstered against?'

'Monstered against. My wife did the most monumental number on me. Something you are going to have to do on your husband, if you want to even stand a chance of getting your daughter.'

'Do you mind telling me?'

'Not in the least. The Buddhists always say you can extract good out of every experience, a view I have to regard as pure bullshit, but in this case they're going to be proven right, even if it did take three years. Besides, I'd like to see her arsenal of weapons deployed on the right side.'

'Should I take notes?' An academic question, really, since I could not handle a pen, nor formulate the written word. What came out when I tried was an infantile scribble.

He shook his head. 'If you're as avid as I think you are, you'll remember every last trick.'

'So shoot.'

'My wife started building up a dossier two and a half years before she filed for divorce. Every school concert or sports day I missed she dutifully noted down. Of course, she failed to note down that I had cancelled at the last minute because I was in surgery, trying to save someone's life. Most accidents are inconveniently timed, damned inconsiderate of people really, but there you go. Missed milestones in my children's lives, occasions when I let them down, when I would have done anything not to let them down, apart from allow someone to die. That I wasn't prepared to do. Every time I had said I'd be home at a certain time, and had been late, she recorded it, down to exactly how many minutes late I had been. Again, the demands of my job were irrelevant next to a broken promise, was how she phrased it. Then there were the times we had arguments, and what I called her. Now we argued, sure, but not as frequently as she claimed, and I never, not once, used the insults against her that she claimed.'

'But this all seems so slight, not to your children, true, but as major ammunition, as a demolition job.'

'You didn't see what she says I called her, time and again. You didn't see the dossier. Two-and-a-half-years' work, with all the keywords, ready to push the buttons of the judge, a woman, in this case. Neglectful, aggressive, cruel husband; neglectful, uncaring father. Her dossier showed all my omissions, real and imagined, and sins of commission I had never committed, but it never showed anything good, remember.'

'And the judge went for that?'

'She did. My wife got custody of Charlie and Emma. She got the house, she gets half my salary, and all because she fell for someone else, didn't want me around anymore, wanted to have easy access to her lover, wanted him to have easy access to our home and her bed.'

'Bloody hell. The whole thing stinks, it's so unfair. But why didn't you fight back?'

'I could have. I could have proved her infidelity easily enough, but our children had already had one parent dragged through the mud. I didn't do it for their sake, pure and simple.'

'Do you see your children?'

'Not as often as I'd like. One weekend a month. And one two-week holiday a year.'

'How does it feel, to lose them like that?'

'It's like a bereavement. To wake up every morning and cuddle them, to be part of their lives, and then to be surgically removed, ejected from the home that you provided for them.'

'I would be so bitter.'

'I am, but what can I do, save get just a measure of cosmic revenge by helping you?'

'But I can't live with him for two and a half years. I'd go crazy.'

'Then you need a quick, knockout blow. Can you prove his infidelity?'

'No. Not unless he carries on now, and I get a private detective to follow him.'

'Do it. If you can afford it. What about money?' he continued. 'Do you want to get any money out of him?'

I laughed. 'That's a good one. No, it's a question of how I can stop him trying to take even more of my money than he and Lady Macbeth already have.'

'What do you mean?'

'I'm the one with money. Too much money. He had access to my money, via a joint account, but I heard her, when I was in my coma, saying they had power of attorney over my money, that she would secure their future from it.'

'How did she get power of attorney?'

'I have no idea. I never signed anything giving it to her in the event that something happened to me, at least not–' I stopped. 'Oh no. Oh God, maybe I did? Archie used to come to me with so many bloody documents to sign, Scottish Heritage, for stuff we were doing to the castle, insurance for the builders. He'd often have a whole pile, and I'd just go through them, never reading them. We'd actually joke about it, that I was signing my life away, my organs away. I could have signed power of attorney. Jesus. I can't believe he would do that. Her, yes, I can believe anything of her, I could believe she'd forged my signature. Shit, I don't know. Maybe she did that, maybe Archie conned me, with all that implies.'

'Either way, it's fair to say they obtained it illegally. Who *are* these people?'

'They worship bricks and mortar.'

'Enough to defraud you while you lie in a coma.'

'Yes, fortunate for them, wasn't it, but now no doubt Rosamond, at least, is cursing my recovery.'

'No doubt.' He got to his feet. 'I feel like I'm about to have an aneurysm, while you're serene.'

I smiled. 'Is that how I seem? I'm not serene, I'm seething inside. I would love to scream at them, to physically have at them both, to curse them from this life to the next.' I shrugged. 'Where would that get me?'

'Fair point. Revenge best eaten cold and all that.'

'Exactly, but revenge is secondary. It's my daughter I want.'

'Then it's your daughter you must fight for.'

'Maybe I should just go to the police, report that, get them done for fraud, for embezzlement, get custody on that basis.'

'Could work, but can you prove it? If your husband conned you into signing it unawares, you'd be hard pressed to prove that. He'd just argue that you signed it voluntarily, and now, because of your accident, memory loss, and blackouts, you simply can't remember, and have turned nasty and unstable. If Lady Macbeth forged it, or got it forged, you might have a chance, depending on how good the forgery is. Your choice, but go down that road, and your hand is declared. You'd better be bloody sure you'll get them.'

'I can't be, can I? And I've made a big noise about not being able to remember stuff, before the accident. They would use that against me.'

'Guaranteed. And they'd haul up an expert witness from my profession to testify to personality changes, et cetera, et cetera. By the time he or she'd finished with you, a jury would think you were demented.'

'Wonderful. Right. So if that's not an option, I'm really going to have to pull out all the stops. I'll have to pretend I don't know they have power of attorney; I'll have to stay out of contact with my bankers. If they think I know, they'll be puzzled why I'm not doing something about it. They'll smell a rat. God. If I do this, this dossier, I'll have to play the part the whole time, pretend I remember nothing about catching him in bed with that woman, pretend I don't know about their power of attorney.'

'Hey, you've come out of a coma, you have trauma-related amnesia, you can play it as gaga as you like, and be credible. Make it work for you.'

'I can, can't I, and they'll happily underestimate me anyway, they're so convinced of their own superiority.' I smiled. 'So, let's get this started. I should get a private investigator onto him, at least when he goes down south, see if I can catch him with some silly tart.'

'At least you won't have a problem with the expense of it.'

'No problem. And I'll keep watch on him at home, to see if I can prove they're defrauding me, that they forged or conned me into signing the power of attorney.'

'All of that. But don't forget the little things. The dossier. Times when he might forget to take proper care of the baby, or be cruel to you, show himself to be unstable in any way, untrustworthy, an unfit father.'

'I don't think he has much to do with her. Sins of omission, I'd say.'

'Find whatever you can.'

I stopped, as an idea fluttered on the edge of my mind. 'What if I find out something about his mother, something so bad that if I expose her she will be ruined . . .'

'And do what with it?'

'Use it to get him to voluntarily surrender custody of his daughter.'

'If he's that besotted, it'd have to be pretty bad.'

'Oh, it's bad.' Now I knew what I had to do, the rest seemed easy. I could act, I could play my part, and I would deliver Rosamond's head upon a plate.

Chapter thirty-six

And so I prepared myself. I relearned to walk. Sounded simple enough. I'm sure it couldn't have been this difficult first time round. But this time I didn't bounce like a baby when I stumbled and fell. I had none of that delicious fat to insulate me when I took a tumble, which I did, too often. My muscles simply couldn't hold me for long they had atrophied so badly, and they were unco-ordinated. Getting the message through from the brain seemed unspeakably difficult. The trauma to my head clearly severed or at least damaged some of the circuits pretty badly. 'Use it or lose it,' said Lyn, my physio, and so I did. I forced myself through four hours of physio every day, until I was running with sweat, and trembling. The more I did the better I got, but God, it hurt and it left me in a pit of tiredness. By eight at night, like a baby, I was fast asleep. But the next morning, I was well ready for more. I was driven; I had a goal. I wanted to get back to the castle, be with my daughter and set my plan into action as soon as was humanly possible. And I was progressing. By the end of a month I could talk pretty much normally, and I could read, just a tad more slowly than before the accident, 'BA' as I'd come to call it in my mind. Muscles were growing on my frail bones; I was gaining some necessary fat. My hair too had grown. It had come to look gamine, rather than skinhead, innocuous, rather than scary, and it suited my purposes fine. My eczema remained, and I suffered too from the return of periodical asthma attacks. They medicated me as much as they could, but the arid air of a hospital was about the worst place for me. These complaints were superficial though, compared with everything else. An irritant I hoped would vanish again.

My mind was on other things. I was clear about what I wanted. After all, I had ample time to think about my plan. The only incognita was Geoffrey. He obviously still hadn't heard about my accident. He couldn't have, otherwise he'd have been here. But surely he would have been puzzled by my silence. And surely he would have tried to get in touch. I tried to remember the red pins in the map, to trace his journey in my mind. Was he on some major ocean crossing? Had his comms gone down? I wanted to ring the bank, desperate to find out where he was, *how* he was, but I didn't dare. I needed him now more than ever, but I wasn't sure I could afford to have him here. He would never have approved of my plan. He would have dragged me away from Wrath Castle by any means he could, but even he, with his money and his ruthlessness could not have extracted Georgie for me. Robert Beeston had spelled it out cleanly enough. I was a trauma case, recovering, but still damaged. *I* had crashed the car that had nearly cost me and my daughter our lives. By fair means, I would never win custody. The only way forward, was to insinuate myself back into my own home, into my husband's life, and to damage them from within. That meant no Geoffrey. That meant I could not call him from hospital. I could only hope that he was fine, that his panic attacks had abated or gone, that he was safe, that there was a simple explanation for his silence. Perhaps there was mail for me at Wrath Castle that would explain it all. Until I got back there, I could only wait and hope. And pray.

Of course, *they* came to visit. I saw my daughter every three days. A form of torture that brought almost as much pain as it did pleasure, but something I could not now imagine living without. The price I paid for seeing her, besides having to say goodbye to her, barely ten minutes after she was brought in, was seeing them.

God knows how I would manage living with them. I treated each visit as a rehearsal. Like most things, practice made it easier: physio for the emotions. And as I got physically stronger, my acting became less arduous to me. I was getting impatient. I could walk, so I wanted to run. I wanted to get out of this prison. I wanted to walk on the hills, sit on the beach, and watch the sea with my daughter by my side.

My hunger for living was ferocious. Beware those who have escaped death. If they recover fully, they will ruthlessly pursue the life they so nearly lost. I smiled to myself. Rosamond had no idea what was coming.

I was counting down the days. I kept pushing Robert Beeston.

'Come on, I must be ready. I feel fine, *please*, sign me out.'

'I will not take the risk of discharging you too soon, only to have you shipped back in here if you collapse. You don't want that do you?'

'Of course not, but it won't happen.'

'I think I'd like to be the judge of that.'

'Well judge, test me, please.'

'When you're ready.'

Long days went by, days when I thought I might go slowly mad in my incarceration, but all I could do was play their game, was do my physio, practise speaking, do mental arithmetic, anything to train my brain as well as my body. And I felt the synapses firing, faster and faster.

Finally, they tested me. I walked for Beeston, for half an hour around the grounds of the hospital. I sat down, I stood up, I tied the laces on the trainers Archie had been asked to bring in, and stood back up without passing out. I lay down and got up without help, without turning dizzy. I could shower, and bath alone, without sliding down into watery oblivion. I could boil a kettle without electrifying or scalding myself. I could make a toasted sandwich without chopping my fingers off. God, Beeston was so obsessively thorough.

'Do you put all your patients through this?' I demanded.

'No. I do not. Not when I know they're going home to a supportive family, when I know they will be looked after, when I know they will not arrive back to a major battle, even though it is to be played out silently. I want you to *win*, Morganna.'

'Why? Why do you care?' I asked.

'Because I cannot sit on my Olympian mountain all the time. If I didn't allow myself to care, just some of the time, I would be a mere mechanic.'

I nodded, chastened. It felt good to have someone on my side, rooting for me.

They gave me another CAT scan, and pronounced my brain healed. But still, Beeston was worried.

'What is it?' I demanded, almost choking with frustration.

'Something's not right. I just feel instinctively that you're not fully healed. I fear you'll get more blackouts.'

'So what are you going to do? Keep me in here for life? Watch over me like a jailor? It's *my* life. I *cannot* stay in hear any longer. I'll go mad. You're worrying about my body, about my brain, but keep me in here any longer and my spirit will atrophy. This is no life. You know what I want. You know how hard I've worked for it. All the tests say I'm fine.'

'Three more days,' he declared, and in those three days, he had me pushed, physically, mentally, emotionally. He made me tired, he heaped on the pressure. He woke me up late at night when he was on call. I knew what he was doing; trying to see if I was susceptible to another blackout, but he hadn't reckoned on my will. I did not black out, and he, despite his misgivings, was forced to sign my discharge.

Chapter thirty-seven

Archie collected me. He had brought some clothes for me. I wondered briefly what had happened to the clothes I had been wearing when I crashed. Had they been covered in blood, embedded with shards of glass? I hoped they had been incinerated. I had requested my favourite old jeans, a heavy sky-blue cashmere jersey, and my Timberland boots. I took them into my bathroom to change. I closed and silently locked the door. It felt exhilarating to wear day clothes after months of hospital gowns. I ran my hands through my hair, all different lengths. It looked as if it had been expensively cut by some boho Notting Hill stylist.

I took a deep breath, and I walked out to Archie. He held out his arm to me. I moved towards him, and took it. We walked out into the corridor. The nurses had lined up to say goodbye to me. I found this incredibly touching, and I started to cry, silent tears. I brushed them away as I said my farewells. We turned another corner, and there was Robert Beeston. He looked at me, ignoring Archie, as we walked towards him. I stopped before him, halting Archie.

'Goodbye, Morganna,' he said gently.

'Goodbye, Robert.'

I smiled. *I'll be fine*, I tried to say with my eyes.

'We'd better be on our way,' said Archie, as if Beeston had had no hand in saving the life of his wife. 'Goodbye, Doctor,' he said brusquely.

'Goodbye,' Robert replied. He raised a hand in

farewell. I mirrored him, then turned and walked away.

Archie and I walked in silence to the lift. We rode down that way. I walked the last five metres to the door of the hospital. It opened automatically, and I felt the blast of cool, fresh air. I walked out into it. I let go of Archie's hand. I could not have this moment polluted. I tilted back my head, opened my mouth, and breathed. I felt giddy, drunk. But this was no blackout. This was ecstasy.

I caught sight of Archie's face. Alarmed, embarrassed, uncomprehending. He didn't know what he had before him. His wife, the stranger. I almost laughed out loud. He had no idea. It struck me then. I was not the only one who was acting. I just hoped I was better at it than he was.

'Morgan, Morgan, Morgan. Welcome *home*, darling.'

Jesus, had she never heard of *over*acting? Rosamond stood at the enormous door to the castle, the chatelaine, arms flung wide. I must submit, I knew it. I walked forward meekly, into her embrace. She squeezed me hard. It hurt. I stepped back, and smiled.

'Now, I've thought about it long and hard, and it seems better to me, for now, if you have the old wing all to yourself, a sort of enormous sick bay. It's quiet, and you'll have your old studio, and view of the sea. I know how you loved that.'

I smiled again. 'That's very thoughtful, Rosamond. I'm sure I'll soon be back to one hundred percent, but in the meantime, it'll be perfect.'

I caught the fleeting look between mother and son. Jesus, they'll have to do better than that.

'Of course, darling. Whatever suits you best. Bad eczema. Poor thing.'

This time, unlike back in Southwold when she had been playing the role of mother manqué, she didn't quite manage to conceal her distaste as she looked at me and my lesioned skin.

'Now, come on up,' she continued, dropping her honeyed words into the silence.

She walked ahead, into the hallway, chattering gaily as she had never done before. I saw it then, whilst I pretended not to, the gilding, the new art, including an Old Master. I could have sworn it was a Rembrandt. I saw my fortune on her walls. Once I had felt that this castle was mine. Now it was indisputably hers, and all I could do was smile as if I neither noticed nor cared.

I was shown to my wing. They led me on up the stairs to the old marital bedroom. I arrived, puffing like I'd just climbed a mountain. God, stairs were something I hadn't practised. Was I that unfit? I would not let myself get depressed. It was a timely, salient reminder that I was feeble still, and I'd better remember it.

I looked around the bedroom, mine alone now. It looked unchanged. It had about it an air of abandonment, as if the occupants had simply vanished one day, which, I suppose, I had. My eyes came to rest on the bed. I looked up to see Archie watching me. I gave him a smile, but I was unable to conceal the sadness in it. Our marriage was dead but there could be no requiem.

I effected to shrug off my sadness. 'It's only for a while, Archie. That's what makes this bearable.'

He reached out, took my hand, squeezed it. 'I know,' he replied, his face torn between smile and grimace.

The clock we had passed in the hallway began its noisy grind, working up to the Herculean task of striking midday. I turned to look at it. Old, beautiful, straining, and new. I loved it.

'How beautiful,' I said softly.

'*Isn't* it?' replied Rosamond with enthusiasm. 'One of my finds.'

I turned to her and smiled. 'Well done.' And there, again, was my salvation. The castle, its restoration and decoration would breathe life into a thousand conversations.

We all listened as the clock pealed out twelve times. As the last chime faded away, Rosamond gave me a brisk smile.

'Lunch at one, if you'd like to join us. I've engaged a cook, so much easier. I've given her instructions to always set the table for three, and cook for three, so you can simply decide last minute if you feel up to company.'

'That's considerate, Rosamond, thank you.'

'My pleasure, Morgan. So,' she rubbed her hands together briskly, 'what now then?'

'My daughter. I can't wait to see her, where she sleeps. Everything.'

'Yes, well, one step at a time, darling. Remember what that doctor thingy said.'

I nodded. 'I do remember.'

'Bear it in mind then, darling, not being alone with her, in case you have one of your little blackouts. And her routine, well, as you'll see, it's quite full.'

'I will be careful,' I said quietly.

'I'm sure. Right, better get on. See you later, if you feel up to it.'

With that, she turned and click-clacked out on her elegant heels. Some ultrachic designer, long coveted, no doubt. How grand and generous she was becoming with my money, about as parsimonious as she was with the time I was to have with my daughter.

Archie folded his arms and gave me what I think was meant to be an avuncular look. It wanted twenty years and sincerity, but hell, it was probably good enough for a recovering vegetable. 'Anything I can get you?'

'Yes. I'd like to see my daughter.'

He frowned, and then tried to morph it into a look of concern. 'I think Georgiana might be having her nap now.'

'How lovely. Then I shall watch her sleep.'

'Fine. Come on then.'

He walked off briskly, trotting down the stairs at a pace he knew I could not match. I walked slowly, securely, burning inside. On top of everything, he lacked compassion. I suddenly wanted to cry, or to slap him, but of course I did neither. I just put one foot in front of the other, and focused on not falling down the stairs.

He waited in the grand hall. I could feel impatience rising off him like steam. I caught up, and off he went again, up the south staircase. So my daughter was housed about as far from me as it was possible to get. He stopped on the second floor, listened outside a door, and then gently opened it.

The room was yellow, filled with light. In the corner, there was a lavish cot. I could see her through the bars, her hair black against the white sheet, her tiny hands flung out. Almost holding my breath, I tiptoed across the carpet. I saw the figure of a woman in the adjoining room, but I ignored her. I had eyes only for my baby, here in her room. I stopped beside the cot and crouched down with awkward effort so that I could see her face to face. Her chest rose and fell with delicate flutters. She looked like a bird, tiny and vulnerable and oh, so beautiful. At that moment, as if aware of my presence, she opened her eyes. But she didn't cry, she just lay there, looking at me. I smiled at her, as the tears coursed down my face.

'Hello, Georgie. It's your mother. I'm home.' I reached out my finger through the bars of her cot, and slowly, curiously, she reached out hers, until the tips of our index fingers touched, and what I felt flow between us was a current of the purest, the deepest love I had ever felt. I stayed like that, just touching her, until slowly she closed her eyes, and fell back to sleep.

I struggled, and slowly managed to get up. I walked into the adjoining room where the woman was standing, watching me. She was, unmistakeably, the nanny. She even wore a starched uniform. She must have been in late middle age, with mousy hair shot through with grey. She stood with feet squarely planted as if to root her solid frame to the floor.

'Mrs. Myot,' whispered Archie. 'This is my wife.'

We shook hands. To give her credit, she ignored my eczema. 'How's she doing,' I asked, 'my baby?'

'She's good and fine. Eats and sleeps and does all her wee business just as she should. Got a fine routine going here, we have too.'

I nodded. God, she made my baby sound like an automaton. 'When does she have her bath? I'd love to bathe her.'

Mrs. Myot shot Archie a look. He cleared his throat.

'Er, is that wise, Morganna, given your blackouts?'

I looked from him back to my baby sleeping next door and saw in that moment the way they would play it.

'You can watch me bathe Miss Georgiana, Mrs. Edge,' said Mrs. Myot. 'No reason why you cannot do that.'

I nodded, not trusting myself to speak.

'Five o'clock is bath time,' she went on.

'I'll see you then,' I managed to say. How was I to spend the day, banished from Georgie, given visiting rights that I had to negotiate by prearrangement? With one last look at my daughter, I followed Archie out.

He closed the door gently behind us.

'The formidable Mrs. Myot,' he said, voice rich with admiration.

'Does she sit there all the time, while Georgie is sleeping?'

'Of course. She was preterm, traumatized by your crash. She needed special care.'

He couldn't have put it more clearly. Your crash. Your ignorance. You know nothing about how to take care of a child, so shut up, stay out of it, leave it to Mrs. Myot. And how did I learn to take care of my daughter if I was not allowed to be alone with her?

'What are her hours?' I asked.

'Twenty-four hours a day, seven days a week.'

'God, that's Victorian.'

'It's how she wants it.'

'And you?'

'I want what's best for my daughter, of course.'

'Of course.' With the minimum inconvenience to you.

'Right. Better get on. Anything else you need?'

A divorce, a hammer?

'Thanks, Archie. I'm fine. I think I'll just lie down for a while. Too much excitement and all that . . .'

'Of course. See you at lunch, maybe.'

'Archie, wait. Where's Jelly?'

'Ah. She's with that chap Ben, the shepherd. I really couldn't take care of her, but he came by, volunteered, so I thought why not? He took care of her before.'

'Yes. He did. Well, I'll get her back as soon as I can.'

He looked at me aghast.

'What on earth's the matter? I asked.

'What about Georgiana?'

'What about her?'

'A *dog*?'

'A sheepdog. Not a ravening wolf. Look, I won't leave them alone together, and I'll keep Jelly on a leash when we're all together.'

'And if you have a blackout?'

Oh God, please.

'When Jelly's with me and Georgiana, I shall keep her tied up.'

'We'll have to see what Mrs. Myot says about all this. I don't think she'll be happy about any of it. Safety, hygiene. You name it.'

'Well, it's a good job Mrs. Myot isn't in charge then, isn't it?'

At that he gave me a slightly pitying look. 'Must go.'

And he trotted off down the stairs with his carefree agility.

I made my way slowly back to my wing. I closed my bedroom door and leaned against it, blowing hard. I shut my eyes. This was going to be much harder than I had ever imagined. When I got my breath back, I moved away from the door, and began to examine my rooms. I picked up objects, the bedside clock, a perfectly struck porcelain bowl, I felt them and replaced them in positions more to my liking, perhaps trying to give myself the illusion that I could control something in this castle.

In my sitting room hung the two portraits of my parents. I walked up to them, as if to greet them. Their presence comforted me, as always, and I began to relax, just fractionally. They were my eyes, my allies, in the court of my enemy.

I opened my door and climbed the narrow staircase to my studio in the tower. My paintings were all there, stacked up. I suddenly remembered Toby Hood. What must he have thought? I'd simply vanished. Had he tried to get in touch with me? He must have done. What had happened to all my phone messages, to my post? Months of them. I didn't want to appear too efficient, too ready to re-engage in everyday life, but I *wanted* my post, my messages, to see if there was anything from Geoffrey. I wanted my things, anything that reminded me who I was, that gave me a link to the world outside, a lifeline. I gave a bitter chuckle. Look where my last lifeline had led me.

I stood before the window, gazing out at the sea, which was eerily calm. Could I do it? Could I really execute my plan? I conjured their faces: Archie, Rosamond. Then I saw my daughter's face, replayed the sound of her laughter, lighting my life, filling me with the most complete joy I had ever felt, and I knew I could, that, whatever it took, I would. But I must do it fast, I knew that too.

Chapter thirty-eight

At twelve fifty-five, I forced myself to go downstairs. The smell of something delicious greeted me before I entered the dining room. God, I felt like I was in a hotel. Everything was gleaming and alien and professional. The scent of food, polish, and flowers mingled. I preferred the smell of the sea that emanated from the old, untroubled walls.

They rose as I approached.

'*Morganna*!'

Jesus, she made it sound like this was an unexpected pleasure.

'Come, sit down,' she exclaimed.

Archie moved rapidly across the room like a marionette and showed me to my seat, next to his. He seated me, pushed in my chair for me. I wanted to scream at his fake solicitude. Perhaps he had to convince himself that he was a gentleman. It was okay to fuck other people, but God forbid you fail to jump to your feet when your wife walked into the room.

A woman hurried in carrying a tray on which stood a tureen. Rosamond ignored her. She flashed me a quick glance, seemed uncertain when I offered a smile.

Rosamond spoke when she had disappeared.

'Leek and potato soup to start, darling. Something to build you up a little. Dreadfully peaky.'

'How delicious. What's her name, the cook?'

'Melissa something. Mouse from Leith's. Cooks like an angel, though, doesn't she darling?'

'Absolutely,' confirmed Archie.

Something squirmed inside me. They were like a double act, each reinforcing the other, like a well-worn married couple.

We dipped our spoons into the thick, creamy soup. It *was* delicious. After months of a tube, and then the solid form of hospital food, this was like manna.

'Mmm,' I said.

They looked pleased.

I ate it all, with alacrity. They finished, and, mysteriously, Melissa appeared right on cue with more lidded bowls.

'Coq au vin,' said Rosamond, 'with runner beans and dauphinoise potatoes. Wine, Morgan?' she asked, rising and click-clacking to the sideboard to help herself.

I shook my head. It was on my forbidden list. Alcohol and blackouts were sadly incompatible. I watched her take a healthy portion. She looked just as keen on good fare as I was. After years of scrimping and saving, this must have been bliss for her. She returned with her plate.

'Morgan?' Archie said, gesturing at the food.

'Yes, please.' So this was to be the order: Rosamond, the alpha female, followed by me, then the gentleman last.

He brought me a full plate.

'Who's the other woman?' I asked, as he took his plate to his seat. He nearly dropped it.

Suddenly, the atmosphere was electric. I wondered what I had said, and then it came to me. I only narrowly stopped myself from laughing out loud. I decided to make it easy for them, not out of pity, but to protect myself. 'Housekeeper?'

'Mmm. Correct,' replied Rosamond, breathing again.

Archie sat down. He positioned his plate with meticulous silence on the place mat.

'Any other staff I should know about? After all, I don't want to scream "intruder" if a butler pops up.'

'Should I line them up, have you inspect them?' she asked.

'There are two local women who do the cleaning,' said Archie, as if aware that his mother had been just a tad too sharp. Melissa, the Cook, and a vastly diminished team of Poles and assorted specialists putting the final touches to things. Oh, and Mrs. Myot, of course, whom you met.'

'Of course.'

We ate for a while in silence. Rosamond then opened up a stream of small talk that it was easy to go along with, mostly about the renovations. Archie chipped in from time to time, visibly relaxing now we were on safe territory.

Our plates were cleared. This time I noticed Rosamond pressing a button on a tiny silver elephant's back to summon the help.

It was tarte tatin for pudding. My absolute favourite. I should have had no appetite for the delicacies laid before me by my enemy, but hunger, like sexual desire, overrode such niceties.

'How did you know?' I asked Rosamond.

'I didn't, darling. I just guessed. This was the stuff I lived on in France. It's always been my favourite.'

'Does Georgiana ever eat with you? If she's on solid food yet, I don't know,' I added sheepishly.

'Darling. Whatever she does or doesn't eat, she does it in the nursery kitchen, of course, with Myot. The appropriate thing.'

'Of course.' Jesus, she gloried in her lack of knowledge, the lady of the house, rising above such things as the sustenance of her granddaughter.

When I'd cleared my plate, I felt exhaustion wash over me. I got to my feet.

'I've got to go and lie down,' I said.

'You all right?' asked Archie.

'Fine. I just need to digest this in a supine position, that's all.'

'You need a hand?' he asked, getting to his feet.

I smiled. 'No. Thank you. Walking up the stairs unaided will count as my physio.'

They returned my smile. It felt to me as if they suddenly wanted to detain me, as if they were itching to ask me something. Let them wait.

'See you later,' I said, raising a hand in farewell as I turned and walk out.

Chapter thirty-nine

The bed was double. Untold luxury after the hospital single, with its crinkly plastic undersheets. I peeled back the quilt that covered the duvet. It was silk, antique-looking, with panels depicting scenes from old Japan. Another thing of beauty. I'd give her that, Rosamond. She had a good eye. I sat and pulled off my shoes and trousers, then my thick jersey. Quickly, for I was suddenly cold, I slipped under the duvet, drew it up to my chin, and awaited sleep.

I thought of my daughter. I wondered if she was sleeping peacefully. I was going to have to add my passion for her to my list of things to be concealed. I prayed for sleep, and it came. I felt myself falling, down, down, down. I didn't dream but somewhere within me I still had a spark of consciousness. For suddenly, as I lay there, in my stupor, I felt that there was somebody in my room, standing over me. I tried, but I was so tired I could not summon myself from sleep. It felt as if it was hours later when I finally managed to wake myself. I was alone, but it seemed to me that something in the quality of the air around me was disturbed. I glanced at the luminous figures on my clock. To my amazement, it was nearly midnight. I'd missed seeing Georgie have her bath. How could I have slept so long? I felt angry with myself, furious with my debility.

I lay back and tried to make myself familiar with this old, new room. Apart from the slight sickly glow of my clock, I was surrounded by almost complete darkness. In hospital, lights blazed all night long in the corridors, and the light always seeped under the door, and through the glass panel at its centre, like a contagion.

Here, just the faintest trace of moonlight found its way through my curtains. And there was practically no sound, save the faintest susurration of the sea. In hospital, there was always something. The soft-shoe shuffle of nurses bustling, or dragging tired feet, the periodic laments of patients, hushed voices whose whispering urgency was more disturbing than a voice pitched at normal level. But now there was nothing. Just me and the sea. And whatever had haunted my sleep of the afternoon. I felt a sudden fear grip me. I had lain there, infinitely vulnerable, while someone had prowled around. I was sure of that. I groped blindly for the light, blinked at its ferocity, stumbled towards the door. There was a keyhole, but no key. No way to keep them out.

I faced them the next morning for breakfast at eight. They both sat at the table, heads ensconced in the papers that lay spread out over the pristine white linen tablecloth, oblivious. Perhaps it was seeing them sitting there, so complacently, perhaps it was the smell of strong coffee and kippers mingling, but suddenly I felt almost violently nauseous. I forced in some deep breaths that alerted them to my presence.

'Goodness, Morgan!' exclaimed Archie.

This constant air of surprise occasioned by my appearance was acutely annoying. I felt like shouting: *No. I haven't died* yet. I'm still alive, and, so far as I'm aware, this is my home too. Clearly, for them, at least one of these statements wasn't correct.

'Morning,' said Rosamond, the more collected of the two. 'Sleep well?'

'Loggishly,' I replied. 'Practically from lunch yesterday until now.'

'What you need.'

'Mmm. You didn't look in on me, did you, either of you?' I asked, looking from one to the other.

It was Rosamond who answered. 'Good God, no. We didn't, did we, darling? We didn't want to go bursting in on you. On your rest. If you want anything you'll appear, won't you?'

I nodded. 'And you?'

'Me what?' she asked sharply.

'Sleep well?'

'Well as ever.'

'Meaning?'

'I'm an insomniac, darling. Few hours at best.'

'Hmm. I would have thought you would have consulted the best in the business. Surely a hypnotist or a herbalist could do something?'

'Darling, I have. They can't.' She shrugged, inexpertly concealing her annoyance. 'I just live with it.'

'Shame. Sleep that knits up the ravelled sleeve of care, and all that.'

'Yes, well I just have to ensure that my sleeves do not unravel in the first place, don't I?'

I laughed. 'You make it sound as if that's in our power.'

'Mainly, it is, don't you think?'

'Perhaps, but then some bloody great truck looms out of the mist, and–' I made a scissors motion with my hands.

'Darling, is that what happened to you? Is that why you crashed?' she asked, biting on the bait with obscene swiftness.

I frowned, looked troubled, shook my head. 'It might have done. I don't know. I can't remember.'

'What, nothing at all?' she continued.

As they waited for my response I was conscious of an almost scintillating silence, broken only by another grandfather clock, marking time in the corner.

I effected to gaze into the distance of my mind, shaking my head again. 'No. There's a great big gap. All I can remember is seeing Toby Hood, saying goodbye to him. Next thing I know, is waking up in hospital, months later.'

Rosamond and Archie glanced at each other. Not even she could hide the triumph in her eyes. When she turned back to me, puzzlement was firmly in place.

'Who on earth is Toby Hood?'

'Ah. He's my secret.'

They both raised playful eyebrows at me. Their delight and relief fluttered around me like butterflies released from their cocoon.

I laughed. 'He's an art dealer. He's the reason I drove up to London. I took some of my paintings. He agreed to stage an exhibition for me. Probably all gone by the board now, but maybe not. I've still got the paintings, after all.'

'Well, how exciting,' said Rosamond. 'Your very own exhibition.'

Yeah, not bad for a vegetable, is it?

'Isn't it,' I replied. 'Did he write?' I asked. 'I must have got loads of post waiting. Part of me wants to ignore it, but part of me feels I ought to be dealing with it.'

'Oh darling, not very restful is it? We have your post, of course, all waiting for you to deal with, when you're up to it. But, might I suggest, just go slowly to begin with? Don't do anything that isn't pure pleasure or relaxation.' She looked so concerned.

'You're probably right,' I said with a sigh. 'Know your limitations, and all that.'

They smiled back at me. They looked delighted. They looked as if they had won the lottery.

'Was there anything from Geoffrey?' I asked. 'You know he's on this voyage, crossing the oceans. Did he get in touch? I'd have liked to have seen him.'

'I gathered, from his postcards,' said Rosamond. 'He's sent some from, oh, I forget where, various places. Didn't like to study your post, after all.'

'He hasn't rung?'

'No, darling, he hasn't. He's probably relishing his freedom. Life on the ocean wave and all that. Months can pass so easily.'

'I can imagine. You've done it, after all, haven't you?'

'Well, not months, darling, not without making port, but, on and off, yes, and you do lose perspective on time, so I wouldn't worry. He'll be having the time of his life. And God, must he deserve it after years slogging in that dreadful bank. Let him rest, darling. You tell him about your accident and he'll be worried sick.'

'I know. I haven't got in touch with him for that very reason.'

She couldn't quite conceal her relief at that one.

'Wise girl. I should keep schtumm, let him have his trip, worry-free.'

I nodded. 'I will.' Convenient for her too, not to have my greatest ally breathing down her neck, scrutinizing her.

Chapter forty

Miss One Percent. What was I now? Twenty-five, thirty? I walked up to my rooms and pulled on coat and boots, then, without allowing myself to stop for breath I walked down again, slowly, slowly. I approached the enormously heavy oak front doors and let myself out. I walked perhaps fifty yards from the castle, and then turned around to look back at it. I could have been standing here with this same castle, this same view at any time in its nine-hundred-year history. I felt a sense of the vertigo of time, the terrifying weight of it. How could I have even felt for a day that this castle had been mine? Its walls were so steeped in the breath and the blood of Rosamond's family. It had always been hers. I was the outsider, and always had been, the only difference was, now I knew it.

I turned and walked away. I looked at my watch; I wanted to walk for half an hour, on the flat, nothing too taxing. Build up slowly, Robert had said, and I would.

But it was hard, walking over the uneven track, and the lumpy heather. Still, the harder it was, the better for me, so I persevered, turning back when I had been gone for fifteen minutes on the dot.

When I arrived back at the castle I was sweating and trembling. I paused a while, and caught my breath. I didn't want to feel exhausted, bedraggled, if I caught sight of Rosamond or Archie. I needed to arm myself for them first.

When I felt ready, I made myself go forth, haul open the doors, and walk in.

I felt like an intruder. There was no sound. I wondered where everyone was, the two of them, Georgie, Myot, the staff, the builders. I looked around cagily, almost feeling silent eyes upon me, but there was no-one, save the paintings, and the suits of armour standing sentry on the first-floor gallery that looked down over the great hall.

I decided to explore, while I could. This place was like a treasure trove. I walked to the first painting: *The Wreck of the Hope*. It depicted a wrecked ship, icebound, a tiny sliver in a sea of ice, so jagged and perfectly delineated you felt your finger would freeze if you touched it. You could almost taste the frigid air. The ruthless sea. The next was *Venus Asleep*. She lay, watched over by an approaching skeleton, apparently unconscious, or perhaps just asleep, legs parted, dreaming of the seduction of death, perhaps. I could tell her about that. Around her, women supplicated, arms raised to heaven. There was a new moon at the top right edge casting sliver shadows on the slate grey scene. Then there was a Hans Baldung that I recognized: an infant, a woman in the splendour of youth, an old crone, and a skeleton — *The Three Ages of Man and Death*. I found it hideous in its accuracy. Death stalked the hallway. And money. This little lot, and the Rembrandt on the stairs, would have cost tens of millions. Of my millions. The sheer audacity of the woman was almost incomprehensible. She seemed almost drunken in her acquisitiveness.

And supremely reckless. Or maybe just confident.

I headed for the south staircase. I mounted it, heart racing from the effort, and from desire to see my daughter. I waited outside her door, listening. At once, I could hear Mrs. Myot chatting to her. She was awake.

I opened the door, and walked in. My daughter lay on a sheepskin mat on the floor. Mrs. Myot scrambled to her feet.

'Mrs. Edge. Come to spend some time with Miss Georgiana?'

I crouched down beside my daughter. 'I have. Hello, Georgie,' I said. There were enough syllables in her name to spare two. I thought shorter was friendlier, and prettier, and I wanted to have *some* say in what I called my daughter. I sensed Mrs. Myot retreat, but only as far as the next room. From the corner of my eye I could see her move a chair into position so that she could sit down, and keep me under watch. Jesus. So much for intimacy with my daughter, but if this was the best I could hope for I'd just have to live with it. For now.

I smiled down at Georgie. 'You're gorgeous, you know that.' She smiled, as if maybe she did. My thoughts suddenly cartwheeled back in time. When I had been as old as my daughter was now, my own mother was dead.

I extended my finger slowly towards my daughter, sadness welling for my mother who had so little of her child. Georgie made flailing gestures to bat my finger. I moved it closer, made it easy for her. I longed to take her in my arms, but her eyes were wary. I was after all a stranger to her.

I stayed with her for ten more minutes, just talking,

just being with her, before Mrs. Myot came back in. 'She's restive. Needs her feed.'

'I'll do it.'

She raised her eyebrows.

'I know you'll be delighted to show me how. Come on, I'll be sitting in a chair. I won't drop her.'

She really couldn't object to that, so off she bristled, her starched uniform rustling officiously, to get the bottle. She returned shaking a bottle vigorously. She took the top off, sprinkled some milk on her arm, and then handed me the bottle.

'Temperature,' she said. 'Always test, inner wrist best place.'

'Thank you.'

Georgie had seen the bottle and was writhing. I picked her up and sat down in a low, high-backed chair.

'Hold her firmly. Tilt the bottle like this.' She angled her beefy arm. 'Up, up, up, up,' she said, as if I did not understand the word.

Georgie lay in my arms, utterly focused, completely contented. The same feeling swelled over me, and I could almost block out everything else. For the first time in a long time, I felt complete bliss. It ran through my body. It seemed to make everything feel better. The aches and pains I lived with almost eased away.

Twenty minutes later, the bottle was drained. Georgie was looking sleepy, eyelids drooping, body loose. Myot reached out her arms.

'Right. I'll take her now. Burp and bed.'

'Just a few more minutes. Let me hold her, soothe her.'

Reluctantly, she backed off.

I held my daughter and softly I began to sing. I don't know where the idea came from, or even the song, it was just something that I seemed to remember, that seemed a good idea. *'Speed Bonny boat like a bird on the wing . . .'*

On I sung, the same song, over and over. Georgie seemed to like it. I felt her soften in my arms.

Finally, I gave her over to Myot.

She sat down, forced Georgie into what looked like an uncomfortably upright position, and proceeded to weigh into her back with resounding pats. She registered my look.

'No point being lily-livered about it.'

'I'm sure. Right, Mrs. Myot, I'll do the same tomorrow. Same time. What time does Georgie go to bed at night?'

'Miss Georgiana goes down at seven, after her bath and feed.'

'Fine. I'll look in then too.'

'She's not to be disturbed. Wound up.' She said it as if it was something unspeakable.

'I'll remember that,' I said. 'Thanks for this. I really enjoyed it.'

She nodded and turned away. I could not afford to alienate this woman, and if sheer bloody-minded graciousness was my price of admission, then I'd pay it happily. I walked out, despite it all, smiling. I had fed my daughter, and the sense of achievement I felt was indescribable.

Chapter forty-one

Archie and Rosamond returned from their ghostly exile at lunchtime. I arrived at the dining room as they did. Archie gave me a formal bow and stood back to let me pass. Rosamond, of course, did no such thing. As chatelaine, she strode ahead. I, of course, did not attempt to compete. My ego was patient, but I was surprised. How was she so sure of her suzerainty? Was I so diminished, or had she somehow grown, like the parasite which has taken over its host? Did she think she would consume me as she consumed my wealth?

Today we had a light green salad, followed by poached wild salmon, tiny new potatoes, and asparagus.

'Where did you go this morning?' I asked.

They look surprised, as if I was not meant to notice anything.

'I was getting some supplies,' replied Archie. He gave me a quick smile. 'Nothing exciting.'

I smiled back. 'Rosamond?' I asked, taking a mouthful of potato, sweet and earthy.

'On my computer, darling. Why?'

I concealed my surprise. I would never have thought her computer-literate. She belonged to the wrong generation. I shrugged. 'Place just felt empty,' I said. I didn't mention seeing Georgie. I was sure Rosamond would be informed of that soon enough.

She studied me for a while, her chin resting in her cupped palm, like a raptor, assessing its prey.

'What you need is a diversion,' she concluded. 'Something gentle, yet occupying. Nothing too strenuous.'

'Mmm,' I prompted. 'Like what?' How about letting me divert myself with my daughter?

'Oh, God, I don't know. Needlework. Piano. Something that daughters of the household did in Victorian times.'

Jesus, she really was losing it. I was meant to be the lady of the house, not the fucking daughter.

'Painting!' she shouted gleefully. She gave a rueful chuckle. 'Never see what's before your nose, do you?'

I smiled. 'No you don't, do you? I suppose it *would* keep me occupied. Of course, that's if I can still do it.'

'Oh, Morgan. I'm sure you can.'

'Painting comes from the brain, Rosamond. Mine's still damaged.'

'I know. All you can do is try, isn't it?'

'All right. I will. But I'm not sure landscapes will hold me anymore. I need something human, living and breathing. I could paint you, or maybe,' I said, striving to keep my voice casual, 'my daughter. I could sketch her while she sleeps.'

Rosamond laughed, but I could see how annoyed she was.

'Do me if you must. Tackle Mrs. Myot when you're a bit better. I'll try to make the time.'

God, she really didn't want me near my daughter. To volunteer for a portrait when last time she had hated it so much.

'Ten o'clock tomorrow?' I asked. 'That way I'm not too tired.'

'Ten o'clock it is. For an hour mind,' she couldn't resist adding.

'It's a deal. Oh, by the way, I couldn't have my post, could I? I want to catch up a bit.'

They exchanged the most fleeting of glances. They just couldn't help themselves.

'Of course, darling,' answered Rosamond. 'But are you sure?'

'It's only post, Rosamond. I shall sit in my bed and go through only those things that look nice.'

'Well, I've saved it all for you. I'll go up to my rooms and get it after lunch, is that all right with you?'

How very magnanimous, I thought.

She gave it to me later, some time later, at least an hour after lunch. Had she misplaced it, or had she been furiously checking for anything unsuitable to her own purposes? Finally I headed downstairs and up again to her rooms. Her door was closed. I knocked, tentatively.

'Who is it?' she called out.

'Morganna.'

'Just a moment.' I heard a scrabbling round, then, moments later, she half-opened the door and handed me a bundle, not very thick, held together by an elastic band. I wondered what she had edited out. I wondered why she patently did not want me to enter her room, or even see inside it. I resolved to have a serious snoop, as soon as I safely could.

'Thanks, Rosamond,' I said, as if oblivious.

She nodded graciously. I headed back down the

stairs, across the great hall and back up my own stair-case. Physio, I told myself, as I arrived panting at my rooms. I tucked myself up in bed as I'd promised, took off the elastic band and rifled through the envelopes, looking for Geoffrey's postcards. I amassed four.

Dearest Morgan,

You were right. This is bliss. Just what an old man needs. Everything fine. Made it to Bermuda, am writing this from a café on the beach. How are you and your baby? Due any day now. Sat phone dodgy, so ring the bank, please.

Dearest Morgan,

Cruising the islands now, Anguilla, Guadeloupe, Dominica. Spending a few days restocking at Martinique. Where is that baby? Please ring bank.

Dearest Morgan,

Congratulations on your daughter. Clever girl, well done. And how is the new mother? Call when you're not too tired.

What? I could scarcely believe my eyes. I was strug-gling out of bed when there was a knock at the door.

'Morgan, may I come in?'

Rosamond. Be calm, be calm, I chided myself. Do not blow this. 'Yes. Do.'

I walked through the bedroom, postcards in hand.

'I wanted to give you time to read them, before I

explained,' she said, eyes flicking over my face, trying to read what I was trying to hide.

'Now's your chance,' I said.

She sat down on the sofa. I stood where I was.

'Come on, sit,' she said, a flash of the maternal charm I had found so alluring showing through.

I sat.

'What good would it have done, to have him give up his trip and come racing back here, hmm, tell me that? Georgiana was delivered safely, and we all knew you'd come through. Better to spare him, don't you think?'

I said nothing. Better to spare him, yes, but what of me, lying there in a coma? What about what I wanted, or needed. It sure as hell wasn't the ministrations of her and her son. I didn't trust myself to speak, I just nodded.

Her face lightened. 'Good. I knew you'd see sense. I rang the bank and told them about Georgiana, said you were fine but too tired to talk. Just a white lie, Morgan–'

My incredulity must have shown for she faltered.

'A big one, I know, but for the best, as we agreed.'

'Was that the only one?' I asked.

She looked guarded. 'Meaning?'

'I'm sure he would have rung here, sooner or later.'

She glanced down at her hands, before raising her face to me.

'He did call, a couple of times. I told him you were travelling with Archie and Georgiana. Again, I didn't want to upset him. He sounded like he was having a ball.'

'You must have done a good job, reassuring him.'

'Oh, darling, I tried, but why do you say that?'

'Because otherwise he'd have shown up here.'

'Would he? Yes, I suppose, he worries about you, his daughter manqué. So, what will you do?'

I thought for a while. 'Get in touch, tell him everything's fine. I don't want him to abort his voyage for me. He can find out about the crash when I'm a hundred percent and it's all just a bad memory.'

'Wise girl,' she said approvingly. She got to her feet and headed for the door. She turned and paused under the lintel. 'I'm glad you understood.'

I nodded, keeping my face blank. Only when I heard the sound of her heels trail off into the distance did I close my door, lean back against it, and blow out an almighty breath. Oh yes, I understood all right, how she wanted Geoffrey off the scene, and how cleverly she had managed that. I wondered if there was anything else she had done, to reassure him, any other little harmless white lies.

I went back to my bed, and read the last of the postcards.

Dearest Morgan,

My damned sat phone's given up. Sorry I haven't been in touch. We'll have to rely on the odd piece of snail mail. I hope you had a . . .

A huge ink smudge blocked out what came next. Was that just coincidence, I wondered, or had Rosamond done a touch of convenient editing? I had to put my money on the latter, but if so, why?

And where was Geoffrey now? Okay, his sat phone was down, and the last postcard was dated six weeks ago? I padded downstairs to the library, hunted around, and found what I needed, a beautiful, old atlas — some valuable first edition, no doubt. I lugged it back to my rooms and opened it on my bed. Where were you Geoffrey? Had you gone through the Panama Canal, were you heading down the South American coast, or plotting a course for the Galapagos? God, what I would give to speak to you, I thought, knowing all the while, that it simply wasn't an option. This endgame I had to play out alone.

I put aside the rest of my mail, lay down, and went to sleep. That night, I took dinner alone in my rooms. I couldn't deal with any more Rosamond or Archie. I had that awful, debilitating sense of unease, where I knew that something was going on that I just wasn't getting. It was a bit like being in a coma again, with partial awareness losing out to a great swirling blackness.

I took comfort where I always had. After dinner, I went to my tower and with the radio playing gently in the background, I went through the ritual of cleaning my brushes, many of which had become hardened and unusable.

I cleaned brushes till my fingers themselves were steeped in turpentine. Then I went down to my bedroom and changed into my nightdress, heavy flannel to keep out the cold I felt too easily. I went to my window. The sea rippled idly. A swathe of sparkling silver bisected it. Moonshine. The moon was not yet half full. It was waxing, I thought. It had the feeling of growth, not shrinkage. It was getting stronger, like me. I had to hold on to that.

Chapter forty-two

She came to my tower at ten the next morning. I was
waiting, a cup of Nescafé warming my hands. I heard
her from far off, the click-clack of her heels on the spiral, stone staircase tapping out a tattoo.

I had positioned a single hard-backed chair in the
centre of the room. She would not relax on anything
less formal

'Rosamond,' I said with a smile as she entered the
studio.

She rubbed her hands, as if keen to start, and finish
an irksome job of housekeeping. On impulse, I took
her hands. They were not the manicured, soft hands of
the lady she was once. They were callused working
hands. I remembered how the day before, when debat-
ing another lie, she had looked down at her hands. Was
this her involuntary reflex when under pressure, when
entertaining which lie would get her what she wanted?
I felt a flutter of excitement, as if I had a key, small, but
crucial, to her soul. As if she knew this, she tried to
drag her hands back from me, but in my determination
I was strong. I kept them captive.

'You have interesting hands,' I said. 'I will paint
them.'

'What, not my face?'

'I'll do that too. It's also interesting, but, I imagine it
has been painted many times before.'

She smiled and order was restored. 'Once or twice,'
she admitted, graciously.

'Who painted you?'

'Oh, darling, they all did, or most of them. The greats. The South of France set.'

'Enlighten me. Picasso . . . ?'

'He did.'

'Where is it?'

'In some gallery, somewhere. I don't know,' she answered vaguely.

Yeah, I'll bet. Wouldn't you like to get your hands on that?

We discussed him for a while. She opened up. She loved to gossip, to relive this part of her life.

I mixed my paints. I positioned her. Tentatively, I lifted my brush, eyes squinting at her. Slowly I drew my brush over the blank canvas, my eyes on her hands. I listened with half my brain, while the other side conducted its own conversation of light and shade. Her hands were ugly, I realized with a shock; they were large, too big for the rest of her fine frame, and the veins stood up, livid blue. They lay there, fingers curved, like she was hanging on to something that might otherwise slip from her grasp. They were avaricious, controlling hands. As I studied her, my own hand moved at its own beckoning, and before me, something began to take shape. I felt electrified. Something that seemed to block my brain was releasing, was cracking apart. Another part of me was coming back to life.

Every day I contrived to paint her. Those hours gave substance to the facade of our relationship. Into the web of conversation, I span my questions, I searched for names.

On the fifth day, she left in a hurry. I listened to her departing tattoo, rose to my feet, and brewed up another coffee. I leant against the window, sipping it speculatively, and my eyes fell upon the glistening stream of gold that was her bracelet. I had made her take it off. I wanted no decoration on her worker's hands. I put down my cup, crossed the room, picked up the bracelet and let it run between my fingers like sand in an hourglass, catching it before it dropped to the floor. It was made of a hundred tiny links, like the lies she told. We all told.

Chapter forty-three

I wanted to return the bracelet, and I wanted to make sure she was not there when I did. I was sure she was going out somewhere. I gave her time to get ready, and only then did I head for her private rooms, and knock gently. There was no response. I opened the door and called out, but still no reply. I glanced around, and then let myself in. I decided to leave the door open. Easier to explain if I was caught. My heart pounded as I crossed the carpet. To the right lay her bedroom, to the left, her office. I could see the computer, screen darkened. I went in. I saw a large map of the world on one wall. It had red pins at various places. I could not work out what they might signify. A planned trip, perhaps? I tore my attention away. Fax machine, scanner. All the paraphernalia of a modern office. What was I looking for? What had she seemed so keen to hide when she had blocked me from her rooms when I had come to her for my post?

I did not like it in there. My mind and body were screaming at me to get out. I left the bracelet on her desk and hurried out.

I went for my daily walk, keen to escape the castle and the constant need to act, to keep up my game. I longed to head down to the sea, but the coastal path down was a challenge at the best of times. I had to get stronger first. I had increased the length of my walks to an hour now, and I could, literally feel my muscles strengthening and my body getting fitter on a daily basis. A few more days, I promised myself, and I would head down to the sea.

I arrived back at the castle in time to play with Georgie under Myot's watchful gaze, and feed her and burp her and lay her down to sleep. My sanity saver, but I could not face Archie or Rosamond, so I dined alone in my rooms on a casserole the kitchen sent up. I headed for bed by ten, and soon I fell into a deep sleep.

I woke up. Not slowly and luxuriously, but suddenly, riven with terror. Something was there. I knew it. Someone. I felt evil. I felt terror. But I could see nothing. I could not even drag myself from the paralysis of sleep. I could not move. I felt the weight of my terror forcing the very breath out of me. Yet still, I could not move, I could not scream. All I could do was lie there with my blind terror. I cried in my head, in my heart, but no-one came for me. I lay still, and I prayed to God to remove this thing, this person. At last, I felt the pressure lessen. I felt eyes taken off my defenceless body. I felt movement, like a prowling. The air stirred. I felt the lightest flush of air that told me a door had been closed. Only then I sat up, my hair wild, gasping in ragged breaths. I reached out to try to turn on the light. My trembling arms knocked it over and it fell to the ground with a smash that could have woken the dead. But no-one came to investigate.

I was exhausted, but I could not sleep. I lay in bed, with my remaining operative bedside light on. Only when I saw the first chinks of light through the curtains I had drawn back, did I sleep.

I joined them at breakfast.

'Sleep well?' asked Rosamond, with a hostess's languid concern. I held her eyes for a moment, seeking any hint of irony or subterfuge. For a moment I was tempted to say, *no, I didn't. I was riven through with nightmares*, but I'd had as much fake sympathy as I could stand. I had become a follower of the Victorian school. Never show weakness or debility of any sort to your enemies.

'Like a log,' I said, beaming. 'You two?'

'Fine, fine,' they answered in chorus, like a couple. I felt a wave of revulsion flow over me.

'Are you all right?' Archie asked quickly.

I winced, rubbed my head. Fabricated pain I would do. 'My wound hurts,' I said. 'It does that. One moment I'm fine. Next it feels like someone's tightening a vice around my temple.'

He frowned in concern. They both watched me.

'I'll be all right,' I snapped. They exchanged a glance and went back to their toast. I waited a minute, and then went up to help myself to kedgeree and coffee.

I spooned in a sugar, stirring it idly, covertly observing Archie as he read his paper. If either one of them did enter my room as I slept, they bore no trace of it. I could detect neither trespass nor guilt. But then perhaps the whole idea of guilt was ludicrous anyway. Surely they should have been drowning in it by now?

I ate quickly, and then headed up to my rooms to collect my sketching pad and charcoals. I carried them down to Georgie's rooms. As I was turning a corner, I nearly ran slap bang into Mrs. McTaggart.

'You,' I exclaimed, staring at her in amazement. 'What are you doing here?'

'Working,' she answered.

'On whose instructions?'

'The mistress's, of course.'

'You mean the other Mrs. Edge?'

'That I do.'

'Since when?'

'Since a while back,' she answered, moving around me, walking on as if I'd ceased to exist.

I just stood there for a while, pulse racing with fury. I could feel my cheeks flushed with humiliation. Damn Rosamond to hell. I began to feel dizzy. I sat down quickly in the hall and forced myself to breathe deeply and slowly until I felt the dizziness fade. Only when my sense of outrage had faded did I allow myself to go on to Georgie's rooms.

I paused outside to listen. The door was closed, but I could hear Myot talking to her. I opened the door gently and went in.

I managed to give Myot a dazzling smile and headed over to the nappy table where she was changing Georgie. I put down my kit.

'Here, let me do that,' I said. Myot stepped back a few paces. I leaned over Georgie and planted a kiss on her cheeks. McTaggart receded like a bad dream as my daughter smiled and waved her hands at me. She was getting to know me. I was slowly becoming Mama, was no longer the stranger and it felt great. I changed her nappy, dressed her in the day clothes Myot handed me, then carried her around the room, over to the window.

'Look, sunshine, see it?' We stood like that for some time, content with each other, just gazing out into the distance. And I sang to her again. *Speed bonny boat*. She quickened in my arms as I began. I think she recognized it.

Myot was behind me all the time, but I was resigned to that. I hadn't had a blackout since I'd left hospital, but she was taking no chances, and, intrusive as she was, her intentions were not bad. I turned and carried Georgie back to the large rug she loved to wriggle on. I set her down and picked up my sketch pad.

'I'm going to draw her,' I announced to Myot. 'Any objections?'

She shook her head. 'Can't see the harm.'

And so I tried to recreate my daughter, gazing at her with eyes filled with love, trying to capture her smile on paper. She had kicked her socks off, so I drew her tiny toes, which curled with prehensile joy when she gurgled. I worked quickly, passionately, and after half an hour I set down my pad, satisfied.

Suddenly the door opened and Rosamond strode in. She stopped when she saw me.

'Gracious, Morganna!'

'Hello, Rosamond.' I wanted to rail at her, but it was neither the time nor the place.

'What are you doing?' she asked.

I held up the portrait. She bent over it, so close to me I could smell her scent. She backed away, looked from my sketch to my child.

'Not bad,' she opined. She walked over to Georgie and smiled down at her.

'She does look so like me, don't you think? She has the Edge bone structure, and eyes. It's uncanny,' she said to me. I felt my mouth open in surprise, but, luckily, she missed that as she turned back to Georgie.

'You are a little me, aren't you? I can see the same look of determination in your little eyes.' She didn't pick Georgie up, I noticed, just talked down at her, as if she were a pet. God, the arrogance of the woman. This was about ego for her, about the perpetuation of a dynasty, not love.

'I'd like that,' she announced, gesturing at my portrait.

Wordlessly, I handed it over. I had wanted to hang it on my own wall, but no matter; I'd just do another one tomorrow.

She walked out, holding my portrait aloft.

'Bye,' she said, her back to us, waving an airy hand, the chatelaine on her busy way.

Quickly, I followed her out.

'Rosamond, wait, will you?'

She stopped, turned to me in surprise.

'I'd like a word,' I said.

'So, shoot.'

'What is that hideous creature McTaggart doing back here? I fired her some time ago.'

'I know you did.'

'So?'

She blew out an angry breath. 'Look, I needed help here, and, however you might feel about her, she is good at her job, and loyal and trustworthy, which counts for a lot with me.'

'Perhaps to you—'

She held up a hand, cutting me off. 'She has instructions only to clean my wing. She won't bother you in yours.'

'Well, she was in Georgie's wing.'

'Morganna, please, don't obsess.'

God I hated this powerlessness, this acting. As I had done so often in this past week, I bit back my pride.

'Just keep her away from me, and from Georgie. I do not like her.'

'Evidently,' replied Rosamond, with a look of thinly veiled amusement. At that, she turned and walked off, leaving me dismissed.

I went back into Georgie's room. I don't know if Myot had overheard any of our exchange, but I suspected she had. Embarrassed enough already, I studiously avoided her eye.

I stooped over Georgie and gave her another kiss. 'Bye, my sweetheart, see you later.'

I headed back to my rooms. I needed to escape. I pulled on my hiking boots and set out for my daily walk. I got to the high tor, farther than I'd managed so far. Then in the distance I saw Ben, with two dogs running around his ankles — Gin, and my Jelly.

My dog literally went wild when she saw me. She leaped up onto me and covered my face with licky kisses. I laughed so much it hurt. Finally Ben pulled her off me.

He leaned down, kissed my cheek, heedless of my eczema. 'Much as I'd like to follow Jelly's example,' he said.

I laughed again. 'Ben, Ben, Ben. How are you?'

'Lambs. Lambing season.'

'Ah. Busy.'

He nodded. 'Jelly knew you were home. She's been pining.'

I hugged her tighter. She'd grown up. Amazingly, she bore no signs of the accident.

'How are you? I was so sorry, Morganna, so sorry.'

'It's all right, Ben. Georgie's fine, and I'm doing all right.'

'I saw her, out with that battle-axe. She's the spitting image of you.'

'Oh Ben, do you think so? I think so, but then . . .'

'She is, no doubt.'

We talked some more, but I could feel he was restive. I knew he was worrying about his sheep, and their lambs.

'Go, Ben. I'll come and visit you soon. I'm building up slowly, but with Jelly I'll get even fitter.'

'That you will.' He stooped to kiss me again, then he ruffled Jelly's neck, and off he went.

Jelly scarcely shifted from my side. I had myself another ally.

I headed back to the castle and towards the kitchen to hunt out some food for her. I halted when I heard Rosamond's footsteps hurtling at brisk pace round the corner.

'Good God. What's that thing doing here?' she demanded, pulling up just short of a collision. Jelly let out a low warning growl.

'Living.'

'Evidently. Well, Myot won't be pleased for starters. She'll want to expel her, instantly.'

'Oh really. I wasn't aware that she ran the castle.'

'Of course, she doesn't, I–' she stopped herself, but too late.

I smiled sweetly. 'Come on, Jelly, let's get some food.'

My dog watched Rosamond click-clack away, and

only then did she follow me into the kitchen. I was amazed by Rosamond. She could always act so well. Now she seemed to be teetering on the edge of revealing what I believed to be her true self. Was she so drunk on her own successes, so confident of her position that she was losing her judgment, or was she holding some hidden ace that she knew would best me whatever I did?

Chapter forty-four

By nighttime a new lamp had appeared at my bedside. It did not match the other. The perfect chinoiserie was lost forever, smashed in a hundred ancient fragments.

I got ready for bed, leaving the curtains open. The moon was full, the sky clear. My bedroom was silvered with moonlight. I climbed into bed and closed my eyes. It is hard to convey absolute terror to someone who has not felt it, but then, perhaps we've all been held in its petrifying grip, at some time in our lives, the source real or imagined. Was it better or worse if it came from a tangible source, the man with the clenched hand, and not some invisible, unseen terror?

I recalled it now. The worst thing was my absolute powerlessness. How do you fight a threat you could not see? I prayed to God that it did not come back.

It didn't. I slept. Jelly slept beside me. I felt sure it was her who kept my night terror, real or imagined, at bay.

When I awoke I went down to breakfast with a light step, believing it was behind me.

'On for painting today?' I asked Rosamond. 'I'd like to finish your hands.'

She reached them out ahead of her, studied them as if she saw them anew. She gave me a dazzling, almost amused smile. It chilled me to the core.

I awaited her, warming myself with my third Nescafé. It didn't help my nerves, which were suddenly taut as violin strings. Jelly, lying at my feet, suddenly sprang up and gave a low growl, then, a few moments later, I too heard Rosamond approaching. Thank God for her early-warning system. I glanced down at my habitual trainers. Tank Girl, I dressed for stealth.

'Good girl,' I said to Jelly, ruffling her neck, 'but shhh now.' She stopped growling, but stood bristling.

Rosamond appeared. 'I've only got just half an hour this morning.'

It's time-consuming, isn't it, spending my money. I shrugged. 'Fine.' She always said something to that effect. Her insurance against boredom. So far, it had normally been I who had ended our sessions. Despite her protestations, our sessions amused her. I think it was more than the enjoyment of the cat, toying with the mouse she thought I now was. She relived her youth when she was with me, and her beauty.

'Tell me where you stayed in the South of France,' I said, painting in some of the age spots that dotted her hands, legacy of her love of the sun. 'The wonderful villas . . . oh I could do with some warmth, some real warmth to penetrate my bones, and the smells, I love the way you describe them, the pine forest baking in the heat, the mistral.'

This was easy for me, because I did love her stories. They transported me. She smiled.

'I stayed with–' she stopped herself, '–on a boat a lot, actually. We sailed around, often a different place for dinner every night, and he painted me, lying naked on deck. He was good at nudes, and that was the time to do it.' She threw up her hands and ran them down her body, as if she could smooth away the evidence of time.

'Did he keep them?' I asked, frowning with apparent concentration.

'What?'

'The portraits.'

'He sold them. Most of them.'

'I'll bet you grace some lovely collections then?'

'One or two,' she replied, with mock modesty.

If she told the truth, he wasn't a jobbing artist then.

'What was his name?'

She waved her hands quickly through the air. 'Oh, he was no-one, darling.'

'Oh, right.'

I finished her hands. For the first time, I allowed her to see. She stood back, frowning.

'I prefer the charcoal. Of Georgiana.'

Of course she did. This portrait showed a kind of virile ugliness, whilst that of Georgie showed innocent, pure beauty.

'That's all right. I'll keep it.'

'You do that.' She glanced at her watch. 'Right. Must go.'

She click-clacked away. Alone with the sound of her heel beats receding down the tower, I studied my work. *Murderess's hands*, I called it in my head.

I cleaned my brushes and then headed off with Jelly on a leash, hoping that I might get to spend some time with Georgie. I could hear the racket coming from her room as I rounded the corner.

'Where's bloody Myot?' Rosamond was shouting. 'Oh, for God's sake, Georgiana, shut up. Here Archie, you take her.'

'I'm no better than you,' he spluttered with indignation. 'Perhaps if you spent more time with her she'd be happier with you.'

'Not my style, darling, babies. Not even you. Until you were sensate.'

'And when was that?' asked Archie, raising his voice not just to be heard over Georgie's increasingly loud wails.

'Five, six, I suppose. Oh for God's sake, Myot,' she roared. 'Where the hell have you been?'

'Oh, Mrs. Edge, give her to me,' crooned Myot. Georgie instantly stopped screaming.

'So sorry,' continued Myot. 'I was in the, that's to say, um . . .'

'In the fucking loo. Spit it out woman,' yelled Rosamond.

'Yes, I'm so terribly sorry.'

Rosamond ignored her abject apology. 'Archie, let's get out of here,' she hissed. 'We *cannot* be late.'

With a quick flash of gratitude to my fashion sense, I backed away rapidly on my silent trainers and headed back to my own wing. I wondered what they could not afford to be late for.

Chapter forty-five

I needed a notebook, somewhere to write things down. I could not trust my memory. I feared a blackout might erase something irreplaceable, like a power cut losing unsaved work. And besides, I wanted to compile my case perfectly, meticulously, like a lawyer. This was to be my Final Settlement. This was to win me my daughter. Full custody. I found a small sketchbook. It would do. I liked the heavy parchment. Now I had to find somewhere to conceal it. Somewhere *she* wouldn't find it. I ruled out under the mattress, in my underwear drawer, medicine cabinet. I stopped and stared around in frustration. This was proving surprisingly difficult. I remembered hearing it said that if you wanted to hide something, you should do so in full view. I looked at my bookcase, the vertical spines of bright books. This *should* fit in, on its side, I reckoned. I resisted the idea, and then tested it and it worked, slipping in easily, achieving instant anonymity. Part of me didn't like it. I felt it should be hidden in some dark recess, but there was no truly safe place for it. I would have to take my chances. Besides, right then, its pages remained blank. It struck me then that for all the vastness of the castle, there was no safe hiding place, for either my things, or for me.

I checked my outer door was closed, and then I took to my desk. I rang directory inquiries.

'A gallery, in London's Cork Street. The name is Toby Hood.'

I began to sketch something on the first page as I waited. A woman's naked form took shape. I stopped, wrote down the number on the next page. I took a breath and dialled.

He answered. I recognized his voice straightaway.

'Toby. It's Morganna Hutton.'

There was a pause. 'Ah! And to what do I owe this honour?'

'Toby, I—'

'You've found a bigger, glitzier gallery, who've promised to make you a star, make your fortune, put you on the pages on every glossy—'

'Toby, hold—'

'Nice of you to tell me. I wrote to you. I bloody rang you. Not a squeak. When can I expect the exhibition?'

I said nothing. I felt punched by his onslaught. Finally I spoke. 'God, you're a queen.'

He at least had the grace to laugh.

'You're also an idiot. Can you shut up for a full minute, while I speak?'

'I'll do my best.'

'When I left you, Toby, I was as happy as I've been for a long time. I drove back to Scotland, and, just as I was approaching home, I crashed. I was in a coma for seven weeks, then in hospital for another five weeks. I've only been home a week or so.'

He was silent. I could almost feel him forming the images.

'Jesus. I'm sorry.' His voice was low, rough.

'Well, I'm alive, Toby, more so than ever. And, thank God, my daughter is alive.'

'Oh, Morganna, congratulations.'

'Thank you. And, Toby, I can still paint.'

'You can?'

'I think so. And it feels better than before, but it's portraits I'm into now, more than landscapes. I've still got loads of landscapes here, as good as the ones you've got, but I thought you should know.'

'Mmm. Are they any good, the portraits?'

'Well, I've only done a couple, but, yes, I think so. Does your offer still stand?'

'Of bloody course it does.'

'Fine. I'll keep up with the new stuff, bring it down when I can, that and lots of my old landscapes.'

We discussed details for a while, and he gave me a date. November thirteenth. As planned first time around. I wrote it in my book in big letters. I wanted to be free, alone with Georgie by then.

'By the way, there's something I'd like to ask you, in complete confidence,' I said.

'Fire away.'

'There was a painter, may or may not be alive still. A man. He was painting in the seventies. Sailed a boat around the South of France. Painted nudes. Other stuff as well no doubt, but he was meant to be best at nudes.'

'Mmm. What about him? You a bidder?'

'In a manner of speaking. I don't know who he is. I need a name. I need to know if he's still alive, and where he is.'

'Not asking much are you?'

'And I need you to tread extremely carefully, and not to mention my name in connection with this. Not at any cost.'

He fell silent for a while. 'I don't suppose you'll tell me what this is about?'

'I can't, Toby. But if you can, do this for me.'

'I can't promise anything, other than that I will be utterly discreet, and that your name will not come into it.'

'Thank you. But I also don't want it getting around that you're asking about him. Okay?'

'Whatever you say, Morganna. I'm sure you have your reasons.'

'Oh, believe me, I do.'

'You still on the same number?'

'Toby, I know this will sound strange, but don't call me, will you. I'll ring you.'

'Yes, it does sound strange. But then you're an artist . . .'

'I am. Might as well exact some dispensation. I'll ring you tomorrow.'

'Morganna, this might take a while, especially since I have to be so discreet.'

'I know. I'll still ring you every day, anyway.'

'Is it that urgent?'

'Yes.'

'Ever thought of getting a mobile?'

'I've always loathed them, but I can see their advantages.'

'Do us all a favour, and get one. Best way of dealing with a jealous husband.'

'Yes, I can see that.'

I smiled to myself. Rosamond, I'm on your trail.

Chapter forty-six

I decided to go for a walk with Jelly. The weather had turned during the day. The sun and a steady breeze had chased away the clouds, and the sky was brilliant.

I grabbed my whistle, Geoffrey's lovely gift, and, Jelly darting round my heels herding me like an ersatz sheep, I headed not for the sea, I was still wary of the cliff, of the rough footing, but for the hills. I wanted to stand somewhere high, and gaze over the landscape. Unconsciously, I headed for Ben's mountain.

I had forgotten how beautiful this landscape was. In the distance, receding into infinity, were row upon row of mountains, some clumpy in outline, some almost serrated. All of them faded to blue on the horizon. In the foreground were the moors, miles of undulating bleakness that remained beautiful. And dotted all around were the sand-rimmed lochs, smooth as a pane of glass, bearing the perfect reflection of the surrounding mountains. This was not the land of Macbeth but it wasn't hard to imagine him here, scanning the landscape for moving forests.

I walked well. The rough trail no longer made me wobble or sweat quite so copiously. I found Ben's tor, and slumped down at the top, against a cairn. Here I sat for half an hour, drinking in the heather and brine-scented wind and the view while Jelly tore about, coming back to me every five minutes to check I was okay.

Then, with that uncanny radar of his, Ben appeared, Gin at his heels.

I smiled. 'How did you know?' I asked. 'Is it you . . . or is it you?' I inquired, turning to Gin.

Ben gave a low chuckle. 'Shepherd's secret.'

'And I'm a sheep, am I?'

'In wolf's clothing,' he said. 'Like some lamb?'

'Anytime you have some, only I'll pay you this time.'

He made a half-gesture to shrug me off.

'Don't even try. You want me to eat it, don't you?'

'You look like you need a whole sheep.'

'Yeah, well, give me time.'

We said nothing for a while.

'You know it was I who found you,' he said.

It felt like the breath froze in me. I could hear his voice echoing down my memory. His kind words. His fear, and insistence.

'I had to pull you out. You were lying in water.'

I could feel it again, pulling me down, like it pulled my parents down. Only it got them. Without Ben, it would have got me and Georgie. A shudder ripped through me.

'If you hadn't been there, Ben, I wouldn't be here now. Neither would Georgie.'

'I wasn't there,' he said.

'What d'you mean?'

'I was asleep. Don't know if Gin woke me, or I woke myself, but I was awake, and I knew something had happened to you. I just pulled on coat and boots and ran.'

'Jesus. Ben.' I tried to decipher this.

'What happened? How did it happen?' he asked.

'I don't know,' I answered. 'I can't remember.'

He looked at me for a long time, and then nodded. He could see right through me. We both knew it. I did-n't want to lie to this kind sweet man, but I was not ready to tell him the truth with all the lengthy conse-quences that implied. He sat there for a while, and we stared out across the moor in silence. He stirred, got to his feet.

'I'll drop by later then, with the lamb.'

He nodded by way of goodbye.

Chapter forty-seven

I had lunch in the splendour of the dining room, blissfully alone. Rosamond and Archie had failed to return from whatever important business they had rushed off to. I'd just eked out an extra hour with Georgie when Melissa the cook came looking for me.

'Someone to see you, Ma'am,' she said to me. At least she seemed to know the proper form of address. I'd have expected her to call me *Miss*.

It was Ben, standing a respectable distance off the front doors, proprietarily hanging onto a plastic bag. Ben glanced aggressively at Melissa as she wheeled off, leaving me with him.

'Tried to take it off me, she did. I won't be feeding *her*.'

I knew who he meant. 'You probably are.'

'Not with my best stuff.'

'Ah.' I glanced around, walked a few more steps from the doors, took him with me.

'Tell me why you hate her?'

'You know why.'

'*Tell* me,' I insisted.

'Trust what's in your head.'

'Ben, there's too much *noise* in my head. And sometimes there's *nothing*.'

He gave me a fleeting smile, and then he was sombre once again.

'Bad blood. The lot of them. Hated her father. She's worse.'

'Mmm.'

'How much longer are you going to stick it out?' he asked.

'Long as I have to.'

'Get out, Morganna. Get your daughter and go.'

'Oh, Ben. If it were that simple.'

'Send her packing for a start. Ship her off in her fancy boat.'

'In her *what*?'

'The *Gypsy Rose*.'

'Hang on, Ben.' We moved farther away from the castle.

'You don't know about it?' he asked.

'No, I bloody don't.'

'A yacht. Arrived Christmas time. Called the *Gypsy Rose*. Great big thing, fifty foot at least, blue hull. She's out on the thing almost every day, on her own, or with Archie, all weathers.' He paused, shifted awkwardly. 'There's something else too. I've been arguing with myself for weeks.'

'What is it, Ben?'

'There was a woman on the boat. With Archie.'

I could feel the blood pounding in my ears. 'What did she look like?'

'Young, long blonde hair. Skinny as a sick lamb.'

I nodded my head. I could scarcely see. So he'd brought his little mistress here, to show off his boat and his castle. To what was meant to be my home. To show off what might be hers when he's divorced me, I supposed.

'Where is it, this boat?' I managed to ask.

'Moored off Crescent beach, couple a miles away.'

I put my head in my hands.

'I'm sorry, Morganna.'

I raised my eyes. 'I knew already, Ben.'

He nodded. 'But not about the boat?'

'No. That's another nice little secret they failed to keep.'

'And you paid for it.'

'Like everything around here, yes. Look, Ben, don't let on that I know about it, will you?'

'I won't tell a soul,' he said. 'But aren't you going to have it out with them? With him?'

I shook my head.

'Why ever not?'

'I can't, Ben. If I start down that road.'

'What, you're just going to let them get away with it, spend all your money, bleed you dry. Betray you, after you've had his child and all?'

'No. I'm not, Ben. But I have to fight this my way.'

He looked at me in silence, gave a slight shake of his head.

'I hope you know what you're doing, Morganna.'

With that, he handed me the plastic bag, turned, and walked away.

'So do I, Ben. So do I.'

I took the bag up to my little kitchen: a leg of lamb, a small bag of potatoes, rosemary, a couple of carrots, a handful of cabbage. He had picked out an entire meal for me. My eyes pricked with tears. Damn him.

I grabbed a coat, and Jelly and I headed for Crescent beach. It would be the longest walk I'd yet attempted, but rage was a wonderful thing. I walked fast, oblivious to the effort. When I arrived at the perfect, golden horseshoe of sand, lungs burning, heart pounding, and legs trembling, all I noticed was what lay before me, like a scene from a picture postcard. Bobbing gently in the sheltered cove, was one of the most beautiful boats I had ever seen, and, being brought up in Long Island, I'd seen a few. Fifty feet of pure speed machine, but stable enough to deal with the Atlantic too by the look of her. What was I looking at? One million, two? The *Gypsy Rose*. The vanity and the sheer ravening greed of it sickened me. I squatted down, looked at that boat, visualized Archie's lover giggling on deck, and I actually began to shake. So he had continued to betray me, my husband, while his mother was mugging me on a daily basis, and all I could do was smile and pretend I knew nothing of it.

Perhaps it was the physical exertion, perhaps the emotion, but I really struggled to get back to the castle. Hauling myself up the stairs I felt like a climber struggling with altitude, battling to the summit of some Himalayan mountain. I sprawled exhausted on my bed, Jelly beside me. I wasn't sure how much more of this I could take. The urge to ring the bank, to summon Geoffrey was almost overwhelming. Just to have him call me, tell me he was fine would have been the best medicine, but I knew I was kidding myself. I wanted to tell him everything, to have him fly over here, sort everything out for me, but those days were gone. This wasn't a problem that he could just click his fingers and throw some money around and solve. It was a disaster of my own making, and only I could find the way out, for me and my daughter.

I started preparing supper, grateful for the distraction. I would eat Ben's treats up here, with Jelly for company. A discreet knock at the door startled me. Knife in hand, I opened it. My husband stood there. He stepped backwards, eyes fixed on the knife. I thought of him, and Rosamond, and his lover aboard the *Gypsy Rose*.

'Preparing some lamb for supper,' I said, lowering the knife to my side.

'From that bloody shepherd, I assume?'

'From Ben, yes.'

'I saw you earlier, talking with him. Deep in conversation you seemed.'

I could hardly believe this, when he brought his fucking woman here.

'And?' I managed to say.

'He's not exactly one of us is he, I mean, to be consorting with so closely. It seems to me you spend an awful lot of time with him.'

I forced in a deep breath, then another. Ammunition, I thought to myself. Do not give him any ammunition.

'He helps me with Jelly; he provides wonderful lamb.' I gave him what I hoped was an innocent look, as if to say, *what else could there be?*

He seemed only partially reassured, as well he might.

'Was there anything else?' I prompted.

'Actually, I came to see how you were.'

'Not bad.'

'Do you think you are completely recovered?'

'I'm getting better. I take one day at a time.'

He nodded. 'Do you still have amnesia, about the crash?'

'Still a black hole,' I said, flicking him a glance. His eyes were sharp, hunting. He found nothing, I thought.

He smiled, aiming for, and missing sympathy.

'I was thinking. Might be nice for you to go out with Georgie and Mrs. Myot in the car tomorrow. Go for lunch in Caithness.'

I was amazed. He had never before suggested that I spend time with my daughter.

'I'd love to,' I said quickly, instantly suspicious, but not about to turn down the chance of a day out with my daughter. If only I could have ditched Myot.

'Good. Leave here at, say, eleven?'

'I'll be ready.'

Was this a reward, I wondered, for not remembering, or something else altogether?

Chapter forty-eight

The next day I felt excited as a schoolgirl. I agonized for the first time in months over what to wear. I was a mother, going out with her child. I wanted to look like a proper mother, only I wasn't sure what one looked like. Not clad in tattered grubby jeans with mad hair, I thought. Finally I settled on a denim skirt, espadrilles, a red stripy T-shirt. I gave my hair a good brushing, and I twirled before the mirror. Not too bad, I thought. The sea air had worked its magic on my eczema, which was getting better every day. I still looked wasted, but not quite so skeletal as when I came out of hospital. I had Rosamond and her cook to thank for that.

At ten to eleven I headed for Georgie's rooms. Myot was there, fussing with a nappy bag. She nodded at me. I nodded back, and then went to my daughter. I gathered her up in my arms.

'We're going out, Georgie, you and your mother, to lunch!'

She seemed to think this was pretty funny.

'I'll take her down,' I said.

'Oh I think not,' replies Myot. 'Not on those stairs.'

'Mrs. Myot, I am not that decrepit I can assure you.'

'If anything happens . . .' she intoned ominously.

'Nothing will happen, I assure you. Everything will be fine.'

'Here, her comfort blanket,' Myot said, only partially mollified by my determination. She handed me a pale pink fleece blanket that Georgie grabbed onto with her own determined fingers. I carried her downstairs, strapped her into the intimidating-looking car seat contraption, made sure she had a good grip on her comfort blanket, and sat down beside her.

And everything *was* fine until we arrived in Caithness.

Mrs. Myot parked the Range Rover, and I got out to unstrap Georgie. She was asleep, had been for most of the journey. She looked almost drugged with sleep, and flushed. Instinctively, I felt her forehead.

'Gosh, you're hot,' I said.

'Babies often feel warm when they've been asleep,' responded Mrs. Myot quickly, coming round to Georgie's side.

I shook my head. 'Not this hot. I think something's wrong with her.'

'Rubbish,' Mrs. Myot muttered, not quite *sotto voce* enough. But she did reach out her hand and touch Georgie's forehead. She withdrew her hand quickly. She looked at me grudgingly.

'You're right. Georgiana has a temperature. A high one. We'd better go back, right away.'

I nodded, disappointed, but worried. Mrs. Myot got back into the driver's seat. I got back in beside Georgie. I watched her all the way home. Then I carried her up to her rooms. Mrs. Myot quickly got out a thermometer and took her temperature.

'Thirty-nine point eight. Not good,' she said. She went to the fridge and removed a bottle of pinkish liquid. She gave it a vigorous shake and poured out a spoonful. She woke Georgie and persuaded her to take it. Then she stripped her down, and began to sponge her body with a cold flannel. This made Georgie cry out.

'Need to get her temperature right down,' she said. 'And quickly.'

'What's wrong?' I asked, feeling sick with worry, relieved for the first time that Mrs. Myot, a trained nurse, was here.

'A virus of some kind, I think. I'll give her half an hour, and if her temperature doesn't come down, we'll call the doctor.'

I nodded. My little daughter, writhing in her nappy, looked unbearably vulnerable. Suddenly I felt cold.

'I'll just go and pull on a cardie. I'll be back in a minute.'

I hurried to my rooms. I wondered where Archie was. There was no sound of him or Rosamond anywhere. Out on the *Gypsy Rose*, perhaps?

I got to my room, pulled open the chest of drawers and dragged out a jersey. Just as I was hurrying out, I caught sight of the rubbish bin. It was groaning with bottles. One of wine, one of gin, and one of whisky. I looked at it in amazement. How on earth did they get there? And then I looked up. Stacked on my bookshelf, a bit down from where final settlement was hidden, there were more bottles, half-full, of gin and whisky and brandy. I stared at them in incomprehension. What the hell? I turned away and headed out onto the staircase. Whatever it was, it would have to wait. I hurried back to my daughter.

I was dimly aware of the sound of Archie's voice coming from the drawing room off the great hall. I shot past and headed for the south stairs, and back up to Georgie. She was lying on her back listlessly.

'How is she?' I asked Mrs. Myot.

'I'll take her temperature again in ten minutes, but I think the Calpol has kicked in. She's a tad happier.'

'She seems so,' I agreed.

I dragged the feeding chair so that it faced Georgie, and I sat down to watch her.

Mrs. Myot looked across at me. 'There's really no need for this. I am quite capable of watching a sick child. I cared for her when she came out of hospital, skinny, sickly preemie that she was.'

I hated hearing my daughter spoken of in those terms, however accurate they might be on the surface.

'This isn't about you, Mrs. Myot, about your competence or lack of it. It's about me, her mother, wanting to be here.'

She gave a reluctant nod. We both sat in silence, and waited. Ten minutes later, she took Georgie's temperature again.

'Thirty-seven point eight. Good. Still too high, but going in the right direction. No need for the doctor.'

I got to my feet. 'Great. I'll be back in a bit. Come and get me, please, if she gets any worse.'

'I'll do that, but don't worry yourself. Babies are funny little things, sick one minute, then suddenly quite all right.'

'I hope so.'

I went in search of Archie. I wanted to tell him his daughter wasn't well, and document what I thought would be his lack of interest.

He'd gone from the drawing room. I headed upstairs to his rooms. I knocked, but there was no reply. Cautiously, I opened the door and went in. I turned right, into his office. The drawing board dominated the room. His beautiful drawings were still pegged up. I jumped as the phone rang suddenly. I waited to see if he would rush in to answer it, but he didn't. The answer machine clicked on. A female voice spoke.

'Mr. Edge, this is Jo Bell. Er, look, I'm really sorry your wife didn't show up this morning. But don't feel bad, I am very used to dealing with people in denial, whether it's drink or drugs. Please just keep telling her we're here to help. I do agree that she really must get help soon. With her drinking as much as she obviously seems to be, especially given the state of her health, this is extremely serious, more so because of your daughter, and how she treats her. Anyway, give me a call, and we'll set up another time. We'll just keep trying until she does agree to see me. Thanks, bye. And good luck.'

I blinked at the phone. I thought I was about to explode with rage. I had get to get out of there. I could hardly see as I made for the door. I managed to get out, to close the door behind me, and hurry across the hall, up my staircase. As I was turning the corner, I literally ran smack into Archie. The plastic bag he was carrying swung into my leg. I gave a yelp. It clinked. Bottles. He grabbed me, steadied me, held me at arm's-length and examined me.

'Morgan. What's wrong?'

I struggled free and ran for my bedroom. I got in, closed the door, headed for my bathroom, and locked myself in. I leaned over the toilet bowl and retched as if my heart would come out. When there was nothing left in me, I straightened up. I splashed cold water on my face; I swilled some round my mouth and spat it out.

So Archie was doing his own final settlement on me, trying to expel me from my daughter's life. Only he was playing dirty, far dirtier than ever I could have imagined, and he was far further down the track than I was. I had thought I was so clever, so devious, but I was a fucking amateur compared to these people. I scribbled in my notebook, while he co-opted social services or alcohol concern or whatever the fuck it was, and he made his case. And how damning was it? Even though I was not supposed to, I apparently drank, heavily, and then I refused to admit I had a problem. No doubt he would get Myot, as well as Rosamond to testify against me. How clever he was. He got me out of the way with the ace he knew could not fail. The only problem was, my daughter got sick, and we returned home early. He hadn't bargained on that. I saw the bottles he meant to remove before I got home, and I heard the message destined for his ears only.

Suddenly I heard my bedroom door open.

'Morganna, open up,' he said.

I must not let him know what I've seen and heard. I opened the door just a fraction.

'You look terrible. What's wrong?' he asked.

'I've been sick,' I said. 'I'd been feeling funny earlier, but I didn't want to miss going out with Georgie, so I just carried on, but it didn't go away.'

I looked at him standing there with his fake concern and I wanted to put my hands around his neck and squeeze till he dropped dead at my feet. I felt I was dancing on the edge of hysteria.

'Er, Archie, I'm going to be sick again.' I turned away, but not before I'd seen the look of revulsion on his face. I raced for my bathroom, kicked shut the door and made retching sounds. Then I sat down on the chair by the bath. I waited until I heard him retreat. Only when I heard my door close did I come out.

I walked to the window, stared out at the sea. It was grey, unforgiving. The sky had the sick purple tinge that told me a storm was brewing. I stood there, and I tried to cool my blood. I tried to chill it, and I tried to think like them.

My phone rang, making me jump. I grabbed it up. 'Don't you ever answer this thing?' asked the wry seigniorial voice.

'Toby. I've been a tad distracted.'

'And I have been busy. I have a name for you.'

I felt my heart quicken. 'Yes?'

'There are two possible candidates. One drunk himself to death ten years ago.'

'And the other?'

'He lives in some squalor from what I gather, in deepest Dorset.'

'What's his name?'

'August Bryanston.'

I closed my eyes. 'Thank you, Toby. Will you be in London tomorrow?'

'Why?'

'I'm flying down, with some more paintings for my exhibition.'

'How wonderful. I'll be here.'

I packed, and then I forced myself to go downstairs for dinner. I had to keep up appearances more than ever.

They greeted me warily.

'Not still sick?' asked Rosamond

I shook my head. 'It seems to have passed. I can't say I'm exactly ravenous now, but I need to eat something.'

'Keep your strength up, and all that,' opined Rosamond.

'Exactly.'

And so we moved on from clichés to the bromide of the castle, the latest building hitch. Halfway through the vichyssoise, I told them.

'I'm flying down to London tomorrow. I want to drop off some paintings for my exhibition.'

I might as well have announced I was going to swim the channel.

'Good gracious me. Do you think you are *ready* for that?' asked Rosamond.

'For the flight, or the exhibition?' I asked sweetly.

'Either.'

'I won't know until I do it, will I?'

'I didn't know it had progressed so far, you and this, what *was* his name?'

'Hood. Toby Hood.'

'Ah, yes. Does ring a bell. Minor gallery in Cork Street.'

I wanted to laugh. A gallery in the country's capital city, in the street that runs through the centre of the art world, and still she had to put it down. Was this the jealousy of an artist manqué?

I sipped my soup.

'So, when's this exhibition then?'

'November.'

I saw her mind flying. She smiled, all jealousy gone. I'd be divorced and exiled by then. 'Good luck, darling,' she said, charm restored.

Back in my room, I rang Ben.

'It's Morganna.'

'Everything all right?' he asked quickly.

'Fine, but I need a favour, Ben.'

'Name it.'

'Could I drop Jelly off with you for a few days? I have to go to London.'

'What time you leaving?'

'Car's coming at seven.'

'I'll wait outside the castle.'

'Oh, Ben, thank you.'

He grunted. 'What're you up to?'

'Oh, just stuff to do with painting. I'll tell you when I get back.' I didn't want to say much on the phone. I could imagine all too easily Rosamond or Archie picking up some hidden extension, listening in.

'Watch yourself.'

'I will.'

I went then to see my daughter. I did this every night before I turned in. I crept though the castle with the furtiveness of an intruder. I stopped outside Georgie's bedroom, and I listened. This was always my stolen time, the only time I could be alone with my daughter. When I was sure the coast was clear, I opened the door as silently as I could, and tiptoed in. Then I crouched down by her cot, and just watched her, listening to the cadence of her breath. I had on a few occasions fallen asleep on the floor beside her, waking hours later. Then I scurried out, back to my rooms. I could not face a midnight confrontation with Myot. Especially not tonight.

'I'll be gone for a few days,' I whispered.

I reached out and touched her forehead. She was warm, but not hot. The fever seemed to have gone. She looked fine, lying there, arms flung out, apparently without a care in the world. She stirred slightly, uttered the slightest moan. As I gazed at her, my heart flipped over with love. Living without her was unthinkable. Allowing her to be taken from me was not an option.

I changed into my pyjamas and slipped into bed. Jelly slept sentry beside me. I had a restless night, punctuated by dreams, some of which I could recall. I saw my mother, walking down a street. She kept glancing back, over her shoulder, at me. Her black hair hung like a curtain, and I could not properly see her eyes. She seemed to be leading me somewhere, but I was not quick enough to keep up. I struggled. I could feel the breath rattling in my lungs, but I lost her.

I awoke rigid. I got up, showered, and dressed quickly. My suitcase was packed. My canvases were ready, rolled individually, and clustered together like a collection of tubes. Ten of them, including the murderess's hands.

The car came for me at seven. I tiptoed softly downstairs, shadowed by Jelly. Of Archie and Rosamond, there was no sign. Ben was standing in the rain, waiting as promised. I took Jelly to him, gave her a cuddle, and him a kiss goodbye.

'What are you up to?' Ben asked.

'I'll tell you when I get back.'

'Be careful.'

'I will.'

They watched me, eyes grave, as I left.

Chapter forty-nine

The taxi dropped me outside Toby's gallery. I stood there, paintings under my arm, case at my feet, and cast my mind back. People walked past, but it felt as if they weren't really there. In my mind, the street was as it was, semideserted, months ago, and I was standing here, full of hope, reaching out for my lifeline. It felt to me that if only I could have summoned sufficient will I could have gone back there.

I pushed open the door and walked in. The cool white walls welcomed me. The door closed behind me, shutting out the noise of the street. Toby was sitting at the desk at the far end of the gallery. He looked up. I walked towards him. His eyes were on my face, but he did not smile. I sat down before him.

'Good God,' he said softly.

I raised my eyebrows and waited.

'I didn't know you.'

'Most people are sufficiently polite to conceal their surprise. I suppose that was asking too much in you.'

'Most people never get beyond the superficial.'

I shrugged. His artistic snobberies were his business.

'What happened to your hair?'

'They shaved it off, for God's sake.'

'And your leg?'

'It broke in two places.'

'Will you always limp?'

'It's half an inch shorter now, so yes, I always will.' I hadn't thought it showed.

'And what happened to your eyes?'

'The scales fell.' I gave him the paintings. He studied them, pausing at the hands.

'This is your best work. I love it. So elegant, yet every sinew, every age spot and shadow is delivered up with a savage eye.'

'Thank you.'

'Who is it?'

'My mother-in-law.'

'Ah. And where does she live?'

'With me. At Wrath Castle.'

'Shouldn't she be tucked away in some dower house?'

I smiled. I relished our exchanges. They were like bitter chocolate to me, but I was too restless to indulge. I got to my feet. 'I have to go. You have the address?'

For a moment he looked blank.

'Augustus Bryanston.'

'You're going there now?'

I shook my head. 'First thing in the morning.'

He reached into his desk, drew out a piece of paper, handed it to me. I read it, pocketed it, and got up to go. He reached out, took hold of my hand. His eyes studied mine and I saw the silent sentences scud across. I knew what he didn't say. The last time I left him, I drove to disaster. I was weary with warnings, with portents of doom.

'See you on the twelfth.'

I smiled. 'Of November,' I replied, while the voice in my head mocked: *of never*.

I took a taxi to the Ritz. I walked through the gilded marble foyer to Reception.

'I'd like a suite, please, overlooking the river.'

The man paused just a second too long before he spoke. 'Certainly, Madame. Let me see what is available. For how long will you be staying?'

'Two nights.'

He consulted his computer.

'We have the Wellington Suite.' He cast a quick look up and down, taking in my jeans, my leather jacket. 'It's nine hundred pounds a night,' he said, almost reprovingly, as if embarrassed to reveal anything so base, but forced into doing so by my patently unrealistic ambitions.

I smiled, and handed over my platinum credit card. It had the desired effect, soothed the wrinkles from his brow, and I was rewarded with a smile of oleaginous warmth as he took the imprint.

'If you could just fill out this form, please, Madame.'

Name, address, signature.

I scribbled in the necessary places.

He scanned it quickly. His eyes widened visibly as he encountered Wrath Castle. What slaves you are still, to wealth and privilege, despising them as you fall to your knees, I thought to myself.

'Any bags, Madame?'

'Nothing I cannot manage,' I replied, as he handed over my key.

My suite was truly magnificent. *The mind a hell of heaven can make, and a heaven of hell.* I tried to enjoy its padded luxury, but I was too impatient. I wanted to be done, I wanted to be free, I wanted to end this game.

I rang down to the concierge.

'I would like a car and a driver tomorrow, ready at nine, to take me to Dorset and then back here.'

'Certainly, Madame. I'll look into it. Would you like me to advise you of the cost first?'

'No, thank you. Just arrange it. Oh, and I'd like a lunch hamper for two, with two bottles of Cristal, two Puligny Montrachet, and two Château Talbot. Have the sommelier pick good years.'

'Certainly, Madame. Both champagnes and the Montrachet chilled?'

'Just one of each chilled. The others are to be gifts.'

As I hung up, I thought of Geoffrey. Fascinated by the sheer concept of it, he always used to say, *it is so wonderfully fungible, isn't it, money?* And so it was. Gift and weapon, delivered in one blow.

Away from Wrath Castle, away from listening ears, I decided it was time to call the bank.

I rang Mary-Beth.

'Hi. It's Morganna.'

'Well heck, long time no speak.'

'I know. Look, how's Geoffrey?'

There was the slightest pause.

'He's been fine. He used to ring in every week or so, check on things, ask if you'd phoned. I tell you, if you hadn't sent all those e-mails he'd have been just a tad worried.'

E-mails. Jesus. So that's what she'd been doing, Rosamond. She'd got hold of my computer, intercepted my e-mails and sent her own, purporting to be from me. I'd completely forgotten all about the computer. I hadn't even used it once, before the crash. I had no recollection of it even being delivered. All I remember was telling Archie I needed one, to e-mail Geoffrey. He'd said he'd order one, and that was the last of my involvement with it. But not Rosamond's.

'Morganna? You still there?'

'Er, yeah, Mary-Beth. Sorry. So Geoffrey's ringing in every week, and he's fine. Where is he?'

'Well, we think he's doing the big crossing, Ecuador to the Pacific, possibly via the Galapagos.'

'And?'

'Well, last time he rang, three weeks ago, he said he was having trouble with his sat phone, and that was after having his computer stolen in the Caribbean. So he's sorta incommunicado. We reckon he's fine, but his phone must of gone down, and he's right in the middle of the ocean, will be for a few more weeks.'

'Right,' I answered slowly. 'So you don't know for sure he's okay, or where he is?'

'Well, we know his plans, and we know he's meant to be right in the middle of that crossing, and we knew his phone was giving him problems, so we're not worried, Morganna.'

I took in a long, slow breath. 'Okay, right, well when he does call, will you tell him I'm fine, but that I need to talk to him. I'm at the Ritz in London for the next two days, so he can reach me there if by some chance his phone gets back up and you speak to him soonish, but otherwise he's not to call me at Wrath Castle. I'll just keep trying you at the bank, and then I'll work out how to ring him. Presumably when he makes landfall he can get a new phone.'

'We've couriered one to Fiji.'

'Good.'

'Is everything all right, Morganna? You sound worried.'

'I'd just like to speak to him.'

'And let me tell ya, him to you, too.'

I hung up and thought about Rosamond, about her climbing into my head, e-mailing Geoffrey, being me.

Chapter fifty

I headed down in the lift and took a taxi to Embankment Gardens. It was quiet. There was no-one around. As I withdrew Archie's key (that's how I thought of it now, his, not mine), I felt like a thief. I let myself in and walked up to the third floor. I unlocked his door, crossed his threshold, and, literally, shuddered with repugnance. Home of my early dreams, I hated it even then. His badger's set, into which I had strayed. I picked up the phone and rang the castle.

Rosamond herself answered. 'Darling, how are you?'

'Fine, I just got to the flat. I'm absolutely shattered. You might have been right, this might all be a bit too soon for me.'

'I *did* warn you.'

'I know. I'll go to the gallery tomorrow, then either fly back, or spend one more night here, depending how tired I am.'

'Do pace yourself, darling.'

'I will. I'm going to have a bath now, then turn the phone off, and go to sleep for a while.'

'Good idea.'

'Give Georgie a kiss for me, will you?'

'Of course, darling. Bye.'

I hung up, and began my search. It took me hours, in which I found nothing of interest, from any perspective, but then, in a box in the tiny attic, I hit gold. An old box with a dusty lid that made me sneeze. Inside were four photograph albums.

They started, as this whole story seemed to, with Wrath Castle. There she was, the steely look and tilted jaw instantly recognizable, even as a young child. She sat in her father's arms, or held his hand as they stood before the enormous front door; the king with his little princess. Of the queen, there was no sign. She had died, of course, giving birth to that princess. But where were the earlier pictures of her, the wedding photos? Had she been so easily forgotten, after she had done her duty and provided a Baby Edge, even if it was a female? Or, did her image lie forgotten in some other dusty attic?

I wondered who had lovingly stuck all these pictures into these albums? Had it been Rosamond herself? They had the patina of age, but it could have been another of Archie's labours of love. I could see him hunting down old albums in some auction house, stripping out the unfortunate subjects with a deft flick of a razor, and pasting over the smudges the history of his mother's life. Why then would they lie untouched in his attic?

I flicked on. Rosamond at her wedding to Archie's father. That is the first time I had ever seen a picture of him, and the oddness of that suddenly struck me. In the castle, there were countless window ledges, side tables, God knows what manner of surfaces on which to display a silver-framed photograph, yet there were none. It seemed almost as if her past was to Rosamond what mirrors were to a vampire.

I studied her husband. He was handsome, elegant in

his tails. He smiled with bland well-being; the groom who had won his fair bride. And how she dazzled, his bride, in the family tiara that I too wore. On his face there was no sign of the fate to which he had married himself, no shadow of foreboding. But then, neither was there on mine. Just joy. In retrospect, I must have looked just as blithe and vulnerable.

I was filled suddenly with a hatred so intense I felt I could burn to a cinder. As the rage abated, a great tiredness welled in like an ebb tide. I had to get out of here quickly. If I blacked out here I too would become dust. I had not looked at all the pictures. I knew it was a risk, but I had to take it. I replaced the albums in the dusty box, and hauled it out of the attic and down the collapsible stairs. With a rod I pushed up the stairs. They rose up and folded away like a circus trick. I closed the trap door, hung up the rod in its place, and headed for the bedroom.

The air was stale, repugnant. I pulled back the sheets, forced myself in, writhed around, and then got out. In the kitchen and bathroom, I ran the taps, wet the towels, left one rumpled on the floor.

Then, confident that the flat would betray only what I wanted it to, I left with my haul.

There was a new shift of staff on duty at the Ritz. They gave me more than a cursory glance as I entered their world, dusty and dishevelled. They actually stopped me.

'Can I help you, Madame?' said one.

'Yes, you can get out of my way,' I answered.

Something in my eyes must have spoken to him too, for he stepped back to let me pass. I felt his eyes on me as I waited for the lift. I could still feel their mark on my back as I travelled up to my splendid refuge.

Inside, I ran the bath, and called room service. I washed off my revulsion in a sea of bubbles. Clean, wrapped in the heaviest of towelling robes, I sat down to a club sandwich and glass of creamy hot chocolate.

I slept as I used to. No presence, real or imagined, stalked my night. I awoke refreshed. I took a wonderful shower in the Art Deco bathroom. I was dressed just as room service arrived with coffee, the freshest of orange juice, and croissants. I sat overlooking the river, and ate with an appetite I could scarcely remember. Only then did the full oppression of the life I was living hit me. The hammer stopped, the weight lifted. I could breathe, I could smile, I could be, and not have to act, or fear. But I missed my daughter with an ache that was tangible. I needed a knockout blow, if I was to stand any chance of getting her. I could only pray that today would provide me with one.

The car, a midnight blue Mercedes, was waiting at seven, hamper and bottles inside. I took with me a bottle of Evian water. The driver greeted me solicitously. I had given the concierge the address the night before, and the driver had already planned the route, which he attempted to check with me.

'I've never been there,' I told him. 'And I'm sure your guess is a lot better than mine.'

'All right then, Madame. If you're comfortable, off we go.'

I had my hoard with me. I sat in the back, flicking through visions of Rosamond's life. In the third album,

I found what I was looking for: a boat, glittering sunshine almost managing to filter through the black-and-white images, Rosamond, head thrown back, laughing beside a man who gazed not at the camera, but always at her. The same man was captured several times, standing before an easel, paintbrush in hand, frowning at the canvas. In one picture, the model too was captured. Rosamond, naked in all her twenty-odd-year-old splendour. I pulled out the photograph. The back was blank. I studied the artist's face. *Were you the right one?* I asked silently. Please be the right one.

Only when we had left London behind did I look up to see the gentle folds of the English countryside passing by me. We could live here, Georgie and I, and here, I thought, as I spied beautiful houses perched on hillsides. I was like a child in a sweetshop. It did not occur to me that I might have been on the wrong track.

Chapter fifty-one

Stiff hours later, we found the house, at the end of a long lane. It was like something that time had forgotten. Brambles climbed untamed over the grey stone facade. An ancient wisteria fought for supremacy.

He might have been out, but I doubted it. It seemed near impossible to gain entry or make exit from that wizened little home. There must have been a back door. Round the side of the cottage, I walked cautiously, heart accelerating. A bramble snared my leg and drew blood. I picked my way to the back door, waited a beat, and then knocked. Nothing. Perhaps I should have rung. Perhaps he was mobile, perhaps this was his day to go up to London, visit his old haunts, but even as I thought that, I doubted it. I knocked again, I called out: 'Mr. Bryanston, my name's Morganna Edge. I've come to—'

A creaking sound from above silenced me. For a moment I feared that molten lead might be poured down upon me, and I jumped back. Instead, a head emerged, grey hair tangled as the brambles. The eyes that pinpointed me were small and sharp and curious. It was the man in the photographs, beauty cruelly betrayed by age. And, I was sure, this was the man who had given Rosamond her alibi. This was her accessory to murder.

'I'll come down,' said a voice gravelled by a million cigarettes.

He opened the door and eyed me again. 'Morganna Edge,' he said, mulling me over.

'You have something of the same in your eyes, but you are more beautiful than she. Are you a daughter?'

'Daughter-in-law,' I answered. She inhabited still, the forefront of his mind.

'Ah. Come in then.'

The place reeked of smoke. I could hardly breathe. All the windows were shut tight against the inroads of the sun as if there were treasures there to protect. And there were. His treasures. His paintings. They covered the walls, some framed, most unframed, perhaps done in the years when penury bit. I stopped to study them. Ahead of me he paused, watching my contemplation. They were magnificent. Just one, surely, would have translated into a gardener, a cleaner, a cook, for God's sake. The man's baggy, thick cords could not conceal the skin and bones beneath. I turned slowly, as if feeling other eyes upon me. There was a staircase, and, looking down from halfway up the stairs, was the portrait of Rosamond, nude on the boat. Her head was thrown back, neck exposed with the blithe confidence of the predator.

'Magnificent, isn't she?'

I turned to the walnut eyes. 'The portrait is magnificent.'

He smiled for the first time, and gave me a tiny bow. 'You know anything about painting?'

'Not much, but I paint, so I know a little bit about what goes into it.'

'You any good?'

'I like to think so.'

'Exhibitions?'

'One in this coming November.'

347

'Where?'

'Toby Hood. Cork Street.'

He dipped his head. 'I'm impressed. Not bad for a . . . ?'

'Twenty-one-year-old.'

'You'll forgive me for saying, but you look older.'

'God, you older men don't pull your punches, do you?'

He chuckled. 'That's because we've given up trying to bed you.'

'Ah.'

His hands fell limp by his sides, as if the joking was over. We stood in the hallway.

'So, on what mission has she sent you?'

'She hasn't. She doesn't know I'm here, and I don't want her to.' That much was true.

'So why are you here?'

'For her birthday. I'm compiling a short book, a sort of memoir, of her youth, recollections, pictures,' I smiled, 'that sort of thing.' That, too, was true.

He eyed me again and I felt his radar, seeking out the truth.

'She is a mythomane, and a fabulist. She always did love records, mementos. You chose well.'

For a while I lost him to his memories. He extracted himself as from a cooling bath, with reluctant speed. 'Come on, we can't stand here in the hallway all day.'

I paused. 'I've got something outside, in the car. I'll just go and get it.'

I negotiated the brambles. The chauffeur wanted to carry the things himself.

'I'll take them,' I insisted. I did not want to draw

attention to him. I wanted Bryanston to think we were alone. I struggled in with the hamper, and then came back for the bottles.

Bryanston's eyes widened, and I saw the hunger, not just for the food and drink I had brought, but for what they represented.

I spread out the baguette, cured ham, tomatoes, lettuce, and Camembert. I hunted in the cupboards for plates. I washed them, dried them, and set them in place. I did the same with knives and forks, all the while watched in silence. I found glasses, but handed the champagne to Bryanston, who held it for a while before opening it, which he did, as I knew he would, expertly.

He poured out two glasses. I should not have been drinking, but I could not have held back entirely if I wanted this to go my way.

'You came prepared,' he said.

'I like to eat well. I thought you would too.'

'Rosamond must be doing well?'

I smiled, but said nothing.

I sipped my champagne. It went like a bullet to my brain. I felt a wild slug of euphoria. And I felt reckless as the sea.

'Where did you train?' he asked.

'Florence. Under Nardizzi.'

He nodded his approval. 'Is that where you developed your taste for good living?'

No. That was born out of a brush with death. 'Here and there,' I said.

'Where are you from?'

'America.'

He raised an unsatisfied eyebrow.

'Long Island.'

'In a house like the Great Gatsby,' he jested.

'Exactly,' I answered, and, for a moment, he froze. He tilted the glass to his lips and took not a sip, but mouthfuls, as if it had been water. I cut some cheese, and pretended not to notice.

'What was your maiden name?'

'Hutton,' I answered.

At this, he got up and walked from the room. When he returned, his face was flushed. I saw damp stains on the frayed cuffs of his shirt. He had been splashing his face with cold water.

'So, tell me about Rosamond,' I said. 'It seems she was the belle of the South of France.'

He smiled. I seemed to have given him a lifeline, and, I hoped, within it, a noose for another.

'She was magnificent. She had this wild beauty, she was *sauvage*, she practically tingled with danger.' He looked at me confidently. 'We were lovers, of course. You worked that out, no doubt.'

'Yes.'

'She was married, but not happily. Anyway,' he ran quickly from the spectre of the husband, words tumbling. 'She had to be in the South, sourcing all her antiques. She was like a magnet. Beautiful things just came to her.' He paused, puzzlement wrinkling his brow. 'But she seemed to like me, favour me against the men with the bigger yachts, the bigger wallets, the grand houses. I don't know why.'

'I've seen pictures of you. You were beautiful yourself.'

He smiled an old man's sweet, wistful smile. 'I was, but time hasn't been kind, has it?'

I looked around, I drained my glass. 'Why not?'

His eyes locked on to mine. 'I lost the knack for painting, and then, I suppose, for life.' He paused. 'No,' he corrected himself. 'I lost the appetite for both.'

'What happened?'

He shook his head. He poured me, then himself, another glass. 'Come on, let's talk of happier things.'

And so we talked, and we drank, and the next thing I knew, I was slipping away. I was on the floor, and he was crouched above me, face contorted with worry. 'Wake up, wake up,' he was saying. 'Oh please. Can you hear me?' he implored. I tried to speak, but I was not sure what was coming out. I was still underwater, trying to surface, flailing. I thrashed about, sat bolt upright, covered my face with my hands. I felt so godawfully bad. Each blackout seemed to get worse. Each exit seemed to get harder, and I feared, I really feared, that one day perhaps I would not manage it. I must have been mad to have drunk anything, but I felt I had no choice, not if I were going to succeed in loosening his tongue. He crouched before me, wizened face etched with concern. He reached out, hesitantly touched my cheek.

'Are you all right?'

I stared back at him. I could say nothing.

'Water?' he said, pushing himself up. He returned with a glass brimful. I took it with a trembling hand. The water splashed down my T-shirt. The cold was like a slap. I drank a sip, then in gulps drained the glass.

Slowly, I felt some semblance of normality return to my body. My face, and my hands, were still like ice. I hugged my hands under my arms, and gazed across at this man.

'What happened?' he was asking.

'Drink. I'm not supposed to.'

'Alcohol makes you black out?'

'Many things make me.'

'Have you always been like this?'

'No. Since the crash.'

'What crash?' he asked in a whisper.

'Car crash. Ended up in a coma. I came out of it but I slip back, that's how it feels when I black out.'

'Can you get up?' he offered me his hand and pulled me up. His skin was papery. He had less strength in him than I did. He got me to the sofa and made me sugary tea, which I drank like it was an elixir.

'Is that why you have a driver?' he asked.

'You saw him?'

'I'm not blind.'

'I'm not allowed to drive.'

'Lucky she has money.'

I gave a bitter chuckle. I could not help myself. 'No, *she* doesn't have money. *I* have money.'

'A lot?'

'A lot.'

'Millions?'

'Last time I looked, yes.'

'How long have you been married?'

Long enough. Too long. 'One and a half years.'

'And where do you live?'

'We live in Wrath Castle. All of us.'

At this, he winced. I watched him in amazement. My words seemed to have acted on him as a bullet. He held his stomach. Finally he spoke.

'She is back in.'

'Yes. It is her son's gift to her. The castle has been renovated.'

'With your money.'

'With my money.' I paused. 'So yes, she's back. Once again, chatelaine.'

'And you are not?'

'Not since my accident, no.'

He got up, and began to pace. He looked agitated, angry even. I could not begin to guess what was going on within him. He stopped, bent towards me, almost hissed at me.

'You have to go. Now. Now.'

Alarmed, I got to my feet. There was madness there, and I wanted to be away. I got to my feet, raised my hands. 'I'm going.'

I gathered up my bag. 'I'm sorry if I upset you,' I said. This seemed to provoke him more, so I moved off rapidly down the hall.

'Your bottles,' he called after me.

'Keep them,' I said. 'That's why I brought them.'

I got to the car. I felt his eyes upon me as I climbed in. The driver closed my door, glanced up, and then moved round and got in. He started up the car, and, with a low growl, it bore us down the lane, and off.

In the back seat, I slumped back. I had failed.

Chapter fifty-two

Back in my suite I paced like a caged animal. I *could* not give up. There must have been something I could do. If I could have another pretext to stay in touch with Bryanston, come at him from a different angle. Anything, just to keep the game alive. I rang Toby Hood.

'What's the story with Bryanston?' I demanded.

'Good afternoon to you too, Morganna.'

'Mmm. Yeah, well, not so good.'

'Did you visit him?'

'I did.'

'And?'

'Looks like he hardly eats. Like he wants to die, a self-imposed sentence, to a long, lingering death.'

'Doesn't surprise me. Word is, he's a bit of a crackpot. Schizophrenic. Quite a bad one from what I hear. Hasn't painted for twenty years. Can't. Or won't.'

'He's starving, yet he's got all these beautiful paintings, *his* paintings, on the wall. Is there no market for them?'

'He's not fashionable, but there's always a market for beautiful things.'

'He has one, a nude woman, on a yacht. It's called *Prelude*.'

'I *know* it. He has it, does he? Caused a furor at the time. His subject, his muse, was married. The portrait practically flaunted their affair. She had an affair with Picasso too, and he painted her, several times. Anyway, husband died soon afterwards, and the whole thing seemed to die down too. Beautiful portrait, beautiful woman,' he added, as an afterthought.

'My mother-in-law,' I said.

He gave a low whistle. I felt the cogs of his mind whirring.

'She wants to buy the portrait, and you are the go-between?' he hazarded.

'How much?' I asked.

He laughed. 'Pluck a figure. Depends how much she wants it.'

'Oh, she wants it.'

'Depends then, on how much money she has.'

It was my turn to laugh. 'Let's just say her budget is effectively unlimited.'

'Then give the old boy a hundred grand.'

'Will you handle it for me?'

He paused. 'Why?'

'Because you owe me a favour.'

'I thought I'd paid in full when I found his address.'

'That was just a down payment. Do this for me and we'll call it quits.'

'When?'

'Tomorrow, of course.'

'Fine. I'll just wipe clean my diary.'

'He's old, Toby. I don't think he has much longer to live.'

'But a few days here or there?'

'Would make a difference to me. What's your bro-kerage?'

'Oh, I'm allowed to charge for my services, am I?'

'As you wish.'

'Two, then.'

'I'll come round now, with the cheques.'

'You're very confident he'll sell.'

'Mmm.'

'I think I'll just telephone him first.'

'As you wish.'

He rang me back ten minutes later.

'You have a deal.'

'Good.'

'Do you always get your way, Morganna?'

'If only.'

'There *is* one condition,' he said slowly.

'Yes?'

'He wants one of your paintings in return. As well as the money.'

'Give him one,' I replied.

'Which?'

'The murderess's hands,' I said, before I could stop myself.

'What?'

'My-mother-in-law.'

He laughed. He thought it was a joke.

'I'll bring the cheques round now, shall I?'

I scribbled them out and hurried downstairs. The doorman whistled for a taxi. Five minutes later I was in Cork Street, dodging the tide of homeward-bound pedestrians flowing towards me with unyielding purpose. Toby let me in. It was quiet, sepulchral and calm in his gallery. He flipped the sign to 'Closed' and locked the door behind me. He was smoking his pipe and the air was rich with the smell of it.

We sat on opposite sides of his desk. I rummaged in my bag, handed over the cheques.

'I wonder what else he might have,' he said, depositing the cheques in a tin that he replaced in a drawer. 'Since I'll be there anyway.'

'What're you plotting?'

'If there's a lot of stuff and it's as good as you say, I might think of staging an exhibition for the old boy. If he'll let me.'

I laughed. 'He will. She won't.'

'Who won't?'

'Never mind. Try, anyway. It might make him interested in living again in whatever little time he has left.'

'You sound like you have the ear of the grim reaper. What makes you so sure he's not long for this world?'

I could see it when it landed on someone, the mark of death. We all can see it, we just choose not to. I shook my head.

'Thanks, Toby, for all of this,' I said, getting to my feet.

'My pleasure. I'm not quite sure what I am doing here, who is doing exactly what for whom and why, but one thing's for certain. I'm not bored.'

'Now *that* would be a sin.'

He smiled, paused, grew serious. 'Do be careful, though.'

'I'm a big girl.'

'A frail girl. Bryanston told me about your collapse.'

'I don't feel frail. Most of the time.'

He gave a snort, said nothing.

'I *don't*. I'm fine. Practically completely recovered.'

'Morganna, confidence is one thing, recklessness another.'

'Meaning?'

'Meaning you *are* frail. A gust of wind could blow you over.'

I shrugged. I knew how my clothes hung off me. What could I say?

'If it makes you feel any better,' he said gently, 'you are still terrifying.'

I laughed. 'How so?'

'You might have the body of a reed, but you have the eyes of Medusa.'

'Now that would be truly useful. But the only person who'll turn to stone is me, if I don't get some rest.'

Toby escorted me to his door, unlocked it, and let me out.

'Good luck, tomorrow.'

'Rest.'

'I will.' I returned to my haven. I should have rung Rosamond and Archie, but I could not face them. And why should I have done so anyway? The time for pretence was over. My game had failed.

I rang the bank. I got Mary-Beth.

'Hi, it's Morganna. Any news?'

'None, but it would be surprising.'

'I know, I know, but if he does get in touch, tell him I need to speak to him. Now. It's urgent. Here's my number.' I gave it to her and hung up. I ordered room service, and I waited, against hope.

Chapter fifty-three

Toby brought me the portrait the next evening. Speculatively, he glanced around my suite.

'Your husband must be a rich man.'

'My parents.'

'Generous.'

'Dead.'

'Ah. I'll just put my foot in it again, shall I?'

'Fearlessly.'

He chuckled. 'Here's your mother-in-law.'

I took the portrait, set it down, removed one of the Ritz's prints from the wall, and hung Rosamond.

'You pleased?' Toby asked, as he appraised it.

'Was he?'

'No. It was strange, watching him. Sad and relieved at the same time, I would have said.'

'What about the money?'

'That's the funny thing. He didn't seem particularly interested in the money, though God knows, he looked like he needed it. He was interested in your painting, though.'

'Did he like it?'

'He loved it. Until I told him the title. Put him off a bit.'

'You *didn't*,' I said, sheer horror almost strangling the breath from me.

He frowned at me.

'I thought it was a *joke*, that he would share it.'

'The murderess's hands,' I said, just to make sure.

'Yes.'

'A joke.'

'A daughter-in-law/mother-in-law thing.'

'*Jesus*, Toby.'

'It *wasn't* a joke?'

'Never mind what it was.' The game really was over now. He would tell Rosamond. She would see it as a message, indirect, but all the more insidious for my choice of courier.

'Shit! Well, that's that then,' I said.

'Are you going to tell me what the hell is going on?'

'You've blown a whistle, Toby. Time's up. Game's up.'

'Are you all right?' Toby asked.

I nodded slowly. 'I'll be fine.'

'Morganna, I'd like to help you.'

'There's nothing you can do.'

'You sure?'

'I'm sure.'

'I'll be on my way, then. But if you change your mind.'

'I'll let you know. 'Night, Toby.'

Feeling the onset of despair, I got ready for bed. Rosamond's eyes watched from her position on the wall. I'd always felt when I painted in the eyes of a sitter, that I gave them an unworldly vision. That's why I preferred to paint Rosamond's hands. Perhaps that was worse.

Just as I was turning off the lights, the phone rang. Damning it, I fumbled in the darkness.

'Morganna?' The smoker's voice rasped down the line.

'Augustus?'

'I want you to come here.'

'Where? Dorset?'

'Yes.'

'When?'

'Now.'

'I'll get there as soon as I can, but it'll be the middle of the night.'

He gave a crackling laugh. 'All the same to me. Don't sleep anyway.'

I could not quite believe his call might have meant what I wanted it to. Was this a schizophrenic change of mind, and would he have changed it again by the time I got there? I wondered, briefly, if he was dangerous in any way. He hadn't seemed so. Disturbed, yes, dangerous, not truly. Anyway, I wouldn't be alone. I would have a driver, close by. Either way, I had to go.

All due credit to the Ritz. They conjured a driver within half an hour. I'd had just time enough to dress, order a coffee, have it delivered, and drink it down when the driver rang to tell me he was waiting downstairs.

He was tall, black, reassuringly tough-looking. He said his name was Jason. He stood beside a Bentley, brown, smooth as chocolate. Quiet as stealth, we cut through the night. I should have slept, but I could not. Caffeine and adrenaline ricocheted around my system.

'Don't fall asleep,' I said to Jason as we pulled up. 'Stay alert, listen out for me. Come if I call.'

He nodded, looked interested.

The moon was full. It lit the way to the back door. I

walked in haste, and the brambles scored my flesh again. The door was closed. I knocked, but there was no answer. Heart pounding, I knocked again. A roosting bird took flight and woke the sleeping forest. But from inside, still nothing. I tried the door. It was unlocked. I walked in, negotiating furniture by the light of the moon.

I found him, slumped on the sofa. For a moment I wondered if she had reached out a diabolical hand to silence him, if I had walked straight into a trap, but then I saw his chest rise, and with it heard his snore.

'Augustus,' I said gently. 'Augustus. It's Morganna Edge. I'm here.'

He woke with a shout. '*Rose, Rose!*' He eyed me wildly.

'Morganna. It's Morganna,' I said, crouching down.

'The car-crash one.'

'Yes.'

He rubbed his eyes, puckering the skin.

'I thought she'd come. Edge. I heard Edge.'

'It's just me.'

He studied me in the darkness. Finally, he spoke. 'He brought your painting, your agent.'

I nodded.

'I asked him what you called it.'

I felt my heart quicken.

'And he told me.' He kept his eyes on mine. I did not veil mine. I let him search and see what was there.

'You think she is a murderess,' he said flatly.

'Yes. I do.'

He nodded. 'And that's why you tracked me down?'

'Yes.'

'Why?'

362

I took a huge breath, blew it out, and with it all caution.

'Because I wanted you to tell me the truth.'

He reached over and lit a cigarette. He inhaled deeply, and then hacked out a great, liquid cough.

'After all these years. Why?'

'Because I need to get away from her, and I need to take back what she took from me, and, because I have to buy myself a safe passage.' I didn't tell him about Georgie, about my real reason. That was too important to risk telling anyone.

He nodded, and smoked. 'And if I do tell you the truth?'

'I'll confront her with it, use it to do a deal with her. She'll return to me what is mine, and I'll go quietly, never breathe a word to anyone.'

'No police?'

'No need to complicate things. Rosamond wants her castle, she wants her freedom, I want what she's taken from me. All I need to do is threaten her with the police, if I have good enough evidence, and she'll deal.'

'Yes. Put it like that, I'm sure she will.'

He looked out into the night. I could almost feel him agonizing. Finally he turned back to me, eyes determined.

'You believe what goes around comes around?'

'I wish. I'd like to think so, but I know it doesn't always happen.'

'She thinks she's immune. She's ridden her luck, trusted too much that other people will be her pawns, once and for always. Well, serve her right if she gets a little scare. Won't harm her, really, will it?'

'No. She'll just have to give back a small fraction of what she's stolen from me. She'll keep her castle, restored with my money, she'll keep much that's in it, and she'll keep her liberty.'

He nodded, lit up another cigarette from the tip of the old one.

'She used to visit me, at least once a year. And send me something at Christmas. First because she wanted to. Then because she thought she should. But then the visits stopped, then the letters, for five years now, nothing. Because she thought I didn't matter anymore. I was ancient history. I didn't matter. I'd been loyal. Played my bloody part. I suppose I always knew she was using me, but she at least had the grace to try to hide it for a while, but then she couldn't even be bothered with the pretence.'

He shrugged and I could see the pain in his eyes, still fresh. 'I loved her, you see. That's why I did it, and that's why she thought I'd stay schtumm for good.'

I kept silent. In the forest I heard an owl cry. For a moment, our faces were cast into sheer blackness as the moon hid behind a cloud, and then once more we were illuminated.

'I sailed her to Cape Wrath. Pig of a storm. Practically flew across the water. Got there at night. Perfect. Pitch black. No moon. I moored up and risked my life rowing her in. I waited for her while she went to the castle. I waited for her while she killed her husband. I think it was amyl nitrate she used, something like that. She knew he had arrhythmia, dodgy heart. Big sniff of this stuff, gave him a heart attack. Trembling with excitement, she was, when she came back to the shore. I rowed her back to my yacht. And we sailed back to the South of France. When the police came, I gave her an alibi. Said we were sailing in the Med. Didn't want to buy it, but they had to.'

I could hardly breathe. He stopped. 'Is that what you wanted to know?'

'Yes. Can you prove any of this, or is it just your word against hers?'

'I loved her, but even I wasn't completely stupid. I never trusted her, not completely. I used to plot my voyages, write down the weather forecast, conditions for the voyage, times, dates, plot my course on tracing paper that I pinned over the charts. I kept all of them. They're upstairs in the attic.'

'Wouldn't she have known that, wanted you to destroy the one for that voyage?'

'She thinks I did. I destroyed an old one, completely unrelated.'

'So, the right one is upstairs?'

He shook his head. 'No. It's in a safety deposit box. Coutts. On the Strand.'

'I don't suppose you have the key?'

He got to his feet, limped over to the clock on his mantelpiece, opened it up, and withdrew a key. He walked over and handed it to me.

'You were expecting her to betray you, or abandon you?'

'That's what she does,' he answered. He might as well have spoken of the scorpion and its sting, or the cobra and its bite. Rosamond's evil was simply a fact of nature.

'She might have done worse.'

'Kill you?'

'Why not? She'd done it once. At least once.'

'She'd killed before?'

He shook his head. 'Suspicions.' He looked away, and I knew I would get more from him.

'Could you write down, what you've just told me, and sign it?'

'No. You'll have to make do with the log. Should be enough.'

'Okay.' It would have to be enough. I got to my feet. I wanted to leave, quickly, before he changed his mind. I'd seen the schizophrenic mood lurch last time I was here. But I could not go without asking him one more thing.

'Listen, aren't you worried about what she might do, when she realizes you've told me all this?'

He laughed. 'Wouldn't make any difference.'

'What d'you mean?'

'I'm dying anyway. Six months max. Throat cancer. Spread everywhere. And the bloody pain. She'd be doing me a favour. Tell her that, will you?'

'I won't. I'll just tell her to leave you alone, that if anything suspicious does happen to you, I'll take your charts to the police.'

'What the hell, tell her that. I don't think I could face her, any road, her in full fury.'

'Look, I'll never be able to thank you, or repay you for telling me all this, but if there is anything you need, if there's anyone you might want me to help in some way, let me know.' I wrote out Geoffrey's home number. 'Ring this number. They'll always know where to find me.'

He took it and put it in his pocket. 'There's nothing,' he said, 'and there's no-one.'

I took his hand and squeezed it.

'Thank you.'

He nodded. He looked grim; the euphoria of betrayal seemed to have worn off. I left, closing the door gently behind me.

Jason was waiting, pacing slowly beside the car, like some animal of the night. He held open the door for me and I slipped in, onto the leather seats. I kept Bryanston's key clenched so tightly in my hand that it left a mirror impression in my flesh. I looked as we reversed slowly down the track, and caught a glimpse of Bryanston in the window, watching me. Dawn was breaking, but in the half-light I did not make out the phone in his hand. It was only my subconscious that registered it, stored it up, flung it back at me later.

Chapter fifty-four

Back in London, I refuelled with coffee and croissants. I rang the concierge, asked him to get hold of a good lawyer for me, and to have him or her come to the Ritz at ten thirty. And then I headed for Coutts. I could not quite believe that simple key would unlock my future, would yield up the secrets that would win me my daughter. I trembled as I walked down the street and turned into the Strand. I tried to calm myself before I went into Coutts. I kept thinking they would eject me, find some reason to keep me from the safety deposit box. I breathed deeply, straightened my back, and attempted to affect the right degree of careless entitlement as I walked in. I beamed at one of the cashiers, a sallow-looking, blonde woman wearing a shocking red blazer.

'Good morning. I've come to open a safety deposit box.'

She nodded. 'If you'll just take a seat, someone will be right over.'

I retreated to a navy leather banquette and flicked nervously through a magazine with lots of advertisements for gin palaces.

'Good morning,' said a thin voice. A pinstriped man little older than me towered above me, willowy as a reed, and pale as white bread.

'You'd like access to a box?'

I stood up. 'Yes, please.'

He nodded. 'Could you show me your key, please?'

I removed it from my purse and handed it over, heart racing. As he examined it, I feared I would be exposed as a fraud, that this key would open nothing more than a garden shed.

'Fine,' he said. 'Would you like to follow me?'

And that was it. He handed me back the key and led me through the foyer, through a series of security doors, and we went down two floors in a lift. He opened a security grill, then another door, and suddenly we were surrounded by security boxes.

'I'll wait outside,' he said. 'I think you'll find number forty-eight on the right-hand side, low down.'

'Thank you.'

My heart was hammering. It took me ages to even find number forty-eight, and then to get the key successfully into the lock. Finally, I did it. I pulled the small door open, and saw before me several large envelopes. I took them all out, sat at the desk in the middle of the room, and opened them up. Share certificates. More share certificates. Then I found it, in the third envelope. A large sheet of thin parchment, with a route traced on it, and then two ragged-edged pieces of paper with, as promised, dates, times, his name and hers, all the details of their murderous voyage. I put the other envelopes away, put the chart and the notes back in their envelope, and secured it inside my bag. Then I locked the little box and went out into the hallway.

'All done?' asked my guide brightly.

'All done,' I replied.

I took a taxi back to the Ritz. I would not risk the street with what I was carrying.

The Ritz's business centre made me ten copies. I immediately posted two to Geoffrey's house in Long Island. I gave the Ritz Augustus's key, with a note to him attached, and asked them to courier it to him. The lawyer arrived at ten thirty, all pristine confidence in her beige Armani suit. I explained what I wanted her to do. If she found any of it surprising, she did not say. Discretion had been schooled into her by the pin-striped legions.

I got to Heathrow at three. I could not wait. I wanted to finish this off, and then escape with my daughter. I had it all planned. We'd fly to New York. Go to Geoffrey's house, wait for him to come home, and then I'd buy a home for the two of us. I'd take no pleasure in besting Rosamond. I merely wanted to get it over, and get away with Georgie. It suddenly occurred to me that she might have no passport. I'd need Archie's signature, or something, wouldn't I, to get her one? But he'd give it, just as he'd allow me to take our daughter. He seemed reasonably fond of Georgie, in a sort of detached, almost academic way, but he loved his mother, and had always been and always would be in thrall to her. Most of all, like her, he loved money.

It was Friday, and the airport was heaving. I shuffled forward in a long queue, backed up at the X-ray machines. I put my bag on the conveyor belt. It rolled away from me. I passed through the check unopposed, but the security men decided they wanted to open up my bag. I did it for them. They inserted prying hands and pulled out the roll of parchment. They looked at the notes, at the plotted line.

'What's all this then?' asked one.

My silver bullet? Deliverance? Enough ammunition to sink Rosamond Edge.

I smiled. 'That is a map. There lies treasure.'

'And you're the pirate, are you?'

'Better believe it.'

With their laughter ringing in my ears, I moved through.

As the plane carried me north through a stormy sky, I thought, *do not crash now*. I thought this on every flight, but more so on this one. I had what I wanted, and I could scarcely believe it. I was waiting for the glitch, the problem, that would make all this real for me. In its absence, I was suspicious.

The landing was rough. A gust of wind as we touched down almost rocked the plane onto one wing. There were gasps, but no-one spoke. Not until we finished our taxi and the seat-belt sign went off did anyone speak, and then it was the hushed chatter of the shocked.

A taxi bore me away through the rain. My carry-on bag sat beside me on the back seat. The driver muttered quiet curses as the rain grew heavier, and the car was rocked by gusts.

'Going to be a bad one,' he said.

'No doubt.'

Chapter fifty-five

There was no-one to meet me as the taxi pulled up in front of the castle. The driver looked from it to me in wonder.

'You *live* here?'

I turned to him in surprise. 'Yes. Why shouldn't I?'

'I wouldn't. Not in that, not if you paid me.'

'Yeah, well, no-one will, so I shouldn't worry.' The castle did look especially forbidding, tall, bleak grey walls down which the rain sluiced.

I paid him, tipping him less than I would have, and struggled with my bag through the rain to the huge doors. I was soaked in those brief seconds. I tried to turn the huge handle. It was locked.

Fuck it. Anger rising, I rang the bell. It was never locked during the day. What was going on? The taxi driver watched while I waited like a penitent come to seek shelter. Finally, Rosamond came to the door. She gave me an odd smile. The taxi driver, reassured that I really did live here, drove off.

'*Darling. Look* at you. Should have rung, we'd have sent someone.'

'It's easy enough to get a taxi, Rosamond.'

'Yes but, we had no *idea*. Anyway, you're here now. Come on in. You'll catch your death.'

I shivered, followed in her wake. 'I'll go and change,' I said.

'*Do* that. See you at dinner?'

'I'll see how I feel,' I answered.

I walked away from her, across the great hall. I climbed the staircase to my wing, and I felt her eyes on my back. The sound of my heels on the stone floors echoed around me. Faraway, I heard the answering echo of hers. I got to my room, closed the door behind me, leaned back against it, and dropped my bag at my feet. How I wished I could lock this door. I had to see Georgie, but first I had to figure out where to hide Bryanston's map and notes, my final settlement. I did not want to let them out of my sight. For want of anywhere better, I shoved the bag under my bed, and then I changed into jeans and trainers and hurried off downstairs.

I padded silently across the great hall, and headed for Georgie's rooms. I stood outside her door. I could hear muffled giggles. Smiling, I let myself in. She was in her bath, with Myot pushing yellow rubber ducks at her.

I nodded a greeting at Myot. Her reign would soon be over.

'Hello, my Georgie. Hello darling, how are you?'

'Quite fine,' replied Myot. I bent down, kissed my daughter's downy head. I stayed a few moments more. 'I'll see you later, my love,' I said, and then with just one backward glance at her, I left.

I went up to my tower, collecting my bag on the way. I needed ten minutes, just to compose myself, and then I would go to confront Rosamond. Now that the time had come, I was resolved, but suddenly terrified.

I closed the door behind me. I could hear the sea. I could almost feel the compression of air as the waves crashed into the rocks below. The wind roared and moaned as if in the throes of torture or ecstasy, I could not tell. I took the bag to my cupboard and shut it in, amidst the jumble of unused canvases and tubes of paint.

I went to the window. Through the driving rain, I saw the sea churning madly below me. A huge wave rolled in with deadly implacability. It hit the rocks and exploded upwards. The spray hit my window and ran down, like blood from a wound. I jumped back. I had never seen such a storm. It was as if all heaven and all hell was in a rage. I turned on the radio. It burbled on. I did not mentally tune in until I heard the shipping news. It confirmed what I saw before me. Severe gales in Fitzroy.

The weather system we were experiencing was the edge of a hurricane system that was currently devastating the Atlantic. The news came on. Many ships were lost. The coast guard could not keep up. One helicopter had crashed at sea.

I took one more look out of the window; then before I could change my mind, I turned off the radio and headed down to Rosamond's rooms.

I stopped every so often, and listened out. I could hear nothing save the storm. I paused outside her door. No sound emerged. I knocked. Nothing. I tried again. Still, I heard nothing, save the sound of my own blood, rushing through my ears.

I tried the handle. The door opened. I walked in.

'Rosamond?' I called out. 'Are you here?'

She was not. I looked around. I saw the red light on her message machine flashing. On impulse, I clicked *play*. And I heard a voice I knew.

Rose, Rose, why won't you call me? I'm sorry, I'm sorry. How many times do I have to tell you. Just call me, please. There was an anguished pause, and then Augustus Bryanston hung up. Oh dear God, she knew. He'd told her.

Frantically, I tried to work out what this meant. I had lost the element of surprise, that much was clear. She knew that I knew, now what would she do? It was then that I felt the first bands of fear close around my chest.

Quickly I left her rooms, pulling the door gently to. I headed down the stairs, past Archie's rooms. I heard his voice, and hers, shouting. I stopped, and over the wind, I strained to listen.

'Archie, we cannot do that. We cannot let it lie, not a moment later. She knows, you bloody fool, God only knows who she might tell. What's she come back here to do, if not spring it on me? She's probably trying to ring the bloody police now. We cannot take that chance. Am I going to have to do it, or will you?'

And then I knew, beyond any doubt, she was plotting to kill me.

Get out. Get out, screamed the voice in my head. I backed away a few steps, and then I turned, willing myself to slow down. My feet wanted to run. They wanted to stampede. The urge to give in to this panic was almost irresistible, but I knew my only hope remained in appearing calm, as if I suspected nothing. If I could just buy myself the minutes to get out. I could take Georgie, I could go to Ben. He would keep me safe.

I crossed the great hall. I stopped at the sideboard, pulled open the top drawer, and reached to grab the car keys. They were not there. They were always there. Three sets. All gone. To trap me, why else. I would have to walk to Ben's. I'd ring him, tell him I was coming. He could pick me up.

Silently, go silently, I willed my feet, terrified I would stumble. I got across the hall, I made it to the stairs, I began to climb. I made the first bend in the stairs, and then I thought I heard their voices. It was nearly eight o'clock. Dinner would soon be served. Were they coming down to await me, or to hunt me down? How would she do it, I wondered?

Up, up, up I went. To my room. I grabbed up the phone and dialled. Nothing. No dial tone. The storm. I was well and truly cut off. It was then that I felt pure, unadulterated terror. I did not allow myself to stop. I pulled on my huge Dryzabone and I crept from my room. I feared my breath would give me away. It raged through my lungs. Oh, God, I began to feel light-headed. If I blacked out now, I was truly dead.

I stopped, tried to summon the calm that would save me. I invoked my dead parents, I invoked God, and I invoked the devil. *Get me to my daughter, get us out of here.*

It seemed to recede, just fractionally, the threatened oblivion. Down, one foot before the other. Down the stairs. I stopped at the last corner. I listened. I could not hear them, just the banshee wails of the wind.

Go. I took a breath and willed myself forward. Down

into the great hall I went. The door to the dining room was three-quarters closed. Were they in there, had I heard their voices, heading that way? I had to pass it to get out. I had no choice. I willed myself to approach, and to pass it. I did not look in as I went. I imagined their faces turning in unison as I crept by.

I willed myself on. I got to the south staircase and headed up. I did not know what I would do if I encountered Myot, as I surely would. Knock her out, was all I could think of. I saw a bronze of a horse on a side table. I grabbed it, carried it behind my back, and headed for my daughter's rooms. I paused outside. Silence. I opened the door. Myot was there, bending over Georgie's cot. She turned and looked at me in surprise. I closed the door behind me and approached her quickly. I did not allow myself to think about what I had to do. Sheer, bloody ruthlessness was my only option. At the last moment, I took the statue from behind my back and smashed it into her head. She uttered a small moan, and then fell like a stone. Georgie sat up, surprised. I grabbed her baby carrier from the back of the door, shrugged off my coat, and pulled the carrier on. Then I took my daughter, and pulled her into it. I grabbed my coat, slipped it on, and did it up around me and Georgie. Saying a silent prayer, I opened her door, and listened. Nothing. I hurried down the stairs, praying Georgie would be silent. I crossed the hall, got to the great door, turned the handle. It nearly smashed into me and Georgie. I gasped, tried to steady myself and hang onto it. Georgie let out a little cry. The wind screamed in. They must have felt that, in their fastness. I moved, dragged the door, struggled to shut it. I could not close it quietly. I could only hope some other sound of the storm would confuse them, perhaps distract them, let me get out of sight.

I tried to run. The wind was coming off the sea. It should have sped me up, but it whirled around me, as if determined to drag me to the floor. I remembered Toby's words: *a gust of wind could blow you over*. Try the tail of a hurricane.

I pushed on. Step by step. The rain sluiced down my face. I stopped, turned. The door was still closed. Perhaps, just perhaps, I had gotten away.

But I still had to get to Ben's house. On a good day, it was a walk of twenty minutes. Tonight, God help me. Let me get there, quickly.

'Georgie, Georgie, are you all right, my darling?' I asked, reaching my hand in to smooth her head. But she was shocked into silence.

I bent double, trying to give as small a target as I could against the harrowing wind. I turned inland slightly, away from the clifftops. I stopped and turned. Still no signs of pursuit. I could feel myself tiring, but I forced myself on. Somehow, I kept going. Walking in this storm, carrying Georgie, was so much harder than normal. My breath became ragged in my lungs. I could hardly see. Five more minutes. I thought perhaps it was safe now. I had put enough distance between myself and them.

And then I saw someone, head down, moving like an arrow towards me. I cried out, turned, and hurried on. I did not know who it was. I could not see. I nearly tripped. I tried to run. I glanced over my shoulder. They were gaining.

I tried to will myself to go faster. My muscles were burning, my chest felt as if it would explode. Oh Ben, Ben. With your second sight, couldn't you see I needed you?

A voice was calling. I could hear it snatched and thrown by the wind. I tried to go on, but the dizziness came, and that time I knew it was irresistible. I sank to my knees.

Please, God, please, let me stay conscious. Help me. Help me.

The figure was there. It pushed back the hood. It was Archie.

I was light. I was like a reed. Not even my Medusa eyes could help me though.

He grabbed me, picked me up.

I could not speak. I was paralyzed, with terror and with the imminence of blackout. I was keeping it off, but just, just.

He walked fast, as if I was no burden. A gust of wind hit us, and he faltered, but still he struggled on. But he was carrying me not back to the castle, but towards the cliffs.

'What are you doing?' I screamed.

He looked down at me, my face inches from his shoulder.

'What do you think? Did you think I would let you go?' He ripped open my coat. He pulled at the poppers on Georgie's carrier.

'You thought you could take my daughter, that Ma and I would let you take *Georgie*?' He unhooked her, laid her on the wet ground, and then he ripped my coat off me, and bundled her up in it. As I lunged towards her, he grabbed me again, picked me up and headed closer to the cliff edge.

Nearer we got. I could feel the wind pulling at us. I felt as if it would rip us from the ground and fling us into the sea. The cliffs were twenty feet away.

He walked closer, slowly now, more circumspect.

'Did you think I would let you destroy my mother? And take my daughter from me?'

'She's my daughter too, you bastard. You don't care about her. You only care about money. Leave her with me. You can have my money, as much as you want. Just leave us.'

He laughed, edged yet closer to the cliffs. 'Georgiana will get your inheritance, won't she. With her, I get everything.'

'Was this the plan? From the start?'

'What did you *think*?'

And all I managed to say is, *damn you and your mother, to hell and back*, before he dragged me off him, and hurled me towards the cliff.

'*Georgie,*' I screamed. '*Georgie!*'

Chapter fifty-six

I tumbled, rolled on the precipitous last slope before the ground gave way. I felt grass, giving way to stone. I tried desperately to stop, to hold on, but the push had been too violent and the slope was too steep. And then I was over, out beyond life, over the edge. I heard the screeching seagulls, surprised by a human where one should not be. I heard the roar of the wind, my own voice, screaming horror, I thought I heard another voice shouting. I felt the rock beneath my fingers and the earth and the scrub of bushes growing defying gravity and I gripped. I flattened my body and I stuck my fingers into the earth and rock like pistons and I rammed my feet against the sloping cliff and with all the life in me I held on. Jutting rock smashed into my ribs, but still I slipped, albeit more slowly. I felt the skin go from my fingers, I felt my coat ripping. And then I stopped. There was a ledge, my fingers fought and scrabbled madly, and my toes curled in prehensile survival as my feet perched and gripped. I could hardly breathe. I dared hardly breathe though I wanted to rake in breaths to scream and flail, but I stayed silent and still, while around me the wind screamed its madness.

Below me I saw the foaming sea. I was less than a hundred feet above it. The next big wave would wash me away. I saw then, that the cliff wasn't vertical. It sloped, horribly, terribly, but it sloped, and there were handholds and footholds. And I had no choice. I began to climb, ignoring the screaming pain in my ribs. Perhaps I screamed too, but you wouldn't have heard it, above the banshee wind. I unlocked the fingers of one hand, stretched and scrabbled for another hold. I found one. I raised one foot, sought out another hold no matter how small, found one, and up I went.

I did not look up, I did not look down. However far up I had to go, I would go. I could have fallen, at any time, but I knew I must move, or die. I don't know how long it took. At one point, a wave hit the cliff below me with a force that vibrated the rock, and sent the water sluicing up to get me. I clung on as it smashed into me, then sucked down, like some hellish retriever. Only that time, it didn't get me.

My hands bled. Skin hung off them in ribbons. I could taste blood in my mouth and my head rang.

I climbed. Fractured thoughts and images went through my mind. I saw my daughter's face, I heard her laugh. I saw Archie. I wondered if I ever made it to the top, would he be there, waiting, to stamp on my fingers? But he was not. No-one was. I took the last hand hold, and then hauled myself over the rock, over the edge. And I crawled away, ten, twenty, fifty feet, until, in a small hollow, I collapsed.

For a few minutes, I tried to get breath into my lungs. Each breath was like a knife wound. I pushed myself to all fours, and, like an injured dog, I crawled. I dragged myself on. I had a mile to go, a distance I normally covered in twenty minutes. I would never get there like that. I pushed myself up. Bent over, I stumbled forward. It felt like hours passed. I was cold, so cold I toyed with the idea of just lying down for five minutes, getting my strength. I knew enough to realize if I did that, I would never get up again.

I conjured my daughter. Like a spirit, like an angel, she kept me going. I saw Ben's cabin, his door. I staggered into it, pounded it with my fists. I grabbed the door-handle, wrenched it open, and fell in. It was empty. Ben had gone.

I saw his phone, but I knew what I would hear before I picked it up. I'd already seen the electricity and the phone wires lying like dead snakes beside the fallen telegraph poles. I checked it anyway. It was dead.

Where were you, Ben? Where would you go with your dog and mine, on a day like this, leaving your car? I tried to think, I tried to breathe. I wanted to lie down so badly, but I knew I had to keep going, somehow. Only adrenaline, and the urgent desire to get to my daughter, and to get her away from her murderous grandmother and son kept me going.

I saw Ben's keys. I grabbed them with shaking fingers, and I let myself out into the storm once more.

Opening the jeep was agony, climbing in was agony. Changing gear stabbed me with another red hot poker. And the ground, every bump was torture. Any suspension in this jeep died many years ago. Twenty miles to the police station. Just twenty miles to go. I thought wildly for one moment, that I should head for the castle, and then what? They would finish me off in a minute.

I drove on. I knew I could black out at any time. I think it was the pain that saved me. Every time unconsciousness threatened, an extra lance of pain kept it at bay. Christ, I could hardly see. The rain fell in an almost solid sheet across the windscreen. As I drew nearer, I wondered if there would be anyone at the police station.

I got there. I left the jeep, walked up to the front door, and opened it. A man in uniform sat behind a desk, listening to his radio crackling static at him. It was the red-headed one who'd come to me after my portraits were stolen. A nameplate stood before him: PC Jordan. He looked across at me and jumped up.

'What happened to you?'

'Just come with me. Please. Come with me, and I'll tell you.'

I thought for a moment he would refuse. 'You need to get to a hospital,' he said.

'Later. Please. You've got to get me to my daughter, before they try to kill her too.'

That got his interest.

'Where is she?'

'Wrath Castle.'

We went in his car. Getting in, strapping myself in, was agony.

'What happened?' he asked.

I gingerly took a few breaths. 'You remember me?'

'Morganna Edge. The one with the stolen portraits. Married to Archie Edge.'

'He just tried to kill me.'

He flicked me a glance. I could see him wondering if he had a nutter in his car. Even to my own ears, my unemotional delivery sounded extremely odd, but then I did look the part. My hands were covered in blood, my clothes were torn and shredded in places, and God only knew what shape my face was in.

'I know, I should probably be screaming. I know this must seem all wrong to you, but all I care about right now is getting my daughter away from those bastards.'

'There's more than one?'

So I told him about Rosamond. He listened, tried his radio, spoke into it. All that came back was static. There was no voice at the end of the line. There was nothing moving on the roads, no people, no cars. Just the wind, and what it caught up in its maw. It felt like the end of the world.

It took nearly an hour to get there. A tree had been blown down on the A99 since I passed ten minutes earlier. This storm was worsening. There was no way past. We had to turn around and go another route. I was beginning to shake. PC Jordan cast quick glances at me.

'I'm worried about you.'

'Worry about my daughter.'

At last, we turned the bend and I saw Wrath Castle a quarter of a mile away. I noticed at once that the Range Rover was gone.

We arrived. PC Jordan jumped out. Awkwardly I followed. My heart was beating so fast it felt like it would burst. Jordan opened the front doors. In I went, shouting, screaming for my daughter, but I knew it even as I shouted. She wasn't there. How could I miss what they had done? I forced myself up the stairs in a hobbling run, clutching my ribs, calling out. I saw the empty picture frames yawning obscenely, their canvases cut out. I got to Georgie's room. Her cot was empty. Her car seat was gone. Her coat was gone. Her comfort blanket was gone. I checked Myot's room. She too, loyal to the last, was gone.

'They've taken her,' I said.

Jordan took hold of my arm. 'We'll find them. We'll find a phone that's working, get the boys out on the road.'

I shook my head as a thought struck me. 'Oh, God. One more place. Come on.'

'You sure they couldn't be here? It's huge, this place.'

'The empty picture frames, the silver Georgian rosebowl. Looted the place, gone. I think, to the boat.'

In his car again, bouncing down the track to Crescent Bay, where the boat should have been. The orange mooring buoy danced wildly on the waves. The boat was gone. The tender was gone from its place on the sand. But the Range Rover was there. I went to it. The key was still in the ignition. Mechanically, I took it out and pocketed it. I opened the rear passenger door, where my daughter had sat. There was no trace of her. No lingering baby smell. They had taken my child, Rosamond and Archie, and put out to sea with her in a Force 9 gale.

'They've gone out in a boat in this?' Jordan gestured at the raging sea.

I nodded.

We drove back, towards the castle. As we drew nearer, on the road that led from the castle towards Ben's moor, I saw something. Two dogs, running around jaggedly. A body lying in the road. Jordan slowed and, engine running, jumped out. Awkwardly, I got out and followed him. I saw Jelly and Gin, yelping. And I saw Ben, motionless on the road. Jordan fell by his side.

'Can you hear me? Can you hear me?' he shouted. Nothing. Ben's eyes were open, but unmoving.

I crouched down, took his hand. Jordan put his head on Ben's chest, listened for a heart beat.

'He's alive,' he shouted at me. 'We've got to get him to hospital.'

'The phone line's down in the castle.'

Jordan had no choice. He lifted Ben into the back of the car. Jelly and Gin jumped in beside him. I squeezed in and tried to hold Ben's inert body as still as I could as we drove off over the million bumps.

'What happened to him?' I asked Jordan.

'If I were to guess, I'd say he was hit by a car.'

I held on to Ben, willing him to live, even as I sobbed for my daughter.

But I could not keep going. Before long, I slid away.

In my head, I saw them, knives in hand, hacking the pictures from their frames, bundling them up, as they bundled up my daughter in her blanket and carried her out. Money and dynasty. Both portable. Then into the car. Myot too. They would have needed her to look after Georgie, while they sailed the boat through that mayhem. Had they forced her to go with them? Was that when they saw Ben, had he come to stop them, and had they simply run him over? Had I heard his voice, shouting when I went over the cliff? Had he seen it all, chased Archie, tried to stop him, and been mowed down by him, or by Rosamond? What was one more death to them, when they were up to their necks in blood? Then they drove to the cove, readied the tender, bundled my daughter in. They got to the boat.

They offloaded her, bundled her into a cabin with Myot, and put out to sea.

I saw waves, high as a skyscraper, bearing down on them. For my daughter's sake, I begged God that they survive.

Chapter fifty-seven

I awoke. Everything hurt. I tried to open my eyes, but then closed them again in a hurry. The light was too bright. And then I remembered, everything, and I opened my eyes and screamed. I heard footsteps running, and then in came Robert Beeston. He gripped my hand. He didn't tell me it was all right. He just held on until I stopped screaming.

'Have they found them?' I asked.

'I don't know. You'll have to ask the policeman. He's here, I think, now. Talking to your friend.'

'He's alive?'

Beeston looked evasive.

'He must be,' I insisted.

'He is now,' Beeston said slowly. 'Look, Morganna, I'm sorry. There's no gentle way to say this. He's dying. He has internal injuries so severe he doesn't stand a chance. It's a wonder he's even come round. But he did, and he insisted on making a statement to the police. We called them half an hour ago. The same sergeant who brought you in yesterday came back.'

'Yesterday. Jesus. I want to see Ben.'

'He wants to see you too.'

I struggled to get up. 'Strictly speaking, you should stay in bed,' said Beeston.

'Strictly speaking, I should be dead,' I replied.

He helped me out of bed. He guided me down the corridor. I tried to compose myself, but how the hell could you?

'Does he know he's dying?' I asked.

Beeston nodded.

Ben was lying in bed, his face drained of colour. I could see and smell death in that antiseptic room. Two policemen were there too. Jordan and someone I didn't know. Beeston conferred quietly with them, and they nodded. Ben was just lying there, but then he seemed to sense me. He looked across at me, and managed a smile. God knows what that must have cost him.

'Morganna. Miracle.'

His voice was so faint, this man with the melodic, deep burr. I went to him and took his hand.

'Oh Ben. What happened?'

'I saw him, Archie. Saw him go after you. I saw what he did. I shouted, too faraway, but he saw me, just after, saw that I'd seen, and he ran.' He stopped. His chest was heaving with the effort of hanging on to life. 'You survived. How on earth?'

'I got a foothold on the cliff. I scrambled up.'

He shook his head. His eyes, normally so brilliant blue, were yellow. They looked amazed.

'Chased him,' he said. 'Had a good ten minutes on me, and he was faster. I got there as they were running from the castle.' He stopped again, struggled for breath. We all waited.

'Rosamond, carrying all these rolled up bundles . . . that bastard, carrying your child, and the nanny, with more loot. Shouted at them . . . but they just got in, and drove. I just stood there, on the road.' He stopped, looked away, and in that look I saw him trying to fathom something, that, despairing, he could not. 'She just drove on.'

I laid my head, light as a feather, on his chest. I felt his hand in my hair.

'I'm sorry. Oh God, Ben, I'm so sorry.'

'Not your fault.'

I straightened up to look at him. 'I will get them for this,' I told him. 'I will get my child back, and then I will destroy them. I will kill them with my own hands if I can. I promise you I will not let them get away with this.'

He was shaking his head. He tried to speak. I moved my head close to his lips.

'Just live. Get Georgie, and live.'

He died, two minutes later. One moment he was breathing, and the next not. That interval of time just stretched out ahead till the thread of his life, till whatever kept him anchored to this world just snapped, without us hearing a sound. I watched him die. I turned. The policemen were bowing their heads. Beeston moved forward, and he took hold of Ben's hand, as if in communion, looking for a pulse that he knew had stopped. I shook with silent sobs.

Sometime later, the policemen visited me in my bed. Beeston was with them. 'Have you found them,' I asked.

The policemen shook their heads. 'Storm's still up. Coast guard have been looking, navy've been looking. No sign.'

'Murder, attempted murder, child abduction,' said Beeston.

'We know. We're looking,' said Jordan. He turned to me. 'I'm very sorry,' he said.

'If I had them here now, I would kill them,' I said.

He nodded.

Chapter fifty-eight

They told me I had no injuries that time would not heal. Hypothermia was the most serious, but they had gotten me in good time. Broken ribs and lacerated hands would heal; the scratches on my face would fade. They said they wanted me to stay in hospital for a week. It was longer than I needed, but Beeston wanted to keep watch. So I lay there, and I waited. Exhausted as I was, I didn't sleep. I refused the sleeping tablets they offered me. I felt I had to be awake, to keep my vigil, that if I relaxed for a moment, then that would be it. Everything would be lost. No news was good news, of a sort. Day in, day out, no news. Geoffrey too had been at sea in his typhoon. Of him too, there was no news.

On the day they were due to release me — God knows where to, I could hardly think that far, or care — two things happened.

Geoffrey arrived. He was thinner, wind-tanned, younger-looking, apart from his eyes, which were harrowed.

'You got here,' I said.

'I stopped over in the Isles Marquises. Wasn't meant to, just had a feeling. Got hold of a phone there. Rang the bank, they said to get in touch with you. Urgently. I rang the castle and the police answered.'

'You know everything?' I asked.

'They told me.'

I nodded. I sat there in my bed and I looked down at my hands which were knitting and separating wildly.

Neither of us knew what to say or do. The ruins of his advice lay between us.

'I'm sorry,' he said.

'I know,' I replied.

There were no possible words of comfort.

The police came in. I knew at once the news was bad. I could not take a breath. Or speak.

They hovered, and then PC Jordan spoke.

'The coast guard found wreckage, off northern Spain. It was the *Gypsy Rose*. Nothing else was found,' he said. 'No survivors.'

Chapter fifty-nine

I knew grief could kill, and I wished it would kill me, but it didn't. I would have walked out in front of the nearest car but for Geoffrey. When I was blinded by grief, incapable of the merest independent action, he took me home, back to Long Island. I never set foot in Wrath Castle again. He himself packed up the things he thought I would want. He sent the rest to Sotheby's who auctioned them, and then he boarded up the castle, as if in doing so, he could board up my past.

But I wasn't ready to parcel up my past. I refused to believe that was it, that I would never see my daughter again. I insisted the police keep searching. Geoffrey made my representations for me. I know I was too wild to convince anyone of my belief that my daughter and her abductors were not dead.

But the police report was unequivocal. Wreckage of the *Gypsy Rose*, including the front board that bore her name, was found in the Bay of Biscay, three days after they disappeared. So many boats foundered in that storm, even huge tankers. What chance did a fifty-foot yacht have in that? What chance did a baby have? But I would not give up. The police of various countries had long since given up. It was not their job to indulge the grief of a rich woman who had lost her child, a woman who had reputedly lost half her mind before her child even went missing. My utter and absolute conviction that my child was still living cut no ice with them. They thought I was deluded.

So then I brought in private investigators: Geoffrey's man, Bud Brascoe of Kroll's, and a small team. They did a good job of disguising the futility they felt. I knew they thought they were performing their service in vain.

Six months in, two good things happened. Not with Kroll, they still offered up nothing save bills, but with day-to-day living, with the rudiments of what was left of my life. After quarantine, Jelly and Gin arrived here, and then I decided to get somewhere of my own to live.

I picked for my new home a wooden-framed house, half a mile down the road from Geoffrey — that was as far as I felt I could go, and it was distant enough to give me the isolation I now craved. It was a simple house, a far cry from the Gatsby-esque splendour of Geoffrey's Mirador, but it appealed to me. It was painted a pale, sea-weathered blue, surrounded on three sides by a wide deck, partially shaded by an extended roof. It had two bedrooms, a large eat-in kitchen, and a biggish sitting room that was airy, but would be cosy on a winter's night. Like the bedroom I chose for myself, this looked over the dunes and out to sea. I bought a car. Oddly enough, since coming back to Long Island, I had suffered no more blackouts, so, after more checks and CAT scans at Beth Israel in New York, I was pronounced fit to drive. I picked a jeep, grey/blue like the sea.

The day I moved in, I felt my spirits flicker. I took my dogs for walks on the beach. Sometimes I would look at Gin and imagine, like me, she was thinking of her master, missing him, and then I would feel that murderous rage rise up in me again, and I would burn with the futility of it all.

For four months more, I paid Kroll to search, and search they did. But they found nothing. No trace of Georgie. No trace of Archie or Rosamond or Myot.

Then, nearly a full year on, I began to wonder if perhaps they were right. As soon as I admitted the first grain of doubt, like a virus it ate away at me. I decommissioned Kroll. If my daughter were dead, then there really was no point in living. It was easy to start drinking, a delicious, effective pain-number, not killer, for nothing killed the pain. But, when you're unconscious, you can't feel, can you? I would have a beer with lunch, and then carry on. At night I would fall into bed oblivious, and that was exactly how I wanted it. And that is how I spent my next three months on Long Island.

And then, when I was well on my way to my chosen goal, a letter arrived in the post. From Toby Hood. He'd written to me many times over the past year. I knew Geoffrey had put him up to it, trying to get me to paint again, to give me some purpose. All in vain. I was about to trash this letter, but some instinct stopped me. It was a miserable, rainy day in March. Even the ocean was listless, throwing desultory waves at the shore. I sat at my kitchen table, and ripped open the envelope.

> *Brace yourself Morganna. I heard a rumour, not fact, rumour, yesterday, that a Rembrandt had come onto the market. The* Widow at the Window. *A group of the*

biggest players were apparently bidding for it, all very
private. I don't know who bought it, probably one of six or
so collectors. If I'm not mistaken, you said that was one
of the paintings cut from its frame at Wrath Castle.

Let me know if there's anything you want me to do,

Love
Toby

I felt as if someone had plugged me into the mains. I
jumped up, knocking over my coffee. Jelly and Gin
leapt up from their baskets and jumped up on me.

'It's all right, girls, I'm all right. Down, now, down.'

They watched me cautiously as I dragged the phone
over to the table, sat down, and rang Geoffrey.

'Geoffrey, Geoffrey,' I shouted. 'The *Widow at the
Window* has come onto the market. It was one of the
paintings they cut from its frame. They took it with
them when they sailed.'

'My God. How'd you hear this?'

'I just got a letter from Toby. He doesn't know who
bought it, but he thinks he can narrow it down.'

'I'm coming 'round,' he said, and hung up.

I stood with the phone still in my hand. I thought of
Georgie, one and a half years old now. 'Where are you,
where are you?' I whispered.

Chapter sixty

'They're alive,' Geoffrey said, hugging me. Tears streamed down my face. It took me a while to speak.

'Can you imagine it, my daughter is alive. She's one and a half years old. And she's out there, *some*where. I just want to reach out, to get on a plane and grab her.'

'So what are we to do?'

'I don't know yet. Talk to Toby, see what else he can find out.'

'Kroll?'

'No, I don't think so. They didn't find them before, did they, and they're bloody good. That means they must be hiding so well I doubt it would be any different this time, although with a lead from Toby it might be. But if they even suspect someone is on their trail they might just up and go again, and then we're back to square one. We lose everything.' I paced around.

He paced too. The dogs watched us, bemused. 'I know. We're gonna have to play this thing so carefully.'

'The police?' I posited, not really seeing how they could be more discreet than Kroll.

Geoffrey shook his head. 'Not what they're best at. We need stealth. We need one person, not a whole team. One person surgically searching, not a crowd tramping 'round.'

'They're short of money, so they sell the Rembrandt, or they get someone to sell it for them. If we can find out who bought it, Toby says probably one of six or so collectors, if we can somehow get to him, find out who sold it to him, trace the money transfer . . .'

'If we find the buyer, we might well be able to trace the money,' said Geoffrey.

'How?'

'Not legally. With a hacker.'

'They can do that?'

He smiled. 'As part of a security operation at the bank, I got hold of the best hacker in the business, set him a challenge. Asked him if he could track a certain sum of money that was set to move round about a given date. They were the only two details I gave him. Took him two days. We tightened up after that, but let me tell you, most outfits are not anywhere near as tight as we are.'

I nodded. 'I'd never have guessed you kept such company, Geoffrey.'

'I'm not as boring as I look, Morganna.'

'I never thought you were.' I felt euphoric, dizzy, wild with excitement that I could not contain.

'Let's walk,' I said. The dogs leapt up. Out onto the beach we went, and we walked and talked.

But we didn't come up with anything that satisfied me. That night, with my dogs sleeping in their baskets, I sat up and I tried to think. I reached, as habit dictated, for my bottle of whisky. I got so far as positioning the glass, tilting the bottle, and then, with the wonderful smell hitting my nose, setting off the Pavlovian warmth in my body, I stopped. Like I was going to come up with the plan to end all plans with a booze-befuddled brain? And what was my excuse now? My daughter was not dead. She lived, somewhere, and if I was to stand any chance of finding her, I had to clean up my act.

I did not have many bottles, so it didn't take long to trash them all. Then I stood in the kitchen, boiling the kettle for coffee. That I would never give up. I took my steaming mug to my planter's chair, and with nothing stronger than the light of the moon, I sat there, and I thought.

All the plans that I had thought so clever, so devious, were like child's play compared to what Rosamond and Archie came up with. But they had the advantage of adhering to no rules. Nothing curbed them. Not morality. Not legality. They stole, they betrayed, they murdered. Did I have to think like them, did I have to go as far as them to beat them? Just what would I do to get my daughter back? I knew the answer even as I framed the question.

As dawn broke, I had my plan.

I took the dogs and went to Geoffrey's for breakfast. Since his precipitate return from his voyage, he'd given up his full-time role at the bank. He was now a non-executive director who worked just one or two days a week. It seemed to suit him fine. His panic attacks were a thing of the past, his heart was fine, he sailed almost every day, and he was there for me. Today was one of his at-home days, so I found him breakfasting in his chinos and lawn shirt. I took my seat to his right and buttered some toast.

'So, tell me,' he said with a smile.

'I need to meet your hacker. I need to learn how to hack, and how to pick locks.'

He laughed and interrupted me. 'And, let me guess, how to kill someone with your bare hands.'

'Yeah, something like that.'

He chuckled. He thought I was joking.

'So what will you do with all these wonderful new skills?'

'Simple. I will get into studies, offices, whatever, wherever there is a computer, and I will hack into it, and search for insurance records, records of purchase, anything that will show me who sold the *Widow*, and what their address is.'

'This would be in the collector's home, presumably,' posited Geoffrey.

'Correct,' I said, getting up to help myself to more coffee.

'And how, pray, will you get access to their homes? I cannot think that even you envisage picking the locks to their front door and strolling in.'

'No. Lacks a certain sophistication.'

'So?'

'We're talking six, max eight, possible buyers here, all super-rich, all art lovers.'

Geoffrey nodded.

'Think of a type of art that adorns the walls of almost all the super-rich, something they cannot resist.'

'Apart from Old Masters?'

'Mmm.'

Geoffrey steepled his fingers, fell silent. He loved this kind of psychological guessing game. And he was good at it.

It took him just a couple of minutes. He smiled.

'Wouldn't be portraits of themselves, would it?'

'Funny you should say that.'

'And you will paint them, I take it?'

'Who else?'

'Fine. Goodish. But how will they be persuaded that a portrait by Morganna Hutton is something they just must have, and now?'

'More psychology, Geoffrey, and some plain, good old-fashioned hard sell. That's where Toby will come in. He will quietly, in the best of ears, spread the word that he is representing a superb new portrait painter, who only accepts the most exceptional people of their generation as sitters, and who charges one million dollars a portrait, and that, if they are very, very lucky, she might, might just consider painting them.'

'I see. And he will also mention, no doubt, that she is young, and very beautiful.'

'Whatever it takes, Geoffrey.'

He buttered himself some toast, ate it before he next spoke.

'And you will not use your real name, presumably?'

'No, I will not.'

'You know, Morgan, it might have a chance.'

'I'm going to go home and ring Toby now.'

'You haven't painted for ages. Think you can still do it?'

'Oh, I'll do it, Geoffrey. It's not gone. It's all still in my head.'

He nodded. 'And, assuming you do find their address, what will you do then?'

'I will get some kind of security backup, and I will go and visit them, and this time, I will take my daughter away.'

'What, just like that?'

'I will get the police involved. Murder, attempted murder, child abduction, and theft. The charges still exist. They will be arrested, I will get custody, and Ben will get justice.'

'You've got it all worked out, haven't you?'

'Look, I know things never go according to plan, but if you don't have a plan, you'll get nowhere.'

'True, but remember, Morganna, they've killed already to keep Georgie, and to stay free. You survived once, against all the odds.'

'And I'll survive again. I'm not the girl I was, Geoffrey. I underestimated them, and their sheer evil. I won't do that again.'

'You be very, very careful. I will help you. I will set up a meeting with the hacker, try and find a lock picker from somewhere, but my condition is that you keep me informed every step of the way. If you do track them down, then I want to know, and I want to be involved in the endgame. I do not want you going off alone on your mission, on your vendetta.'

'God forbid.'

'Morganna, this is serious.'

'Geoffrey, this is about getting my daughter back. I've never been so serious about anything in my life. And don't worry, I'm not going to go and shoot Rosamond and Archie, although I won't deny I have dreamed of doing just that a million times over. I want to track them down, go to them, get my daughter away from them, and get them banged up for life. But I'm not going like a lamb to the slaughter this time. I am going to learn how to take care of myself, really take care of myself, and then, and only then, if they try anything, then Geoffrey, I *will* kill them.'

Chapter sixty-one

I saw his worried face in my mind as I drove away, as I truly began the first day of the rest of my life.

I dragged the phone to the kitchen table and I rang Toby. He answered the phone himself.

'It's the woman you threw the lifeline to,' I said.

'Morganna!'

'Not anymore. Now you will know me only as Inca.'

'Inca?'

'As in Incognita.'

'I see. Or rather I don't.'

'You got any customers in?'

'I don't, as it happens. This bloody recession's vicious.'

'Then lock your door, flip the sign to closed, and listen.'

And listen he did. The only time he interrupted was when I said the portraits would go for a million a time.

'Listen, Toby. If I price it at ten grand, they wouldn't be interested. I know these people. I grew up around them. They live and breathe exclusivity. They don't want something if it's not through the roof. You want to create a buzz. A million dollars a shot will do it, that and the fact that they get to meet, they get to find out who Inca is.'

'And who are you?'

'I'm nobody, and I'm whoever they want me to be.'

'Do they get you, too, for a million?'

I laughed. 'That's what Geoffrey was worrying about, but unlike you, he was too polite to ask.'

'So?'

'No, they don't. They get my time at the easel, and they get to put me up in their house for a few days. That I insist upon. That I paint them in their primary home.'

'So that you can hack into their computer.'

'Exactly. Directly. Oh, and Toby, if you get me in to these people's houses, you get the full mill.'

He let out a whistle. 'No half measures with you, are there?'

'No room for them.'

'I'd better get to work, then, hadn't I?'

'You'd better.'

I hung up, and I sat, riven with excitement. This thing could work. I knew it could. The dogs could feel my excitement. They were pacing around my house, agitating for a walk. I took them out, onto the deserted beach, and we walked for miles. Then I went to my garage, and dug out my paints.

I wondered what she looks like, Rosamond, over one year on? Had she disguised herself, had Archie? Where had she gone that she could blend in so easily as to be invisible?

I tried to paint her with different hair colours. I broke for lunch, and then I went and stood before my mirror and examined myself. I was nearly twenty-three, but I looked older. My black hair was streaked with the odd grey strand. I didn't like the way I looked. I was like a wraith, washed out. Major work was needed. I headed for the car. Jelly and Gin jumped up to follow me.

'Not this time, girls. I'm going to a dog-free zone.'

Michael's was Long Island's most chi-chi hairdresser. This was where the ladies who lunched, who could not spare the time to nip back to Bumble and Bumble in Manhattan, came to get their roots done and their ends trimmed. I had never been there. For the past year, I'd been cutting my own hair when it got too long.

I opened the door and crossed the threshold into what I imagined was meant to resemble a Roman bordello. Marble columns, murals, a water feature tinkling soothingly, and the reek of hair products.

A skinny blonde made her way slowly towards me.

'Yes?' she asked.

'I'd like a cut, and a colour,' I said.

'Mmm-hmm. Have you been here before?'

'No.'

'Really?' she replied, as if it wasn't evident.

'So?' I said. I felt as if I should have offered her a password, the name of some friend who had recommended her, but I could not be bothered.

'When would you like to come in?' she was forced into asking.

'No time like the present,' I replied brightly.

'Let me check the book,' she said. That was rich. The salon was empty, save her, me, and a thin black man sitting in the depths.

'Fine,' she said. She picked out a black cape. 'Would you like to put this on, and follow me.'

I walked after her and sat where indicated, before a huge mirror.

'So, what're you after? Cover up the grey?' she asked, fingering my hair, somewhat reluctantly.

'No. Something completely different. I want a new look. I want to go light. Chestnut blonde.'

'Chestnut blonde?' she said with the slightest curl of her lip. 'From black, well, blackish?'

'Why not?'

'You'll need to come in every four weeks to have your roots done, that's why not. If you don't, it'll look real tacky. And I gotta warn you. It'll be expensive.'

I laughed out loud. Why do these people feel that in the company of those they perceive to be poor they need show no tact? Are they still so impressed by a designer wardrobe that its absence fills them with contempt? I suddenly saw myself as she saw me. An unkempt woman, in off the street, with paint stains on her baggy jeans.

'Sweet of you to be so concerned, but don't worry. I'll manage, somehow. The streets pay pretty well, I understand.'

I was rewarded with a bark of laughter from behind the water feature, but my stylist, she said nothing.

It took three hours. When the two of them had finally finished, even they looked impressed.

'Wow,' said the skinny blonde, whose name I had discovered, was Sheena. 'You scrub up pretty good.'

I was amazed. I stared at the transformation they had wrought. My hair was now shoulder length, layered so

409

that the natural wave came out, and it was a dark honey blonde. I no longer looked so washed out.

'Get yourself a tan, and you'll be set.'

I got out my credit card. Never had four hundred dollars been so well spent.

'Been dumped, have you?' asked Sheena.

'In a manner of speaking. But that was way back.'

'So you're going fishing, that it?'

'That's exactly it.'

'Well, remember, back here in a month now.'

'I'll be here.'

I walked out, stunned by the alchemy performed on me. I headed for Tim's grocery. I'd been going in there every week for over a year, but that day there was no cheery wave of recognition from Wendy at the till. And that day, unlike every other time in there, I shunned the booze, and filled my trolley with a selection of foods a nutritionist would have been proud of. I pushed it up to the checkout. Wendy literally did a double take.

'My God, Morgan. Is it really you?'

I smiled. 'No, it's not. It's someone quite different.'

'No shit, Sherlock.'

As she was ringing up my purchases, I scanned the notice board. Every corner of life was there. Psychic cleansers, colonic irrigators with do-it-yourself kits on offer, astral readers, homeopaths, reflexologists, yoga teachers, and, what I hoped I might see, a tae kwan do instructor, available for groups or individual tuition. I wrote down his name and number, collected my brown paper bags, and headed home.

The dogs were not impressed. They barked at me

and sniffed me repeatedly — only then did they quiet down.

'It's me, girls. It really is. And I know you've been stuck here for hours. Sorry. Look, how about a walk on the beach, no, even better, a run, then dinner?'

This they liked. I pulled on ancient trainers, sweat-pants, and a T-shirt, and off we went. I was not as unfit as I should have been, and I managed to keep up a good pace for fifteen minutes before I had to slow to a walk.

That night, I fell into the deepest sleep I had had in years. I didn't even dream.

When I awoke, I just lay in bed and listened to the sound of the ocean. Today, it was just a gentle wash. I'd never really listened to it like this before. Normally when I woke up I was in the throes of a hangover any-way, and in no position to enjoy any sound. But that day, everything was different. Now that I had some-thing to live for, it was as if a switch has been flipped inside me and everything felt new and brilliant.

I got out of bed and my muscles groaned. I'd forgot-ten to stretch out after my run.

'Hey, Gin, Jelly, want to go for another run?'

They galloped round me as I dressed and stretched painfully. Out we went. The day had dawned clear. There was the first hint of spring warmth in the air. Soon it would be time to swim. I walked for a bit, to warm up, and then, pursued by my dogs, I started to run.

After breakfast I rang the tae kwan do man.

'Pete Marshall,' said a surprisingly high-pitched voice.

'Marshall?'

'Yeah. Marshall. What can I do for you?'

'Er, this is Morganna Hutton. I'm ringing about tae kwan do lessons?'

'What d'you wanna know?'

'Can you teach me?'

'Teach you to what?'

'Defend myself.'

'I can try. Want to meet up, talk about it?'

'Are you any good?'

There was a polite laugh. 'I'm a black belt, seventh degree. That good enough for you?'

'Sounds all right.'

Pete Marshall sounded about fourteen. I wondered if I was being had.

'Look, I'm teaching tonight at Bethesda Hall. Seven till nine. Know it?'

'Yeah, I do.'

'Come and watch if you like. Satisfy yourself, if you think I'm up to it, or not.'

From the outside, Bethesda Hall looked more suited to a women's institute fete than a martial arts session. It was seven thirty, and I was fully expecting to find the hall deserted, but I could hear the shouts and grunts from outside. I pulled open the door and headed in quietly.

There were about twelve white-clad men and women, mainly men, performing a series of kicks and punches at invisible opponents. Standing opposite them, demonstrating, was a figure I assumed to be Pete Marshall. He did look a bit older than fourteen, but not much. He was about five foot four, maybe a hundred and forty pounds, wiry and lean, with dark, curly hair, but boy, did he know his stuff. I supposed, looking like he did, tae kwan do was a smart option.

I took a seat and I watched. He kicked, he punched, he took blows and deflected them. He made his class sweat, laugh, and curse. This whole subculture existed, half a mile from my home. All these people, all their lives. I was conscious again of how I had scarcely lived in such a long time — of my own self-imposed isolation. Were it not for my dogs, and Geoffrey, I would have gone mad.

When the class had finished, I looked at my watch in surprise. An hour and a half had flown by. Slowly, people trekked out. Marshall said goodnight to them, and made his way over to me.

'The skeptical Morganna?' he asked.

I nodded, abashed.

'So?'

'I'd like you to teach me,' I said. 'When can you start?'

'Well, am I glad I passed your test. You want private tuition?'

'I do.'

'Hundred bucks an hour.'

'Two hours a day?'

'Whoa, there. What's the hurry? You on some kind of mission?'

'I just want to be able to look after myself.'

'Yeah. Right. Well listen up, for starters, two hours a day would kill you. I don't wanna get too personal here, but you don't exactly look like you've been doin' much with that body a yours, so let's do an hour three times a week, and see how it goes.'

'All right.'

And so we set it up.

I drove home. While I was waiting for my pasta to cook, I called Toby.

'Hi, just checking in.'

'Nothing new to report yet, I'm afraid. You're going to have to be patient, Morganna. Softly, softly, catchee monkey.'

'I'm no good at softly, softly.'

'Then get good,' he said, and hung up. I laughed. I loved his rudeness. He hadn't been rude to me in ages. This was infinitely better than kid gloves and a padded cell.

Geoffrey called just as I was tucking into pasta alla carbonara.

'You talk, I'll eat,' I managed to enunciate.

'I've got your computer consultant all lined up,' he said. 'Want his number?'

'You bet. Let me grab a pen.'

He gave me the number. I scribbled it down and rang him as soon as Geoffrey was off the line.

'Yep?'

'Er, it's Geoffrey Warrender's friend here,' I said. 'You spoke with him about giving me some lessons.'

'That's right.'

'When can you come?'

'End of the week. Friday?'

'Sounds good. Afternoon?'

'Thousand bucks an hour.'

'God!'

'Five thousand corporate.'

'Bargain then.'

'You better believe it, honey.'

'Look, let's get one thing straight, shall we. A thousand bucks an hour is fine. Honey is not.'

He laughed. 'Ten o'clock, *honey*?'

Who said I had to like the guy? 'Ten o'clock Friday is fine. By the way, I don't know your name. If I'm to be *honey*, shall I just call you *nerdy*? I imagine you must be, all that time in front of a screen.'

He laughed again. 'Whatever the hell you like. You're payin'.'

And in this way, I convinced myself that I was doing something, however remote, to bring Georgie closer, while she kept growing up, a stranger, in an unknown place, not even aware that I existed. And then I wondered, had Archie got another woman, someone Georgie called mother? Only then, as the thought burned its way through my mind and into my heart, did I learn the real meaning of jealousy.

Chapter sixty-two

Pete Marshall arrived the next day at three. Gin and Jelly started up a real commotion. Rarely did strangers pull up here. They were good guard dogs, these two.

'Down girls, sit now. Quiet.'

They quieted down, but refused to sit. They flanked me as I opened the door.

'Hi!' said Marshall. He was wearing old sweatpants and an army-green tattered T-shirt.

My outfit was almost as decrepit. 'Hi. Don't mind my dogs here, they're friendly enough.'

He gave me a wry look. 'Might not be near so friendly when they see me kicking at you?'

'I take your point.' I led them by their collars. 'Girls, you are going to need to hang out in the kitchen for a while, and be good.'

They cast me reproachful looks as I shut them in. I returned to find Marshall surveying my large living room.

'We need to move some stuff.'

'Okay.'

And so together we moved the sofa, two armchairs, and two side tables, and a standard lamp.

He surveyed the space

'Better. Let's get my mats.'

I followed him out to a beat-up red Chevy. He let down the back and hauled out two large, heavy-duty mats from atop a blanketed floor. We lugged one each into my house and laid them out in the newly vacated space. They just fitted.

'Great.' Now he appraised me. 'Got any injuries, any health conditions?'

'Old injuries.'

'Like what?'

'A few breaks.'

'Where?'

'Uh, ribs, legs, arms, and fractured skull.'

'Jesus Jones. What the hell happened?'

'Car crash.'

'Fractured skull?'

'Mmm. Look, that was years ago. I'm well over it.'

'You sure?'

'Absolutely.'

'Need to sign a disclaimer. All my students do.'

'Fine by me.' I was glad I didn't tell him about the coma, or about rebreaking the same ribs on the cliff at Cape Wrath. I had a feeling he would have packed his mats and sped off.

He pulled a sheet of paper out of his sports bag and handed it over. I read it carefully. No longer did I ever, ever, sign anything on trust.

Finally I signed and handed back the paper. He dropped it into his bag and took a long swig of water from a sports bottle.

'You ready?' he asked, dropping the bottle back into the bag.

'I'm ready.'

'Warm up, first.'

He fell into a number of stretches, legs, hips, arms. I followed his moves, aware how stiff I was. It took a good ten minutes to go through all the poses, many of which looked like yoga to me.

'Right, let's get the blood moving,' he said, launching into a series of star jumps. I followed suit and then we changed to jogging on the spot. I could feel the colour rising to my face. Boy, was I glad I'd given up the booze. I'd have been throwing up by now.

'Good. Now we can play this two ways. The conventional, where I take it slow, a real methodical buildup, or I can teach you certain short cuts, specialize in a small number of techniques. Won't get you a belt, might just get you out of trouble, if you're stupid enough to find it in the first place.'

I laughed. 'Oh, I'm stupid enough.'

'Thought you might say that. So, short cut?'

'Please.'

'Right. We'll start with kicks, then punches, then evasive action, how to get out of a neck lock, that sort of stuff.'

'Sounds good.'

One hour later I could hardly move. We went through an even longer stretch out than the one we opened with. I knew that without it I probably wouldn't be able to get out of bed tomorrow.

'Have a hot bath tonight,' he said. 'Get a rub down, if you can.'

The bath would have to do. 'Okay.'

'You will be stiff tomorrow. Go through the stretches I've shown you, morning and night, or you'll be even stiffer in two days when we have our next session.'

'Great.'

'Don't say I didn't warn you.'

'I think I'll swim in the sea. That always sorts me out.'

Marshall looked at me incredulously. He nodded towards the breaking waves. 'In that? In March?'

'Cold water's even better for you.'

'If you say so. I hope you can swim.'

'That I can do.'

'You're not bad at this gig, either, for a complete beginner. Got a real dose of aggression.'

I smiled. He had no idea.

Chapter sixty-three

The next day dawned sunny. The good spell continued and my mood was on a high too. I eased out of bed, stiff, but not chronically so. I did a few of Marshall's stretches, and then, watched by my excited dogs, I pulled on my swimsuit and robe. They knew what this meant. A dip for all of us.

I jogged slowly down to the water's edge. There was hardly a breeze, and the swell was uncharacteristically muted. Suddenly I was assailed by a memory of the waves I used to watch from my tower at Wrath Castle, the great, terrifying behemoths that smashed into the cliff face, and sprayed my outstretched fingers with brine. I sometimes wondered if I ever did live that life, or if it was just some schizophrenic dream. And then I thought of Georgie. Unconsciously, I reached down to where my Caesarean scar lay hidden beneath my swimsuit. A legacy of proof that cut through any doubt.

I was drawn back by my dogs, nosing my legs, whimpering and barking with excitement.

I turned to them.

'All right, girls, you ready?'

And together we ran into the icy grip of the water. Swim, swim, I commanded shrieking limbs. In two minutes, I had adjusted. I did not feel the cold, just the exhilaration. My dogs swam gamely beside me, rising and falling with the gentle swell. I looked at them and I laughed out loud, with pure, almost forgotten happiness.

I swam every day. I added that to my regime of running and tae kwan do. Friday came, and with it a double dose of my program. At ten, the hacker was coming, and Marshall at three.

I was curious about the hacker. I sat in front of my flickering computer screen, nursing my coffee, wondering what a desktop outlaw looked like. The answer surprised me. The roar of what can only be a Harley-Davidson drew me to my door at one minute to ten. Off got a leather-clad figure, well over six feet tall, and sturdy. He pulled off his helmet, and, I kid you not, shook out his hair. Long, wavy, black hair, shiny as a raven's feathers. He regarded me for a moment and then strode up to me.

'Hi,' he said, shaking my hand.

'Hi,' I replied. 'You must be Nerdy.'

He grinned, showing off pearl-white teeth. 'That's me. And you're Honey.'

I gave a half-grin, half-grimace.

'Andreas,' he said, still holding my hand.

'Morgan,' I replied.

I led him in. My dogs eyed him gravely. They could not quite believe the new traffic that had hit this house of late.

'Coffee?' I asked.

He looked at the cup in my hand. 'Only if you have something decent.'

'I take it instant doesn't do it for you?'

He shook his locks. 'Nope.'

'Tough. That's all I have.'

'And I thought you were classy.'

'Got that wrong, didn't you?'

'Maybe not,' he replied, looking around. 'Nice sketches.'

I shrugged.

'You did them?'

'It's a hobby.'

'You could sell stuff like that, go pro.'

'Yeah, well, I nearly did, once.'

'What happened?'

'Shit happened. Come on, time to meet my computer.'

He sat down in front of it. 'Pull up a chair,' he commanded. I pulled one over, and he turned to look at me.

'Right, now tell me exactly what is it you're planning to get up to?'

So I told him. Just the hacking bit. He grinned. 'With ninety-nine percent of the computer-literate population, it's a breeze.'

'And the other one percent?'

'Let's hope you don't run into that.'

So he taught me, for nearly three hours. It was meant to be two, but, amazingly, once we got started, we both lost track of time. He looked at his watch in surprise.

'Gotta go. You got my dough?'

'Cash or cheque?'

'Whichever.'

'How much? We ran over.'

'Consider it goodwill. Two grand.'

I handed over a cheque. He folded it and tucked it away into a pocket of his leather jacket.

'Next Friday?'
'Can we do two lessons a week?'
'You in a hurry?'
I nodded.
'Tuesday? Same time?'
'Fine with me.'
He pulled on his helmet, and, with a roar and a wave zoomed off.

Chapter sixty-four

On Saturday, after my swim, I took my dogs round to Geoffrey's. He always looked somewhat pained when I arrived with them. I knew he was worrying about a tail lashing into a Ming vase, or some such insurance nightmare. He tried his best to conceal it, but I knew him too well. But that day, he just looked wide-eyed at me.

'My Gaad. Morganna! What have you done?'

'*I've* done nothing. Michael's have tried their best to transform me into . . .' I shrugged, 'I don't quite know what.'

He stood back to study me. 'Close up, it's you, but, hell, from a distance, I wouldn't know you.'

'Good. That was part of the plan.'

He thought for a moment, oblivious of the dogs. Then he broke into a wide smile.

'Got it. Inca. As in Incognita.'

'Very good.'

'Toby told me. He thinks it's a great name. Pure and simple. I knew it had to mean something, above and beyond.'

'You should be a full-time crossword-solver.'

'Bank goes down, I probably would be.'

'No chance of that, is there?'

'You don't read the papers, do you?'

'Not for a while. Who needs it?'

'You might have a point. Steve Welland, Moon Systems?'

'Steve Welland, Rembrandt collector?'

'One and the same. Just got served the most godawful massive antitrust suit.'

'Ah. Might curb his collecting?'

'Might curb mine. We have over three hundred mill out to Moon Systems.'

'Painful, but that won't sink you. Even I know your balance sheet can handle that.'

'That on its own, sure. That with all the other stuff hitting us, who knows?'

I paused. I could not imagine the bank going down, the smooth money-making machine I'd always thought it.

'You're not serious?'

'No,' he said with a faint smile. 'I *am* worried, but we *can* handle it.'

'Welland might not be too keen to sit still for a portrait, is that what you're thinking? Or feel he has a spare mill?'

'He's cocky. Nobody gets where he is if they're not. He'll play it cool. He'll lobby, he'll throw everything and everyone he owns at it, and he'll probably win. But hell, he's also vain. He might just appreciate the distraction, that's if he takes the bait.'

I smiled. 'Well, nice to know he's a client, that we can have a go at him from two directions.'

Geoffrey eyed me narrowly. 'He's well known as a collector of Old Masters, of Rembrandts particularly, but we have no evidence he's one of the half-dozen, do we?'

'None, save pure probability. And hell, we have to start somewhere.'

'I hope you're not suggesting that I set up something where you go in and hack one of my major clients.'

'You know me, Geoffrey, that's exactly what I'm thinking.'

He mused on it for a moment. 'Looking like you do, might not be too tough.'

'Meaning?'

'You looked in a mirror lately? You look sensational. Not just your hair, but something in you. You're glowing.'

'That's because I'm alive again, because I have hope.'

He smiled. 'You breakfasted yet?'

'Nope.'

'Come on, let's go eat.'

Jelly and Gin slunk after me, and sat obedient and still at my feet, silently scoffing the bacon bribes that rained down.

Chapter sixty-five

Another week passed with no news from Toby. I rang him on the Monday, only to be cautioned to patience. By Friday, what little patience I had managed to cultivate ran out.

'This isn't something I can just pick up a phone and arrange, like that,' he snapped when I rang again.

'I know that,' I replied. 'It's just agony sitting here waiting. I wish there was something extra I could do.'

'Paint the president. That'd be a good sell, not to mention keeping you busy.'

I laughed. 'I don't think my connections are quite up to that, but how about a NASDAQ chairman?' I asked, thinking about Geoffrey's contacts. 'What about Murdo?'

'As in Global News?'

'That's him.'

'You get him to sit, my dear, and you make my job a lot easier.'

'Why didn't you say?' I asked, unable to conceal my irritation.

'I didn't bloody say because it didn't occur to me that you might be connected.'

'I'm rich, Toby, you know that. And here, and I can't believe it's not the same in Britain, despite all your aristocratic pretensions, money connects.'

'Silly me,' he said with all his queenly indignation, and hung up.

I rang Geoffrey straightaway. 'Geoffrey, I need Andrew Murdo, delivered on a plate, for me to paint.'

'He's not on the list, is he?'

'No, he's not. But I need a name, someone to add to my CV. Somewhat to start off my CV, let's face it. And Murdo's is one of the biggest in town. Because he's not on the list, we don't need to be so subtle.'

'Hmm. Let me think about it. I'll get back to you.'

And that is how my next week of preparation passed. The following one was pretty much identical. Murdo was on some world tour, the financial equivalent of a rock band's touting for business. Not even Geoffrey could get to him. And so I ran, I swam, I hacked, and I tried to kick ass. And, hardest of all, I tried to be patient.

March ran into April. The weather grew suddenly cold again, and the breakers became huge. Sometimes my heart was in my mouth as I hurled myself in, watched from the safety of the shore by my worried dogs. But I was getting stronger with all the training I was doing, so I emerged, battered and exhilarated, from the waves. My body was changing. Where once I had been thin, I now had muscles. And my skin was no longer pallid. All the time I spent outside had given me a wind tan.

I was painting too, honing rusty skills. I'd taken my two teachers as sitters. My opportunity for revenge if they were too tough on me. They were pleased with the results, Pete and Andreas, and I was pleased that I could still conjure a likeness, and capture something of what lay beneath.

Then one Saturday morning, the first to dawn warm and sunny for weeks, Geoffrey arrived just as the dogs and I were trekking back across the sand after our dip.

'Hey, Morgan.'

'Hi, Geoffrey. Aren't you the cat that's got the cream? What's up?'

'Clean your brushes, Morganna. I've got you a commission.'

'Murdo?'

He nodded.

'You are a *star*.'

He grinned. 'Well, if you insist.'

'How, when?'

'He's coming round, two weeks today, to meet you, go for a sail, lunch, the whole gig.'

'Wow. I'm amazed he can schedule a whole day.'

'All a question of how ya sell it, Morgan.'

'I never knew you could hustle.'

He barked out a laugh. 'I'm an investment banker, for Chrissakes.'

'Well, yeah, but a refined one.'

He was still laughing. 'All that means is we hide the hustle under pinstripes and a tony suit.'

'Fine. As long as I'm not supposed to hustle him.'

Geoffrey gave me a wry look. 'I think, Morgan, that all you need to do is just be.'

That night, I got another piece of news. Toby called. He was in Tokyo. It was the middle of the night and he said he'd just got back from a club.

'I just heard something you might find interesting,' he drawled. 'Had a drink or three with some friends in the insurance game. Fine art insurance. They just got a nice new piece of business.'

'Come on, tell.'

'This is why I told you to be patient, Morganna. You play the game, slowly, you get around, keep your ears open, and hey presto . . .'

'I'm listening.'

'They just insured the *Widow*.'

'Who for?'

He told me.

It was late, but I rang Geoffrey anyway. When I told him, he whistled. Next I told him my idea.

'Listen, Geoffrey, you know the Saturday when Murdo's coming?'

'Yes?'

'Why don't you make it a corporate thing? Ask, say, your top ten clients, see who can make it, say that you've commissioned a group portrait of your most important clients. All they need to do is mingle, drink vintage champagne, snuffle canapés, even go out on the yacht together, while I snap away. I'll paint a group portrait from the photographs.

'Morgan, the diplomatic fallout of choosing some, leaving others out, is gonna be a nightmare, for one. Second, how the hell am I meant to get them all together with two weeks' notice, and third, assuming I get even half our top ten clients out here, if *Hurricane* goes down the NASDAQ'd tank and my memory would be dirt.'

That was when I laughed. That was when I knew he'd do it.

That night I did not sleep. I sat in my Long Island planter's chair and watched the moon traverse the horizon, and then I watched the sun come up, hesitant at first, then triumphant in a blaze of glory, all the while trying to see my daughter in my mind's eye.

Chapter sixty-six

Geoffrey had pulled it off, as I knew he would. I didn't dare think how he had hustled behind the scenes, what promises he had made. Perhaps he had just thrown down an invitation with such casual aplomb that, from a man known to be socially reclusive but to live like Gatsby, it was irresistible.

I found myself agonizing for the first time in years over what I should wear, and furious that it mattered. I had gone shopping on the Friday, inexpertly trawling Long Island's boutiques, hunting for I wasn't sure what. Anyway, I bought five different outfits, all of which lay strewn on my bed. I finally selected a pair of black cotton pedal pushers with scalloped edges and a black T-shirt, with black espadrilles. I added some gypsy-hoop gold earrings Geoffrey had given me for my last birthday, and finally stood, armed with my camera and twenty rolls of film, on his emerald green lawn, waiting for Steve Welland to arrive, pretending I was even the slightest bit interested in anyone else who was there.

As I aimed and snapped, I discover that it was rather wonderful to hide behind a camera. It was far less intimate than painting a portrait. I could move around, camera obscuring my face, snapping away, and be largely ignored. Those men, and, yes, they were all men, were so used to having their picture taken they affected indifference. I say affected because I did glimpse the odd flash of vanity in the tilt of a chin and the sucking in of a stomach, and I knew it was in part vanity that had brought them there that day.

Suddenly, the men I was snapping became more self-conscious, they talked more animatedly, laughed a little louder. Then I saw why. Into their chino'd midst strolled Welland, hands in pockets, leaning back slightly, the picture of nonchalant power. I saw Geoffrey stride forward to greet him, to take him into the centre and introduce him, not that he needed any introduction. There was most definitely a pecking order at work, and he was right at the top. Intrigued, I snapped away, moving around the group like an animal circling its prey. I took six rolls of film over the next fifteen minutes, and then I had to go inside to label them all, store the used films, and load up with fresh supplies. I had made Geoffrey's office my centre of operations. I was sitting spread-eagled on the floor, sorting my gear, when the door opened behind me.

I assumed it was Geoffrey, coming in to get something, but another voice altogether spoke.

'Good yoga pose. Could straighten the back a tad, though.'

I whirled round. Welland was standing there, a self-satisfied grin on his face.

'So you're a yoga guru now, are you?' I carried on labelling my films, trying to blank out the irritation he provoked in me.

'I wouldn't say guru. Practitioner, maybe.'

'Really.'

'And you're the artist?'

I was finding it difficult to pursue the conversation in that position. I drew my legs together and got up.

'I am.'

He gestured at the portrait of Geoffrey that I painted years ago.

'That one a' yours?'

I nodded.

He studied it for a while in silence.

'Pretty good,' he pronounced.

'Thank you.'

'So how come you know Geoffrey then? You his mistress?'

I laughed at the thought, and also at the man's impudence.

'No. I'm not.'

'That's all right,' he said. 'I know who you are.'

I tried to keep my eyes from widening.

'You're his charge, aren't you? If that's still the right word to describe you.'

I was horrified. So much for a cover story.

'It's all right. Your secret's safe with me.'

'How did you find out?' I asked, fuming.

'Easy. I have a whole team of security people. They won't let me go anywhere without checking the place and the people out first — unless I manage to sneak off, which I sometimes do to keep sane.'

'Geoffrey didn't say anything about this.'

'Geoffrey didn't know.'

I sank down onto a chair.

'Just how much do you know about me?'

'Not a whole heap. You're Geoffrey's charge. You grew up here, went to Florence to learn to paint, spent some time overseas, came back . . .'

'Is that it?'

He nodded.

How could I know what to believe?

'Don't take it so bad,' he said grinning. 'Nothing like a bit of nepotism, is there?'

At this, and at my casual exposure, the tattering of my plans, my anger flared.

'What, nobody ever helped you on your way up?'

'Nope. Did it all myself.'

'We all have luck, good or bad.'

'Luck is impersonal, isn't it?'

'Never feels so to me.'

'So, your guardian got you other commissions?'

'Has anyone ever told you that you can be really obnoxious?'

Oh shit. This was not going the way I had choreographed it in my mind.

He laughed. 'Plenty of people, but none so charmingly.'

'I didn't mean to be charming.'

He laughed again.

'So tell me, why paint when you can photograph?'

'Painting is so much more subtle. It's not a machine capturing a likeness, it's a human being trying to represent an image, but to capture something from within too.'

'You paint people's souls?'

'I wouldn't put it so grandiloquently as that.'

'So how would you put it, then?'

'I try to paint what lies hidden.'

His eyes widened. 'Now we're getting interesting. Want to paint me?'

'I'm going to.'

He shook his head. 'Not with the rest of these jokers. On my own.'

My heart started to race. I was sure colour was rising to my face. 'Where?'

He looked puzzled. 'Wherever you like,' he replied.

'Where do you live? I asked. 'I mean, really live?'

'My favourite home, where I keep all the things I really care about, that's a sort of holiday home, where I go whenever I can.'

I nodded. 'Where is it?'

'Wyoming.'

I waited. I could hardly breathe.

'So, will you paint me?' he asked.

I smiled. 'You sure you can afford me?'

'I think just maybe.'

'There's a condition,' I said. 'In addition to the money.'

'Shoot.'

'You don't tell anyone who I am.'

'Why?'

'Because I want to make my own way, without connotations, associations.'

He thought about this for a while. He pondered. I prayed.

'All right. I'll meet your condition. But tell me something. What shall I call you?'

'Inca,' I said.

He looked straight at me, silent for all of five seconds, and then he grinned. 'Incognita!' he said with triumph.

Despite myself, I was impressed. 'Faster than Geoffrey,' I said.

'I should be. It's what I do,' he replied. 'Write codes. That's all software is.'

'Break codes,' I replied.

'Breaking's just the flip-side of making, isn't it?'

Suddenly I felt nervous. This man's brain was like a laser, and I felt I was being unpicked.

'I'd better get back.' I grabbed up my kit.

'So when will you paint me?' he asked.

'You tell me. You're the one with the schedule.'

'Next weekend?' he suggested.

I nodded. 'Fine with me.' I tried to keep my voice nonchalant.

He grabbed up a piece of paper, scribbled down an address, and a phone number.

'Would you like a ride?'

I looked at him uncomprehendingly.

'My plane,' he said. 'We can travel down together, if you like.'

'Yes, thank you. That would be very convenient,' I replied, sounding to myself like an Austen heroine.

I played out the day, doing my stuff, dodging the odd advance. Sun and alcohol were great levellers, bringing the CEOs down to earthier levels. Geoffrey took us all out on *Hurricane*. It was a perfect day, clear blue sky, stiff breeze, but smooth waves. I caught Welland looking at me from time to time. I smiled, and hid behind my camera. I did not want to talk to him again. I did not want to give him any chance to change his mind, to tell me he was suddenly busy, that he didn't really want a portrait after all.

Finally they all left. Geoffrey and I sat down to a light supper. Only then did we have a chance to speak.

'So, how'd it go?' he asked.

I smiled. 'I'm going to Wyoming. Next weekend. To paint him.'

'Good Gaad. How'd you pull that one off?'

'I didn't really. He sort of came to me. I practically had to do nothing.'

Perhaps that should have made me suspicious, but I was so keyed up, all I could see was next weekend, and a computer in an office, waiting to offer up its secrets to me.

Geoffrey studied me carefully. I could see him weighing his words.

'Be careful, Morgan. You've got your access all right, but to just about the worst individual in the world you could want to hack. This goes wrong and you could finish up in the lock up.'

If this went wrong, I thought, jail would be irrelevant.

Chapter sixty-seven

I prepared myself as best I could. The prospect of hacking into the computer of the man who designed its brain worried me just a tad. It would have to have been him who bought the *Widow at the Window*, wouldn't it, not some beef baron or plastics manufacturer. But a plan was a plan, and I couldn't think of a better one. For an exorbitant fee, Andreas gave me some software he had written, which he promised would deliver up the password of ninety-nine-point-nine percent of all users, and get me where I needed to go. I could only pray it worked. I booked him every day of that week, three hours a time. I told him to teach me every last trick he possessed, and I opened my chequebook.

I continued too with my tae kwan do, my swimming, and my runs. I hardly had time to eat, or to think, which is just how I wanted it. When I crawled into bed at eleven, I was so tired that sleep usually came mercifully fast. Except for Thursday night. Then I could not help myself from playing out in my head the exact way I wanted it all to go. I would emerge on Sunday with the address, I would buy the plane ticket to wherever, I would arrive. I would see my daughter playing in some kindergarten yard, or riding in a car. At that point my thoughts dissolved. The yearning to see her, the fear of getting it all wrong was so great that I literally could not see straight, even in my mind. I knew that somehow, I was going to have to distance myself, just so that I could function, if I was to have any chance.

On Friday morning, early, I took my dogs to Geoffrey's. I'd never left them for a single day, let alone night, since I came back to Long Island. They knew something was up and were whiny and subdued. Geoffrey looked worried. I put it down to dog sitting. I had a car waiting outside to drive me to the airstrip in New Jersey. I used it as an excuse to drop them and run. I don't want any more warnings. My stomach was churning already.

Welland's plane was huge, not one of those dinky executive toys you expected to fall apart if it hit turbulence. Apart from his two pilots, a cook, and a steward who was built like a bodyguard, we were alone. Which is just how I didn't want it. I had imagined he would have with him a phalanx of secretaries and bodyguards. When I told him this, he laughed.

'It's Friday afternoon.'

'I thought you'd be a workaholic.'

'Even workaholics need downtime.'

I nodded, gazed out of the window as we soared over Manhattan.

'You like my jet?' he asked.

A smile snuck up on me before I could conceal it. The boy was father of the man.

'It beats cattle class.'

'That's it?'

'And it's reassuringly solid.'

'You been in one before?'

'A few times. Geoffrey uses one sometimes.'

'Money doesn't impress you, does it?'

I shook my head. 'I was born with a fair bit of it

myself, enough to remove the mystique and the novelty value.'

'So what does impress you?'

Suddenly I thought of Ben. He impressed me, with his quiet dignity, his goodness.

'Integrity. Humour.'

He nodded. 'My experience, there're only two types of people don't care about money. The very rich, or the true mystics, guys who have their minds focused on a higher plane.'

I laughed. 'You don't think that's me?'

'You're not a mystic, no. But I've got a feeling your mind's focused on some pretty serious shit.'

I pulled out my book. 'I'm tired,' I said. 'You don't mind if I read?'

He looked momentarily surprised, and then he shook his head.

'Go right ahead. There's a cabin back there, if you want some privacy, or a sleep.'

I thought that would be too rude. 'I'm fine, thanks. Just got to an interesting bit,' I said, gesturing to my book.

If he noticed that I opened it at page one, he was too polite to say.

His house was high on a mountainside, nestling in its own small plateau, looking out across the Teton Valley at the snow-capped peaks beyond. It was honest to goodness beautiful, built of stone, timber, and glass, sited amidst some of the most stunning scenery known to man. By this I was impressed.

'You like it?' Welland asked me.

'I love it. How could I not? Everything about it is beautiful.'

'Thanks. Designed it myself.'

'What, no architect?'

'Sure I had an architect. Thing would have looked pretty but fallen down without him. I know nothing about joists and weight-bearing walls and all that caboodle. I just drew the look I wanted.'

'Is there anything you can't do?' I asked.

'How long you got?'

I grinned. I hadn't expected humour, and it took my mind off another building, another architect.

He showed me to my room. The picture window opened onto a balcony that hung out over space. Standing on it, I felt as if I were floating.

'Would you like to eat alone, or with me?' he asked. God, I hadn't realized I'd given off quite such *I vant to be alone* vibes. But perhaps he just didn't want dinner with me?

'Would you like to eat alone?'

'Not unless you want to.'

'Well, no. I'd like to eat with you.'

'Great. Drinks in half an hour?'

'Sounds good.'

He was waiting for me in a room at the top of the house. The ceiling was glass, partially covered with blinds.

I craned my neck and looked up.

'For the stars,' he said. 'In winter, I like to lie here in front of the fire and just gaze up at the night sky. If it's clear, you can see the Milky Way.'

'Wow.'

'What'll you have to drink?'

'Er, just water, please.'

'You don't drink alcohol?'

I shook my head.

'Why not, or is that too personal?'

'I used to drink. I stopped before it got too much.'

'What made you drink?'

I laughed. 'What makes anyone drink?'

'So why stop?'

'Didn't need it anymore.'

'Mmm-hmm.'

He could see I would go no further, and retreated gracefully to pour me a water. As I took the glass from him, I froze. Beyond his shoulder, on the far wall, was the painting. He turned and followed my gaze.

'Fantastic, isn't it?'

I walked over to it. I stopped before it. I could not speak. In my head, I saw it in its place in the great hall, and then I saw the empty frame. I could almost hear the sound of the wailing wind.

I felt Welland's hand on my shoulder. 'Are you all right? You're white as a sheet.'

'What?' I looked at him as if he were a stranger, morphed out of nowhere. 'Oh, I'm fine. It's nothing.' I took a gulp of water. 'It's admiration, despair,' I improvised quickly, 'that I will never do anything that even approaches this.'

He looked at me carefully. 'Would you like to see some more, or is that enough for one night?'

This was my chance of a guided tour, the opportunity to search for his computer.

'I'd love to,' I replied.

So he led me through his house. He had five Rembrandts, including *Widow at the Window*, a clutch of Picassos, three Titians, two Gauguins. I could have gone on. And, in his study on the second floor, he had a computer. I dragged my eyes from it.

'You live like a Venetian king,' I said.

He shrugged. 'I'm lucky enough to be able to buy some of the things I love.'

'Can I ask you an indiscreet question?' I asked him.

'You can ask.'

'The *Widow at the Window*. How much did you pay for it?'

'Thirty mill,' he said.

Low. Lower than what they could have got on the open market, but enough to let them hide forever and a day.

'What, you think that's too much?' he was asking me.

I felt a sudden panic. I could not have it getting back to Rosamond that someone was showing an unhealthy interest in that painting.

'Whatever it takes,' I said with an airy shrug. 'God, I'm hungry.'

'Bored with my art?' he asked.

'Yeah, that's it.'

He led me down to the dining room.

'I wasn't sure what you liked, but I thought I'd take a risk. You like Vietnamese cooking?'

'I love it. Only had it a few times. Ages ago.' I thought of the Vietnamese restaurant just off Sloane Square that Archie and I went to a few times.

'My cook's Vietnamese. Does the best food outside Saigon, I like to think.'

He pulled out a chair for me and I sat down. He took a seat opposite me. I looked across the table at him, relaxed, smiling, and I was hit by the force of his attraction. I wished he were old and ugly, or, better still, young, obnoxious, and brash.

His air steward brought in bowls of soup and laid them delicately before us. Layer upon layer of flavour hit my tongue as I drained the bowl with almost indecent haste. Welland watched me, smiling.

'That was absolutely delicious.' Helped by the fact that for over a day I had hardly been able to get anything beyond black coffee down, but I didn't tell him that.

And so it went on, course after course of utterly delicious food, finished off by the most delicate lemon sorbet I had ever eaten.

Our plates were cleared and we got to our feet.

'Thank you. That was truly spoiling.'

'Can I get you anything else?'

I wondered what he was offering me.

'Coffee, herbal tea?' he added, as if reading my mind.

I shook my head. 'No thanks. I'd better get some sleep. Busy day tomorrow.'

'What time d'you want to get going?' he asked.

'Soon as we can. Say nine?'

'Suits me. I'm always up early. We can start before then if you like?'

'Nine's fine.'

'Room I showed you's okay?'

'North-facing, huge picture window. Could have been designed as a studio.'

'That's me. Mr. Perspicacious.'

I smiled. ''Night then.'

'Sleep well,' he said.

I had no such intention. I disappeared with a yawn.

Chapter sixty-eight

It was eleven thirty. I sat in my room by the open window, lights out, and waited. I knew he said he woke early, but I reckoned he was probably the kind of man who only needed a few hours' sleep. I could feel my heart racing all the time I was waiting. There was no risk I would accidentally fall asleep, no matter that I ought to have been exhausted, that I had hardly slept the night before. At two o'clock, I got ready. I went to the loo for the tenth time, slipped Andreas's disks into my pockets and slowly, stealthily in my bare feet, I let myself out of my room.

The floors were wooden, but so well built they did not betray me by creaking as I passed. Spotlights in the ceiling burned gently, thoughtfully lighting my way. At a window I saw a sliver of new moon. I made a wish.

It felt as if I was moving like an automaton, along a predestined path. The idea that I could turn back was a theoretical impossibility. I was like a runner, looking to the tape.

I found his office. As I reached for the door, I entertained the thought that it might have been locked, hand hovering. But the security here was external; he did not perceive threats to come from the inside. I took the handle and turned it. With a polite click, it opened and I moved inside. I closed it gently behind me. Now it was almost completely dark, save for the thread of light coming from the moon. I had to wait until my eyes adjusted before I risked moving. Two, three minutes later, and the contours of the room and its contents slowly emerged from the darkness. I moved over to his desk, pulled out his red-leather, ergonomic chair, and sat down. I turned on his computer and screen and waited, imagining bells ringing. But the only sound was a murmuring whirr as the machine warmed up.

I slipped out Andreas's disk and pushed it into the floppy drive. Figures scrolled down the screen before me, so fast I could not read them. It reminded me of *The Matrix*. Then the mayhem stopped and a message flashed up. Password accepted. Up came the desktop, with about forty icons. I searched for anything that sounded like art. After three false starts, I opened a file called Log. It listed paintings, artists, purchase value, insurance value. I started to scroll down. My heart began to really race. I could see the finish line, so close. I imagined Georgie standing there, willing me on. And then I heard a quiet click as the door opened. I wheeled around. It was Welland. His face was rigid with fury.

'What the *hell* are you doing?'

I felt as if I were falling. I wanted to scream out in despair. The figure of my daughter ran away, vanished. What could I say? How could I even begin to explain?

Welland flicked on the light, closed the door behind him, and crossed the room to me.

'Silence won't cut it. You are going to tell me what you are doing. And why.'

I rubbed my hands over my face.

'Put it this way. You tell me, or I turn you over to the cops. That make it any easier for you?' he said.

'How did you know I was in here?' I asked.

'Certain areas of the house are protected at night. Any movement is picked up.'

'Who monitors it?'

'Tonight, Brian.'

'The steward.'

'Yeah. He woke me, asked me if I wanted him to deal with you. Luckily for you, I said no. So, spill.'

'Could I have a coffee?' I asked.

'What, the executionee's last wish?'

I looked at him long and hard. 'I don't think so, Welland, and before you throw around any other threats, realize this. There is precious little you can do to me that hasn't been done already. And there is practically nothing you could do that would frighten me.'

'But there is something?'

I thought of my daughter. 'There is something, but nothing you can get at.' Nothing I could get at. 'Can I have my coffee now?'

He looked at me with his laser scrutiny, and seemed to relax a fraction. 'Come on.'

He led me out of his study, down the hall, down two flights of stairs, trotting down fast, confident that I would follow, that I would not attempt to deliver a killer blow from behind. He stopped inside a huge kitchen, closed the door behind me. It was a mixture of stainless steel and oak. Over by the window there was a large old refectory-type table. I sat down on the bench and watched Welland make a large *cafetière* of coffee.

'Black?'

'White, please. Sugar too.' I needed it.

He spooned in two sugars, handed me the cup, and sat down opposite me with his. I looked across at him.

'What gives?' he said.

'I don't know where to start,' I answered.

'There's always a beginning. We know when things start.'

'All right. But listen to me. You must not tell anyone any of this. If you do, I really will have nothing left to lose, and then I will come after you and I will get you.'

'You mean kill me?'

'Yes. That's exactly what I mean.'

'You know, I really think you would too.'

'So, will you make me a promise?'

'That's not so easy is it, upfront? What if you tell me stuff I think should go to the cops?'

'I *will* be telling you stuff like that. But I'm the victim, not the perpetrator.' I took a mouthful of coffee, and blew out the breath that seemed to have lodged in my lungs.

'That's what I'm doing here. Going after the perpetrators.'

He leaned across the table towards me, the picture of concentration.

'All right. I promise.'

I paused for a while, listened to the sound of the wind rustling the leaves of the aspens outside, and then I spoke.

'Will you come with me?' I asked him.

'Where to?'

'Upstairs, the top.'

So we walked in silence, up to his great den, where the best of his paintings hung. I walked up to the *Widow*, and stood before her.

'This painting, the *Widow at the Window*, you know why I am so interested in it?'

He shook his head.

'It belonged to me. Strictly speaking, it still does. It was bought a couple of years ago, with my money. It used to hang in a castle in the northwest of Scotland, Wrath Castle. I lived there, with my husband, Archie Edge, his mother, Rosamond Edge, and with my daughter, Georgie.' I moved away, turned my back upon the *Widow*. I sat down on the low sofa, across the room. He followed, and took a seat beside me. And then I told him. I told him about meeting Archie, about falling in love, about Scotland, the castle, my pregnancy, the crash, the coma, my daughter. Then I told him about Archie ripping my daughter from me, and hurling me over the cliff. I had not spoken of this since I told Geoffrey. Now I relived it, in all its brutal horror. The tears cascaded down my face and I could do nothing to stop them. He brought me some water. I drank, and carried on.

'So he tried to kill me. He thought he had, trouble was, there was a witness, my friend, a very, very good friend. Ben. He chased after Archie. But Archie had a good start on him, got to the castle first. Had just enough time to round up his mother, and the wretched woman who they'd imposed as Georgie's nanny. Oh, and they just had enough time to amass their horde, their running-away money. She took jewels and art. She cut a Millais and that Rembrandt from their frames, bundled them up, and they set off in the car. But Ben caught up with them, tried to intercept them, stood blocking the road. And you know what they did? You know what they did? They just drove right over him. He managed to live for two days. He managed to tell me all of this, to speak, to get the words out, and then he died.'

'Jesus H. Christ. Where are they? What happened?'

'They fled on a boat, a fifty-foot yacht Rosamond had bought, again with my money. They put out to sea in a Force 9 gale. The outrunner of Hurricane Bert. Wreckage was found three days later in the Bay of Biscay. *Gypsy Rose* sank, all those aboard presumed drowned.' I turned to him now, talked directly at him. 'I never believed my daughter was dead. For nearly a year I paid Kroll to search. They found nothing. Finally I had to accept she had gone. That was when I decided I didn't really want to live anymore. So I drank. Not enough though, and thank God, because then I heard something, someone told me that there was a rumour that *Widow at the Window* was being touted around a small group of megabucks collectors. And I knew. She was alive. They were all alive. Then I was told that you were the buyer. So I engineered, with Geoffrey's help, that whole day on Long Island. Now here I am.'

'And you did all this to find out where they are?'

'Yes.'

Welland got up. He walked away from me, stared at the portrait, and then came back to me, sat beside me.

'Why didn't you just ask me?'

'What, just saunter up to you at Geoffrey's and say, hi, you don't know me, but do you by any chance own a painting that was stolen from me?'

'No. Here. You could have told me tonight.'

'And run the risk that you would tip them off? You don't know how clever they are, how they are always one step ahead, how unbelievably ruthless they are. If they get even a whiff that I might be searching for them, they'll disappear again. Shit, they have an extra thirty mill now, thanks to you. They could go anywhere, and I would never see my daughter again.'

'You could have trusted me.'

'Trusted you? Are you insane? I trusted my husband and all the while he had married me for my money, had an affair while I was pregnant with our child, and then when I was lying in a coma, more dead than alive, he and his mother systematically fleeced me of over a hundred million dollars. And then he tries to take my daughter from me. He makes it look to social services that I am drinking, when I didn't touch a drop back then after my accident, and then, when I get my evidence that proves that my darling mother-in-law murdered her husband twenty years earlier, they decide they have to do away with me. So my husband tries to murder me.'

Welland bowed his head.

'So you tell me, please, because I'd like to know: how the hell can I trust anyone, ever again?'

He turned to me and I saw in his eyes a look of such compassion, such gentleness, that I was calmed into silence.

'You can trust me. You don't have to believe me, but you can. I will not sell you out to them. I will give you their address. I will help you get your daughter back in any way I can.'

I nodded. I could not speak. My shoulders started to heave with sobs I could no longer hold in. He took hold of me. He pulled me in to him. He held me firm and hard against him. Through my sorrow, something else rose in me, and, I could feel, in him too. A hunger, a yearning born of pain and the need for comfort, and of the joy of being alive, possessed of hope. Slowly at first, and then feverishly, we began to kiss each other. We tugged off our clothes, and lying on the floor, watched by the *Widow*, we made love. I had forgotten how it felt. My body had been dead to that kind of passion for so long, but it awoke quickly enough, and the pleasure ran deeper and harder than ever before.

The pale light of dawn woke us a few hours later, lying entangled in one another's arms. He looked at me and I smiled, but then, slowly, regretfully, I pulled myself free of him. I put on my shirt and jeans and sat down beside him again.

'That was something so absolutely wonderful, I will never forget it.'

'But?' he said.

'But,' I replied, 'it can never happen again. You know why. All there's room for in my mind now is getting my daughter.'

'Just one beautiful night?' he said.

I nodded.

He got up, drew my face to him, kissed me softly on the lips. 'Whatever you say, but everything else stands. I will help you in every way I can.'

'Thank you.'

'And it's only fair you should know, when I want to be, I can be a very patient man.'

I smiled. Another part of me that I'd thought was dead registered that it was nice to be flattered. I thought no more of it than that.

'Come on,' he said. 'Let's have breakfast, then we'll go into my computer together, and I'll print you off the address, everything I have.'

Chapter sixty-nine

They were in Mexico. On the coast. A place called
Santa Christina, a few miles outside Mazatlan. I saw in
my mind a dazzling white house, a courtyard with
jacaranda and frangipani, the flickering blue of the
ocean, and a small, brown girl chattering away in
Spanish, wholly unaware that a few thousand miles to
the north lived her mother. I held the piece of paper
Welland had printed off for me as if it contained the
secret of life, as, I supposed, to me it did. How did they
get there? Did the *Gypsy Rose* really sink, leaving them
to find refuge aboard another boat, or was that staged?
And once they got to Mexico, how did they hide so
well? Had they been planning a flit, had it all worked
out? They had stolen so much money from me that
they could easily have bought themselves a bolthole in
Mexico, a clutch of false passports to go with it, and
official protection. The Mexican police were not exactly renowned for their probity. And Rosamond spoke
Spanish, after all, Archie too. With their colouring,
their European looks and accents they could easily have
passed for émigré Spaniards.

'Like to fly home?' asked Welland, breaking into my
thoughts.

I looked at him and nodded.

'I'll stay here,' he said. He scribbled down two num-
bers and gave them to me.

'You can use either of these, day or night, and you
will get me. Anything I can do, I will.'

I reached up and kissed his cheek. 'You have been so kind to me.'

With infinite gentleness, he took my face in his hands, and he kissed me, long enough and deeply enough to send fire through my entire body. Then he stopped.

'I'm not being kind. I'm just trying to even out the odds a bit.'

His plane, and then his helicopter, ferried me home. I landed at Geoffrey's at cocktail hour. I saw him striding indignantly towards the 'copter, then pausing and breaking into a smile as I stepped out, ducked under the whirring blades, and ran across to him. The helicopter rose in a great roar and flew off overhead. We waited for it to disappear and the noise ebb and blend with the sound of the waves breaking on the shoreline and then we spoke.

'Sorry,' I said. 'Tried to ring. Nobody picked up.'

'James's day off, and I needed to escape the phones for a bit. How'd it go?'

He knew from my grin. I rummaged in my pocket and took out the piece of paper, although I know the address by heart. I gave it to him.

'Senora Mercedes Benavides. Casa de Carmona, Santa Christina, near Mazatlan, Mexico.' He turned and looked out to sea, as if he could spy them faraway.

'All this time.'

'I think so, yes.'

'So, what now?'

'I go there,' I said, 'and I bring Georgie back.'

He gave a bitter laugh. 'Just like that.'

'No. With immense planning and contingency, blackmail and bribery. Whatever it takes. I am going to plot and plan and counterplot and put my head into the mind of that witch until I have thought of every angle and every possibility and every problem. And this time, they will not get the better of me.'

'By which you mean kill you, and run off again with your child.'

I nodded.

'Why not just ring the police, let them get onto it.'

'You think she doesn't have half the local police in her pocket? And quite possibly someone in Interpol too? I'm not trusting anyone with this.'

'How'd you get the address?' he asked suddenly.

'Long story.'

'Come and get your curs, sit down to dinner, and tell me.'

Chapter seventy

Later that night, with Gin and Jelly asleep at my feet, I sat in my rocker on the deck, wrapped in a blanket, coffee in hand. I rocked and I thought. The night was clear and dark. There was a sliver of new moon. A faint breeze carried to me the briny seaweed scent of the ocean. Could they smell it, where they were? Did they sit out under the new moon too? Could my daughter peek from her bedroom window and see it and make a wish? What would she wish for I wondered, my daughter whom I loved so much, whom I did not know.

And then I turned from her and my wistful, melancholic longing. I turned to Rosamond, to my enemy in all things, and to my husband. The dead could not divorce and I truly hoped that he thought still that I was dead. I could not keep from my mind the wisp of pleasure as I visualized my reappearance in their lives — a ghost, come to do more than haunt them. Come to shear them of what they had stolen from me.

I tried to see, I tried to pack my mind with evil, to banish anything that resembled a scruple. Either of them would kill me without a second thought. That I knew. The insurance policy I needed, the blackmail, the bribe, the deal would have to be so watertight, and, ultimately, impossible to renege on. I would not let them go after I took my daughter from them. For what they did to Ben, they must rot in hell. A Mexican prison would do.

Only when the first crack of light appeared from the east, did I give up for the night. I'd got the beginnings of a plan, and my heart raced with it. I did not go to bed. I could not sleep when I had so much to do, when I felt so glitteringly alive.

I woke up my slumbering dogs, changed into my swimsuit, and ran with them along the beach. When we had all built up a sweat, we plunged into the waves, and I swam out beyond the breaking point.

Showered, dressed and breakfasted, I rang Andreas on his mobile.

'Wha the fu–'

'Rise and shine, hacker-man.'

'Shit! Morganna. You have any idea what time I got to bed?'

'I really don't want to know, but if it makes you feel better, I didn't.'

'What, go to bed?'

'Exactly. Now, I need your help.'

There was a silence and I could almost feel him rubbing his eyes and coming to.

'How'd it go?'

'It went well.'

'You got in?'

'In a manner of speaking. But forget that. Something new.'

'Shoot.'

'Not on the phone. Can you come here?'

'When?'

'Now.'

'Aw, Morganna. Have pity.'

'No room for pity. No time. Come. Please.'

There was another silence. I imagined him checking a diary.

'This afternoon,' he said, and hung up.

He looked rough, disgruntled, but interested. His face glowed pale against his black hair, but his clothes were clean and well pressed, this immaculate outlaw.

'Give me coffee,' he said.

'Anything. Pancakes?'

He seemed to turn slightly washed green at the thought, but then broke into a smile.

'Yeah. Great. If only to watch you cook.'

I laughed. 'You are so unreconstructed.'

'Maybe. But I'm here.'

'You most certainly are.'

'Don't talk to me till you've fed me.'

'That bad?'

'Mmm-hmm.'

'Look, why don't you go for a swim. That'll sort you out.'

He raised a thick eyebrow. 'You mad?'

'Go on. It works, I promise you.'

'Got nothing to wear.'

I smiled.

'That kind of thing's illegal 'round here, case you hadn't noticed.'

I could not suppress a smirk. 'God forbid you break the law.'

'Hey, stay clean, that's what I say. They never get you on the big things anyway.'

'Go in your underpants.'

To my surprise, and his credit, he did. He came back ten minutes later swearing and grinning.

'Get in the shower,' I said. 'Pancakes in five.'

When he reappeared before me, he actually had some colour in his skin.

He ate and drank, and then wiped his mouth with a napkin, leaned back in his chair, and fixed me with a look.

'So, shoot. By the way, thanks,' he nodded at his empty plate.

'You're welcome. I want a passport, different name. One for me, possibly couple more for two other women.'

For a while he said nothing, just fixed me with a calculating stare.

'What makes you think this is my territory?'

'Guesswork. Nothing more.'

'Where you going?'

I shook my head.

'All right. When?'

'Soon as you get me the passports. I don't need to say, top of the range.'

He took the bait, gave me a disparaging glare, and I smiled.

'Cost you.'

'I know.'

'Who're the other chicks?'

'Don't know yet.'

He nodded, filing that away.

'Got a camera?'

'I have.'

'Get yourself up, like you wanna look. Want my advice?'

'Yeah.'

'Dye your hair.'

'I do.'

'Ah. Then thin your eyebrows, get 'em bleached to match your hair. Eyebrows make a real difference.'

'You, Andreas Hacker, are a man of many talents.' I got to my feet.

'Where you going?'

'Hairdresser. Back in an hour.'

'And just what am I meant to do?'

'Come with me if you want.'

'Think I'll stay here. What about your dogs?'

'They'll be fine, provided you don't snoop.'

'Yeah, right.'

Michael's was full.

'Next week,' said Sheena prissily.

I smiled, slipped her a hundred-dollar bill. 'I really, really need to fix my brows, like now,' I said, in my best valley girl voice.

She grimaced, caught between avarice and the gate-keeper's love of denying the public. I slipped another hundred into her palm. 'For the stylist,' I said.

She hurried over to Kevin and they moved away from the aging blonde he was attending and had a hurried conference in the corner. I saw him nod, glance at me, and tip his head again. Sheena hurried back.

'Come with me.' She ushered me through the salon into a back room. 'VIP room,' she said with a smile.

My, had I made it. I took a seat, got robed up. Five minutes later Kevin came in, bowl of bleach concealed under a magazine.

'Let's go,' he said by way of greeting.

'Thin,' I said, 'and matched to my hair.'

He regarded me, head to one side. 'Manhattan look.'

'I know. Won't suit me, but hell, we all have to experiment.'

He shrugged. 'Your face.'

Half an hour and another two hundred dollars later, I was done. I hated my new arch, undefined look, but, hell, it was different, it did change me and that was all I needed.

I went back to Andreas. He contemplated me, turned down his mouth, and nodded.

'Worse, but better,' he opined.

Twenty minutes later, he left. He took with him a cheque for fifteen thousand dollars, plus two rolls of film. How would I even stand a chance, I wondered, if I were not rich. I thanked God for my parents. And their money.

Then I rang Bud Brascoe at Kroll.

'Hey, Morganna. Long time no hear. News?'

'None,' I said. 'Something different I need from you.'

'Name it,' said Bud, ever ready to do me a favour for a fee.

'Two women. One a bodyguard, the other a bounty hunter.'

He let out a hiss of breath.

'Come on, don't be precious. You might not have one on the payroll, but I can't believe you don't have access to them.'

'Not quite our thing, Morganna. Bounty hunters.'

'For the amount I've paid you over the past twelve months I think you can damn well make it your thing.'

'I'll try.'

'Good. I want them both to look low-key. Like tourists, not hired muscle. And I want the best.'

'Hmm. When?'

'Soon as you can get them.'

'Let me look into it. How long d'you need them for?'

'Couple of weeks, say.'

'Call you back.'

I waited. It was a whole day before he did get back to me. A day of pacing, of tae kwan do, of agonizing waiting.

At four the phone rang. I snatched it up.

'You got it, Morgan,' promised Bud, the bounty deliverer. 'One's finished a job today, the other in two days.'

'The best? Low-key?'

'Guaranteed.'

'Send them here, to Long Island.'

Chapter seventy-one

The first one arrived the next day. A bodyguard and no mistake. She was six foot, efficiently short-haired, and she was wearing a blue business suit. She might as well have been wearing a badge that screamed hired muscle. I was as polite as I could be, impatience seething through me like heartburn.

'I'm sorry,' I said, pretty much as she crossed my threshold. 'This isn't going to work. Nothing personal. They just got the brief wrong.'

She looked pissed off and I couldn't blame her, but neither was I prepared to compromise.

'Scream at Bud,' I said. 'He messed up.' She directed a mean look at the ether. I smiled. Bud deserved all he was going to get.

I drove her back to the jitney stop and hurried home to ring Bud.

'What the hell were you thinking?' I demanded. 'I said low-key. Shall I spell it out this time?' I know I was being rude but I could not help myself sometimes. Bud had no idea what was at stake for me. Still thought of me as the grieving mother who'd lost all hope, and he was still patronizing me, still not listening to me.

'I want someone who looks like she might be a friend of mine, a travel buddy. Someone who looks like a Manhattan advertising girl on a week off, or a divorced Long Island rich girl looking for kicks. Not portable muscle.'

He was silent. I could just see the look of indignation on his square-jawed, turning-to-pudge face.

'Do you read me, Bud?'

'Loud and clear,' he said. 'I'll look for someone else.'

'Please do that.'

'Lisa'll be with you, day after tomorrow. You will like her, I promise.'

Waiting was sheer agony for me. As I lay in bed at night and tried in vain to summon sleep, I imagined Rosamond and Archie somehow getting wind that I was onto them. I saw them preparing once again for flight. I saw them provisioning a boat, taking my daughter and setting sail for some unknown destination. I imagined myself arriving at Casa de Carmona to find it deserted, my footsteps echoing through stone halls. Somehow I did sleep, but then it was worse because I dreamed, and it was always the same dream. I saw my daughter off in the distance and I called to her. I cried out, louder and louder, but she didn't turn, she didn't hear me, and when I tried to run, to get closer to her, she just receded into the distance until she was lost to sight.

Lisa arrived. She looked about twenty-eight, five seven, well-highlighted blonde hair, and a fun smile. Bud had got it right. She looked perfect. And, according to her CV, she was pretty damn near perfect. Jujitsu black belt, third dan, glowing references from names you normally see in the celebrity columns testifying to her abilities in seeing off trouble, and to her discretion.

I showed her the guestroom. 'I'm expecting someone

else today. German. Katrina something. A bounty hunter. Know her?'

Lisa shook her head. 'Nope, but there're lots of players in this game.'

'Growing business, huh?'

'This world isn't getting any more peaceable.'

'That's a comforting thought, but you're probably right. Look, if you don't mind waiting, I'll brief you fully once Katrina arrives, okay? If you want to go for a swim or a walk or anything, that's fine. Just say you're an old friend of mine who's staying for a while if any-one happens to ask. Most people here just keep to themselves anyway.'

'Sure thing,' she said, dropping a compact sausage bag on the floor.

'I'm paying you as of now, but until you're briefed I won't regard you as fully working.'

'Might just take that swim,' she said. 'I love the water. But, swim apart, I have to regard myself as work-ing. You're payin', I'm workin'.'

'Fine. Better to err on that side.'

So I waited again, until five when the doorbell rang. Lisa was in her room, discreetly reading. I went to the door. Before me stood a petite, wiry, nut-brown woman with sleek, shoulder-length brown hair.

'Hi. I'm Katrina,' she said, the trace of a German accent mingling with the American English that so many Europeans seemed to speak.

'I'm Morganna,' I said, shaking her hand.

I'd read her CV too. German champion at karate for three years in a row. Spoke three languages fluently. She'd been bounty hunting for eight years, with great success, given the roll call of desperados she'd collared. I was curious about these women's lives, but I pushed it, like everything else, to the background.

She followed me in, sat down delicately on my sofa.

I called Lisa out, introduced the two women, and watched them quietly size each other up. They did not seem displeased with one another, thank God. But I knew the next bit would not go so smoothly.

'Drink?' I asked. 'Water, coffee, soda?'

They both opted for water. I brewed myself a coffee, returned with their waters, and sat in my favourite arm-chair, across from them.

'Right, this is the job. Once I've told you what it is, you either commit one hundred percent, or you go. Either way, you do not, ever, repeat one word of what I am about to say to you. Is that clear?'

They nodded. I did not like to sound so stentorian, but they seemed quite used to it, and really, I had no choice.

'We need to go to Mexico.' I saw both of them react infinitesimally at this. I carried on. 'We will go as, appar-ently, three friends. We are going to Mazatlan, a holiday area. We will stay in a nice hotel, in three adjoining rooms. We will all travel under false passports.' Again, I saw unease flicker across their features. 'Your job will be twofold. One, you must appear to be nothing more than friends on holiday. Two, you must take up position, a safe distance from a house where I will be going in alone to negotiate with some people. You will not be straight bodyguarding or bounty hunting at that point, but your existence, and your proximity, will, I hope, deter these people from killing me.'

At that, they began to look really unhappy. They sat there, still, composed, and fiercely resistant.

'I will sign letters absolving you both of any culpability if things go wrong. You will not be left with blemishes on your career.'

Please let them be more receptive than they looked, I thought, watching their faces set. I fell silent.

Lisa was the first to speak.

'I'm sorry,' she said. 'There is no way I can take a job like that. It's going in blind to something that I have no handle on.'

Kat nodded. 'I don't go in blind either,' she said. 'You've told us nothing.'

'Damn,' I said, getting to my feet. I paced around for a while. I tried to consider all my options. I knew I could not go to Mexico alone. I knew, without my having backup, that Rosamond and Archie would happily kill me. I really had no choice.

I stopped pacing and sat down again, bracing my elbows on my knees.

'Look. I'll tell you the truth, the whole bloody story. Then you make up your minds. I'm going to trust you, but I swear, if either of you betrays me I will—'

'I won't,' said Katrina quickly.

'Neither will I,' added Lisa.

I nodded. I think they read the message in my eyes.

'Okay. Here goes. We're going to Mexico to get my daughter back from my husband, who thinks I am dead, who thinks that he killed me, over a year ago, by throwing me over a cliff in Scotland.'

That got their attention. And so I told them the

whole, wretched story. When I finished, a long time later, no-one spoke.

'Wow,' said Katrina finally, running her hands over her face and getting to her feet.

Lisa just looked at me. She shook her head. 'I'm sorry,' she said.

I nodded.

'I'll drive you to the jitney stop,' I said, glancing at my watch. 'There's one in twenty minutes.'

She got up. 'No. I don't mean I won't do it. Of course I'll do it. How could I not?'

Katrina came up to me. 'Me too,' she said. 'Count me in.'

I smiled. I felt waves of relief wash over me, and something else too, like a tremor inside, my nerves twitching as the countdown began.

Of course, Geoffrey had wanted to come, to mastermind things, to watch over me. I could imagine him all too easily losing his famous detachment and piling in.

'You think you can disguise yourself?' I asked him. 'You're six foot seven, for God's sake. The giant American. The right height, the right age. I'm sorry, Geoffrey, but no way. If, and I have to assume she does have some kind of early warning system, Rosamond heard you were in the locale, do you really think she'd buy it that it was just coincidence? She'd be off with my daughter before you could get near her. I can't take that chance. You cannot want me to risk losing Georgie again.'

There was no way he could fight against my logic.

He had to give in and finally, he did. We went over and over the plan until he was as satisfied as he would ever get.

'What if it goes wrong?' he asked, again and again.

'I could do nothing, of course. That is the only way to guarantee nothing goes wrong, isn't it?'

'I just keep thinking there must be a better way,' he said.

'Tell me, and I'll do it.'

But he couldn't.

'When you get her, and you have her, safe, ring me. Let me come then.'

'I will get her, won't I?' I said it like a prayer, like a child asking for the ultimate reassurance only a parent can give.

'If you are careful and clever. Yes, Morgan. I truly believe you will get her.'

'I'll ring you the moment I do. Promise.'

So, leaving my dogs with Geoffrey again, one sunny day in June, I said goodbye.

Chapter seventy-two

The plane circled low over a dazzling sea, then came in
steeply to land. Half an hour later, Katrina, Lisa, and I,
and our false passports were shuffling forward slowly in
the arrivals hall. Finally we took our turn before a lech-
erous immigration official.

"Olliday?' he asked.

We nodded enthusiastically. 'You bet,' said Lisa.

'Chav a goood time,' he said lasciviously.

Hell, we'd convinced him, so I forgave him, smiled
at him, and passed through, officially into Mexico.

We walked out of the erratically air-conditioned
building and the true heat of Mexico hit us. Desultory
palms dotted the road and the parking lot beyond. The
air was arid and carried with it the taste of dust and
baked earth. The buildings dotted around — car hire,
tourist information — were built of dazzling white
stone. The sun glinted off car windscreens. I screwed up
my eyes and looked for my sunglasses. The smell of fry-
ing food drifted through the air; the cries of reunited
families and excited children competed with straining
engines and car horns, energetically used. Kat, Lisa, and
I towered above most of the women and many of the
Mexican men milling around in the crowd. We looked,
and I felt, indisputably foreign. We were just a few
hours from the border, but we felt a long way from the
US of A. A clever choice, Rosamond had made.
Cleverer still to remain invisible.

I noticed a small, wiry man holding up a nameplate — Sta's Kim, Janey, and Tara. That was us. I waved to him and he led us to the hotel car — an old white Mercedes, stately amidst the gleaming four by fours and the rustbuckets that lined the roadside plying for trade. Silently and efficiently, our driver loaded our bags and held the doors for us. We slid in, smiling, girls ready to have some fun. I had pulled on my baseball cap and my sunglasses. I might have been overestimating Rosamond's scrutiny, her reach, but better that way . . .

Soon the driver escaped the airport and the hooting mayhem, and he took us on the scenic route, along the cliffs. Arid countryside stretched away to one side, dotted with what looked like newly built, lower-end houses in the inevitable white. Ribbon development for the locals. Definitely not tourist or Rosamond class. On the other side, beyond the cliffs, the sea shimmered and heaved in its never-ending dance. I rolled down my window and breathed in the hot, briny air.

'Good, huh?' said Katrina.

'Very good,' I replied.

A while later, we passed a large marina, glistening with expensive boats, sleek yachts, bulbous gin palaces. Inland, in the middle distance was a large, walled village with villas rising up on a small hill. Beyond that stood a large, gleaming white building: *Opitale Privado de San Sebastian*. We were moving upmarket. Closer. But another few miles beyond was a small, industrial-looking port, with a boat chandlery and repair yard. I noted it all, encyclopaedically hungry for detail.

After another fifteen minutes along a now deserted and wonderfully undeveloped stretch of coastline, we came to our hotel. It rose from the arid earth like a great monolith, the creature of some architect's dream and developer's millions. It was huge, white, adorned with swimming pools and verdant palms and frangipani, smelling of air-con and sun cream. We were shown to our rooms. We agreed to congregate downstairs by the main pool in twenty minutes.

My room was large, airy, and furnished in rustic chic style. The walls were rough, sponge-painted in a vivid sea-green and orange-yellow. The bed was covered in a geometric Aztec-style quilt and on a dark, wood-carved table sat a huge bowl of yellow roses. In an alcove, behind the bed, stood a collection of vicious-looking cacti — a surprising choice, I thought, liable to spike restless sleepers or energetic love-makers. Fine for me. I couldn't imagine even being able to sleep. I thought of Steve Welland, and our one glorious night together and then, before I could get carried away, I pushed him ruthlessly from my mind. But I did offer up a quick *thank you* for all his help. One day I would try to repay him for his kindness.

I was restless, adrenaline was already coursing through my system. My body and brain were on super-drive. It took me five to shower, dig out my bikini and sun cream. Then I stood at my window, gazing out at the beach below and the sea beyond. Off to my right, about two miles away as the crow flew, by my calculations, was Casa de Carmona. Was my daughter. Could she feel me, I wondered? Could she feel a flutter of something, of someone?

God, how I wanted to just run there, abandon my carefully wrought plan, just go there to see her, if only from a distance. But of course, I did nothing of the sort. I put on my baseball cap, my sunglasses, picked up my book, and took the lift down to the pool terrace. I asked the attendant for three loungers, and I waited there for my 'friends.'

It was 5 p.m. Not too many hours of sunbathing left, but we would enjoy them, and be seen to. Lisa and Katrina appeared, gym goddesses in their bikinis, Katrina perfectly tanned already. Heads turned as they made their way to join me, but for all the right reasons.

All of us went through the motions. Hell, it was not that hard to conjure fun at a five-star hotel on a still beautiful stretch of the Pacific coast, but as we sipped our virgin Margaritas my mind didn't even stray.

That night, as I knew it would, sleep eluded me till dawn. I got two hours before I woke, groggy-headed, electric-stomached.

At breakfast on a terrace overlooking the sea and shaded by large parasols, the girls and I 'decided' what to do.

'I feel like exploring,' said Lisa. 'Think I'll hire myself a jeep and go for a cruise.'

'I'll join you,' said Kat.

'Count me out,' I said. 'I'm just going to stay here and hang out by the pool.'

'Lazy girl,' they said, laughing.

I could hardly wait till they got back. I tried to read my book, to fall asleep, to swim, but I was just going through the motions. It was three in the afternoon by the time they got back.

'Hey, girl, you look like you've had enough sun for one day,' said Lisa.

I got up slowly. 'Maybe you're right.' I gathered up my things, and together we went up to our rooms.

'How'd it go?' I asked.

'We got lucky,' said Kat. 'She's here. The mother-in-law. For sure.'

I saw her in my head. I felt the sheer raw power of my rage, and my hate. All this time, and it was fresh as a new cut.

'We didn't have to hang around long before Lady Macbeth came out in her black Land Cruiser,' Kat continued. 'I picked her up, Lisa hung back. Between the two of us we tailed her five miles, to a small harbour, to a boat.'

'Of course. She would have one.'

'Big, sleek. Real number,' says Lisa. 'She took it out with some guy, not Archie. Mexican-looking, some sort of flunky I'd have said. They were out for a couple of hours, came back in, and then she seemed to be having a real go at the guy. Couldn't hear any of it, but it looked like she was tearing a strip off him.'

'She's good at that. What was the boat called?'

'*Belladonna*,' replied Kat.

I laughed. 'God, she's vain. That boat. Another get-away boat. If anything goes wrong, if she thinks she can get away, she and my loathsome husband will head for that boat.'

'So what do we do? Scupper it?' asked Kat. I loved the way she'd gone from rule-bound to outlaw.

I shook my head. 'Tempting, but what if we get caught? We blow the whole thing. No, we stick to plan A. At least we know where the boat is, we can always intercept them there if necessary.'

Lisa and Kat had shown their faces enough for one day, so we stayed in the hotel for dinner. I couldn't wait for my turn, my chance to see the faces that had haunted both my dreams and my nightmares for a long year.

Chapter seventy-three

Over breakfast next morning, Lisa turned to me. 'How about we drag you out today, do some sightseeing?'

'Not with either of you two at the wheel.'

'Fine,' replied Lisa, as primed for the benefit of any eavesdroppers. 'We'll get a driver and cruise around.'

'You mean actually leave the hotel?' I said.

'If you don't do it today, you never will,' replied Lisa.

'You've got a point,' I said.

'Okay. What time?' asked Katrina.

'Ten?' suggested Lisa.

'Fine by me,' I said.

At ten our car was waiting. 'What you like to see?' asked Benito, our driver.

'Nothing touristy,' said Katrina. 'Nice little local villages or towns. You can drop us off, wait for us while we have a walk round.'

'Whatever,' he said.

'Not too faraway,' I added. 'Don't want to spend all the time in the car.'

He nodded, digested this, and set off. There was only one place that fit our description. Santa Christina. He drove across the arid plain. It took ten minutes. The little town nestled inside high walls at the foot of some rough hills. It must have been a natural oasis of some kind because I could see the greenery from some way off. It looked old, this place, not some tourist construct but the kind of place people would have lived for generations. However, I could see the sprouting of new villas too. New money, newcomers, enough of them to allow Rosamond and Archie and my daughter to fit right in.

Benito drove us in through the large stone archway that rose up from the old walls. He took us to the town square. He dropped us by the fountain.

'Nice town,' he said. 'Nice little shops, churches, cafés . . .'

'Wait for us here,' said Katrina. 'We might be a while.'

Benito shrugged. 'Got me all day.'

We left him; we wandered, checking out leather goods in an artisan's shop, stopping for diet Cokes at a café, my heart and mind churning, all the while. The girls seemed to know how I felt. They cast me covert looks of encouragement. Lisa squeezed my hand. Katrina became more crisply Germanic.

After an hour, I said softly, 'Let's explore the outer part of the town, shall we? Stretch our legs before the midday sun hits us?'

'Sounds good,' replied Lisa.

Katrina nodded keenly.

We all set off casually. We knew exactly where we were going, although we meandered slightly to get there. We had all memorized the map, and Kat and Lisa had been in the vicinity yesterday in their jeeps. We knew precisely where Casa de Carmona was. We had even brought snacks and a drink, so that we might sit on the small hillock that overlooked the house, sip and eat and watch, with some sort of cover.

It took us ten minutes to get close. I felt as if everyone we passed must surely have heard the drumming of my heart. I forced myself to breathe surely and slowly. Then we turned a corner, and there it was below us, looking out over the Pacific. My daughter's house.

What the map hadn't shown was the pair of trees that stood on the hillock, and the bench that sat conveniently in their shade. We flopped down like exhausted tourists, unpacked our fruit, and nibbled away. Behind us we heard people passing, provisioning housekeepers, retired old gentlemen on the way to chess or the barber, if the human traffic we'd passed so far was anything to go by. We sat, we chatted. I said little. The girls filled in for me.

And then I froze. I would have known that voice anywhere. In my grave, or beyond. Now it spoke Spanish, but it still rang with the same timbre of sardonic humour. The voice that answered it in baby talk, toddler talk, was high, bell-like. I heard the clack, clack, clack come closer. I did not breathe. The girls talked. I waited. The click-clacks passed, perhaps fifteen feet behind us.

I could feel scrutiny raising the hairs on the back of my neck. Then the clacks passed. I couldn't hear the girls, obliviously chatting away. All I could hear was the clacks and the pounding of the blood in my ears. I felt emotion rise up in me like a wave that would swamp me. I could not resist it. Like a machine, I slowly turned my head.

Rosamond walked away in high heels and a tan cotton skirt and sleeveless shirt. By her side, wearing a yellow-checked dress with a ribbon round the middle, was my daughter. Was Georgie. And then, she too turned her head, looked right at me, her stranger mother. She was brown, honey brown. Her hair was blonde and long. Her legs were chubby and her arms were like little sausages sticking out from her dress. Her eyes were green, like mine, and alive with curiosity. She was the single most beautiful thing I had ever seen in my life, and my heart, my whole being yearned for her. *My daughter, my daughter*. Moving, breathing, living. I almost uttered a sound but it was stillborn in my throat. Then she turned away, back to her grandmother. I wanted to run to her, to grab her up, to call her name and hold her to me, grip her so tight I could feel her heart beating. To sit there and let her pass was almost more than I could do, was superhuman, was inhuman. I began to sweat, rivers, and to shake. The emotion of a year's dreams and nightmares was too much.

The girls kept talking, but, *sotto voce*, Katrina hissed: 'Are you all right?'

'You heard those people pass?' I asked, my voice high pitched.

They both nodded.

'That was my daughter, and my mother-in-law.'

'Cripes,' said Lisa.

'Fuck,' said Katrina.

'What now?' asked Lisa.

'We get the hell out of here, as unobtrusively and as fast as we can, making sure we do not bump into them again,' said Kat. 'Come on. Let's loop round in the opposite direction.'

'And fall in behind them, way behind them, or risk coming head to head,' finished Lisa.

As for me, I could not speak. Mutely, I followed them.

We got back to Benito with no sightings. 'Had enough sightseeing. Need the pool, Benito,' said Lisa.

He ushered us into the car, drove us away. Only when I was back in my hotel bedroom, did my heart slow down. I dried the sweat from my body, and then I wept.

I allowed myself to weep, with yearning, with sadness, for all the time I had lost, and then, slowly, I forced myself to stop. I could not function like this. I thought of Rosamond, of Archie, and of Ben. I tried to steep my mind in cold evil. I tried to switch off love and yearning, to make myself, just for now, into another person.

It was my hatred that saved me. I conjured it and the fury that flowed through my veins gave me the strength I needed.

It took several hours until I could face Kat and Lisa again, until I could enter their rational world.

I knocked on Kat's door. They were both in her room, waiting for me. I sat down by the window, looking out at the sea beyond.

'Look, I don't think I can wait beyond tomorrow. I think we should go there, first thing, 8 a.m., before they get moving, assuming today was in any way typical. And I think we need more of an entourage. We need Benito, and let's ask for a translator, a secretary or two. Enough people to make a small crowd of witnesses on that hillock.'

'While you go in there,' said Lisa.

'While I go in there,' I agreed.

'And what will you say? You'll ring the bell, and say,

483

hello, it's Morganna, I've come to take my daughter away?' asked Katrina.

I shook my head. 'You know, I've played this scene a thousand times in my head and I still don't know what I'll say. But that'll be the gist of it, yeah.'

'And they'll just give her up, without a fight?' Katrina went on.

'Listen, they love two things, above all. Money, and freedom. They will choose both, over Georgie.'

'You're certain of that,' asked Lisa.

No, I was not. Not one hundred percent. How could I have been? Nothing ever went the way you thought it would, but that was not a good enough reason for the inaction that was the alternative. A tiny voice in my head goaded away at my certainties. I silenced it.

'As much as I can be,' I answered.

'But how does it play out?'

'I don't know. I try to see it, try to choreograph it, but I can't.'

'That's short for anything could happen in my book,' said Lisa.

Katrina nodded. 'I should go in, collar them at that point.'

'When I've safely got my daughter out of the way, yes. You can do whatever the hell you do, however the hell you do it, and get those two banged up for life. And yourself a nice bounty in the process.'

'Sounds good. In theory.' She looked hungry, predatory. She was enjoying herself.

'Sounds a tad short on theory,' said Lisa.

'Give me a better plan and I'll follow it,' I replied, exasperated. 'Jesus! First Geoffrey, now you. Everyone keeps going on as if there is such a thing as some perfect plan, always there, just waiting conveniently for us to discover it. It doesn't exist, can't you see that? I'm amazed you think it does. Only the truly naïve think it does, that the brain can construct something that fits real life, that moulds real life into the exact shape they want it. You know, we could have an army here, and it'd still all go wrong, or go differently. Anyone who's read any history knows that War is a cock-up. Every war. You start with a plan, an imperfect plan and it all goes wrong. And all the while, all those perfect planners are just sitting on the fence, growing old, getting bitter, dying, just waiting for some false perfection that will never come.'

Lisa turned red and said nothing.

'Most of this stuff *is* winging it, in reality,' said Kat. 'You can plan the hell out of something and then the shit hits the fan and it's all change. If you're not used to winging it, you'll be dead.'

'That's comforting,' said Lisa, finding her voice. 'What about the cops?' she continued.

'You know, in a town this small, I'll be prepared to lay a large bet that Rosamond has them in her pocket,' I said. 'We tell them anything it'd be like screaming our intentions from a loud hailer. They'd be gone on the next boat. On the *Belladonna*.'

'Say they give her up, how'll you get your daughter out of the country?'

'Then it goes legal,' I said. 'At that point, Geoffrey

flies in with a phalanx of lawyers. DNA tests to prove I'm her mother. Interpol reports on Rosamond and my husband. They get banged up, I get formal custody.'

'That simple,' said Lisa.

'I'm not expecting it to be simple,' I said. 'I'll stay here and do whatever it takes for as long as it takes and then I shall leave with my daughter.'

Lisa and I started when the phone rang. Calmly, Kat got up, answered it.

'I'll be right down,' she said.

'Where are you going?' I asked.

'Give me a minute, and I'll explain, but first I have to go downstairs.'

That I didn't like, but I could see she was unstoppable, and that I would just have to trust her.

She returned a few moments later with a large package wrapped in brown paper. She sat down calmly on the bed and unwrapped it. A pistol. Ammunition.

'I cannot do my job unarmed,' she said.

'And who the hell gave you that?'

'Someone I've worked with many times before. Someone I trust.'

'Who could still blow, have blown, your cover.'

Kat shook her head. 'No way.'

I got up and paced around. 'I hope you're right,' I said.

'Trust me, Morganna. Please.'

At that point, I didn't have much choice.

Chapter seventy-four

Morning came. I was as ready as I'd ever be. I still didn't have answers for all of Lisa's questions, but then I never would. There was no perfect time. There was no perfect set of circumstances. There was just the here and now, and, two miles away, my daughter.

Two cars drove us to Santa Christina. Katrina, Lisa, and I were in one, a secretary and a translator were in another. The cars parked by the hillock, temporarily out of sight of Casa de Carmona. The girls and I had our walkie-talkies, and our mobiles, all primed. Kat also had her persuader. They and I had the number of the local police station, and, at Lisa's insistence, a private ambulance service. The drivers, secretary, and translator looked on, bemused.

'You ready?' asked Katrina.

I nodded. My mouth was dry.

'Good luck,' said Katrina. Lisa echoed her.

I glanced briefly at them, turned, and walked down the dusty track towards the house. The sky was dazzling blue, cloudless. Even at eight in the morning the reflection of the sun on the whitewashed walls of the house was hard to look at. Everything, the few blades of surrounding grass, the stones on the path, seemed drawn with a greater clarity. I was superconscious, as I knew I needed to be, in the presence of my enemy. I focused on her, on my husband. I tried not, perversely, to let my thoughts go to Georgie, for then I would soften, become distracted, and I could not afford that.

I had my mobile in one pocket, my walkie-talkie in another, and on my wrist a bracelet mounted with a panic button, but other than that, I was unarmed. And, folded up small in the breast pocket of my shirt, I had my letter, with two copies.

I got closer. Twenty yards. Ten, five. I walked round to the large archway into which were set two, heavy, studded wooden doors, both closed, and I assumed, locked. I breathed, reached out my hand, and pressed the bell.

Seconds passed. A surprised voice spoke to me through the intercom.

'*Si?*'

'*La Senora, por favor.*'

'*Quien es?*'

'*Una amiga.*'

I heard a click, but the door didn't shift. I debated buzzing again, when I heard footsteps. I heard keys being turned, bolts being drawn back, then the door opened inward, and a small Mexican woman stood there, studying me. She apparently decided I was all right.

'*Un momentito,*' she said, and hurried off.

I dug my fingers into my pocket, pressed transmit on the walkie-talkie.

'I'm in,' I uttered. 'Waiting for the lady.'

I released the button, looked around. Before me was a courtyard, fountain at the centre. Delicate plumes of water spiralled up and tumbled into a small pool. Off to the left was what looked like a well. The house was built around the courtyard, two stories, some windows shuttered, others open.

Georgie, Georgie. Where were you?

The Mexican maid reappeared. With Rosamond. Rosamond strode towards me, clacking shoes on already. She stopped before me. I took off my baseball cap, and my dark glasses.

'Hello, Rosamond.'

She gasped. Her eyes riveted themselves on my face. Disbelief, then shock spread over hers.

'Morganna.' She said it like a growl, low in her throat, her body unwilling to pronounce the syllables of my name.

'You're dead,' she managed to say.

'I am, aren't I, and, in the best tradition, I've come back to haunt you.'

'What do you want?'

'My daughter.'

She laughed. God, she recovered fast.

'And what, we're supposed to just give her up?'

'In return for your freedom. In return for me not handing you over to Interpol. Oh, and before you think of any of your wonderful dirty tricks, you might want to look up on the hillock. You'll find a small crowd of bodyguards and lawyers, all ready to hand you and your son over if you try anything.'

'Got it all worked out, haven't you.'

'I've had time, Rosamond.'

'Oh, I think we can assume you'll have missed something, anyway, if your past performance is anything to go by.'

I wanted to reach out and rake out her eyes.

'Hubris, Rosamond. Never wise.'

'We'll see.'

It amazed me. She acted like she was still holding all the cards.

'So, you think your daughter will just go to you, a stranger?'

'I'm her mother, despite her father's best efforts to rob her of me.'

'Typical of him that he should fail. Never could complete a job.'

'No, you'd have killed me properly, wouldn't you, Rosamond? Just like when you killed your husband.'

She actually smiled. 'Killed him. And got away with it.'

'Well, not so lucky this time round.'

'Maybe not. So, let me get this straight. I just hand your daughter over to you?'

'Yes. You and your son sign a form saying that you formally relinquish all claims to Georgie, or whatever you're calling my daughter these days, and you grant full, one hundred percent custody to me, her mother, and the ability for me to travel with her anywhere in the world without recourse to you.'

'My, my. You certainly have gone to town.'

I took a step closer to her. 'No, you're the one who's gone to town with your lying and your stealing and your killing. But it ends here.'

'And haven't I done it well, darling? I'll still walk free under your little proposal.'

'I think it's called an ultimatum, Rosamond.'

She smiled, as if humouring me.

I sensed movement. I whirled round. Framed by an archway, stood my husband. I watched as the colour drained from his face. I took a few steps towards him.

'Yes, it really is me. You failed, Archie, when you threw me over that cliff. You couldn't even manage to kill me.'

He tried to say something. His eyes darted to his mother. His face was taut with barely suppressed panic. She responded with a look of scorn.

'But you're well used to failure, aren't you, Archie?' I continued. 'Never succeeded at anything until my money bought you a ticket to ride.'

I saw anger flare in his eyes. I wanted him to step forward, go for me. Then I could show off all my new tricks, break his arm. Break his neck. I goaded him further.

'And all that money you stole, doesn't seem to sit well on you. Slim is one thing, but my God, you're addled. What is it? Alcohol? I can't believe it's guilt, eating the flesh from your bones.'

He took a step towards me. I could smell the tobacco on his breath. Another new prop.

'What do you want?' he hissed.

'What you took from me.'

'Your money, your paintings, your stuff.'

I laughed aloud. 'My stuff, yeah, much of it's gone I'm sure. You idiot. Do you think I care about my money? You think I survived everything you put me through because I wanted my money? I want my daughter.'

God curse him forever. He actually looked relieved.

Rosamond took this as her cue. 'All very touching, this matrimonial reunion, but I think we can terminate the posturing, don't you?' She proceeded to fill in Archie on my demands, and on the sanction standing on the knoll of the hill. I saw his mind working. Freedom in return for his daughter. He didn't even attempt to keep her. I felt such a cold loathing for him, and I could have wept for what Georgie must never know.

'So,' concluded Rosamond, all business. 'Your daughter.'

God, she didn't even call her by her name.

'Yes.'

'Don't you think you should have a nanny? Someone to show you how to take care of her?'

I felt the barb sink home. Pretend mother.

'Get Georgie, one of you. Now. And, while you're out of my sight, don't think about trying any tricks. I have backup on the knoll. They'll pick you up and haul you off, and no, Rosamond, don't look so smug. It's not the local police who you no doubt have in your pocket. It's my own people, bodyguards, lawyers, and a bounty hunter, keen as mustard to have both your hides. Check them out, will you.'

I led them to the outer door. They looked up to the knoll. I waved at the team. They waved back.

At that, Rosamond lost her smugness. And Archie began to sweat. I could smell the animal stench coming off him. He was cornered. They both were and they now knew it.

'Right. Get back in. Rosamond, you stay here with me. Archie, get Georgie, please.'

He looked to his mother. She nodded. He walked away. I imagined him going to her bedroom, waking her, carrying her downstairs. Would he be weeping, I wondered, at the last embrace.

It took minutes. Agonizing, electrifying minutes. Rosamond just stared at me. I stared back at her. She refused to look away, so I just looked straight back, trying to reflect the evil that I knew lay just beneath the arrogant contempt. But then I took my eyes from hers. I heard movement. I froze. I could not believe what my eyes were seeing.

I saw my daughter, barefoot, in a white nightdress, toddling awkwardly, sobbing gently. Behind her walked Archie, her father. In his hands was a snub-nosed machine gun. He was pointing it at his daughter's head. He took hold of her arm, pulled her to a halt, and, with the gun still levelled on her, he turned to me and he actually smiled.

'Get the car, Ma,' he said quietly. I saw her move way from the corner of my eye. I could not drag my horrified gaze from Archie. My daughter was looking up at her father, squirming in his grasp, still sobbing gently, incomprehension on her tiny features.

'Shall I spell it out for you, seeing as you're looking just a bit out of it?' said Archie. 'You keep your posse up their away from us, and she lives. If you try to stop us, I will kill her. Do you understand?'

I nodded. Mute.

Then, keeping the machine gun on Georgie, he half-dragged her backwards. Any moment that gun could have gone off. I tried not to think of the bullets spraying out. Oh God, oh God, help us, help us, I prayed. But neither he, nor this time the devil, came to my aid. I could do nothing but watch Archie disappear at the back of the courtyard with my daughter. I heard the roar of an engine. I heard doors slamming, wheels spinning, a burst of an accelerator being floored, and a car roaring away.

'Get the jeep,' I yelled into my walkie-talkie. 'Pick me up here. They're getting away.'

I heard another roaring engine, the squeal of brakes, and then Kat appeared. I ran, jumped in the jeep.

'I saw them come out. White Mercedes,' she said. 'What happened?'

'They've got Georgie, with a gun to her head. He'll kill her if we try to stop them.'

She turned and looked at me. 'Your call. What do you want to do?'

Agonizing seconds passed. Their car drew farther away, my daughter in it. This was my last chance, and I knew it.

'Everyone else stays back. You drive, I'll duck down. Try to find them, and tail them without them seeing. Can you do that?'

'Yes.'

'You promise me. It's my daughter's life.'

'I can. But no guarantees. Your call.'

'Follow them.'

We sped over the grassy knoll, and joined the coast road. I heard Lisa's voice, shouting into the walkie-talkie.

'Stay back,' Kat shouted. 'Do not follow on. They've got her daughter. Hostage.'

Kat drove fast, but not conspicuously so, overtaking where she could. Of the white Mercedes, there was no sign. We raced on, climbing up a long hill.

I felt cold, so cold that movement, thought, seemed impossible. I wanted to drown in that coldness, to simply stop being, and I felt a terror so great it seemed it would obliterate my heart.

We soon reached the brow of the hill. To our right, the cliffs tumbled away to the Pacific a thousand feet below. Ahead of us, switching back and forth along the hairpins, was the white Mercedes. And Georgie.

'There they are,' I shouted.

Kat nodded. She sped up, fractionally. Slowly, and I prayed, inconspicuously, we were gaining on them.

I crouched down on the floor.

'Where d'you think they're going?' she asked.

'Boat. Got to be.'

'Yeah. I reckon.'

She was calm, ice cool.

'We're gaining,' she said. 'What's the plan?'

'We track them, to the boat. We have to let them go, sail away, then we get U.S. Customs on them, we say the boat's laden with drugs, we get Interpol, we get someone who Rosamond hasn't bought.'

She said nothing. I glanced up at her. She was frowning.

'I think they might have seen us.'

Oh no, please God no.

'Slow down,' I shouted.

'Holy shit.'

'What's happening?' I leaned up, and then I saw.

Ahead of us, perhaps a quarter of a mile away, the Mercedes had stopped. A door opened, arms reached out. I could see thrashing movement, and then my eyes defied me for the second time. I saw Archie. He was holding Georgie. Then with a shove, he pushed her from his arms, and he left her on the side of the road. The door closed, my daughter hurled herself against the car, but it brushed her off. She fell by the roadside. I could hear her screams as the Mercedes accelerated away.

'Hurry, hurry,' I managed to say, as my daughter stood screaming at the roadside, as rush-hour cars hurtled past.

I did not breathe. I tried to shut my mind to the images forming.

'Get there, get there,' I screamed.

Every second was like an unbearable eternity. We got there. While the car was still moving, I leapt out. I grabbed Georgie who screamed even louder, and I carried her into the back seat.

Katrina turned to me.

'What now?'

'The hospital,' I shouted. 'She's bleeding.'

'What, just let them go, after everything?'

My daughter was bleeding. Frantically, I looked her over. Blood had soaked her nightdress and she was looking at me with wild eyes. For as long as I live I never want to see that look again in a child's eyes.

'The hospital,' I said, my voice a whisper.

Katrina turned the car around.

I held Georgie in my arms, and then I found it. A knife wound, about two inches long, on her right thigh. And in that instant I understood what they had done. They had cut my daughter, dumped her on the roadside, to buy them the time to escape.

I held my screaming daughter to me. 'You'll be fine,' I said, not even sure she could understand English.

'You'll be fine,' I promised her, as I prayed like I had never prayed before.

I ripped off part of my shirt, and I tied it over the wound in her thigh. I could see Georgie was in the grip of shock. She looked at me with dead eyes. I did the only thing I could think of. I held her tight, and I began to sing.

'Speed bonny boat, like a bird on the wing . . .'

I felt her move in my arms, and she leaned away to look at me. In her eyes I thought I saw the stirring of memory.

Chapter seventy-five

We got to the hospital fifteen minutes later. I didn't remember much of the next few hours, save Kat literally throwing money around, barking at people in fluent Spanish. Then an English-speaking North American doctor arrived. With quick efficiency, Georgie got treated. I thanked God the hospital was clean, ultramodern. It was, I discovered, one of the new seriously upmarket hospitals for plastic surgery that were springing up on that coast. North American doctors. The best of everything. Thank God for the vanity of women.

Georgie's wound looked worse than it was. She was bandaged, given shots of tetanus and antibiotics.

I rang Geoffrey.

'I've got her,' I wept. 'I have her, Geoffrey.'

'Morgan, oh, Morgan.' I could hear the catch in his voice, knew that he too was in tears.

'Come now, please.'

'I'm on my way,' he said, and hung up.

We were kept in for two more hours, and then the doctor allowed us to go.

Katrina drove us back to the hotel. My daughter lay in my arms, limp with exhaustion.

Lisa was waiting for us, frantic. Kat and I filled her in.

'The police are looking for them,' Kat concluded. 'I told the hospital it was a domestic incident.'

I nodded. I could not imagine that they would be caught. I saw them away, at sea, laughing.

Georgie was asleep in my bed. In the flickering of her exhausted eyes, I saw the enormity of what I had done, of what had been done to her. I sat on the floor, just watching her, listening to her breathe. Kat and Lisa sat in the adjoining room, drinking coffee. After a while, Kat appeared at the open door, beckoned me through.

Geoffrey was on the line, calling from the plane. The wheels were turning. He was bringing a lawyer specializing in family law over with him. They were due to arrive in a few hours. After we'd finished speaking, Kat updated me. She had rung Interpol and the local police who had reported no sign of Archie and Rosamond.

'What now?' she asked.

I longed for sleep, for oblivion. I had my daughter. That's what I came for. To take her back. Seeing the ease with which her father and her grandmother endangered her life, and then abandoned her, removed the lingering doubts I had harboured but never allowed myself to acknowledge about setting out to remove her from their lives. I had her, safe, and I thanked God for that. I so desperately wanted to stay with her, to watch her sleep, to hold her when she woke, never to leave her side again, but I knew I could not. Not yet.

'Long ago, I made a promise to a friend of mine as he lay dying from the wounds he received when Archie drove a car over him. I promised him I would not let them get away with it.'

'You want to go after them?' asked Kat.

'Apart from my promise, I think if I didn't, and if we didn't somehow get them, I'd spend the rest of my life looking over my shoulder, waiting for them to come back, either to pay me back, or to take Georgie.'

Kat snorted. 'You think they care a damn about her?'

'They don't love her as a daughter, as a grand-daughter, but I think they'd want her as a pawn, as a possession.'

'So what do we do?' Lisa asked. 'Don't you think they'll be well gone by now?'

I shook my head. 'They should be, but I've got a feeling, don't ask me how or why. I just don't think they are, and as long as I feel that, I have to have one last look.'

'And Georgie?' she went on.

'You stay here with Georgie. Look after her with your life. Geoffrey'll be here in a few hours. There is no-one in the world I trust more. He will look after her, keep her safe. Hook up with him and the whole legal stuff will start. Kat and I will head for the boat. I'll bet it's sailed, but there's always a chance.'

'And then?' asked Lisa.

'We'll play it as it goes,' I said.

Kat was pulling on her trainers and checking her kit bag as I went into my room. Georgie lay sleeping on her back, arms thrown out, oblivious, but for the crease of a frown linking her eyebrows.

'I'll be back soon, Georgie,' I whispered. I watched her for a minute. It was the hardest thing I have ever done to turn away, gather up my shoes and jacket, and leave.

It was ten o'clock when Kat and I headed out. A sliv-er of new moon hung high in the sky. We drove in silence to the small harbour where Kat and Lisa had seen the *Belladonna* moored.

We stopped on the clifftop and gazed down at the harbour below. We could see from a distance she was gone. Four boats were bobbing gently in the water, and they were all thirty-footers max. Kat hauled up and thumped the steering wheel.

I felt the welling of despair. They'd gone, as logic had said they would. I got out of the car, stood there gazing out to sea. A faint sound of music wafted up from the harbour.

I turned back to the car. 'Kat, I want to go down there, take a closer look.'

'Morgan, the boat's gone. They've gone.'

'Humour me, please. Let's leave the car here, go down on foot.'

'All right, let me just get my rucksack.'

She closed the car door gently, locked the car, and together we headed furtively down the road towards the harbour. There was a small dry dock, with a large warehouse building, alongside the water. That was where the music was coming from.

We walked closer to the dry-dock area, crouching low, silent in our trainers. The pounding beat of a heavy metal anthem thumped through the night as we drew near. Whoever was listening to the radio was making no attempt to be covert. Kat pulled her pistol from her jacket. Together, we skirted the shadows of the warehouse, stopping every so often to listen. Before we rounded the corner of the building we paused, and then we heard something besides the radio: the breathy hiss of a blowtorch. Slowly, we took a look round the edge of the rough wooden frame of the warehouse. About thirty feet away, moored up in the lee of the warehouse, was the *Belladonna*. On her decks, I could see two swarthy men, one was working with a blow-torch, and another was hauling up on deck what looked like supplies. They were gearing up for a voyage, a long one given the mountain of tinned food.

'Bingo!' I mouthed.

Of Rosamond and Archie, there was neither sight nor sound.

But they could have come, at any time, in the darkness sneaking up behind us. We were exposed there, against the salt-caked wood. When we were sure the workmen were fully engaged on their tasks, we tried to melt along the building's front. We found cover behind a great pile of rubbish — old planks, engine parts, and rotting refuse. Unpleasant, but the uneven contours allowed us to blend in and to peek at the boat and the approach path. Behind us was the harbour. The sea sloshed against the dock, lulling, susurrating, as if to say sshh, shhh, all was well. There was no lulling us. Kat was as tense as I was. She still had her pistol at the ready, eyes gleaming in the darkness.

'Funny the police didn't find the boat,' I whispered. The noise of the radio and the blowtorch almost drowned out my words, but still I felt uneasy speaking.

'Maybe they didn't want to?'

'Being in Rosamond's pocket?'

'It's what you always suspected. I think the fact the cops haven't found and impounded the boat is all the proof you need. They're meant to be on their case.'

'So what the hell do we do with them when we get them?' I asked. 'We hand them over, I have a very strong feeling they'll somehow just slide away from whatever cell they're thrown into. They sold the Rembrandt for thirty mill. That greases a lot of palms. And as for getting them across the border, they'll scream kidnap.'

'I have a plan,' she said. 'You might not like it, but it's as surefire as we can get.'

'Shoot.'

She smiled. 'We stow away. We wait for our moment, surprise them, make them sail into international waters. Meanwhile, we'll have rung the U.S. Coast Guard, the FBI, Interpol, the whole shooting match. They'll meet us at sea. We'll hand them over.'

'Shit.' I thought of Georgie. 'Could take days. Risky as hell.'

'Got a better idea?'

I thought of Georgie, asleep in my hotel room. I ached to be back with her, to shut off my mind, just fill it with her. But would she and I ever have a moment's true peace while they were still at large?

'I guess it all boils down to how much you want them,' Kat went on.

I thought of Ben, dying in his hospital bed, I thought of Archie holding a gun to his own daughter's head, dumping her on the highway, and I made up my mind. I was sure that this was going to be the only chance I had of getting them.

'I want them.'

Kat nodded.

'Right,' I said. 'Let's pick our moment, and get on board that boat. I have a feeling Lady Macbeth and her spawn will show up any minute.'

'You know anything about boats?' Kat asked.

'A bit. C'mon.'

Chapter seventy-six

Like assassins we crept through the darkness to the stern of the *Belladonna*. She was a fast-looking ketch, fifty foot long. The dockside was high, and although it appeared to be high tide, it was still eight feet or so to the *Belladonna*'s deck. Kat stirruped her hands and I was half-launched, half-self-propelled aboard. I fell into a crouch and listened. The welding and banging contin ued. I hung over the side, dangled my arm down. Kat grabbed hold of my hand while I locked onto the side rail and hauled her, scrabbling, aboard.

Ominously, the banging ceased. A voice called out. The other workmen answered. They paused, listened. If they had come to investigate we'd have been like rats in a barrel. Seconds passed. The hammering resumed. The scorch of the blowtorch making contact with metal sounded out. We breathed again. I scouted out the deck area before us. We needed somewhere concealed, where we wouldn't asphyxiate ourselves. Spare cabins were one option, but there was no way we would have got round to the foredeck and the pilot house that gave down to the living quarters below. That was right where all the work was going on. I inched round to the port side. A large dinghy was lashed to the deck. I reckoned there might just have been room for us to squeeze underneath and slump down. I nodded at it. We had to struggle with the ropes and flatten ourselves, but we both managed to squeeze under and find enough space to semi sit up. The dinghy wasn't lying flush to the deck, but angled against the roof of the cabins, so that gave us a sort of backrest and allowed for air to circulate. We fell silent, made ourselves as comfortable as we could, and sat back to wait.

The luminous hands on my watch showed eleven thirty. Still the welding and the hammering and the radio droned on. Another hour, and the sounds faded. The last hammer blows echoed out into the dark ocean. The blowtorch was extinguished and the radio was silenced. The men seemed to be discussing something. They argued, and then clearly came to some decision. It sounded as if they were disembarking. I followed the sound of their voices as they moved away along the dock. I could not see Kat's face, and I dared not speak. So we held our silence, and we waited. It suddenly occurred to me that if we needed to pee, or worse, we were in trouble. I had water in my backpack and I had a fearsome thirst, but I could not risk a sip.

We waited. Every sound, save the low murmur of the waves, etched itself into my consciousness; the creak of the dock that might have betrayed a footfall, the distant sound of a car engine, the breeze flapping a loose sheet of plastic somewhere — oilskins, or just an innocent tarpaulin?

Hours passed. I wanted to move, I wanted to escape that prison, I wanted to go back to Georgie. But I didn't. Then I heard something else — the distant squeal of the axle as a car took a corner a little too sharply, the low rumble of an expensive engine coming closer. The engine was killed. I felt Kat stiffen beside me. We reached out, found each other's hands, gave a quick squeeze. There was a click of a door opening, and another. Then two dull thuds as they were closed. Something wicked this way came, and I knew it was them. I imagined them scanning the dock. They must have known the police wouldn't have been there. I wondered how much that little operation had cost Rosamond. Wouldn't have made much of a dent in thirty mill. I bet they had another bolthole. Question was where? Where would they sail us? My thoughts stopped abruptly as I heard the creak of the dock, then a muffled voice — Rosamond.

I smiled in the darkness. Come into my lair, why don't you? She thought this was her territory, but I had been practically reared on a boat. I might not have known the *Belladonna*, but together with Kat, I could lash these two to the guardrail and sail into international waters, and deliverance.

I was surprised at myself. I'd never felt like this before. Perhaps it was just that everything that Rosamond and Archie had visited upon me, my daughter, and Ben had coalesced. I had become predatory. I found myself entertaining new thoughts, different endings for Rosamond and Archie than the sanctioned ones. I thought of Archie's face as he pulled me off him, as he threw me over the cliff. He had been smiling. Now I waited in the darkness. It was my turn.

Another creak of the dock, then another as they crossed the gangway and came aboard. I could hear their hushed voices, edgy, staccato. I heard the low thump as they dropped baggage on deck, then footsteps. They seemed to be walking round, checking everything. The footsteps split up. One set came closer. I wished I could see, but I just froze and listened. A heavier step. Archie. He stopped, just feet away. I could practically smell him. He didn't move. Shit, what was he examining so closely? I held my breath. Another step, and suddenly he was rattling the dinghy. I stifled a gasp in my throat, but then the movement stopped. Apparently satisfied, my husband moved off. Kat and I breathed, ever so softly. I heard them go below. Ten more minutes of stowing and checks and then I heard the low rumble of the engines, and the *Belladonna* and her four passengers slipped from harbour and headed for the open sea.

Chapter seventy-seven

I sat in my cramped rubber prison, breathing in salt freshness and synthetic staleness and I wondered where we were going? Were we hugging the coast, bound for Central America, or the drug republics of the South? Or were we striking out to sea in search of a far-flung island in Indonesia? Some bolthole beyond the reach of the authorities, insulated by remoteness and bribery, of that I was sure. Either way, we needed to ring, soon, while we still had signals on our mobiles. The elements conspired against us. It must have been one of the most silent nights at sea. Hardly any breeze, the gentlest of waves. The minutes passed. I heard footsteps on deck. They called to each other now, voices still tense, but ragged with the edge of jubilation. They thought they were on the cusp of escape. I heard cranking, then the idle flap of sails in a low wind. 'Mainsail up,' called Archie. 'All we need now is a stiff breeze.'

'We'll get one,' called back Rosamond. 'Weather fax just came in. Force 5 forecast. Should hit it soon.'

'Great,' he replied, moving forward. I could hear them talking at the helm, but couldn't quite pick out their words.

I had to risk a whisper. 'Kat?'

'Yeah?' She sounded completely alert.

'We have to ring soon.'

'I know, but it's so damned quiet.'

'You heard what Rosamond said. Wind's freshening.'

'Let's give it fifteen minutes.'

Ten minutes shimmered past in the darkness. Abruptly, as if we had left one room and entered a different one, the wind picked up. The rigging began to creak, the boat started to rise and dip, the waves and the wind slapped against boat and sails. Archie went forward to adjust the sails, and then returned to the stern. Kat pulled out her phone, hit memory dial. We waited, interminably. Finally she spoke.

'Joe. Kat Chasen. I'm on a boat. Fugitive situation. Interpol number eight three six FGU, and FGW. Planning to take over controls and sail into international waters. Can you get coast guard on standby, pending co-ords?'

She listened in silence. Joe was clearly biting. I wondered briefly if she shared her bounty with him, and frankly I didn't give a toss if she did. As long as he played his part.

'Great. Hold hard,' she said and clicked off.

'He's on. I reckon we have no more than another fifteen minutes or so guaranteed signal. You ready to rock?'

'I am. Plan is we immobilize them both, okay?'

'And who sails this thing?' she asked. I heard the first tinge of nerves in her question.

'I do.'

'You can handle her solo?'

'If it's not too rough, yeah.'

'Let's hope it's calm then. I'll keep the pistol on them, you tie them.'

'Fine.'

We waited, we listened. They were both astern, talking animatedly. They had no idea what was coming. We eased out from the dinghy, our sounds masked by the sea. We took a few moments to stretch, to make sure blood reached cramped muscles. We looked at each other and nodded.

Kat went first, pistol ready. We crept along the side, screened by the cabin roof. Then round we went.

'Hands up,' said Kat.

Archie and Rosamond wheeled round towards us, mouths opened in shock. They looked from Kat to me, and back to her pistol. I smiled at them.

'In the air, high,' said Kat. 'Try anything, and I will shoot you, happily.' Her voice was wondrously calm.

'*You*,' spat Rosamond.

'Yes, me. Surprise.'

Her face contorted. It was like looking at the picture of Dorian Grey: the true ugliness revealed.

'Turn around, slowly,' I said. 'Hands behind your backs.'

They took their time.

'My finger's getting twitchy,' said Kat amicably.

Slowly they complied.

'Who'll sail the boat?' asked Rosamond

I took the cuffs from Kat's bag, grabbed Rosamond's wrists, locked her in, and then locked Archie back to back with her.

'Fuck,' said Archie.

'I won't, thank you. I have a boat to sail.'

'You?' hissed Rosamond.

'Yes. Me. You weren't the only one to grow up by the sea, Rosamond.'

She laughed. 'You have no idea, do you, what's heading our way.'

I felt a momentary flicker of alarm.

'Some rough weather. Nothing I didn't sail in off Long Island.'

'Oh, I think this one might be special, even for you. You'll be begging us for help.'

'We'll see.' I turned to Kat. 'I'm going down to check our bearings, and plot a new course.'

She nodded. 'I'm happy baby-sitting. Long as I don't have to change any nappies.' She laughed, and I saw a stroke of cruelty in her I hadn't known was there.

I went below. I checked the GPS, and the course Rosamond had charted. She was bound for Nicaragua. I plotted a course that would take us northwest, across the Tropic of Cancer and into international waters. I set the autopilot, and then did a full manual check of our position, in case anything happened to the instruments. Then I checked the weather fax. A new one had just come in. My stomach contracted. The weather was worsening. A Force 9 was forecast. Due to hit in the next eight hours. Could I sail the *Belladonna* alone? Probably not. I'd need Rosamond, or Archie. I felt sick at the thought. What I could not have done was to turn back to the Mexican coast. Rosamond would have had the local cops in the palm of her hand, of that I had no doubt. She and Archie would have been allowed to 'escape' in a heartbeat. I had no choice. I had to sail on, for international waters, where the U.S. Coast Guard could take over.

I went back up on deck. Archie and Rosamond turned to glare at me. I smiled. They turned away. Mobile, I mouthed to Kat. Surreptitiously, she gave it to me and I went down to the pilot desk again. I pressed last number redial. Joe answered promptly.

'Hi, Joe. My name's Morganna. I'm with Kat.'

'Shit,' he said.

'Shit what?'

'You're the one they murdered.'

I chuckled. 'Nearly. I've plotted a course. You might want to tell the coast guard.'

'Give it over.'

I relayed it to him. He checked it back to me. 'We'll be out of mobile range soon,' I said. 'I'll talk direct to the coast guard on the ship to shore. And I'll see if there's a sat phone tucked away.'

'Okay.' He waited a beat. 'Good luck. Be careful.'

'Oh, don't worry I will be.'

I clicked off, walked back on deck, circled back to the stern. I stood, gripping the guardrail, watching the slick of the wash behind us. The stars burned above me, the water was black below me. The *Belladonna* scudded along in the wind. It was going to get bad. But right then, it was a perfect night for sailing. Off to the west, on the horizon, there were no stars. That's where the clouds were. That's where the storm would hit.

Chapter seventy-eight

It was getting rougher. The waves were peaking at about fifteen feet, and they were stiffening and increasing in frequency. The *Belladonna* was taking them well. She was the best of her size money could buy, but Kat was beginning to suffer. I could see she was trying her best to suppress her nausea, but mind over matter could only take you so far, and things were only going to get worse. I needed to tie Rosamond and Archie somewhere they'd be safe, could pose no threat to us, and where they wouldn't need supervision from Kat. I decided upon the rail in the galley. It was steel, bolted in. I took Kat's extra sets of handcuffs. Together we forced the two of them down into the galley way. With Kat training the revolver on them, I unlocked them, and cuffed them again so that they could sit at the table, with each hand separately shackled to the rail behind them. They sank down with ill-disguised relief, animosity reeking from them.

I went back up with Kat. 'How are you?' I asked.

'Not good. I keep trying to–'

'I know. Listen, Kat, the forecast's not good. It's going to get very rough. You need to keep yourself safe.'

'Shit, Morgan, I'm not going to huddle myself away and–'

'I don't think you're going to have much choice. Ever been at sea in a storm?'

She shook her head.

'Best thing you can do is not have me worry about you. Stay below. If you need to come up on deck, tie yourself on.'

I showed her the safety harness. 'Do not come up without tying on. If you're washed overboard, the chances of me finding you in the night in a storm are zero.'

She nodded. It was beginning to dawn on her, the shit we were in. Strangely enough, at that point, I wasn't afraid. There was too much to do.

'I reckon we'll hook up with the coast guard in the next eight to twelve hours, depending on how quick off the mark they are, and on the weather,' I said.

'The weather might speed us up, though, mightn't it?'

'Depends. If it gets really bad, we'll have to forget all about plotting a course and just go with the storm. Now go down,' I said gently, 'and keep your eye on Lady Macbeth. See if you can find any other weapons tucked away, and chuck them overboard. Keep an eye out for a sat phone too. I didn't see one, but it might be tucked away.'

She'd just got down when a wave hit us full on and washed over the deck. I grabbed onto the guardrail and hung on. I was soaked. I hurried down, past the glowering figures, and pilfered Archie's wet-weather gear from his cabin. I went back up on deck and clicked into my safety harness. The wind began to roar. The waves were cresting twenty feet. I tried to reef the mainsail, but it was slow, hard going. The *Belladonna* began to lurch. The seas were coming in all directions now. I was going to have to take the *Belladonna* off autopilot soon, and helm her myself. Which meant I'd need help.

I called down to Kat. She came up looking rough. I clicked her into a safety harness.

'What's up?' she asked.

'I can't sail single-handed in this sea. I'm going to have to release Archie.'

'Shit.'

'I think you'd better give me the revolver.'

'You know how to handle that thing?'

'No, but you'll show me.'

'Not good, Morgan, if you don't know what you're doing and you have a boat heaving up and down you could shoot anywhere, get your own foot, take a ricochet.'

'That's a chance I'll have to take.'

She thought for a while, and then handed over her weapon. She pointed out the safety, let me get used to the pressure on the trigger.

'Fire it,' she said, 'out to sea. You need to know how it feels, how hard to squeeze, how the recoil kicks in.'

I took it, moved to the guardrail, tried to fix my stance with the boat rolling beneath me. I squeezed back the trigger and fired into the blackness.

'Aim for the chest, if you want to kill,' said Kat. I nodded, clicked the safety back on, and shoved the pistol down into my sou'wester pocket.

'D'you find any other weapons?' I asked. She shook her head. I wondered what Archie had done with the machine-gun.

Together we went down. I took my keys and released Archie.

Rosamond smirked at me. 'Can't handle her on your own, can you?'

'Could you? If I held a gun to your son's head? But no, that's more your family style, isn't it, and besides, you wouldn't care a toss about that kind of sanction, would you? You'd sacrifice your son for your freedom any day of the week.'

She laughed. 'No. I wouldn't. But I would sacrifice your daughter.'

I saw a haze of red. I was almost blinded by rage. Beside me I sensed Archie moving. My hand was in my pocket and out with the revolver before he got anywhere. I took a step back, levelled it at his chest. I caught Kat's look of worry out of the corner of my eye. For a moment, I saw in my mind's eye the cliffs of Cape Wrath. I saw him holding his own gun to my daughter's head. I considered pulling the trigger.

'Get up on deck,' I said. I saw in his eyes both fear and loathing.

'Tie in,' I said, as he went out on deck before me. He clicked himself in, and then I did the same.

'What do you want me to do?' he asked with scorn.

'Whatever I tell you,' I replied.

'You're enjoying this, aren't you?' he said, bracing himself as *Belladonna* reeled under a huge wave. He was soaked. I wiped the water from my face.

'I'm doing what I have to do.'

'And what's that then? Where are you taking us? Out to sea, to shoot us, throw us overboard?'

I smiled. 'Now that is seriously tempting.'

'You know, I did love you once, at the beginning,' he said, taking the breath from my lungs.

I remembered. Despite myself, I remembered. 'Maybe you did, but not for long, and never as much as you loved my money.'

'Don't you remember?' he asked, reaching out his hand towards me. 'How it was. You and me, Morganna.'

I leaned down towards him. 'Carry on like that, Archie, and I might just change my mind about shooting you and throwing you overboard.'

He wheeled away, as if slapped. The change in him was so abrupt. Manipulation having failed, he turned ugly again.

'Go and check the rigging,' I said.

With a backward sneer, off he went. I watched him. I didn't like this, but what could I do? I took the wheel and tried to steer round the worst of the waves. I craned up, checked he was where he should have been. Ten minutes later, he came back. It did occur to me that he might have tried to scupper us instead of help, but I didn't think he was suicidal. He stood, watching me. I took my eye off the sea, and out of the darkness loomed a monster wave. It washed over both of us. I lost my footing, and then next thing I felt was Archie's fist in my face. I felt a searing pain in my nose. I hit back, with my fists, with my elbows, with knees and feet, with everything Pete Marshall had taught me, and with a viciousness all of my own. I heard him gasp with pain. I got to my feet as he struggled up and I got him with a leaping kick that hit his shoulder and spun him across the deck and thumped him into the guardrail.

'That was for holding a pistol to my daughter's head,' I screamed.

'She was fine,' he shouted back.

I walked up to him, the boat pitching wildly and kicked out again, hitting his knee. 'And that was for knifing her and dumping her by the roadside.'

He lunged at me again. I spun out of his way, launched another flying kick that took him full on in the ribs. He slumped down on the deck. 'And that was for throwing me over the cliff,' I finished.

He looked at me. He was utterly helpless, at my mercy, and I could practically smell his fear.

'Don't, don't,' he said, voice whining

'Oh, I could kill you now, with a kick to the throat, or I could simply throw you overboard. But I won't. I'm not you, Archie. I don't go in for cold-blooded murder, but I'm not the dupe I was when I married you. I'm not the same girl at all. Remember that and I won't have to hurt you again.'

'You have hurt me,' he moaned. 'Badly.'

'Get up.'

'I can't. I think you've broken my ribs.'

'Try.'

'My harness is caught.' He fumbled with it, unhooked it, and at that moment the biggest wave of all hit us. The *Belladonna* keeled over, the water washed over us. I was knocked off my feet, swept against the pilot house. But Archie was unhooked. I saw him, face contorted with fear, desperately trying to grab onto something, anything. And fail. And then I saw him caught up in the full sweep of that awful wave, and swept overboard, and away. The *Belladonna* righted herself and I rushed up to the guardrail. I could just make out a hand, rising through the waves, and, briefly his face, contorted with fear, and then Archie went under, down to oblivion.

I had no time to think, to mourn or to rejoice. My husband, my would-be murderer, the father of my child was gone, but I was numb. I would think and I would feel later. I went back below, to Rosamond.

'Archie's not up to it,' I announced. 'You're going to have to help me.'

'Now that will be fun, won't it, eh, Morganna? Me and you up on deck, working together to save your skin. How pleasant.'

'And your skin, and your son's skin,' I kept lying.

'If, as I suspect, you have captivity in mind for us, I don't really give a toss for anybody's skin.'

'Ah, the milk of human kindness. No wonder Archie's so fucked up. Stay here then.' I turned to go, betting on her survival instinct, on her love of life, and on my belief that she would gamble to the last.

'Unlock me,' she said in her slow drawl. 'Someone needs to sail this boat.'

I turned slowly and smiled. 'And of course, no-one can do it as well as you. Can do anything as well as you.'

'Glad you got there,' she said as I freed her.

'Kat, here's your pistol. Take Rosamond up to the helm. I'm going to bring Archie down and lock him out of the way in one of the cabins. Toss me the keys, will you?'

She did as I asked. I let her and Rosamond go ahead of me. I followed them up, and doubled back towards the stern.

'Archie,' I called out. 'Time to go back down.'

Rosamond kept walking straight ahead, oblivious,

fooled by my deception. I had thought that perhaps some deep-rooted, well-hidden maternal instinct would have told her that her son was lost forever, or, at the very least, in trouble. But she just moved blithely, arrogantly on, no doubt still plotting how to best me and escape.

I went through the motions of going down below. I took sufficient time to account for locking Archie up in a spare cabin, and then I went back up, tied on, and relieved Kat, who was looking not just ill but terrified.

She gave me back the pistol. I moved out of Rosamond's earshot.

'Archie's been washed overboard. Don't let on, whatever you do. Pretend he's locked up in a guest cabin. Okay?'

Her eyes widened, but she nodded and went unsteadily below.

I moved back towards Rosamond. I knew, sooner or later, she would try something, but hell, I really didn't have much choice. I needed her help if I was to sail this boat. The storm was worsening. Soon the issue would-n't be following a course, but staying afloat. I didn't know what this boat could do, how much she could withstand. Every so often she took a huge wave and once her mast dipped on the water side before she righted herself. She was halfway between a nymph and a cow in the water. I didn't know her and I couldn't trust her. One thing I knew for sure was that I would not go down in that boat. So I needed Rosamond, and she knew it. Trouble was, with her arrogance she prob-ably thought she could sail this boat alone, with Archie incapacitated, and me overboard. All she needed to do was take a knife to my safety harness and wait for the right wave to hit.

'Take the sails,' I told her. 'I'll hold course, you trim as I say.'

'As you wish. You know what you're doing?'

'You'd better hope so.'

We sailed on into the night. I needed to raise the coast guard, confirm a rendezvous. We were in the thick of the storm now, no way to change course and escape it. The coast guard would need spotter planes as well as a vessel to find us in the mayhem. Hell, they might not even want to launch into the storm. After all, it was not a mayday situation. I could only hope the storm eased, and that the FBI and Interpol wanted Rosamond and Archie enough. Frankly, given what they were dealing with day to day, I wondered whether one murder and one attempted murder in a distant country over a year ago were going to tip their switch. Kat's guy had sounded keen, but unless he had some major muscle I doubted whether he was going to be able to push all the right buttons.

I had to risk leaving the *Belladonna* on autopilot for a few minutes.

'Rosamond, get over here, we're going inside.'

'Are you mad?'

'Yes. Now get moving.' I pulled out my revolver. She eyed it and moved.

In the galley I cuffed her. 'Kat, five minutes.' She nodded. I went through to the navigator's desk, tried my mobile. Miraculously it worked. Geoffrey answered as if he'd been waiting for my call.

'How's Georgie?'

'Fine. Lovely. Great. What the hell are you up to?'

'No time for that. Listen, here's the plan, here's the rendezvous co-ords. I need you to pull some strings, make sure the coast guard gets a vessel and whatever air cover it needs to make the rendezvous. You're gonna have to pull some serious strings on this, Geoffrey.'

'Do my best. Now—'

I clicked off, uncuffed Rosamond, and gestured her up the companionway steps. Just as we got up on deck, before we got our harnesses on, the most godawful wave hit, washed right over us. I was on deck, in the sea, floating free towards oblivion I reached out my hands and scrabbled for whatever I could get. The *Belladonna* heeled over. Shit, I thought she was going to do invert. Next thing I knew I slammed into the guardrail so hard the wind was knocked from my lungs, but I grabbed on, and I held on like a vice as water sluiced over me, trying to dislodge me into the churning ocean. For I don't know how long, the *Belladonna* wallowed on her side. I heard a cry from below, but put it out of my head. All I could think about was hanging on. All I could do was pray she righted herself. If we were hit again now, we'd capsize. And then, slowly, she did right herself, just as another wave hit her. But this one was smaller; she weathered it. Now I just had to get myself back to the wheelhouse, find my safety, and click on.

I made a frantic run in as we were riding up another wave. I got there. Rosamond was standing, latched on, holding the other harness in her hand. I'd seconds to get it on, but she wouldn't hand it over. I did the only thing I could. I launched myself on her, grabbed hold of her, and waited for her safety to hold me on deck. It did. The wave receded and as it did I pinioned her arm and grabbed the safety from her. She coughed; she was winded. But she gave me a look of pure hatred. She would have watched me float away with glee.

'Sorry to disappoint you,' I said.

'You won't,' she replied, as if she could see the script of her own writing playing out, just as she wanted it.

Chapter seventy-nine

Hours passed. I could feel the dull ache of exhaustion in my limbs but my mind was buzzing with adrenaline. Somehow or other I managed to keep the *Belladonna* on my pre-set course. Rosamond actually helped, which was deeply worrying. At the current rate, we were due to be at the rendezvous in two hours, just before dawn. I had to find out if there would be anyone there to meet us.

'Time to go down below,' I yelled.

'What?' she yelled back.

The wind just stole our words away, leaving us mouthing at each other. I got out my pistol. She got the message. She went down ahead of me. And gave a sudden chuckle.

I elbowed her out of the way. Lying on the floor of the galley, a gash at her temple, was Kat.

'Sit down,' I yelled at Rosamond.

I turned back to Kat. The wave that broadsided us must have rocked her across the companionway and knocked her out. I bent down, checked for her pulse. It was beating all right, racing away, but she was out cold. I cuffed Rosamond, and then I half-carried, half-dragged Kat into the nearest berth. I heaved her in and strapped her down. That was the best I could do for her.

I felt the boat begin to lurch. I could not leave her on autopilot in seas that needed constant monitoring. I rushed back to Rosamond, uncuffed her, and motioned her up. We strapped up — she went to the sails, I went to the helm, tried to steer my way over and round the biggest waves. I offered up a sudden prayer. If the engine died, for whatever reason, we would be lost. You could not ride out a storm like this without the power to navigate the waves as best you could, let alone make a rendezvous. And there was a limit to the time I could sail this beast in a storm like this, and try to keep Rosamond under control, all single-handed. I could not go below again. I could not ring Geoffrey, or the coast guard. I could only pray the rendezvous was set up.

An hour and a half later I looked up to the sky. I could hear an engine, somewhere near. Please God, let it be the coast guard, I prayed, let them see us in this mayhem. Then, suddenly, the plane broke through the cloud cover and circled low over us. That was the net, suspended over Rosamond. I wondered if she recognized it for what it was. She must have done. Now, like any trapped animal, she would become truly dangerous. I set off a flare and gave a whoop of delight.

I tried to sail the boat. I tried to keep watch on Lady Macbeth, I tried to search out the lights of a coast guard vessel, and I worried about Kat. Please let her be all right. I thought of Georgie too, in my bed, with Lisa and Geoffrey watching over her.

I turned from the helm to check on Rosamond and it was at that moment I realized she was not there. Instinct, pure gut-clenching instinct made me fall to the deck. As I fell I heard the bang and the hiss as the flare gun was discharged. The flare flew over me at what would have been chest height. The heat seared my hair, my face. I could hardly breathe for the acrid stench of magnesium. My eyes were blinded by the searing white light. I pulled myself up to the raised deck; I squinted, trying desperately to see Rosamond. No-one was steering this boat. In a minute, maybe less, she would be turned broadside by the waves, and she would be over. Where *was* Rosamond? I knew she'd be reloading, and I was a sitting duck. I hauled myself up onto the roof of the pilot house and I saw her, two yards in front of me, creeping round, aiming to get me from behind. I pushed off, launched myself through the air, and landed on her back. She fell on the flare gun, groaning. I wrestled with her, and she screamed at me and fought ferociously, but I was younger and I was stronger and this time I was more vicious. I punched at her head until she stopped fighting. Then, very carefully, I turned her over, grabbing her wrist, pulling the flare gun from her. It was loaded. I pointed it at her.

'Get up.'

She was rubbing her head.

'Get up and get to the fucking sails before I decide you're useless and push you over.'

She must have seen something in my eyes that told her I meant it. And I did. At that moment, I would have happily fired the gun, unleashed her, and pushed her off. No-one would ever have found her body. She'd be eaten by sharks before she washed up on some beach. It was only because of Georgie that I held back. I didn't want her mother to be a murderer too.

Rosamond moved back to the sails. I wondered what other weapons she might have secreted round the place. What Kat had missed.

I got back to the helm and then I saw a beam of light cresting a wave in the distance.

I watched it, transfixed. Rosamond, I knew, was watching it too. So Geoffrey had worked his magic, and perhaps Kat's guy had worked his. Problem now was, how the hell did I offload Rosamond onto another vessel in these seas? And then, how did I sail this thing single-handed? I'd have to see what the coast guard came up with. All I could do now was steer my course and watch Rosamond.

We got closer. The other vessel must have been a quarter of a mile away. I needed to talk to them. I lashed the rudder, shouted for Rosamond. I took out my pistol, gestured her inside. Slowly she walked past me, and headed down into the galley. I cuffed her and then went into the pilot house. I could hear the radio crackling with static.

'*Belladonna, Belladonna*, do you read?'

I clicked on. 'This is the *Belladonna*.'

'Hello there, *Belladonna*. Coast guard vessel *Euphrates* here. What's your current situation?'

'One prisoner on board. She has to help me sail. One ally, but she's unconscious.'

Rosamond was shouting. I tried to tune her out.

'You all right?' asked the *Euphrates*.

'I'm fine. What's the plan?'

'Not sure we can launch a craft to get to you to take off your passengers. Might have to wait until the storm passes.'

'I'm not sure I can control the boat and the prisoner for too much longer.'

'Hold hard. We'll come as close as we can, and reassess. Over and out.'

'*One prisoner? Where's Archie? Where is he?*' Rosamond

screamed at me, as the light of comprehension dawned. 'Archie, answer me. Where are you? Archie, Archie?'

'He's gone, Rosamond, swept overboard. There was nothing–'

'You killed him, you murdered him, you–'

I shook my head and walked away. I did not want to bear witness to the spectacle of a mother robbed of her child, and nothing I could say would make any difference. I hadn't killed him — I couldn't have saved him if I tried.

I left Rosamond screaming and lashing against her cuffs. One thing was sure, now I really did have to sail solo. I hurried back on deck.

I could see the *Euphrates* getting closer. One hundred feet of coast guard cutter, powerful as hell, as she needed to be. Five minutes later, we were three hundred yards apart. I checked in from the pilot house.

'Hold your position,' said the voice from the *Euphrates*. 'Think the storm's abating. Give it half an hour, and we might just be able to launch.'

I watched and I prayed. It was still dark — dawn must have been an hour away. I was getting really tired, that almost hallucinatory tiredness where all adrenaline is spent and all that remained was pure exhaustion. I hadn't eaten or drunk anything for eight hours or so, and the physical toll of wrestling the boat in the storm was telling. As for my emotions, I was in total shutdown, and there I tried to stay.

Half an hour later, the radio crackled into life again.

'How's it going, *Belladonna*?'

'All right, *Euphrates*. But I have to say I'm getting tired.'

'We're gonna launch.'

I felt my spirits soar.

'We'll send over an extra man who'll stay with you, see you into port, and we'll take the prisoner off.'

'That's fantastic. Thank you. Thank you.'

'Hold your horses, Ma'am. We haven't done it yet.'

I tried to hold my course. Out there, in the deep, I couldn't just drop an anchor. It would have just dangled dangerously in the water, thousands of feet above the ocean bed. I watched for the launch. A great spotlight shone out from the *Euphrates*, picking it out. I saw three men on board. All I had to do now was get Rosamond on deck.

I went below.

'I'm taking you up. Please don't try anything, or I will have to use this,' I waggled the revolver at her. She watched me with dead eyes, and said nothing. I uncuffed her from the guardrail, rapidly rebuffed her hand behind her back, and gestured her up. I followed as she ascended the stairs. Up on deck I lashed her in, but it was obvious I'd have to free her hands to let her hold on to something, otherwise she'd be thrown off-balance and smashed around the boat. Warily, I uncuffed her.

Chapter eighty

She stood in her harness, leaning against the guardrail, the madness of the ocean heaving and falling away behind her.

'So this is the grand plan,' she said, her voice raw and low, the old honeyed tones long gone. 'Hand me over. Interpol, FBI?'

'Something like that.'

'Why not just kill me? Like you did Archie.'

'I didn't kill him.'

'No. Haven't you got the stomach?'

'I'd kill you if I needed to.'

'Then why don't you?'

'Georgie had a killer for a father, a killer for a grandmother. I think that's enough bad blood in the family, don't you?'

'Bad blood,' she spat. 'Better blood than you and your stinking whorish mother.'

I felt the lash of her fury, and my stomach turned over with rage. 'She just got what you wanted, didn't she?' I asked. 'My father. You know I never realized how very true it is.'

'What?' she bit.

'That hell hath no fury like a woman scorned. You've harboured it all this time, shrivelling you, twisting you.'

'And now you think you have me, that you'll just hand me over on a plate? Have the final victory?'

The *Belladonna* heaved under the onslaught of a particularly huge wave. We were both thrown to the deck
and soaked as the wave washed over us. I got up quickly, revolver still gripped.

'Something like that,' I said.

What happened next occurred so quickly I had no
chance to stop it.

'You'll never beat me,' said Rosamond. And with
that, she unclipped her harness, and with a great flip
backwards she went over the side and was gone. I heard
the splash as she hit the water. I rushed for the rail and
peered over. At first I couldn't see her, and then a wave
raised her up. She looked up at me with the gleam of
triumph in her eyes for just a moment and then she was
swept from sight, down into the unravelling trough of
the wave and away.

Chapter eighty-one

That bleak, desperate night was six weeks ago. Of course, the coast guard didn't find her. It took them ten minutes to get to us, and in that time the sea would have carried her body faraway. The sheer scale of Rosamond's madness haunts me still. That she would choose death, not just to evade capture but to thwart me, was almost impossible to comprehend. In the absence of her body, part of me refused to believe she was dead. There was something indestructible about her spirit. In other circumstances, it would have been admirable. I had no doubts that Archie was dead. That sea would have sucked him under in seconds. He hadn't stood a chance, and he lacked the indomitable spirit of his mother that threatened to live on beyond the body.

I told my daughter that they had gone to live in heaven with the angels, but I had no doubt it was the devil who claimed them.

Georgie came home with me here, to Long Island, to our home. And it feels like a daily miracle. Geoffrey and his lawyer and a doctor who extracted a DNA sample, and Interpol, all played their part, all allowed me to be legally reunited with my daughter. The process was mercifully quick. I have no doubt that money changed hands too. Steve Welland played his part. Unbeknownst to me, he had made his plane available to Geoffrey, so that when I called from Mexico, it was sitting on the tarmac at JFK ready to fly him straight to

Georgie. One day, when things have settled down, I might just pay him a visit, thank him face to face, show him my beloved Georgie, so that he can see the joy and the perfection his help has returned to my life.

But for now, there is no-one with us, no-one now to dilute or distract us from our new reality: mother and daughter. She is one and a half. She understands so much. She knows I am her mother.

Of course she is resistant. Of course she misses her old home, her father, all the people gone from her, but we are making progress. I think it was my dogs that did it. When she first arrived here, they fell on her, sniffing and licking. I swear they remembered her, her smell, the sound of her voice. And she too, I think remembered them. They are her playmates, her guardians, her link with a past that was almost completely severed. And I am this new figure in her life. But I think too that she remembers something of me. We take it gently, this mothering thing. I try to let her come to me. Bit by bit, week by week, slowly she does.

When the season here finished and the renters of the big houses went back to Manhattan, and we had the beach to ourselves, we played together with our dogs, racing in and out of the sea, chasing seagulls, and then she first called me Mama, ran to me with joy in her eyes, and hugged me.

Sometimes when I sit alone on my deck at night, with Georgie safely asleep in her room, dogs lying sentry at her door, I wonder how all this happened. My money brought it about, drew Archie and Rosamond to me like magnets. But, without that, Georgie would never have been conceived. And without the massive exercise of money and power, I would never have got her back.

Where that leaves me I don't know. But I got the most final settlement of all from my husband, and from his mother. I have my daughter. And that is all that matters.

The End